SINGAPORE!

Jack DuArte

To: Nick
A member in good
standing of the gift of gab club!
Thanks
John DuArte
Lexington, KY

ISBN: 978-1-883589-97-4

Book Design by Kelly Elliott
Cover Design by Chris Inman, Visual Riot

ALSO BY JACK DUARTE

The Resistance

DEDICATION

This novel is respectfully dedicated to my late friend, Donald Bryson Kurfees, who died in late 2006, just prior to the completion of *Singapore!* Don was a wonderful man and a good friend who strongly believed in my ability to communicate to others through means of my novels. Through his encouragement and support, *Singapore!* became a reality. Without his urging and support, I am not sure it would have ever been completed. Along with his beloved wife Zee, I miss Don each and every day. As he looks down on us, I hope he enjoys this book that is dedicated to his memory.

Also, for their help in getting this work finished.

My wonderful wife Susan, who is also my best and most credible critic. Bill and Ellen Uzzel, Tony and Jane Rabasca, my old friends and supporters. Pat and Monty Joynes for their insight.

To Joan Tan in Singapore and Jason Davadason in Malaya.

To Denice Ruddle, Steve Smith, Kevin Uzzle, Beth Aretsky and Bob Whitaker.

And to my incredible editor Florence Huffman who has enabled me to become a much better writer.

FOREWORD

The rough-featured, visibly weathered Asian figure shifted his weight uneasily as he waited under the umbrella shade of a large frangipani tree. He was just outside the iron fence that controlled the main entrance to the command headquarters of Great Britain's Far Eastern Fleet. A pair of white-clad naval sentries stood wearily just outside a small shelter that served as a guardhouse for the installation. The profound heat and incessant humidity caused drips of sweat to drip off the ends of their noses.

The man glanced at his smaller companion, the second officer of his vessel the *Oshima Maru*. He pulled out his captain's watch and glanced at the time, noting that another ten minutes had elapsed since the last time he had checked. The captain made eye contact with his second officer who shrugged his shoulders in disgust.

"When you are forced to deal with people like this, you are forced to work on their timetables, Captain."

Capt. Hioshi Sujito nodded his agreement, but said nothing. He glanced again inside the naval compound that was practically deserted at this time of day.

No need to become impatient, after all, today's visit would be the last if everything went according to plan.

Thinking back, Sujito mentally calculated the time he had spent in building up the relationship with the Singapore man he was waiting for and who still remained inside the building. In all, Sujito had made five trips to the island of Singapore during the preceding year, and each trip wound the relationship with Jeffrey Soon Yapp a little tighter. After first being approached about the assignment by a member of the Japanese Army Intelligence Office, Sujito had planned his course of action very carefully. The Japanese captain made use of information supplied by another trusted JAIO informant who provided him with directions to Yapp's favorite bar. Yapp was a long-time, civilian British civil servant with an alcoholic intolerance that caused him to voice his political preferences whenever he drank socially, and, Jeffrey Yapp was quite social.

On his first Singapore trip, Captain Sujito waited at the bar until Yapp showed up around his daily scheduled time. Sujito immediately gained the unsuspecting man's confidence with the simple offer of a friendly drink. Yapp accepted the seaman's gesture graciously and the two became friends later that same evening. After several rounds of drinks, Yapp suggested they depart for another place Yapp knew well, where they could order a splendid dinner. During the meal, Yapp and Sujito detailed to each other the facts about their careers along with other salient facts about each other's lives.

Sujito was pleased to learn that his intoxicated new friend genuinely despised the British as a whole, deplored their brusque colonial attitude and generally resented their presence on Singapore and throughout South East Asia. The fact that Yapp owed his livelihood to the British mattered little to the unconcerned man.

"After all," Sujito recalled Yapp spouting out early in their relationship, "Malaya has had nothing but a succession of masters for the past five hundred years. The original people here were peaceful Polynesians, content with their lot in life and totally naïve in the ways of the world.

Then invaders came from Sumatra came and took over the area; other raiders from Java in turn conquered the Sumatrans. Some time elapsed and next the Europeans came. First it was the Portuguese and their magnificent ships, but they didn't last too long and were replaced by the powerful Dutch who came in even greater numbers.

Finally, the British arrived. Sir Stamford Raffles founded Singapore and the British period began. That was over one hundred and twenty-five years ago, and nothing much had changed since then. All of the original peoples are still here, but most are still extremely naïve and willing to accept whatever the Lion hands out to them."

Captain Sujito reported the conversation in its entirely when he returned to Tokyo and the decision was made to concentrate on Jeffrey Yapp. That determination suddenly became the most important aspect of Sujito's current intelligence gathering mission.

The wily sea captain continued to gain Yapp's confidence on each succeeding visit and had finally made a proposal to Yapp on his previous visit. Yapp agreed to the arrangement after a bit of minor haggling and a price for the information was agreed upon. Sujito was initially prepared to appeal to Yapp's rather misguided sense of nationalism, but found it unnecessary to do so. In Yapp's case, his disloyalty to his employer was strictly a case of a sufficient amount of Japanese money coupled with his pent-up abhorrence for his British masters.

Captain Sujito's thoughts returned to the present as he observed Yapp exiting the main door of the Far Eastern Naval Headquarters building. He looked closely and observed a briefcase in the Jeffrey Yapp's right hand.

Yapp passed through the guard gate without a word from the sentries; an action Sujito knew would never be allowed to occur at Japanese Imperial Naval Headquarters in Tokyo. Yapp initially turned in the direction of Sujito and his second officer, and then turned back and headed in the opposite direction.

This was all according to plan and after a short interval, Captain Sujito and his second officer proceeded in the same direction that Yapp had taken. According to the routine, Yapp was to proceed to the same bar where he and Sujito had first met, a busy public place where the transfer of information would take place.

Five minutes later, Yapp entered the seedy establishment closely followed by the two Japanese merchant seamen. He selected a table against a wall and sat down. He motioned for the Japanese to sit down next to him and produced a handkerchief from his hip pocket. Yapp patted his forehead as he attempted to dry his moist skin.

"Very hot at this time of the day, maybe we should have made our rendezvous for later."

"No, Jeffrey," Sujito answered, "even though it is quite hot, this is the proper time. No one at your office will suspect you going for a late lunch. Later in the day might have proven more difficult, you might even have been checked."

"Little chance of that, Hioshi, " Yapp remarked, using Sujito's first name familiarly. "The British are much too secure to think that anyone would ever attempt to steal anything from them. I have never been checked when I go through the gate. The guard inside the building is another story, and some of them are quite suspicious. I waited today until the guard was occupied with a pretty girl and wasn't interested in me. He barely glanced in my direction as I passed through the door."

"Good, Jeffrey, very good. It is not in our best interests to bring attention to ourselves in this matter."

"I understand all that. I am doing what you wanted strictly for the money. If something bad happens to the British, it serves them right. Damn superior attitude to everyone, especially the natives. Whatever comes from all this, I could not care less."

"Whatever you say, Jeffrey. Did you get everything?"

"Yes, it wasn't all that easy. The photographs were all taken during the past two months and are the best views of the airfields that I have seen. Luckily there were two copies, so I borrowed one.

You agreed to give them back to me tomorrow so I can replace them, right?"

"Certainly," Sujito agreed. "We can all go to our ship right now where the copies can be made."

"What about my money? I want it right now."

"As you wish," Sujito nodded to the other man at the table. The man produced a small cardboard box that was tied together with string. Sujito nodded again, and the man handed the box to Yapp.

"You can count it right here if you wish."

"Not on your life," Yapp returned. "No one in this place has ever seen this much money. I am content to wait until we get aboard the ship to check its correctness."

"Very well, let us be on our way."

The three got up from the table and filed out of the bar. Yapp and

Sujito walked next to each other and the second officer trailed a few yards behind. It took about fifteen minutes for the trio to reach the waterfront where the *Oshima Maru* was berthed. By the time they arrived at the ship, all three men were bathed in sweat.

Captain Sujito led the way up the gangplank and paused at the top. He spoke to the second officer in Japanese and instructed the man to take the photographs below. The man bowed politely and departed through the nearest hatch door.

"And now, Jeffrey, we can go to my quarters and have a toast of sake to your accomplishment."

Jeffrey Yapp followed the captain through the hatch where the pair entered a modest room that served as the stateroom's outside area.

"Not very large or elaborate," Jeffrey Yapp remarked, observing the surroundings.

"This is but a simple merchant boat, Jeffrey. Under such circumstances, one is not given to extravagance."

Yapp noted the captain's reply but did not respond. He sat down at the wooden desk and fumbled with the cord that tied the box together. After a few moments, he unloosened the cord and spread the money out on the table before him.

He began counting and placed the bills in small piles on the table in front of him.

After a few minutes, Yapp completed his actions and looked up at the captain.

"It is all here," he exclaimed.

"Surely you didn't doubt our sincerity, Jeffrey. I wouldn't want to believe you don't trust us."

"It's just that I have never done anything list this before. I guess I am a little nervous."

"That is to be expected, Jeffrey. I take no offense at your caution."

A knock sounded on the outside door and the second officer reappeared. He nodded to Sujito and took a place to the side of the pair.

"Good. My second officer says that everything you brought with you is in order."

"I am sure that the photos were exactly what you wanted. I told you the quality is the best that I have seen since I started working there."

"You were most certainly correct. I am most pleased."

"Well then, it is time for me to be getting back. I wouldn't want to stay away too long and be missed."

"About that, Jeffrey. I am afraid I have a little bad news, " Captain Sujito replied sourly.

"Bad news?" Jeffrey looked into his friend's suddenly serious face. He started to rise from his seat.

"Yes. I am afraid my country cannot take the chance of your being found out and possibly being linked to you."

"But, I am not about to be found out. I am much too smart for that."

"Yes, Jeffrey, but we cannot take the chance."

"But . . ." Jeffrey was suddenly aware of a cold hard object being pushed against the back of his head. He started to turn to face the second officer who had silently moved behind him.

As the bullet exploded into his temple, Jeffrey Yapp realized his terrible mistake and that his life was at its end. A white blur passed before his eyes as he tumbled to the ground.

"It is unfortunate we had to do this, second officer, but we have our orders," Captain Sujito reflected. "Place his body in the meat locker for the time being. We will give our friend a proper burial when we get out to sea. After all, he did die on our vessel."

The second officer nodded and started to drag Jeffrey Yapp's lifeless body though the hatchway. A thin trail of blood followed as the slumped body disappeared around a corner.

I

THE SOUTHERN ROAD

January 1, 1941, Taiwan Army Barracks, Japanese Imperial Army, Formosa, 1315 hours

The uncomfortable midday heat that teetered just above the seventy-five-degree mark and engulfed Chinese Taipei was difficult for the small group of Japanese Imperial Army officers to bear; a fact made even more arduous considering the men were attired in their winter dress uniforms.

Most of these men had just transferred from the heralded Japanese Kanto Army that was still serving the emperor and Japanese people in the empire's war against the Chinese in Manchuria. Manchuria's northern latitude and the officers' prolonged duty in that harsh locale had toughened each man individually and made each one impervious to the bitter cold and rugged vastness of that far northern area. When word came from the Japanese Army Imperial Staff that they would relocate, most officers considered their unexpected transfers to the much milder climates of the Island of Formosa as a true blessing from divine providence.

The officers said little as they walked, this first day of the western New Year having little meaning to any of them. As they continued their walk, they paused as the ranking officer who walked slightly ahead stopped at a crosswalk inside the military barracks. A new sign had been recently erected. The sign's plain black letters clearly read:

TAIWAN ARMY
NO. 82 UNIT

The ranking officer in the gathering, Col. Masanobu Tsuji, a graduate of the Imperial Japanese Army Military School at Ichigaya, studied the marker as it swung gently in the warm, humid breeze, framed by the brilliance of the temperate afternoon sun.

Tsuji turned back to the men standing behind and remarked, "Remember this day my dear fellow officers, for I think our small unit is destined to provide the Empire with some extraordinary accomplishments. Fate and the deities have brought us together, for our nation is about to embark upon a most challenging path."

Following military tradition, the officers formally nodded to their leader and then to each other, even though each was as yet unaware of the precise meaning of Colonel Tsuji's prophecy. The band departed the signpost and continued their journey towards the unit's barracks, located some two hundred yards ahead. It was not customary in the Imperial Japanese Army for junior officers to ever question a superior's remarks even if such curiosity was warranted. When and if the superior officer felt the necessity to explain his comments, he was always free to do so at his own convenience. Japanese military officers had observed such formality for hundreds of years.

January 10, 1941, Taiwan Army Headquarters, Taiwan Army Research Department, Taiwan, 0700 hours

The oddly clothed selection of Japanese Imperial Army officers stood stiffly as the unit commander entered the room and offered the traditional Japanese perfunctory bow. The assembled officers returned the bow and waited until their commander assumed his seated position.

When the group was finally settled in, an action that according to Japanese military custom would take but a few seconds, the officer looked across the room and began to speak.

At fifty-one, Col. Yoshihide Hayashi was firmly in control of the most significant assignment of his entire military career. For the past two years, he had served as a staff officer connected to the Japanese Imperial Army

General Staff. His work ethic proved to his superiors the fact that he was a trusted and capable staff officer. Hayashi had recently completed several important assignments under temporary duty with the Japanese forces in China, and his success in these matters allowed his superiors to determine Colonel Hayashi's true value to the Imperial Army.

His new command position required ultimate resourcefulness and attention to detail, two of Yoshihide Hayashi's abundant leadership qualities. Tireless in the pursuit of his duties, Hayashi was the type of individual who inspired his subordinates through many of his own individual traits and characteristics. These facts and his unblemished military record weighed heavily in his assignment to the important post as Commander of the Taiwan Army Research Department Unit.

"Honorable gentlemen," Colonel Hayashi addressed his officers in a tone that was carefully controlled, " I must begin by saying that Divine Fate has brought us all together here in Taihoku (Taiwan) for our most important undertaking. As you all are most surely aware, we are now in the fifteenth year of Showa, the reign of our glorious Emperor Hirohoto.

"Because of various political and military circumstances, it has become necessary for our leaders to consider possible alternatives to our ongoing struggle in Manchukuo (Manchuria). I know that a number of you have served in that most intolerable area of the world and I welcome your honorable expertise to our table. You have served the Japanese Empire well and your past actions and military records have brought you here to aid in our present mission."

"The attention of our general staff has now become directed southward, toward the countries that presently control a large percentage of the world's supply of tin, rubber and fuel oil, not to mention huge resources of food and other important things."

The officers in attendance sat intently around the table, attempting to absorb the solemn parameters of their leader's words. Not a single eye was raised or a question formed, for such behavior would be considered disrespectful until Colonel Hayashi had completed his remarks.

The diminutive, pie-faced, bespectacled career military officer continued: "The job we have been given here in Taiwan will be entirely new for all of us. You are all aware that for the past decade, all Japanese military preparations and training have been associated with our fight in the north against the Chinese. Since the locations where this war has been conducted are mostly cold and barren places, our tactics and equipment have been developed with that particular arena in mind. Our efforts there have proven quite successful due to our superior strategy and planning.

Army activities in other areas, however, provide us with a most different and difficult challenge. When I was first approached about this assignment, I found myself questioning the wisdom and sincerity of even attempting such an undertaking."

First, it was first explained to everyone in staff school that whomever controls the seas and supplies from Southeast Asia controls the fate of the eastern world. I had always known of Japan's reliance on the sea and shipping in particular, but I had no idea of just how critical the entire scenario had become. As a nation, Japan will shortly have our backs to the wall, to borrow an old expression. If we are to continue our divine role as a dominant country in the world, something must be done to insure the safety of the Imperial Empire and her ability to supply herself. We are here because our leaders have embarked on a solution to this impending problem. After much thought and consideration, I became convinced that our leaders were totally correct in their initial planning.

"The entire strategy has been referred to as the "Southward Road," because Japan's real future lies to the south. When I first became involved in planning for Southward Road—the name you will all henceforth use in referring to our mission—I was appalled that no one within the entire Japanese Imperial Army seemed to know anything about warfare and fighting in warmer climates. All our manuals and directives are designed to help our troops fight in the cold and snows of the north, but nothing is written about wartime conditions and equipment for the south."

"Honorable officers, we have been given the incredible responsibility of preparing our Army for the eventuality of fighting in the tropics. Our job will not be an easy one and we have not been given much time. We must all make personal sacrifice to insure our mission's success."

Hayashi paused, consulting his hand-written notes. Satisfied he had covered all the contents, he raised his gaze and continued.

"I believe this is an excellent opportunity to introduce a special staff officer to the rest of you. I am extremely pleased that Colonel Tsuji has joined us as staff officer in charge of operations and planning for the Malayan Sector. It is a great honor to welcome him to our unit."

Colonel Tsuji rose, and bowed slightly in the direction of Colonel Hayashi, his superior in rank who had preceded him at Ichigaya by two years. Tsuji was pleased with his old friend's kind words and smiled warmly while formally acknowledging the gesture.

Hayashi bowed back briefly and continued his diatribe.

"Each of you have been assigned here for a special purpose and each officer at this table brings a special ability to our unit. I will not try and deceive you by saying our task will be easy, for that would be foolish and unproductive. I must also share with all of you that I feel privately that an action such as this should have been initiated several years ago when there existed sufficient time for such data to be collected."

Colonel Hayashi paused, as if in deep thought and finally returned his glance to the attentive collection of officers seated in front of him.

"Gentlemen, it is our duty to immediately begin the most urgent task of gathering together all conceivable data that relates to tropical warfare. It will be necessary for us to incorporate pertinent details into a plan that will provide for the organization of all the army forces that will be involved in the actual campaign. We must list all equipment that will be required to conduct this possibly prolonged mission, and finally, we must plan the actual course such a mission must follow in order to prove successful.

"Along with these major areas of concentration, we must additionally address the ongoing problems relating to management and treatment of our army's weapons and ammunition, proper sanitation for our troops and a realistic assessment of the supply needs for everyone involved. In gathering our facts, it is important that we take nothing for granted. Our work is so important that we must assume from the start that we know nothing about the terrain or the people we will encounter."

The room was totally silent as Hayashi adjusted his glasses slightly and continued.

"The military strategies we are now most familiar with must be discarded, for they pertain to a different environment and, in most probability, will be useless to us in the tropics. Special attention must be given to the seriousness and consequences of dealing with malaria, for we are all aware of its disastrous consequences if not treated with the respect and care due its heinous nature."

"We must also keep a constant eye toward the accomplishment of our goals for the empire. If our actions are blessed by the deities and prove to be successful, we must also develop a plan for the administration of the occupied territory. There will be numerous political and cultural factors to consider, and each of these must be dealt with on a singular basis. We cannot afford to make mistakes in this most sensitive area."

"The Japanese High Command feels that if certain circumstances are met, it will be possible to convince many of the Asian natives that we are actually liberating them from centuries of British and Dutch colonial rule. One of the members of the High Command actually feels that some ethnic-allied soldiers might even be convinced to change their allegiance and fight on our side for the remainder of the war. I personally believe that thinking is a bit far fetched, but I am open minded enough to concede that such an idea is possible."

"As you can all see, our unit had been designated the Taiwan Army Research Department, but I am delighted with the informal name that seems to have developed on its own. For our own purposes, we will refer to ourselves as the Dora Nawa Unit, but that name can only be used informally among ourselves. It will be a rallying point for each of us and for our subordinates as we try to accomplish this most responsible task."

He stopped for a moment, reflecting on his notes, insuring he had not forgotten any important points.

Colonel Hayashi looked up once again, his face frozen in its intensity. "Oh yes, gentlemen, I almost forgot."

Each officer's face tensed as they waited for their leader's final words.

"The Imperial Staff had given us but *six* short months to complete our work on the Southward Road."

Not a single eye blinked as the gravity of the situation penetrated each man's comprehension.

II
RUMBLINGS

January 22, 1941, On maneuvers with the 2nd Argyll and Sutherland Highlanders, Northeastern Kelantan Province, Malaya, 1345 hours

It had been a usual, rainy day that was mostly expected on this day's edition of the monsoon in northeastern Malaya. The torrential rains had come a bit earlier than usual this Wednesday morning and by 1000 hours everyone involved with the maneuvers was completely drenched.

Today's scheduled exercise was but one of a number of such maneuvers that was intended to get the 2nd Argyll and Sutherland Highlanders into a top-fighting mode—in an environment its leaders believed would make them superior to any other jungle fighters in the British Army.

Even though the unit had been in Singapore since 1939, this new attitude involving jungle warfare and ultimate preparedness emanated directly from the unit's new commanding officer, Lt. Col. Ian Stewart.

Stewart was a no-nonsense leader who believed that adequate training and preparedness on the part of his officers would ultimately benefit his men, if and when they were called on to fight an enemy. The proud traditions of the original Scottish regiment could be traced back as far as 1799, and included such memorable engagements as the Battle of New Orleans in 1815, and the Russian Battle of Balaklava in 1854, where the regiment had earned its famous nickname in military history, *The Thin Red Line*.

Lieutenant Colonel Stewart was also a confident, pragmatic leader. When he arrived in Malaysia, he surmised that his troops would benefit from extended jungle activities since the country was comprised of practically ninety-nine percent jungles. He developed a series of tactics that were new to the British army—methods that involved aggressive, fast mobility and the use of squads that he called 'Tiger Patrols' due to their pugnacious nature.

The 2nd Argyll and Sutherland Highlanders' main mobility came from a number of older Lanchester 6 X 4 armoured cars that had been sent to Malaysia from Great Britain in 1939. Even though the Lanchesters were too big for the area's secondary roads, Lieutenant Colonel Stewart liked the fact that they were very reliable and easy to maintain, and could reach speeds exceeding fifty miles per hour on decent roads (if rapid deployment became a necessity). The Lanchesters were armed with a 12.7mm Vickers machine gun and two 7.7mm Vickers machine guns that provided a singeing amount of firepower whenever called upon.

It was clear to see why Lieutenant Colonel Stewart had invited Air Chief Marshall Sir Robert Brooke-Popham, commander in chief of the Far East, as his guest for the maneuvers in spite of the failing weather conditions. He was expecting his crack troops to perform well despite anything the monsoon could throw against them.

The two stood on an observation platform atop a small hill overlooking a series of small valleys, some four miles from the Malaysian coastline. It was almost possible to see the water from this spot, but, with today's overcast and rainy skies, such a feat was impossible.

Brooke-Popham lowered his binoculars and turned to Stewart.

"I am very impressed with your unit's progress, Colonel," Brooke-Popham remarked. "I think you are on to something with your hit and move tactics. I must say it is a bit unconventional, but then, we *are* in a jungle setting. It is also smart to always be prepared to make allowances for the environment. I've always been a strong proponent of knowing what is the keenest way to handle a challenging scenario."

"Yes, Sir Robert," Stewart replied, also dropping his binoculars. "I knew you would appreciate what we are trying to do. If only the blinkin' weather would cooperate, we could accomplish even more. These days we spend as much time getting our equipment out of the mud as we do in deployment. It's a bugged shame."

"It is part of being in Malaysia during the monsoon, that's all. It's a bloody mess but there's also a good side to it."

"Good side, Sir Robert?"

"Yes, the same rains and weather would affect an invader's plans as much as it does ours, I believe they would have the same problems with their heavy equipment as we do. I would imagine that following such logic would prevent any invasion from occurring during the northeast monsoon, and that lasts for several months each year."

"I guess you are right, Sir Robert," Steward answered back in an unconvinced tone. "Unless they were able to figure some way around it."

"Some way around it?" Brooke-Popham chuckled, amused at the thought. "You must be kidding, man. You have been here long enough to know what happens during the monsoon–everything comes to a grinding halt."

"I'm just saying, Sir, if they were able to travel light, I mean *really* light, then it could be a different story."

"Really now, Stewart, you can't be serious."

"Oh, it wouldn't be easy, Sir Robert, but I'm convinced it could be done. I just haven't figured out how to do it yet, but you can see what I mean." Stewart pointed down the hill where a number of men were attempting to pull a stuck Lanchester out of a mud hole that appeared to be in the middle of a nearby road.

Brooke-Popham readjusted his binoculars and stared at the scenario below. At length he dropped his gaze and readdressed Colonel Stewart.

"That sort of thing happens all the time, Stewart. It just tends to support my last argument. Whenever it comes to a case of man versus nature, nature usually wins out. It's something I've believed for my entire career. You find me someone who doesn't agree with that and I'll show you a fool."

"Quite, Sir Robert," Stewart agreed. "I guess you have a point."

"By the way, Colonel," Brooke-Popham inserted. "It is my understanding that your men have *already* accounted for a couple of battles."

"Battles, Sir?" Stewart inquired deliberately, hoping the air marshal wasn't implying what he expected.

"You know what I mean, Colonel, don't play coy with me."

Stewart flushed, realizing the AIC was prying good-naturedly.

"Oh yes, you mean the two *recent* battles."

"Precisely," the AIC smiled broadly. "It seems the last one is the talk of all Malaya."

Stewart held his ground in the face of such overwhelming fact.

"I would say we upheld the honour of the regiment, Sir Robert." Stewart was referring to the Battle of Lavender Street (Singapore's red-light district) and the Battle of the Union Jack Club when soldiers of the 2nd Argyles and the Royal Australian Army chose to voice specific disagreements about each other. It was also generally conceded that *both* sides upheld each other's honor during the melees.

"Those type of things are sometimes good for the men's morale," Brooke-Popham offered. "As long as no one really got hurt, it is better to look the other way."

"Some cuts and bruises, but no real harm done. And, the men's attitude was decidedly better after the engagements," Stewart chuckled.

"I can see the improvement, they have turned into a most effective fighting group. I wouldn't want to face them in a conflict," Brooke-Popham concluded. "In fact, I am going to suggest you share some of your tactical ideas with some of the other units that are facing the same type of potential problems."

"Of course, Sir Robert, I would be honored to do so."

Brooke-Popham turned as if to depart and Stewart spoke once more.

"Ur, Sir Robert, there's just one more thing I would like to mention."

Brooke-Popham turned around to face the Argyll's commander.

"Yes, Colonel. Please go ahead."

Stewart thought for a moment and said, " I do hope, Sir, we are not getting too strong in Malaya, because if so, the Japanese may never attempt a landing."

Brooke-Popham smiled and said nothing.

6 March 1941, Inside Officer's Quarters, British Army 16th Punjab Regiment, north of Brinchang, Malaya 1730 hours

It was very nearly this time of each day that British Army Capt. Patrick Stanley Vaughn Heenan enjoyed the most. By this point of the afternoon, most of his routine duties with the 3/16 Punjab Regiment of the British Indian Army were completed and Heenan was able to drift over to the Officer's Bar and have his first refreshing pint of the day. Heenan savored the tasty brew and sometimes drank as if it would be the last beer he would ever have. He was generally one of the first of the Punjab officers to arrive at the club and usually one of the last to leave.

As he tipped his glass into his still parched throat, Hennan glanced out the large, ornate colonial windows that bracketed the Officer's Bar. From his seat, he could see a good distance down the road in the direction other officers would take in making their way to the bar. He always kept an eye out to identify who was coming, just in case one of the snots that made his existence in Malaya uncomfortable was on his way in. Lately, it seemed to him that practically *all* his fellow officers were of a mind to make his duty at Brinchang an unpleasant experience.

He reflected back into his memory and was soon deep in thought.

Not bad for a bastard New Zealander who became commissioned in the British Army despite so many disadvantages.

He checked his mind's progress and recanted to himself segments of his earlier life. He did this periodically to remind himself of his base beginnings.

The initial pieces were told to him by his mother, a woman who genuinely loved him and who in turn was loved by her young son. Never married to his father, Heenan's mother, Annie Stanley, was Irish, and was instrumental in sending Heenan to Great Britain for schooling at the age of sixteen. She chose a place called Sevenoaks School for his early training.

The youth only lasted there a few months and was then sent to Cheltenham College where his natural father had once attended. At Cheltenham, Heenan started to excel in athletics but was always a disappointment to his teachers in any academics.

Heenan was exceedingly tall for his age, and soon developed a wavy head of blonde hair that accentuated his natural good looks. He was also a Roman Catholic, definitely a minority in the school and the local area. Patrick Heenan was not popular with his classmates and tended to consort with a number of the local girls, something strictly forbidden by the strict Cheltenham rules.

He joined the Officer's Training Corps at the school, something for which Cheltenham was well known. When he left the school, his academic woes left him unsuitable for a military career or for admission to any of Great Britain's military academies.

Heenan used a forged baptism certificate to apply to the Supplemental Reserve, the only officer path left open to a man in his position. To his surprise, he was accepted and finally commissioned in the Supplementary Reserve at the age of twenty-five, unusually late for a British Army officer.

He was then placed on the unattached list of the Indian Army while attempting to persuade a regiment of the Indian Army to accept him. It was six months before the 16th Punjab Regiment finally received him into its ranks.

During the winter of 1938 and into the spring of the following year, he took his long annual leave in Japan, a time and experience he now considered as the most rewarding and fruitful of his entire life. In Japan, he met a number of people he found most interesting, and reveled in the fact that several of them treated him better than anyone had in his entire life. His new Japanese friends built up his deflated ego and made him feel he had true friends for the first time in his life.

One of those people was an observant Japanese Military Intelligence agent who spotted Heenan's outspokenness as an easy mark. After several weeks of partying and companionship, the man approached Heenan about intelligence work for the Empire of Japan. Heenan's long-standing dislike of the British and, in particular its snotty officer corps that made his life miserable, made his decision quite easy. When he returned to the

16th Punjab Regiment in late March, Heenan was already a more-than-willing informant.

Heenan glanced out the window as his concentration returned to his surroundings.

If only these officers knew how important I am to the Japanese, they would probably split a gut. Too bad it has to be this way, but it serves them right. All that snobbery and self-importance, and also the fact that the British Crown is <u>always</u> *right—no matter what! Well, if war ever comes, as some people are saying, it will be nice to be on the winning side. I know the Japanese will take great care of me, they already have.*

His awareness again returned to the present, as the Malay waiter replaced his pint with a fresh one. Heenan tipped his brow to signify he already had started a chit with the bartender and the waiter departed.

A small group of officers entered the bar and surveyed the premises. They looked directly at Heenan and then turned in the opposite direction.

Heenan saw this obvious disregard and smiled to himself.

Soon, quite soon! It is important to just ignore those types. I will just keep to myself and continue doing what I have been trained to do. If everything goes as expected, I will undoubtedly have the last laugh. They will never know what hit them . . .

He finished his pint and decided it was time for a walk, the air inside the club now smelled musty and of old beer. Normally, that sort of scent compelled Heenan to have another pint, but today he found the smell unpleasant and so he decided to leave.

Capt. Patrick Heenan rose from his chair and headed to the bar to settle his tab. He noted the four marks on the paper, each signifying a pint, and took out a few coins that he dropped on the bar. When the Malay bartender face remained quizzical, he dropped a few more coins in favor of the native barman. Pleased, the Malay man smiled and turned his back.

So did Patrick Heenan, suddenly pleased that a few small coins had made someone so happy.

March 15, 1941, Doro Nawa Unit, Taiwan Army Headquarters, Taiwan, 1010 hours

The perfectly bent man in tattered civilian clothes bowed stiffly and waited until Col. Masanobu Tsuji finished reading the documents in his hands. The slight, bald, mustachioed officer carefully considered the papers' contents and finally raised his head, adjusting his steel-rimmed glasses on his small nose as he moved.

"It is nice to see you again, Captain Asaeda. Our first meeting in China years ago was much too brief."

"It is kind for the colonel to recall such a minor meeting."

Tsuji bowed his head softly and continued, "So, Captain Asaeda, your service record contains a most interesting personal history. In fact, I can honestly say that I have never seen anything quite like it in all my prior military experience."

The tall, angular man remained silent; his eyes firmly fixed on the ground directly in front of his superior.

"Come on, man, be at ease. I see no need for such silence. We are all friends here."

Asaeda slowly raised his head as his eyes met the smaller, bespeckled Colonel Tsuji for the first time.

"If that is your wish, Honorable Colonel."

As the man stood erect, Tsuji regarded the man's unusual height, certainly more than six feet and unusually tall for a Japanese. It was the first thing that had brought Asaeda to his attention in China, where he towered over most other Japanese troops. There was also something else about the man's bearing that demanded respect and so, the Colonel opted to choose his words carefully.

"I know you have a good explanation for your appearance, and I want to know what that is. I think it is best that you tell me straight away. Our Doro Nawa Unit is quite specialized and I know if you were directed here, there must be a good reason."

Capt. Shigeharu Asaeda chose to maintain his silence, but shifted his weight uneasily. Tsuji noticed the hardened man's discomfort and addressed him again.

"Captain Asaeda, I am also informed of the fact that you have volunteered for this duty. Since it was impossible for you to know anything about our mission, may I inquire as to exactly why you chose to cast your lot with such an unknown group of men?"

Asaeda looked directly into Tsuji's face and replied. His words came in short bursts, but Tsuji noted the man was now much calmer, and completely in control of his senses.

"I will try and explain to you, Sir, the unfortunate circumstances of my miserable career."

Colonel Tsuji returned his gaze to the documents he held in his hand as Asaeda continued.

"After my graduation from military school, I entered the service of the Emperor and spent several years in a number of routine positions that I was ordered to do by the Army. I was elated when the news finally arrived that I had been accepted to attend the Army Staff College. The work there was quite enjoyable and I was blessed with graduation and presented with my set of swords.

I was next assigned as a staff officer in Shansi and was honored to be able to serve my Emperor and country in a number of battles and engagements."

Tsuji followed along, reviewing Asaeda's service record that showed several notations for bravery in the face of enemy action. In fact, the more Tsuji read, the stronger the wording and descriptions covering Captain Asaeda's exploits became. According to his superior's accounts, Captain Asaeda was a true hero officer, famed for his courage and particularly gallant in saving the lives of a number of his men on more than one occasion.

"Captain Asaeda, I can certainly see that your gallantry is well documented."

"Thank you, Sir, but I am afraid that I was given too much credit by my honorable senior officers for my ordinary actions."

Tsuji looked at the man and immediately developed a close kinship for the fellow.

Here is a true warrior, someone unafraid for his own safety, someone who can be counted on to accomplish the most difficult of jobs. He would have fit in well with the former world of the samurais. I will have to use him carefully.

Asaeda shifted his weight uneasily, attempting to choose the correct words. "After my China duties were completed, I was selected for the War Office Army Officer's Bureau and began my duties there."

Tsuji nodded his agreement at the mention of the important posting that was noted in the records in his hand.

"But your records show that you left after only a few months."

"Yes," Asaeda replied, "I did not enjoy the office work. I am afraid I am a very poor staff officer. I needed more of a challenge than sitting around Tokyo shuffling sets of papers and drinking lots of green tea and sake."

Impressed with the man's candidness, Tsuji suppressed a chuckle. "Go on, Asaeda, so what happened next?"

"There were rumors everywhere in Tokyo about the course the Empire would follow and some of my fellow officers in the Officer's Bureau had developed theories about what and where the Army would next act. I made my own assumptions and guessed that our needs and logic would send us on a southward course.

I caught a freighter bound for Taiwan and came here of my own accord. When I arrived I took off my uniform and bought some peasant clothes. I have spent the time since then trying to learn about our enemies' plans from the Europeans who live and work here. I finally decided to approach the Army about my activities and I was sent directly to you."

"And all this was done of your own accord, Captain Asaeda?"

"Most definitely, Honorable Colonel, I take all the blame myself."

Tsuji considered the discussion for several moments and finally asked, "And what have you heard about our unit?"

"Practically nothing, Sir. I have heard it referred to as *Doro Nawa*, and I am sorry to say that I do not understand the meaning of such a thing."

"I will attempt to explain. Maybe I was a little too clever in developing such a name.

Doro as you know, means robber and *nawa* means rope in our language. I wanted the phrase to refer to our work here. First you catch the robber and afterwards you begin to make the rope. Our unit was formed very recently and given a minute amount of time to accomplish its mission. I guess you could say we were formed at the eleventh hour. I know that most Japanese will think our name is some sort of joke and in our language *doro nawa* also means 'no time', but that doesn't really matter. I want our name to stand out. Does any of this make sense to you?"

Unsure of how to answer, Asaeda blinked and said wearily, "I think so. As long as you are pleased."

"Our name also gives us a sense of purpose, quite unlike being called Number 82 Unit or something similar. I think our unit's name will be meaningful in the end."

Asaeda did not reply, since Tsuji's remark was more of a statement that did not seem to require a response.

"And now, Asaeda, I have some good news for you. I think your former bravery and war record, and the ingenuity you displayed in figuring all this out, should be rewarded. I have great need of a man with your capabilities in *Doro Nawa*. There is much to be done here and I believe I can make great use of a man with your unique capabilities. If you agree, I will notify our headquarters and have you permanently assigned to us."

"It would be a great pleasure, Sir."

"Good. I can see you helping us a great deal. Now to briefly explain our mission at *Doro Nawa* Unit."

Captain Asaeda leaned forward as Colonel Tsuji continued speaking.

"Much of our activity involves gathering intelligence information from our enemies. The job I have in mind for you requires a man with great ingenuity and intelligence. It will involve an undercover operation that could provide the Empire with a great amount of information."

"The job sounds much like what I have been doing since I arrived here," Asaeda replied, shaking his head affirmatively. "When do I begin?"

"Today if you wish, you are dressed perfectly for your role. I want you to go into the general population and seek out information. But, now I want you to be more specific. You will seek out British officials and act the part of a common coolie."

Asaeda smiled, understanding fully what was expected of him. His new assignment lifted his spirits and propelled his life and career back to a course that he considered meaningful to himself and to the Empire of Japan. He liked his new commander and felt his new organization was important within the Japanese Imperial Army. Yutaka Asaeda was immensely pleased. He was finally blessed with a duty in which he could possibly excel. His family and ancestors would be pleased.

He suppressed a desire to smile openly, bowed respectfully to Colonel Tsuji, and departed the colonel's small office. The battle-tested captain had already begun thinking about his method of gathering even more important intelligence on the British military in Malaya.

March 17, 1941, Headquarters, 8th Division, Royal Australian Imperial Force, Kluang, Malaya, 0700 hours

It had already been a bad morning for Maj. Gen. Henry Gordon Bennett, Commanding Officer of the 8th Division of the Royal Australian Imperial Force, known to everyone in Malaya as simply the AIF.

Things had been sticky since Bennett and his forces had first arrived in Malaya almost a month before on the liner *Queen Mary*. At first, a round of parties and nightlife in Singapore extended the British Crown's welcome to Bennett and his Aussies, but the newness soon wore off. The move northward to Kluang was a step back in Bennett's considered opinion, and the fact that his brigades were actually encamped some distance away at Port Dickson and Malacca, both semi-remote sites with little to offer, made the situation worse.

Plus, the news that was delivered on February 28 by the deputy general of the Australian General Staff, Maj. Gen. John Northcott, was not well received. Northcott's report that the 8th Division was not getting additional troops to bolster its numbers was taken as almost a personal blow by the fiery South Australian. Like a number of other recent happenings, Bennett considered it part of a plot by the Australian High Command to limit him in his pursuit of higher honors, not to mention the greater glory of Australia and Maj. Gen. Gordon Bennett.

With his fifty-fifth birthday less than a month away, Bennett was aware that others considered him a bit too old for a battlefield command, but he dismissed such personal affronts as "jealous rantin' from my contemporaries." His combative stances throughout his military career had negated his combat bravery, and his continuing bickering with his staff and fellow officers had relegated him to command of the 8th Division, while in his own words, "the real war was bein' waged in the Middle East and elsewhere."

He was also currently embattled in a nasty fight with Brigadier Harold B. Taylor, the commander of the 8th Division's 22nd Brigade. Taylor was a rotund senior officer who had received the Military Cross and Bar for his bravery and actions during World War I. He knew Bennett well, but wanted to be able to command his own troops, and was willing to fight his commanding officer for that right.

He realized the plight of the Australian fighting man in the nearly intolerable conditions of Malaya and sought to provide them with a training regiment that would enable them to compete with the enemy, if and when asked to do so.

It was a simple training exercise that drew Bennett's ire, when the movement went unreported to 8th Division Headquarters. Bennett summoned Taylor to his offices in Kluang and read the doughy general the riot act. He insisted that *every* future order must first pass through his divisional headquarters and failure to do so could mean immediate replacement. Taylor buckled under and promised to work together with Bennett "for the good of the AIF."

With such surroundings and limitations facing him everywhere, Maj. Gen. Gordon Bennett had summoned his new Chief of Staff, Col. Harry Rourke and also his senior administrative officer, Col. Ray Broadbent, to his office for an early morning meeting.

The three sat around a small, circular serving table off to the side in Bennett's office.

Bennett began in his thick accent.

"I asked you two here to insure we get off on the right foot, gentle-men. I know you have just arrived, but I thought this meetin' made a good deal of sense."

"Certainly, General," answered Rourke. "It's never too early for an important meeting."

"Good, at least we agree on that."

Rourke looked for a brief moment at Broadbent, who acknowledged the look with a faint glance of concern. Bennett had not looked up from a stack of papers he held in his hand.

"I want you both to know where I stand on everything," Bennett con-tinued. "An informed staff is a productive staff, don't you agree?"

Rourke glanced again at Broadbent and said softly, "Certainly Gen-eral, it makes all the more sense."

"Right. Now. Let us get down to business. I believe it is necessary for us to 'ave complete control of all our resources here in this blasted jungle, and that may require some doin' since we are somewhat spread out. I have little confidence in our British chums' ability to properly support us and, if I am correct, this will require us to be self-sufficient. Understood?"

Neither Colonel Rourke nor Colonel Broadbent moved an eyebrow, unsure of what was expected from them in the form of a reply.

"Er, General, I'm not too sure . . ." Colonel Rourke replied weakly.

"For heavens sake, man, isn't it clear? Must I explain myself again? Just what sort of chaps are you to have been assigned to me in a leadership position."

"Now, just a minute, General Bennett. We are new here and this is our first briefing. Just what are we supposed to know?" Rourke asserted himself.

"I would have expected my new chief of staff and senior admin of-ficer to have brushed up on what we are up against," Bennett fired back. "It seems that all I am surrounded with are incompetent officers who are incapable of following orders. Just like Brigadier Taylor, but he has 'is coming and I will see to that."

"But, Sir," Colonel Broadbent replied, attempting to mitigate the situation. "Colonel Rourke and I have just arrived and there has been no time to familiarize ourselves with anything, you must realize that. And since the mission of the 8th Division is somewhat secretive in nature, there wouldn't have been much chance to delve into anything of substance before we left home."

Bennett considered the officer's argument and suddenly changed the direction of the conversation.

"Now that I have your *full* attention, let us get down to brass tacks."

The two staff officers stiffened and cast a worried glance at each other.

The rumors we heard about Bennett were mostly correct. Our leader is nearly off his rocker and unable to really focus on anything. This is going to be even drearier than we expected. We can only hope for the best.

"Since I have been informed we are not gettin' the two extra battalions I was promised earlier by the General Staff, I have decided that it is necessary that we change our mission 'ere in Malaya."

Both officers stared at their commander in disbelief.

"I have already contacted the GOC in Singapore about changing our area of responsibility and gettin' us off the Command Reserve status. General Percival seemed to understand my position and the fact that we Australians have distinguished ourselves in battle for many years. He is to be back to me in the near future, and then we will swing into action. If there really is something that starts up around here, it doesn't take the smartest person to figure out where the action will be. I have asked for us to be given the defensive positions around the Alor Star Air Centre and also Mersing near the east coast. These are our best chances of bein' involved with the fightin', one way or another."

The two colonels continued to be totally speechless.

"Also, we need to get our men better prepared for the type of fightin' the jungles around here offer. That means more fitness and more accuracy with their weapons. I don't trust the battalion officers to get the job done, so I am expecting you two to shoulder some of the responsibility, sort of look over their shoulder with a 'elpin' hand if you know what I mean."

Both men nodded, finally beginning to understand what Bennett expected of them.

Bennett continued.

"I want both of you to realize that this can be a truly wonderful situation for us if and when a battle actually erupts. Right now, all the action is in another part of the world, and I have tried my damndest to get myself assigned there, but with no luck. I want to stick it out here with the snakes, leeches and scorpions and hope to hell one of 'em deals me a mortal blow. Well, for now, I've decided to make the most of it even if it means I'm totally uncomfortable for long periods of time.

But, I know this for sure: gentlemen, I will mold this division into a fightin' machine that will make us all proud, and no one will stand in my way. Of that, you can rest assured."

The two colonels blinked, unwilling to display any real sense of their true thoughts.

Bennett paused again, and returned to the wad of papers he was holding.

"And, now, gentlemen, if there is nothing else. "I have other important matters to attend to."

The officers stood and offered a perfunctory salute. When General Bennett failed to notice, they lowered their hands and stepped back from the table.

Their first meeting with Maj. Gen. H. Gordon Bennett, Commander of the 8th Division, Australian Imperial Force, had been concluded.

April 5, 1941, Doro Nawa Unit, Taiwan Military Headquarters, Taiwan, 0855 hours

Capt. Shigeharu Asaeda of the Imperial Japanese Army picked up his pace as he approached the building that served as headquarters of the Research Department of Imperial Japan's Taiwan Army, unofficially called by its men the *Dora Nawa* Unit. He adjusted his uniform, assuring himself that everything was in order. The uniform felt strange to the muscular six-footer, and served as sharp contrast to the peasant's rags he had worn for the past five weeks. As he neared the unit's building, Captain Asaeda reviewed in his mind the upcoming the meeting with *Doro Nawa's* dedicated commander, Col. Masanobu Tsuji. The meeting was scheduled for 0900 and Asaeda knew he could not be late. Since joining *Doro Nawa* and resurrecting his failing military career, Asaeda had found his commander to be more precise and punctual than any other officer he had ever served under.

He entered the building's door and removed his cap. Glancing at his watch, Asaeda noted that he had made the appointment with more than thirty seconds to spare. He looked around the room and saw that several officers and a few enlisted men were busily engaged in writing and examining documents that were laid out across a number of desks that occupied the building's anteroom.

At precisely 0900, a phone rang on one of the desks. The sergeant seated behind the desk picked up the phone and spoke into the mouthpiece. He shook his head once in agreement and replaced the instrument.

"Colonel Tsuji will see you now, Captain Asaeda. You are to go into his office."

The tall twenty-nine-year old acknowledged the instruction and approached Tsuji's office, the first door down a short hall. He knocked once on the door.

"Enter," came the reply from within.

Asaeda opened the door and stepped inside. He walked three steps toward the desk and the figure seated behind it. He bowed and offered a greeting.

"Captain Asaeda reporting as ordered, Colonel. I hope this morning finds you well and productive."

"It most certainly does, Captain Asaeda, thank you for your good wishes."

Asaeda nodded slightly, but did not reply.

"Sit down Asaeda, you will be more comfortable."

Asaeda nodded and took a seat in a chair in front of Tsuji's large teakwood desk.

"I am very happy with your reports so far," continued Tsuji, his narrow eyes continually blinking. It was a negligible characteristic of the colonel that Asaeda had forced himself to get comfortable with early in their relationship.

"In fact, you have already succeeded in getting us some very pertinent information about British intentions for the future."

Asaeda answered self assuredly, "I seem to have a special knack, Colonel. I am happy that you are pleased with my efforts."

"You can rest assured, Asaeda, but now I have something really special for you to do. This mission will again be undercover and will require you to travel first to Thailand and then to Burma. You will disguise yourself as an electrical engineer on a survey for one of our leading Japanese electrical companies. This cover should get you into many areas that could prove useful to us. I want you to take a new camera with you that has been developed specially for our use by the Nikon camera company. It takes three times the number of pictures of a normal camera and utilizes special film. I also have a good supply of that film for you to take with you. You are to use the camera on every occasion you feel necessary. I want you to photograph everything of interest, from airfield to electrical stations to police garrisons. You are also to commit a number of the areas in which you travel into rough maps; I'm afraid that many of our maps of these areas are horribly unusable."

Asaeda remained silent, fascinated with the implication of Tsuji's words.

Is this really happening to me? What have I done to be worthy of all this? I must be sure to thank the gods the minute I have time . . .

"When you reach Bangkok, there are two men that I want you to be sure and rendezvous with. The two men are Japanese Intelligence officers that are on a special mission in Thailand that would seek to promote social unrest within the Indian population of Thailand. I need to know first hand if they have been successful, as this could have a beneficial effect on our efforts after the invasion. Remember, many British army units are composed of Indian conscripts that are Asian by origin. If we are able to turn any of these men against their British masters, our job will be that much easier.

Anyway, their false names are Yamashita Koichi and Yamada Hajime and this is their address in Bangkok. Explain to them who you are and the fact that you are working for me and they will give you the information you want. They can also help you with the information you need for your own report, since they travel throughout Thailand quite freely.

I also need a thorough estimate of the beaches and tides along Thailand's eastern coastline that may be suitable for our use at a later date. This might be the most useful information you can provide, so I need you to be very thorough in gathering the necessary figures and information.

You may take as much time as you need, but, as I just said, it is imperative that you are thorough in your work. During your travel, please talk to as many people in each country as you feel feasible. People tend to say more than they should and are usually proud of their country's accomplishments and generally willing to boast about them. Play on their egos and you will learn a lot from them.

Your report will be very important to our future planning. We also need to know if the Thais will put up any real fight if our General Staff decides to invade them.

I have taken the liberty of having some new papers prepared for you." Colonel Tsuji handed a stack of papers to Asaeda.

Captain Asaeda took the papers and opened the passport. He was surprised to find an older civilian picture of himself inside.

"Where did this come from?" he asked, genuinely surprised.

"Believe it or not, it came from one of your fellow students at the Ichigaya Military Academy who now happens to work in Military Intelligence at Tokyo. He says the photo was taken at an outing one fall afternoon. You haven't changed much since your school days and everyone agreed it would be better to have an old photograph for the passport."

"You are most thorough, Honorable Colonel," Asaeda answered back. "It seems you have thought of everything.

It is my profound hope that such actions will serve to distance us from our British foes who I am hopeful are not so thorough. Remember, under any set of circumstances, the British will outnumber our Army by a significant number. In order to win we must have a better plan and be much better organized."

"I am sure that will not be a problem," Asaeda added. "I know there is no one on the British side that can match your skills in these areas."

"You are too kind Asaeda, but your thought is pure. Now, finish your preparations and get under way as soon as possible. I will rely on the information you develop to make my report to the General Staff. Keep that in mind and make your journey as quickly as possible. I will be waiting."

"It will be done." Asaeda rose and bowed as he departed Tsuji's office.

A moment later Col. Masanobu Tsuji was deeply involved in the paperwork piled on his desk. He was already past the point of being pleased with the fact that he had chosen Captain Shigeharu Asaeda for this delicate job. Asaeda was the perfect person to insure that the job would be done correctly.

April 6, 1941, Headquarters 3/16th Punjab Regiment, Northern Malaya, 1400 hours

Lt. Col. Franklin Edward Moore, commanding officer of the 3/16th Punjab Regiment, reread the papers in his hand for the third time that afternoon. The particularly muggy day had already been problematic for the career British officer and this latest unpleasantry was almost enough to push him over the edge.

Moore's concentration was interrupted by a knock on the door of his small office.

"Come," he commanded stiffly, and the door quickly opened.

A tall, muscular officer stepped into the office, executing a casual salute.

"Captain Heenan reporting as ordered, Sir!"

Lieutenant Colonel Moore chose not to return the salute, but replied, "Stand at ease Heenan."

"Sir!"

"Captain Keenan," Moore began slowly, attempting to control both his tone and temper, "It seems you have managed to stir things up again."

"Don't know what you mean, Colonel," the New Zealander retorted.

"Captain Keenan, you will remain silent until given permission," Moore snapped at the younger officer.

Keenan glared back at his commander, but remained quiet.

"I have another report here of a problem you had with some of your men," he paused for a moment. He stared directly at the almost rigid Keenan and continued. "This is the third such report I have received in the last six weeks. I must admit is it all quite upsetting"

"The blokes I have in my unit are all lazy and disrespectful, Colonel. I just want to make them get their work done."

"That's quite enough Heenan. I'm afraid I don't agree with your rather unique assessment of your men. Before you arrived in Malaya, these same men were good troops, they were praised by their commanding officer, and performed their duties quite well. There were few problems and the unit was progressing nicely. Then you arrived on the scene."

"Colonel, I . . ."

Moore's icy stare cut off Keenan's reply.

"Captain, the way you choose to conduct yourself, in my official opinion, is no way to manage troops in the field. You choose to brutalize them for even the slightest infraction. No wonder you are unable to get them to cooperate."

"Colonel, I admit my ways are sometimes a bit basic."

"Basic, hell man, you are nothing more than a schoolyard bully, and I have had just about enough of your attitude."

"So what are you going to do?" Heenan said, almost daring his commander to act.

"For the first thing, you are officially out of the 3/16 Punjab Regiment as of this moment. I wish I had it in my power to kick you out of the military, but that would take some doing. Next best thing is to transfer you elsewhere, to a duty posting that won't involve you being in charge of soldiers."

"Whatever's your pleasure Colonel, I'm just here to serve," Heenan answered in a sarcastic tone.

"Balls, man. I've had it up to my eyelids with your trash."

Moore handed a set of papers to the towering figure still standing in front of his desk.

"These are your orders temporarily transferring you down to Singapore where you will train as an Air Liaison Officer. At least there you won't be able to misuse your rank any more. You are ordered to take the next train down, later this very afternoon if at all possible. I want you out of my regiment as quickly as possible."

Heenan snapped to attention and offered a salute to the seated officer.

Moore frowned at the braced officer but refused to acknowledge Heenan's gesture.

"Get out of here, man, before I loose my temper!" Moore barked.

Heenan dropped his arm, turned and walked out the door. As he departed, a crude smile crept onto his rugged face.

April 18, 1941, Headquarters AIF, Kluang, Malaya, 1410 hours

It had been well over a month since Royal Australian Maj. Gen. H. Gordon Bennett had petitioned GOC Malaysia, Lt. Gen. Arthur E. Percival, to be designated a more specific and militarily significant area in Malaya—from which his 8th Australian Division could show its mettle in the defense of Britain's Colonial Empire.

The fact that Percival was slow in getting back to him on what he considered so critical an issue genuinely irked Bennett, along with a host of other trivialities that tended to make his command more work than fun for the veteran Aussie leader.

His fifty-fifth birthday had come and gone two days before with little fanfare and, to his astonishment, absolutely no celebration. Bennett had expected a minor celebration at least, and was somewhat crestfallen as the afternoon and evening of the sixteenth slipped by without as much as a whisper about his special day. He even held out hope for a small celebration by his officers, but by 2000 hours, he had become resigned to the fact that he would spend the remainder of his birthday by himself.

Bennett convinced himself that such were the rigors of command, along with the ultimate loneliness of always having to issue orders that no one liked.

It never really occurred to him that practically every officer serving directly under his command genuinely *disliked* him.

Bennett retired early to his quarters and resolved to call Percival the following morning and ascertain what the problem was with his pending request for transfer in status for his forces.

At precisely 0700 the following morning, he summoned his administrative clerk into his office and ordered the man to get General Percival on the division's secure telephone line.

"At once, Sir," the staff sergeant replied, "I'll put through the call immediately."

Bennett busied himself with the daily reports that were always waiting for him when he arrived in the morning, and was surprised nearly an hour later when the sergeant reappeared at his door and knocked.

Bennett looked up and nodded the man in with a wave of his head.

"General, I'm sorry to say that General Percival is not available at this time. I was able to talk to the general's chief of staff, but Percival himself was not available."

"He's ducking me, by God," Bennett shot back. "The skinny bugger is afraid to talk to me."

"Sir, I don't think . . ."

"I'm not asking you to think, Staff Sergeant, I just want you to do your job."

The staff sergeant, long used to Bennett's frequent rants, remained silent.

"I simply can't believe that the person in charge of this bloody fiasco refuses to talk to someone who has made an offer to help. It's not like I am asking for the moon or anything."

"Sir, I . . . "

"And furthermore, we are getting quite good at the art of jungle soldiering according to my commanders. It's not as if he doesn't need our help.

If I could only figure a way to show him how important AIF soldiers are in his plans, then he would be quite willing to have a conversation with me."

This time, the sergeant was able to get out a subdued "Yes, Sir."

Bennett turned his attention back to the papers and spoke more to himself than to the sergeant standing in front of him.

"Look at all these reports, the units all seem to be making genuine progress. Even old chunky is making things happen," referring to Brigadier Harold B. Taylor of the 22nd Brigade. "If he can succeed in getting his men whipped into shape, then everyone else should be able to do the same."

I wonder if I should try another course of action, one that is a bit outside of military channels. If I raise enough of a stink, Percival might reassign us just to get me out of his hair. I don't really like doing it that way, but following the rules doesn't seem to be getting me anywhere. Besides, there's really nothing of note going on around here except these blasted training missions, so it probably wouldn't hurt anything to see if I can get Percival's attention.

The general returned his attention to the man waiting in front of his desk and spoke.

"Staff Sergeant, I've changed my mind about something. I want you to see if you can get me an immediate appointment with Sir Shenton Thomas at Government House in Singapore. I'll see if I can stir up a little something with the lads over at the Straits Settlement Office."

"I'm afraid the call will have to wait a bit, General."

"For what reason?"

"It's the time, Sir. It's just a bit after 0800 and you know the schedules those Colonials usually keep. They won't even be at work this early."

"No problem," Bennett replied with a broadening smile. "Do it as soon as you think best. This morning it seems that I have nothing but time on my hands."

"Yes, Sir, " the staff sergeant replied, relieved he has finally hit on something to Bennett's liking. "I'll let you know as soon as I've reached the Straits Office."

"You do that, Staff Sergeant, you just do that."

Bennett returned to his reports, satisfied he had possibly found a new course of action for the road ahead. He also found that his spirits had improved for the first time in days.

May 19, 1941, Flagstaff House Officers Quarters, Singapore, 2200 hours

Even though he was still in an exhausted state of mind and body, temporary Lt. Gen. Arthur Ernest Percival sensed his system was beginning to acclimate itself to its new surroundings in hot and sticky tropical Singapore. He adjusted his position in the comfortable old covered Chippendale chair that was the centerpiece of his private quarters at Flagstaff House, and which had quickly become his favorite reading and resting spot.

By actual count, the arduous trip from London had taken him the better part of fourteen days time, which, in his personal opinion, could have been much better spent. He had arrived at Singapore's Kallang Airport on the island's southwest shore some three days earlier, absolutely sure he never wanted another long plane ride during his military career.

At well over six-feet tall, Percival was almost bony to any outside view. An abnormal set of front teeth that protruded when he smiled had given him a humble approach to matters that required photographic evidence of his presence.

He was also the atypical British army officer. Rather than choosing his career through the conventional route at Sandhurst, Percival enlisted on the first day of WWI and was immediately sent to France as a lieutenant with the 7th Bedfordshire Regiment. He soon received numerous decorations and by war's end was definitely on his way to becoming a career military officer. Along the way, he had earned the respect of both his men and his fellow officers—both for bravery and also the way he obeyed his superior's orders. He had been awarded the OBE for his actions relating to the IRA during the 1920s, an action that had made him a marked man in Ireland for several years.

During the long plane ride to reach Singapore, he admitted to himself that his posting at Singapore wasn't exactly what he had hoped for as far as a significant career move was concerned. If the Japanese decided *not* to attack targets in the Far East, he would be stranded in what amounted to an inactive command post. If the Japanese did indeed attack, chances were his new command would be severely limited by both resources and troops with which to defend it. He found neither possibility to his liking, but accepted his posting like a career military officer should.

He had agreed to the position at the urging of his longtime friend and mentor and Chief of the Imperial General Staff, Sir John Dill. Dill fervently believed the Singapore posting would prove to be of great importance to the Crown and therefore equally important to its commanding officer.

Percival had waded through the endless possibilities of his new predicament and had repeatedly reread the accumulated intelligence information given him during his London briefings. As far as he could tell, the army resources were adequate at best while the air and navel resources were decidedly below what would normally be available for so important a strategic site as the Fortress of Singapore.

Percival wrestled with the figures he had committed to memory and again fingered the small, framed picture that rested on the adjoining Victorian side table. Included in the picture were his wife Margaret Elizabeth and their small family. They had all been sent back to his ancestral home in Hertfordshire to wait out the European war's conclusion after he received the news of his Singapore posting. The parting, he recalled fondly, was typical of many military families, a minimum of tears and a number of promises to write as often as possible. Making a mental note of the fact that he had yet to write his first letter home, Arthur Percival returned to the latest intelligence dispatches that he had received from the Far East Combined Intelligence Bureau just a few hours before.

He looked up as a series of soft knocks resounded from the front door of his quarters.

He arose and walked to the door, which he quickly opened.

His adjutant, Lt. Col. Ashley Ambrose, came to attention.

"Sorry to disturb you at this hour General, but I saw the light under the door and I hoped you were still up."

"Still haven't been able to set my internal clock on Singapore time," Percival replied truthfully, "I don't know how long it will take. I find myself taking naps here and there and even falling off while in meetings."

"Perfectly natural, Sir. Happens to all of us who take the trip down under."

"Well, it is becoming a bit annoying to me personally . . . I find I am having trouble concentrating on numbers and conversations I am having. Damndest thing, it's not like me at all."

"One good night's sleep is all it will take," Ambrose promised. "Now, if you can spare a minute."

"I can always take the time for something important," Percival replied. "Come in and have a seat."

The pair returned to Percival's Chippendale that was adjacent to an Indo Portuguese Royal Sofa that was clearly the centerpiece of the entire room. Ambrose waited for Percival to sit then took a seat nearest to his commander.

"Now, let's have a go," Percival offered.

"It's all about General Heath, Sir," Ambrose replied, referring to Lt. Gen. Sir Lewis Heath, the Commander of the III Indian Corps. "It seems as if he already resents taking orders from you."

"Ah, yes," replied Percival. "I know about Piggy Heath. I was already warned about him in London. Some of the people there feel he will be difficult since he once outranked me.

If you look at his service record, he is the first real hero of this war for his actions at Keren, Italian East Africa, and that fact cannot be denied. He is also a Sandhurst product, and for some reason, the Sandhurst types never seem to give other officers their just due. I'm afraid there's no getting around the fact that he will be hard to convince on certain issues. I just hope he's sensible enough to let us get our job done."

"I'm not so sure, General. Here, Sir, see what I mean."

He handed a communiqué to Percival.

"His headquarters are objecting to the initial personnel requirements we have established for guarding our new airfields here on Singapore. Normally, this is the type of stuff that proceeds routinely through channels. Sir Lewis had this dispatched directly to us to show how displeased he is with the numbers. It is important enough that I thought you wouldn't mind being disturbed."

"Quite," Percival assured his adjutant. "It certainly is out of the ordinary process for handling such things. Leave the document here and I'll look it over. We will simply have to learn to deal with him."

"Yes, Sir," Ambrose replied as he rose. "Again, sorry for disturbing you at this hour."

"Comes with the territory, Colonel. Have a restful evening."

"Thank you, Sir. You also . . ."

"I will try," Percival sighed, closing the door behind his adjutant.

He returned to the Chippendale and looked again at the picture of his family.

May 20, 1941, Raffles Hotel Main Bar, 1 Beach Road, Singapore, 1800 hours.

The Inside Bar at the stately old Raffles Hotel that was Singapore's finest watering hole was filled with its usual assortment of high ranking civil servants and military officers, a nightly occurrence on the Island of Singapore. Brigadier Ivan Simson and his small party carefully threaded its way to a small table that had been reserved for their use.

The party's initial orders had already been taken by a white-coated Asian waiter when Simson first became aware that another officer was attempting to get his attention from the direction of the long bar area.

Simson recognized the officer as a full colonel assigned to the Far East Combined Intelligence Bureau named Gordon Grimsdale. If Simson's memory was not mistaken, Grimsdale served as the bureau's director of military intelligence.

Sensing a degree of urgency in the man's manner, Simson rose and approached the officer.

Colonel Grimsdale spoke first as Simson approached, "Sorry to bother you, Brigadier, but I wanted to make this little talk as unofficial as possible. You know how it is in intelligence, the right hand not knowing, etc, etc."

Simson nodded apprehensively and replied, "Right. But I have no idea what it is you might want from me."

"Fact is, Brigadier, since you arrived here on the island the brass has paid little attention to you and your requests. The upshot of it all is that some of us in MI have come to feel that some of your ideas make a great deal of sense."

"Thanks for the confidence, it is quite difficult getting anyone to pay attention around here."

"As long as everyone is following London's premise that the Nips will never attack Singapore, it will be practically impossible to get anyone to listen."

"Er, Colonel Grimsdale. Forgive me but I am still unaware of what you want or exactly how I fit into all of this," Simson countered. "I might be the chief engineer, but as far as intelligence is concerned . . ."

"Leave that up to me." Grimsdale cut in. "I just want to make you aware of something that might or might not be useful to you. You will see what I mean."

"Fair enough," came the reply. " I'm all ears."

"It seems that our Special Operation Executive branch has had the foresight to set up a local unit of their spook operation here in Singapore. It is called *Oriental Mission* and is operating under the guise of attempting to influence our trade with a number of East Asian countries.

Oriental Mission is run by a chap named Killery who reports directly to Hugh Dalton at the Ministry of Economic Warfare in London. He's in the process of setting up a 'training school' in Tanjong Balai, at the mouth of the Jurong River. The idea is to train guerilla fighters to stay behind if the island is ever overrun. But they are capable of many other things and they have some very interesting chaps assigned to their unit.

Furthermore, it's all to be as unobtrusive as possible, and the place will simply be called No. 101 Training School.

Most of us in MI have no idea of what they will be able to accomplish but it became clear to me that some of their people might be able to do a little behind-the-scenes work if the right party inquired."

Simson was still at a loss and replied, "I still don't see . . ."

"Sorry to cut you off, Brigadier, but time is of the essence. What would happen to some of your suggestions if they were backed up by firsthand intelligence information? You think the brass would pay more attention? What if you were able to send someone to Saigon, for example and let him look around? It might be interesting to see their responses then.

Not much attention would be paid to sources that are mostly Vietnamese or Chinese. Credibility gap, or something like that . . ."

"I see what you mean," Simson agreed. "A British civilian or military person would be more credible with regard to information. Such an undertaking would provide a most unique approach."

Grimsdale continued. "I met a fellow named Elliott, a lieutenant in the Royal Navy who is attached to *Oriental Mission.* He was also said to be fluent in a number of regional languages. Seemed like a positive chap who is very mature in the ways of the world and someone who seemed to have very little to do about now, know what I mean?"

Simson smiled back. "Couldn't hurt to make a discreet inquiry now, could it?"

"Never can tell what might happen" was Grinsdale's reply.

"I'll take it from here, you can count on it."

"Happy to be of help, Brigadier. Fact is, I totally agree with most of what you say."

"Have a wonderful evening, Colonel, and thank you very much."

The two shook hands and Simson returned to his party at the nearby table where everyone had already begun to give him up as lost. Simson's evening had just taken a decided turn for the better.

May 22, 1941, Engineering Headquarters, British Malaya Command, Fort Canning, Singapore, 1115 hours

The young officer nattily attired in a British Naval lieutenant's uniform knocked crisply three times on the outside door of Brigadier Ivan Simson's office at Fort Canning and waited for permission to enter. When he heard the permissive "Come in" from behind the door, he twisted the door handle and swung open the portal, following the door's movement into the room.

"Good morning, Brigadier," the officer stated politely and stood at attention.

"Good morning Lieutenant Elliott," was the Brigadier's soft reply, "thank you for dropping what you were doing to get here so quickly."

"Happy to oblige, Sir. The note I received sounded rather urgent."

"Almost everything these days is urgent, Lieutenant, or at least soon will be. I was delighted to learn about your capabilities from our friends at *Oriental Mission* and that your leader, Mr. Killery, was keen on lending you to me for a specialized mission. With the actions our little brown friends seem to be taking daily, heaven knows when they will be breathing down our necks."

"Sir?" Lt. William M. Elliott had only partially understood the general's reference to the Japanese, since it was popular to refer to them in Malaya as 'our little brown friends.' It was the remainder of the statement that was unclear to Elliott. He stood expectantly as the brigadier carefully chose his words.

"With all the political shenanigans going on in South East Asia at this time, it is becoming quite clear to me and to many other staff officers, that trouble might just be lurking right around the corner. What's more, if problems do arise, it doesn't take the brightest star in the firmament to point out that Singapore is going to be at the top of the Japanese military's hit list. It is simply much too strategic for them to avoid.

Since they are an island nation, no matter which scenario you draw, it will be necessary for them to draw from the natural resources of South

East Asia for any wartime venture, and that would require control of the seas in this area of the world. Control of the Western Pacific involves the control of the Malacca Straits and that, of course, is entirely dependent on who controls Singapore."

"Exactly, Sir, but I am still a bit unsure . . ."

"I'm getting to that part Elliott, I just wanted to be certain we were both on the same page of the narrative."

"Certainly, Sir."

"It is my personal opinion that the Fortress of Singapore, and indeed, the entirety of the Malayan Peninsula, is grossly under defended and therefore quite accessible to the Japanese if they should decide to come calling on us. I also realize that there are a number of military opinions, bolstered by even more voices from the Colonial Office that feel the Japanese would never dare to strike out at us, no matter what the circumstances might be.

I am the person assigned the duty of defencing Malaya, and that includes Singapore. Since I am a practical man and not given to a great deal of speculation, I think it is about time that I find out for myself exactly what is happening in the rest of our South East Asian backyard. And that precisely, my dear fellow, is where you fit in."

Elliott digested Simson's last words, still uncertain of his own role in the undertaking. He chose not to ask any questions as Simson started again.

"I realize that you are a Naval rather than Army officer who is, by some wonderful rational, presently attached to my staff here. I need to utilize you in a special way. I have decided on a plan that will take advantage of your natural aptitude for these regional languages. I am told that you are quite fluent in Mandalay, Thai, Vietnamese and several Chinese dialects, something remarkable for an Englishman."

Elliott blushed slightly, unprepared for the praise.

"I'm still not sure if I understand your meaning," Elliott stared rather blankly back at Simson.

"It will soon become clear, Lieutenant, please bear with me if you will.

Elliott nodded and focused again on Simson's words.

"I want you to take a little leave of absence for the next few weeks, and do a bit of traveling. I've arranged for some papers to be drawn up and have had a new passport issued for you." He handed the passport to Elliott.

"You will assume the role of a missionary and I've even arranged introductions to several of the mission organizations in the countries you will visit, just to keep the pretenses up. What I really want you to do is to go to three countries, Thailand, Vietnam and Formosa and see what you can find out. What I'm really interested in is the actions of the Japanese military in each of these countries. I want you to snoop around and see what it is they are up to. If they have imported any heavy military equipment, I want to know about it. Lord knows, they are way too far from us here in Singapore to mount any real attack without a staging point much closer to our location. All that preparation takes time and, if it is happening, I want to know about it.

I need to know just how much time I have to really get the defenses of this island prepared, and that is if I can get anyone in command to actually listen to me. I need you to be my eyes and ears, but I don't need you to get caught. You're to take no perilous chances, because I need your report finished on which to base my judgment. Do you follow me now?"

"Perfectly, Sir, but you realize that I've never been involved in any of this shady stuff before."

"Lieutenant Elliott, I consider you a resourceful, intelligent officer in His Majesty's military service, a person with rare language skills. I think you will be amazed at just how much information you can absorb by simply poking around the right places. I believe this to be an important and exciting mission of extreme importance to our country. If I were your age and was offered such an assignment, I would think of it as truly great sport."

"Yes, Sir," agreed Elliott, albeit hesitantly. He straightened himself up and stiffened to attention.

"That will do for right now. Please stop by tomorrow morning before you head out. I've scheduled you to depart tomorrow on a commercial flight to Bangkok at three in the afternoon. That gives you almost a full day to get your affairs in order."

"Very well, Sir," Elliott saluted smartly.

"Well then, dismissed. Remember to stop by tomorrow before you leave."

"Yes, Sir," Elliott turned and executed a crisp about face. He turned and left the room as Simson returned his attention to the paperwork on his desk.

Simson glanced at the stack of papers and pulled out several of the more important sheets. He could take care of these before he left, but the others would have to wait. He sighed silently as he contemplated the work before him.

Time he pondered. *If there was only enough time.*

The very same thought entered Lt. William Elliott's mind as he exited through the doors to the Engineering Headquarters Building.

He realized that time was no longer his to command. And then, Lt. William Elliott also thought about his beloved Pai Lin, and the story he would have to invent for her so that she wouldn't worry.

May 22, 1941, Bungalow just off Beach Road, Singapore, 1730 hours

As Lt. William Elliott of His Majesty's Royal Navy waited for his dinner to be served, he smiled lovingly at the attractive creature in front of him patiently dishing out this evening's soup course. His eyes slowly traveled the soft, feminine contours of her body, perfectly balanced in the bright orange and pink colored native sarong she was wearing. It was incredible for Elliott to realize that this lovely human being was also a pediatric doctor at Singapore's General Hospital on New Bridge Road.

What an advantage Southeast Asian women have against their European counterparts. By simply being smaller of statue, Asian women's bodies seem more uniform, with much less chance for imperfection. And as for Pai Lin, well, everyone who has ever met her thinks she sets the standard . . .

His attention was interrupted as Pai Lin glanced over at him, having caught him looking over at her partially revealed legs. A bit embarrassed, she asked, "What is it my love, tonight you seem to be a little distant from me."

"It's not true," he lied. "I always enjoy looking at you. You have known that for a long time."

"Yes," came her reply, "but tonight is a little different. It's as if you are in another place and time. You can't fool me, I can always tell when something is on your mind. Need I go any further?"

Elliott looked up at her and smiled. Pai Lin was right. She was *always* able to tell whenever he grew distant or contemplative. It was definitely one of her most remarkable assets and he appreciated her for it.

"I won't even begin to try and fool you," Elliott smiled and pulled her close. "You are much too smart for that. I'd be wasting my time if I did."

"Good answer. As long as you realize that . . ."

"Now, let's get down to dinner. I'm actually starving tonight. Is that your special soup I smell?"

"Yes, your favorite my love, my sweet and sour soup that my mother taught me when I was young. For some reason I thought you might enjoy it."

"I always do," he added, sipping some of the steaming broth. As the exotic mixture of sugary and tart flavors filled his mouth, Elliott glanced over with a truthful smile.

"I enjoy you almost as much as I enjoy your cooking."

"Almost," Pai Lin replied naughtily. "That's not what you said to me last night. Then you were much surer of yourself."

"I must have had a weak moment, and you caught me with my guard down."

"I caught you with your pants off," she retorted playfully.

"Never quote a man with his pants off; men are basically weak and are given to say flighty things. When my pants are off, it's mostly in self defense."

Pail Lin sighed and stood to sit on Elliott's lap.

"Now, are you ready to tell me what's really going on? She said, staring directly into his bluish green eyes.

"Yes, I guess so. Earlier today, I was sent to a meeting today with Brigadier Ivan Simson, the chief engineer for the Fortress of Singapore. He is a most interesting man, one of the brightest I have met since I arrived here in Singapore. We had a most incredible meeting and discussed a number of things that are really important to every person here on the island and also to everyone in Malaya."

The young officer paused for a moment and wondered how much of the morning meeting he wanted to relate. Deciding against telling her anything that could haunt her later, he stopped his thought process abruptly. Then, choosing what he considered to be the correct combination of words, he continued.

"Pai Lin, I have been ordered to stop what I am doing and have been temporarily assigned to the Brigadier's staff. I'm perfectly fine with all that, it looks to be a great deal more promising work than what I have been doing.

And, after this morning's meeting, it seems as if the Brigadier intends for me to take a little trip. If you can believe it, my trip will be under the guise of a missionary doing God's work."

"A missionary? William, I don't really understand."

"Simson just doesn't want me to attract any attention. In his opinion, no one will pay a lot of notice to a simple member of the clergy in the service of the Lord."

"I still have no idea what you mean, William. Maybe it will become clearer to me one day."

"And I hope that day never comes, my love, and I mean that truly."

"You had better stop talking and eat your soup, it's already getting cold."

"All right, my love, soup it is."

He raised his soup spoon and dipped into the still steaming liquid. He wanted to savor the wonderful taste for as long as possible.

May 26, 1941, Singapore General Hospital, New Bridge Road, Singapore, 0100 hours

Dr. Pai Lin Song cherished the quiet hours of the very early morning above all others. By this time of night, most of her patients in the Pediatric Unit of Singapore's General Hospital had put themselves to sleep, either naturally or by crying. Ever so often, these patients achieved their sleep by means of a small injection of drugs administered by the hospital staff to help them overcome the pain.

When all was quiet in her Pediatric Ward, Pai Lin was able to get to the myriad of paperwork that accompanied her job; the endless attention to detail that thrust her work above the norm in her field of child injuries. It also placed her work well ahead of her colleagues. She preferred to make most of the clerical entries herself, even if the nurses around were willing to help. Pail Lin could never forgive herself if one of her darling little patients were to come to harm through some staff member's careless mistake.

She finished making the final entry on a ten-year-old-girl who had burnt herself badly while playing with a hot candle. The youth had spilled the hot wax on herself in her home and was confined to the hospital while her burns healed. Pai Lin replaced the chart in the stand next to the nurse's greeting station on the General Hospital's second floor. She sat back in the big, stuffed soft chair the doctors usually sat in to do their reports, and thought for a moment about the man in her life.

Her dashing (at least she thought him so) British lieutenant had come into her life about six months ago at one of those dreary hospital socials and had swept her off her feet, quite literally to her way of thinking.

She was standing at the affair talking to some friends when he approached in his incredible white British Navy uniform. She saw that he was an officer, a lieutenant if she was right about his gold epaulets, who introduced himself as Lt. William Elliott. After a minute amount of small talk, he came right to the point and immediately asked her to dance. Pai

Lin initially refused, but he proved to be so persistent and actually sweet about it that she finally gave in. The song was just ending when they arrived on the dance floor so they stayed for the next. This proved to be a much faster song and he warned her up front.

"You had better pay attention, I'm not really good at this."

Pai Lin laughed and they started moving around. As the music increased in tempo, Elliott's movements increased as he tried to keep up. He swung her around once and caught her at the last second. Emboldened, he tried the move again.

This time he was a bit tardy in catching her hand and Pai Lin went sailing into the distance and off her feet.

Chagrined, Elliott charged over with a smile on his face and offered her his hand up.

"See, I told you I wasn't too sure of myself. Are you okay?"

"No harm done," was Pai Lin's reply. "However, I suggest we tone it down a bit from now on. I'm not sure my body can absorb too many falls like that in one night."

Elliott took her hand and looked over her striking body.

"I see what you mean," he replied. "I certainly wouldn't want to be the cause of breaking anything that beautiful."

Pai Lin blushed. She found his manner absolutely charming, in fact the most appealing man she could remember meeting in quite some time. Considering that she had little time for dating given her hectic schedule at the hospital, Lt. William Elliott was the first man in a number of years that elicited even a shred of interest from the enormously attractive woman.

But, she realized as she returned to the present and her hospital ward, he had now been gone for the past two days and she really missed him. She knew the mission he had been sent on was probably more dangerous than he let on simply from the fact that he did not really want to talk about it on the evening they shared their last time together.

Pai Lin also reflected on their relationship in the way women always cherish that which is good for their hearts.

She had decided almost three months ago that she loved this man, and was prepared to spend the rest of her life with him, and make him happy if he would have her. They had talked briefly of love and of marriage at some distant point, but something about his work had made him a bit hesitant. She had inquired about his job in the Navy, but was always answered with a phrase such as "naval things," or "help run boats" or something equally nonsensical.

She finally stopped asking, knowing that when the time came he would confide in her. Until then, she was content to continue to build their relationship on whatever terms and conditions that were possible.

Pail Lin contemplated her future a bit longer and finally felt a sense of fatigue creep into her mind. She ultimately settled down for a quick nap in the inviting big chair. Since she was called on to be responsible for the night shift once every four days, she found that a few well-placed catnaps were sufficient to overcome the need for sleep the following day.

Before she dozed off, she thought one last time about Lt. William Elliott and where he was at that exact moment. She unreservedly wished she were there to nestle with him through the night as she so often did when she visited his bungalow off Beach Road.

With such wonderful thoughts to keep her company in her passage to slumber, she was able to quickly doze off.

Her last thought was that she really had no idea when William Elliott would return to her arms.

May 29, 1941, Than Son Nhut Airport, Saigon, Indochina, 1100 hours

Royal Navy Lt. William Master Elliott's first week in the guise of a Southeast Asian missionary had gone just about as he had expected. His trip from Singapore to Bangkok's Don Muang Airport on an aged British Overseas Airways Corporation deHavilland commercial aircraft was uneventful, but it was the aircraft itself that caught Elliott's attention when he first stepped aboard.

The aircraft looked strikingly similar to the old deHavilland DH4 Light Bomber that had proved itself so often during the Great War but had since been outdated by a number of newer bombers. Elliott had always considered himself a fancier of wartime aircraft and was always keen to properly identify any aircraft he flew in, civilian or military. Satisfied he was correct about the plane's origin, he had settled back for the tedious trip.

Bangkok itself was a bit of a disappointment. The British colonials his mission had caused him to meet were polite as expected and most tried to be helpful, but were seemingly out of touch with the day-to-day politics of Southeast Asia. He managed a series of day trips to various potential areas of Japanese interest, but was able to find little documentation that the Japanese would utilize Thailand or her facilities for any purpose.

The Thai airfields were something unto themselves. To use the term archaic would be polite, for the general demeanor he found around such places was idle at best and lethargic at worst. Few maintenance vehicles were visible and the Royal Thai Air Force's presence was nil as far as Elliott was able to discern. For the most part, the airfields were all neatly laid out but suffered from general neglect and would require a good deal of effort if they were to be put to anything other than light civilian use.

Even though he had intended to spend ten days in Thailand, Elliott cut short his visit when a seat opened up at the last minute on the morning Imperial Airways flight from Bangkok to Saigon. Since there were only two daily flights, the frequency of which was always in doubt, Elliott chose to make the trip a few days earlier than expected. The aircraft was an older Armstrong Whitworth AW15 Atalantas that cruised at about 130 miles per hour. The AW15 did however possess sufficient room for Elliott and the other passengers to get up and walk around, a fact that made the flight a great deal more comfortable for Elliott.

His landing at Than Son Nhut Airport was a real eye opener for His Majesty's Royal Navy Officer Lt. William Elliott.

In addition to several construction projects that appeared to be of the runway lengthening variety, Elliott was amazed with the level of activity at the airfield. Workers in coolie hats buzzed about carrying and pushing carts filled with every sort of product, including a good many perishables that Elliott observed were poorly packed in ice and dripping noticeably in the midafternoon heat of Indochina.

He scanned the remainder of the field and settled on a particular section that was guarded by military personnel at one end of the main runway. Along the tarmac at that point, rested a collection of at least eight military-designated aircraft, each one bearing the rising sun red logo of Imperial Japan.

Elliott took special note of the types and was able to identify several Nakajima Ki-34 transports and a pair of Mitsubishi Ki-15's, a plane that was generally used for long reconnaissance flights. There were even a few Japanese Imperial Navy planes, including a Kugisho B4Y1 and an Aichi E10A1, both of which Elliott was easily able to identify. Another aircraft caught Elliott's eye, and bore striking resemblance to a Douglas DC-3, an American transport aircraft. He committed the plane to his memory but was unable to recognize its Japanese designation. The remaining aircraft was a small fighter-type craft that Elliott was also hard pressed to recognize due to its distance from his vantage point.

The presence in Indochina of so many Japanese aircraft signaled to Elliott that Brigadier Simson's intuition about the Japanese and their ultimate intentions wasn't all that far fetched. While Elliott recalled the fact that Indochina and Japan enjoyed a loose relationship concerning the deployment of troops on each other's soil, the number of Japanese military aircraft at Than Son Nhut on the Thursday morning of his arrival meant that a significant increase in Japanese troop strength would be apparent in Saigon. Lt. William Elliott also realized that he had better put his available time in Saigon to good use. His superior had entrusted an important job to him and Elliott wanted to make sure he didn't let Simson down in any regard. He tightened his clerical collar and put on the grey coat he had carefully carried on the airplane. He correctly supposed that his next few days would prove to be very interesting, potentially the most interesting of his entire young military career.

———

THE NONE-TOO SUBTLE RAINS THAT HERALDED THE ONSET OF THE precursor of the southwestern monsoon season had already begun to pelt Saigon with its daily blast of rain and wind. While Singapore experienced similar weather patterns during the same basic periods each year, Lt. William Elliot was hard pressed to recall the ferocity and duration that he had been subjected to since his arrival in Saigon.

At about three o'clock in the afternoon, sinister black clouds and gusting winds had preceded a virtual avalanche of water. The weather had been like this for the three days Elliott had been in the city visitors and natives alike called, "the Paris of the Orient."

Saigon's stately tree-lined boulevards and avenues were thoroughly soaked as was the British naval officer turned missionary. By the third day, it was apparent to Elliott that no matter what information he would be able to glean that day, he would have to have his travel completed by early afternoon. If not, it was entirely possible to suffer the probability of becoming stranded in a particular neighborhood when the cyclos or pedicabs, as they were referred to by visitors, and tiny Renault taxis stopped doing business due to the onslaught of rain.

Even given the obvious weather impediments, Saigon had been a bountiful source of military information for Elliott. Once he was able to extricate himself from the very center of the city and its dominant Ben Thanh Market, his visits to the outlying sections of the city were quite rewarding. Along the banks of the Song Saigon or Saigon River,

Elliott observed various army units of the Imperial Japanese encamped in neat, tented formations. Thousands of soldiers engaged in various training exercises marched in formation along the narrow streets.

It was also quite amazing that none of the Japanese seemed to care if anyone observed the military's daily actions.

Once, when Elliott's ancient and stuffy taxi was forced to pull off to the side of the road and allow a platoon of soldiers marching in formation to pass, Elliott had drawn the icy glare of a Japanese infantry lieutenant. Seeing the religious collar around Elliott's neck, the Japanese officer bowed stiffly and continued marching his men at a sprightly cadence.

Elliott had inquired of his taxi driver and was told that the Japanese had begun arriving in Saigon in mid-March and the number of military personnel had continued unabated to the present. Elliott made a mental note to check the Saigon harbor for the presence of any Japanese shipping the following day.

The officer made notes in his small notebook, not wishing to trust such important details to his memory. He had devised a simple code that would come in handy if he was ever stopped and searched. He used a series of bird names and numbers, which, if questioned, would prove to everyone that he was nothing more than an avid birder recording his daily sightings.

Satisfied that he had made the correct entries for what he had just seen, Elliott replaced the notebook inside his coat pocket. He sat back and took in the local color of a place he conceded was one of the most naturally beautiful he had ever seen.

June 2, 1941, Japanese Imperial Army Staff Headquarters, Tokyo, 1710 hours

The long airplane trip from Formosa to Tokyo had been one of the most arduous Col. Masanobu Tsuji could ever recall. The flight was filled with numerous bumps and unevenness due to bad weather the military aircraft encountered throughout its flight. Normally a good flier, Tsuji was ready to admit the ordeal had taken its toll on both his psyche and stomach.

When classified orders summoned him to a top secret meeting in the offices of the Imperial Army General Staff at 1100 hours on June 3rd, a time span of less than thirty hours, Colonel Tsuji literally moved heaven and hell in an effort to arrive in Tokyo on time.

First, his aide located a supply plane scheduled to depart for Okinawa in about two hours, the only aircraft heading in the general direction of Tokyo that entire afternoon. The aide skillfully secured a seat for his superior with minimal difficulty. Once in Okinawa, Tsuji's aide hoped the Colonel's top priority status could secure a seat on a regularly scheduled flying boat heading toward Tokyo. All that was necessary was a small push from the proper gods, and Colonel Tsuji's timely presence at the ostensibly important meeting would be assured.

The initial transport was more than an hour late in departing and severely turbulent weather began buffeting the craft almost as soon as it cleared the Island of Formosa. For several hours the inopportune conditions prevailed and soon nearly all the passengers strapped around Tsuji in the rear of the cargo plane became sick to one degree or another.

Colonel Tsuji considered himself an experiences air traveler, and was able to control the urge to heave but realized the flight was taking a toll on his nerves. He glanced at his white knuckles on his seat handles and found himself unable to concentrate on anything except the pitching and falling of the aircraft and the unevenness of the propellers as they struggled to maintain the craft's altitude inside the storm. When the transport finally settled into some less turbulent air, Tsuji glanced at his watch and calculated the time the plane had been in the air. Unless the horrendous conditions had adversely affected their progress, Tsuji correctly summarized the flight was nearing its conclusion.

Seven minutes later, the pilot pulled back on the power and the craft began its long descent into Okinawa's lush greenness and seemingly unending steep hills. After another ten minutes, the pilot provided a near perfect landing and the plane taxied up to the transient aircraft parking area of the Naha Airport on the southernmost tip of the Island of Okinawa.

As he exited the plane, Colonel Tsuji was met by an excited young man stiffly dressed in the neat black suit preferred by those in the service of Japanese government consulates.

"Colonel Tsuji, I am Mr. Kato with our Empire's consular service. I have been waiting for your airplane to land," the young man exclaimed hurriedly. I have called ahead and asked for a brief delay in the schedule of the flying boat. If we hurry, we can still get you on board today's flight to Tokyo."

"I do not understand," Tsuji replied weakly, "I was not expecting . . ."

"Excuse me, Honorable Colonel, but there is little time to explain. There is a Kawanishi flying boat we have held here to allow you to board. The message we received from Tokyo was of highest priority."

Sensing it was futile to argue, Tsuji ordered, "Then get my baggage from the transport or I will have to appear in this soiled uniform." The bedraggled colonel shrugged toward the transport behind him, looking down at the rumpled condition of his uniform.

"*Hai*," was the consul officer's reply. He walked quickly back to where the baggage was being unpacked, spoke to a laborer and a moment later headed back with a medium-size bag that he held up to Tsuji.

"Yes, that is the correct one, now we can go."

The two men hurried in the direction of the terminal where several aircraft were parked. Immediately adjacent was the area that served the flying boats with a large paved runway that provided access to the water. Within fifteen minutes, Col. Masanobu Tsuji of the Imperial Japanese Army's *Doro Nawa* Unit was comfortably seated aboard a four-engine Kawanishi H8K2L transport headed for Tokyo.

As he slumped into his stiff backed seat, the exhausted intelligence officer removed his steel rimmed glasses, which he then wiped clean with a tissue he carried in his wallet. Tsuji was finally in a position to stop and consider the circumstances surrounding his upcoming meeting. Prior experience told him that it took intervention at extremely high levels to prompt such treatment as he had just experienced, the reason for which was beyond his present comprehension.

Could international events have caused the plans of the Japanese Imperial Staff to accelerate and if so, how would it affect the Doro Nawa Unit's mission?

Had the Imperial Staff received his latest reports and did the leaders of his Empire's great army correctly understand these reports?

Could a problem have developed and was he being summoned so that he could be reassigned to the coldness and obscurity of Manchuria and its hardened battles?

He summarily dismissed the latter thought as a product of his weariness and generally fatigued condition and settled back in an attempt to catch a nap. The weather outside the Kawanishi had settled and the huge transport's four Mitsubishi engines whirred smoothly as they cut through the cold, crisp air at 15,000 feet altitude. In a little less than four hours he would be in Tokyo and could enjoy the comfort of a warm bath and even a few hours of necessary sleep before the meeting the following morning.

His weary head propped to the side, Col. Masanobu Tsuji was soon fast asleep.

June 5, 1941, 23rd Imperial Japanese Army Headquarters, Fuchow, China, 1205 hours

The pilot of the antiquated Mitsubishi Ki-30 military aircraft that was assigned to fly Colonels Yoshihide Hayashi and Masanobu Tsuji of the *Doro Nawa* Unit to the 23rd Japanese Imperial Army's secret war games in Southern China finally located the small dirt field in China's Jiangxi Province. This particular Ki-30 was actually a single engine light bomber that had been specially fitted to hold two backseat passengers who rode piggyback during the flight. There was little room for either Hayashi or Tsuji to stretch, but neither complained. A back seat intercom existed that allowed the two to communicate, but little was said during the flight. Hayashi did remark when the Mitsubishi flew over several particularly ravaged sections of China that had been fought over since 1936. He was of the opinion that war did little to enhance the fragile beauty of the land below and Tsuji agreed.

As the Ki-30 taxied to a stop on the all but deserted strip, its pilot informed his two passengers that he thought the field was about five kilometers from that part of the city where the Japanese Imperial Army's 23rd Army presently maintained its headquarters. Tsuji was aware that the 23rd Army's permanent headquarters were in the Pescadores Islands, immediately outside Taiwan. But he was somewhat surprised to learn that the army's headquarters had been transferred here for the fortnight.

He discussed the matter with his commanding officer Colonel Hayashi, who was equally unsure of the reason for the move.

As they alighted from the Mitsubishi, an open car bearing large Rising Sun insignias turned a corner and came careening onto the airstrip in a cloud of dust. Both officers were dressed in full field outfits, an uncomfortable occurrence that had made their trip from Taiwan in the crowded cockpit even more unpleasant.

As the car approached and stopped, a young *Minari Shikan* (officer in training) jumped out and greeted the two officers. He saluted and bowed.

"Welcome Honorable Staff Officers to the 23rd Army. I have been sent to bring you to our headquarters. Will you please come with me?"

Hayashi looked toward Tsuji, not at all pleased. He decided to wait until they were inside the car before he spoke to his friend.

"Is a *Minari Shikan* all we rate for such an important mission?" he asked once the car had started its journey. "Surely there were officers available to come and meet us!"

"I would certainly agree, Colonel. I think we should find out about it when we arrive."

"Humph," was Colonel Hayashi's only reply.

The drive over semi-improved roads took only ten minutes and the tented headquarters of the Imperial Japanese 23rd Army soon appeared to the left of the road. There were few guards or sentries apparent as the car pulled to a stop in front of a large tent near the center of the complex. A general's flag hung on a small stanchion outside the tent.

The two alighted and a staff officer wearing adjutant's epaulets appeared from inside the tent. The officer bowed formally and raised his head.

"Good evening, gentlemen, how was your flight?"

"Uncomfortable as possible Captain," Hayashi replied noting the officer's rank. The cockpit was not designed for two people to have much room."

"I understand, Sir. I trust you will be more comfortable on your return flight."

Hayashi chose not to respond and the adjutant started to speak again.

"Please take us to our quarters," Colonel Tsuji interrupted, "we are both quite tired from our journey."

"Certainly, Colonel. I hope you will find everything here to your liking."

"We are not here to enjoy ourselves," Hayashi injected abruptly. "The quality of these secret maneuvers will determine the pace for our Empire's future actions."

Hayashi knew his somewhat cavalier statement meant nothing to the junior officer and was probably a product of his own exhaustion and general frame of mind. He knew however, that the next few day's activities in China would go far toward determining the readiness of the Imperial Japanese Army and the recommendations he and his *Doro Nawa* Unit would be prepared to make.

———

BOTH OFFICERS HAD BEEN ALLOWED A LONG REST OF NEARLY SIX hours before a messenger arrived to summon them to a meeting with the commander of the 23rd Army. The man was a *Chu-i* (First Lieutenant) who bowed correctly when he delivered the invitation to Hayashi and Tsuji.

"You can tell the military academy graduates," Hayashi said to Tsuji as the two finished dressing, "they are taught military bearing and social etiquette. I was beginning to wonder if we had made a mistake and wound up in another country's army."

Tsuji laughed at his commander's pun and replied, "It is nice to see good manners. I have always felt that good manners precede good officers."

Hayashi nodded his agreement as the pair stepped out of their quarters.

The *Chu-i* addressed them once again." I have been instructed to show you right in to the General's quarters. He is currently enjoying his evening tea. If you will please follow me."

The same adjutant who had greeted Colonels Hayashi and Tsuji smiled dutifully as he greeted the pair at the entrance to a large sectional tent. The adjutant noted that the two colonels were still dressed in full battle gear.

The captain turned and held the fold of the tent open for Hayashi and Tsuji to pass through. The large tent was made up of several sections and the trio passed into a large general area where several small bamboo tables and a number of large pillows and cushions were neatly arranged.

The young officer gestured toward the cushions and Hayashi and Tsuji settled themselves around the center table. A large tea serving pot and several cups were centered on the table. The adjutant departed and went toward another section of the tent away from the area from which they had entered. Hayashi and Tsuji sat and looked at each other. Neither uttered a word.

In about a minute, a singular figure emerged from the far side of the tent and approached the table.

The man was in his mid-fifties, slightly balding and markedly overweight. His clean-shaven face was moon shaped and puffy. He was wearing a bathrobe and a narrow belt. He bowed slightly to the two visitors.

"I am General Sakai, commander of the 23rd Army," he offered stiffly. "You are here with your reports, am I correct?"

Hayashi was taken back by this breech of military and social etiquette, but said nothing.

"Yes, General Sakai, I am Colonel Hayashi and this is Colonel Tsuji." Both officers bowed in unison.

"I know who you are," Sakai replied, almost offensively. "I saw your orders. What I don't understand is *why* you are here in the first place. I am perfectly capable of judging the merit of my men and their maneuvers."

Hayashi adjusted his position on the pillows and calmly retorted. "We are here to see if the timetable that the General Staff has chosen is feasible or not, Sir, and we were told to offer you our viewpoints on your activities. Since these war games are actually under the direction of the Taiwan Army Research Unit, its commander thought you might find our notes useful."

"What can you tell me that my own staff do not already know?" Sakai shot back, not caring about his tone or meaning.

"General Sakai, we have made a number of observations with a general view toward tropical fighting," Colonel Tsuji explained, hoping to appease the scantily clad officer.

"I will listen if I must," came the reply. "But, we will have our tea before we start. First things first, Gentlemen."

Tsuji looked over at Hayashi and shrugged. He had never expected this sort of reception from an Japanese Imperial Army general officer. He could overlook the breech in manners and social customs, but the offensive attitude of the commanding officer was another matter entirely.

He knew that their report back to the Imperial General Staff would be well worth reading.

June 5, 1941, Legal Offices of Ross and Samuel, George Town, Penang, Malaya, 1100 hours

The day had begun pleasantly enough for Charles R. Samuel, a partner in the Island of Penang's leading legal firm, Ross and Samuel. He had arrived promptly at his offices on Union Street near the waterfront in George Town a minute before ten as was his usual custom. Then he settled down to a cup of freshly brewed Kona Coffee. The coffee was an annual present from a satisfied plantation owner client who Samuel had helped out of an embarrassing predicament nearly three years ago.

At first Samuel was taken back by the strength of the coffee grown in Hawaii's Hualalai and Mauna Loa mountains but soon warmed up to its obvious merits and distinctive full flavored taste of the dark roasted delicacy. He would be heartbroken if the client decided to stop the Kona supply, as it had definitely become a main part of his early morning regimen.

Samuel had come to Penang in 1908 and along with his attractive wife Vi had flourished in Penang's provincial atmosphere. He had formerly served as a municipal commissioner for the island off Malaya's western shore and was presently involved in a minor role with the Straits Settlements Volunteer Force, the quasi-military group charged with backup duties in the event of any problems on Penang Island.

He finished shuffling the morning's paperwork and was about to call his assistant to his office when his telephone rang from atop the low the filing cabinet located behind his large monkey wood desk. He half swiveled his wooden chair around and picked up the phone.

"Samuel here," he intoned in a deep base voice.

"Charles, its Martin Ogle on this end." Ogle was a mid-level manager in the Straits Education Service who Samuel had known for a number of years and was also a social friend to Samuel and his wife Vi.

"Good morning, or at least what's left of it," replied Samuel lightly.

"How's everything on your end?"

"Well, Charles, I went to another Volunteers' drill last night. Unfortunately, it was more of the same."

Samuel noted the disappointment in his friend's voice and asked, "What are you going to do about it? You are certainly not happy with the progress."

"Progress, you mean lack of progress don't you?"

"Of course, Martin, more of the same?"

"Right. We went to the field and a chap from the Great War marched us around for about an hour. Most of us are professional types and I must tell you that I'm not the only one who is disappointed. I asked to see someone in leadership and was told my request would be passed along, but you know how that is."

"Yes, bureaucracy in its finest setting. I've seen it rear its negligent head before."

"But this is getting ridiculous. If anything important ever happened, we would be totally unprepared to really react to anything."

"Quite, old man. And that's the problem. I don't think you will find many people around here who think there's even the slightest chance of anything happening to Penang. If you read the periodicals and listen to the informed Straits' officials, anything that will happen around here will certainly be directed to Malaya's eastern coastline."

"I don't really disagree with that line of thinking," was Ogle's reply. "To me it's simply a case of being prepared and using the talents of the people involved in the Volunteers.

Lord knows there's a wealth of talent available, talent that is currently marching around an open field with wooden guns or poles in their hands."

"There's not much I can do, Martin. I have such a insignificant role in the Volunteers that I doubt I could be much help."

"I guess I just needed someone to vent to. It seems I feel like this whenever we drill. I'm sorry that I had to bother you with my misgivings."

"You know you are never a bother, old friend. I just wish I could do something about it. Perhaps a call to the Colonial Office?"

"I've already tried that. The Colonial Office immediately refers you back to your local Volunteer Office for matters of that sort and our local officials are too old or too disinterested to really care."

"Well, I hope for everyone's sake that the time never comes when the Straits Volunteers are actually called into action. From what you and others tell me, that could be a calamity of major proportions."

"I'm beginning to regret ever signing up. I was told that efforts were being made to modernize both our equipment and training when I enlisted. I guess that was all talk and very little action."

"Cheer up, Martin. Maybe some changes are in store. If I were you, I certainly wouldn't stop trying to get things done. You might be surprised at what you can accomplish."

"Yes, I truly would," Martin Ogle replied truthfully. "But I keep getting disappointed. Some of the others are actually talking about dropping out when their enlistment is up. I'll admit I have had the same thought."

"You must do what is right for you, and I know you will make the right decision."

"Thank you Charles, you always say the right thing for each situation."

"All part of being a barrister, Martin. I am usually paid for using the right words in my arguments. It sort of comes with the office, if you know what I mean."

"I do Charles, and thank you so much for your time."

"See you at the club."

"Right. My wife is thinking of going this weekend and I'll undoubtedly tag along."

"Well, see you then."

"Right. Bye now."

"Bye." Samuel replaced the phone in its hanger and returned to his desk's scattered array of papers. He selected a small pile, picked it up and called out softly for his assistant to come into his office.

June 13, 1941, Taiwan Army Research Section, Dora Nawa Unit, Taiwan, 1320 hours

A little more than six weeks had passed since Col. Masanobu Tsuji had given Capt. Shigeharu Asaeda orders that sent him on a secret intelligence-gathering mission deep into Thailand, Burma and Northern Malaya disguised as an electrical engineer.

During the entire period of Asaeda's absence, Colonel Tsuji had not received a single piece of information from his subordinate, but that fact did not even cross the veteran intelligence officer's busy mind. Due to the quality of Asaeda's earlier work, Tsuji had soon developed supreme confidence in Asaeda. Even more importantly, the battle-toughened Tsuji had even started to consider Asaeda as the son he was never fortunate enough to have. Tsuji saw a great deal of himself in Asaeda, an officer whom he knew could be alternately reckless and brilliant. Totally devoted to the goals of the Empire of Japan, Tsuji knew that Shigeharu Asaeda was one of a handful of men who were ruthless enough to do whatever was necessary to accomplish their goals while in the field on any given mission.

Tsuji often recalled his first meeting with Asaeda some years ago during Japan's war in China. The towering Asaeda had distinguished himself on several occasions with exceptional feats of bravery and Tsuji decided he wanted to meet this young officer whose military reputation was definitely on the rise.

Tsuji summoned the then young Lieutenant to his tent after a particularly bloody battle. Asaeda appeared as ordered with his uniform still smeared with splotches of blood and mud from the battle. When standing before him, Tsuji surmised that the officer was one of the tallest he had ever seen in the service of the emperor.

"You have had a most interesting battle, Lieutenant," Tsuji spoke to the young officer whose head was still bowed, "I hope all that blood is from our Chinese enemies' dead bodies."

"You are probably right, Honorable Lieutenant Colonel, I myself was not wounded but I remember killing many Chinese soldiers. This was a particularly bloody engagement and our men fought bravely."

"I am sure they did Lieutenant Asaeda, and from what I understand, a good part of the success the Empire enjoyed today rests on your broad shoulders."

"Not so, Sir, I was just one of many," Asaeda replied hesitantly.

"Good, Asaeda. True modesty is an natural companion to gallantry."

Asaeda did not reply and chose to keep his head slightly bowed.

The remainder of the conversation flowed stiffly, with Asaeda eventually revealing details of his early schooling and career. He was born of a poor family in a rural setting but was pleased when his teachers said that he exhibited a high degree of intelligence during his early school days. He accepted an appointment to the Ichigaya Military Academy mainly because it was free. After graduating, he received his commission and was sent directly into Japan's long-term ongoing conflict with China where he was able to distinguish himself.

When the visit was finished, Tsuji dismissed the young officer but committed to his mind the fact that he had found a true warrior in his midst. He felt that he had found another person who regarded life and tradition as absolutely as he did. Tsuji was sure the gods would favor the fact that his path would again cross with that of the young warrior, but could not say when.

Tsuji's thoughts returned to the present when a distinct knock on his door stirred his attention. A moment later, the door opened and a huge familiar figure appeared. A uniformed Capt. Shigeharu Asaeda now approached his desk. Tsuji stood up and each bowed.

"So, Asaeda, you are finally back from your vacation. I certainly hope you have had a good time."

Having grown used to Colonel Tsuji's backhanded humor, Asaeda replied. "Yes, Honorable Colonel, but I managed to think thought about everyone here at *Dora Nawa* Unit a good deal of the time."

Tsuji blinked softly and offered a rare smile. "I know your mission must be successful since you were gone for so long a time. If you were having problems, I would have heard from you before now."

"Exactly, Sir. The fact is, I was actually able to travel quite freely. The disguise we agree on, and the papers you had made for me, were accepted everywhere I went."

"And did you see the intelligence officers I wanted you to meet in Bangkok?"

"Yes, Sir, they were quite happy to see me. They wanted to know what was going on with our forces. It seems there are a lot of rumors circulating around as to exactly what is going to happen."

"I'm sure there are, it seems that rumors make up a great deal of what we call *war* in intelligence circles."

"Yes, Sir. I agree. But, I wasn't able to tell them very much since I really have little idea of what is planned. I simply do what I am ordered."

"It is better that way Asaeda, less trouble to get into and less information for them to have should they ever be compromised."

Asaeda started to reply then decided better. He waited for his superior to continue.

Tsuji motioned for him to have a seat in front of his desk and moved back to his own wooden chair behind the desk. He then opened a file that held a number of pages. Tsuji looked through the pages and placed several on his desk in a particular order."

"Now Asaeda, share your report with me."

"It was mostly as you expected Colonel, but perhaps even a bit better. It appears to me that we will have little opposition in any of the places I visited. Thailand seems a bit militarily backward and has only some regional police offices that also loosely serve as military units. Their airfields are primitive at best and offer little in the way of military capability or installations."

"Were you able to observe preparations on the part of any country regarding an invasion?" Tsuji inquired.

"No, Sir, in fact there was hardly any talk of anything even closely related to the prospect of an invasion. I got the idea that none of the countries wanted to be involved in international politics."

"Even Malaya?"

"Even there. I did see a number of British military units in Malaya, but they seemed engaged in ordinary work. The ones that were in proximity to the coastline were not engaged in any sort of defense activities, in fact they were fairly casual in their work ethic. Not at all like Japanese soldiers who take their work seriously."

Tsuji smiled as Asaeda's blatant pride and patriotism and made a few notes on one of his papers. He then directed another pointed question to his subordinate.

"Please go back to the two intelligence officers, Asaeda. What have they been able to accomplish?"

"According to what they related to me, Sir, they are making some real progress. They have successfully contacted a number of Indian nationalists who seem to have some inroads into the British Indian Army units. According to our agents, some of these Indian Army units are unhappy with their British commanding officers and that makes for an excellent environment in which to produce discord. Our agents feel that when the time comes, some of these units will either come over to our side or will not put up much of a fight if an invasion comes. Either way, it seems as if Japan will benefit from the soldiers' unrest."

"I thought as much," Tsuji offered. "It is time that the Asian races band together to rid ourselves of the white menace." His tone chilled Captain Asaeda, who had never witnessed Tsuji elucidating on the subject.

Tsuji became silent as he peered through the remainder of the papers on his desk. He scratched his chin and pinched the edge of his thin moustache in deep thought.

When he finally rearranged his thoughts, he looked up at Captain Asaeda who had waited patiently for his superior's attention.

"Asaeda, I want you to write down everything you experienced on your entire trip. Leave out nothing, for there is no telling when even the smallest bit of information can prove valuable to us. When you are finished, bring all your notes to me. I already have your next assignment in mind, and I believe it will be one that you will enjoy."

"Yes, Sir?" Asaeda asked. "What do you have in mind for me to do?"

Tsuji paused again, then answered.

"The one big question that still remains concerns the beaches and tides of the areas we plan to disembark upon. We have practically no information that is truly usable to our Navy. I have promised them that we will secure enough pertinent information about these specific areas as to make their mission somewhat easier. I am entrusting you to gather that information."

"*Hai*," Asaeda answered, his enthusiasm again breaking out.

"I knew you would enjoy this. It will be like going to the beach as a youngster."

"Yes, Honorable Colonel, I had almost forgotten."

"And, Asaeda, one more thing."

"Yes, Sir, what is it?"

"This time you will be going as *Major* Asaeda. I've taken the liberty of securing your immediate promotion from Tokyo."

This time it was Shigeharu Asaeda's turn to smile, the broadest smile Tsuji had witnessed since he had first met the young officer.

"Thank you, Sir, I hope my present and future actions will make you proud."

Tsuji knew that they already had.

June 13, 1941, Civil Engineering Headquarters, Fort Canning, Singapore, 0930 hours

Lt. William M. Elliott of the Royal Navy was again in his correct tropical white uniform when he reported in to Brigadier Ivan Simson. His trip back from Saigon had taken several days longer than expected thanks to a detour through Thailand that Simson had directed if Elliott felt he had the time. He had arrived early this morning and had only stopped at home to change into uniform before reporting.

Simson was in good spirits when he entered his office where Elliott was waiting. Elliott snapped to attention as the Brigadier stepped around his desk.

"See here, old chap," Simson remarked uncomfortably, " no need for all the formality, seeing as we are only people in the civil engineers office in this environment."

"Right, Sir," Elliott replied with a smile, "I guess it's sort of a habit I picked up along the way."

Simson returned the smile, noting the playfulness of his subordinate's statement.

"I see you had the extra time to stop back on Formosa. That's good, and if you were able to find out what I wanted, that will make your little expedition all the more rewarding."

"Yes Sir, I did." Elliott replied. "The entire trip was quite worthwhile. Indochina was even more than you expected, and Thailand, well, it might be quite correct to say that Thailand was probably less than you expected. And, my last stop on Formosa, well, it too, proved to also be productive."

"Quite, I follow you so far. Now, if you don't mind I would like to immediately start with some facts. I thrust you managed to take some notes."

"Yes, the system you suggested worked out quite nicely, and I was able to condense the information on my return flight from Formosa."

"Lieutenant . . . oh blast, I hate such formality. I will call you William from now on, if you don't mind. Let's start with Indochina, if you will."

"Certainly. I must say you were right on target, Brigadier. If the Nips aren't building up for something big, I'll eat my hat. Let's start with the air forces I was able to observe, if that is okay with you."

"Fine. What have you got?"

"Well, it seems the Japanese are amassing a huge force, both in Saigon and other airfields close by. When I first arrived I counted over a hundred-fifty aircraft, mostly bombers and reconnaissance-type aircraft. There were so many that they were parked in every conceivable location, sometimes nose to nose. I noted some of the squadron numbers and watched to see if they returned from their missions each day. Some did and some did not, signifying to me that they were using additional airfields. I asked my cab driver and he said that new planes were arriving each week, and that there were four times more now than just a month ago. To me that is a sizeable buildup. The cabbie said it was great for his business, so many new people in Saigon. He wasn't happy though, because the Japanese weren't very nice to the native Indos. Very little tipping and not much conversation. Seems they feel a bit superior.

And, I also saw that there was both Imperial Navy as well as Army aircraft present. Their markings are quite different, not to mention the type of planes themselves. Anyway, I counted well over three hundred planes of different types, not to mention the ones that deployed to other bases."

"That's consistent with what I had heard through the grapevine," Simson commented. "Only the numbers were somewhat smaller. With those numbers their use couldn't be strictly for military exercises, which is the excuse the Japanese always use in these matters."

"No, Brigadier," Elliott retorted. "These were permanent change of stations. The Japanese are even having a hard time finding places for everyone to stay. All the hotels are filled up and I understand a number of private homes have been secured for the purpose of giving officers a place to live."

"What about the Imperial Japanese Army? More of the same I suppose?"

"Quite, Sir. I passed the headquarters of something called the 25th Army if the sign was correct. It was a big operation, with many thousands of soldiers. They made no attempt at concealing anything, even marched the soldiers out onto roads whenever they felt like it.

I saw a wide variety of troops and a lot of them appeared to be battle hardened. The soldiers were older, not like a conscripted army with plenty of youngsters. These were veterans, and proud of it. You could see it in their faces. Their officers have told them something, and they believe what they have been told. You can see it in the manner they conduct themselves.

And, oh yes, I even saw a number of Imperial Marines present; they really stand out from the regular Nip soldiers. Since they are considered elite soldiers, they always seems to act differently from regular soldiers and thus are easy to spot."

Simson weighed carefully the information Elliott had produced.

Such large numbers of both troops and air support are in direct conflict with what British High Command expects from the Japanese in this particular part of the world. If the Japanese are massing so many troops in one place, there must be a specific reason for all the activity. Realistically, the Japs' target could be Hong Kong, The Philippine Islands or Malaya and of the three, Malaya and Singapore are certainly the most strategic.

Simson returned his gaze toward Elliott.

"And what about the other part of your mission? What about out little friends in Thailand? And you mentioned some success on Formosa? What was going on there?"

"Thailand is another story, Brigadier. It's a country where no on seems to be thinking about anything that's going on in other parts of the world. Formosa is a different story entirely, and I will get to that last."

Simson nodded, and Elliott continued.

"I went to the two largest airfields around Bangkok, and there wasn't much going on. There were very few military aircraft apparent and limited training exercises. I also went to the largest Royal Thai Army base near Bangkok and it was much of the same. The place seemed quite lethargic and laid back to say the least."

"I was hoping for more of a change in attitude from the Thais," Simson admitted. "Our chaps in the Colonial Office and our consular delegation there have warned them of the possibility of a Japanese buildup affecting their sovereignty, but no one seems to believe in such a thing or is willing to take our warnings seriously."

"From what I understand, there are many in His Majesty's service that aren't yet convinced either, Brigadier. I know several of the intelligence types here that treat such items as purely speculative. I have no idea what would really convince them that the Japanese are really serious."

"The day a Nip soldier sticks his bayonet in their rear end might do the trick, William. Until then, we must still make the effort. Now, what about Formosa?"

Elliott looked back at his notepad and fixed some facts firmly in hi mind.

"Formosa is an interesting place, Brigadier. I saw a number of fairly high ranking Japanese officers there, more than it would seem needed for peacetime occupation."

"You must remember that Japan and China are still involved in a little conflict at this time," Simson said factiously. "That might explain it."

"I considered that aspect, yet it seemed there were a unusual number of field grade officers around. These were not combat types, but mostly administration and logistics fellows.

I also spent some time around the docks and in particular paid attention to some of the Japanese flag ships. One in particular caught my attention since there were armed guards stationed around it. I found a Chinese supervisor having a beer after work and managed to find out what the cargo was and where it was headed."

"So, what was it Elliott? Guns and ammunition, supplies for an army?"

"No, Sir, that's the strange thing. The cargo was bicycles, some fifteen thousand of them. Took the entire ship."

"Bicycles? How very novel. And what made you think this was something out of the ordinary?"

"The ports of call, Sir. The vessel was to sail for Haiphong and then on to Saigon. I thought it too much of a coincidence."

"Fifteen thousand bicycles, huh? I agree that might be a bit unusual. I wonder what to make of all of it?" Brigadier Simson put his hand to his chin in thought.

"I don't understand all it all myself, Brigadier, I even intend to share part of my little expedition with my fellow workers at *Oriental Mission*, and see what they think of everything. They will probably feed it right back to the other intelligence chaps who will undoubtedly say they already know all about the troop buildups."

"Perhaps so, William, but it also shows we are willing to be part of the team. That might be very important later on."

"If you say so, Brigadier, you know I'd be delighted to help."

"And so you will, William. I am going to ask Mr. Killery to extend your term of loan to me on an indefinite basis. I need someone who is comfortable slipping in and out of certain circumstances and who is adroit enough in doing so to not get caught."

"Whatever you say, Brigadier, I have a feeling you are on the right track for snooping out the details of what's coming up in the future."

"Possibly, William, quite possibly. But let's hope I am wrong about my gut feelings and potential projections. For the sake of everyone here on the island and, indeed, all of Malaya, I sincerely hope I am barking up the wrong tree."

Elliott looked over at Simson, unclear as to the exact meaning of Simson's last words.

June 13, 1941, Bungalow off Beach Road, Singapore, 1600 hours

Lt. William Elliott had decided to surprise her and have her favorite dinner prepared when Dr. Pai Lin Song returned home to her neat little bungalow off Beach Road. If his calculations were right, today was Friday, June 13th, and he was not the least bit superstitious. If Pai Lin held to her schedule, she would arrive home in about an hour and would have the next day off, which meant the two could stay in her comfortable bed as late as they liked.

This thought pleased Royal Navy Lt. William Elliott a great deal. He had just returned to Singapore after several weeks in Indochina and Thailand where his sleeping quarters usually consisted of a hard floor mat or antiquated bed of some sort. He rubbed his back in a spot that had started aching a week ago and showed no signs of getting any better. He made a mental note to ask Pai Lin about his back when she came home later this evening.

Before he reached the bungalow, Elliott had made a swing by Pai Lin's preferred neighborhood shop that specialized in fresh fish and had secured a pair of nice freshwater Barramundis for their evening meal. The fish were a local delicacy, deep bronzed in color and Pai Lin's favorite. He had also found some excellent pineapples and papayas at an adjacent shop and had chopped them up to serve as a topping for the fish. By placing the fruit on top and around the whole fish and allowing the melange to slowly bake, the resultant fish dish was a joy to the taste buds. Even though Elliott silently abhorred the sight of the fish head looking back at him, he chose to respect Pai Lin's preference of serving the treat in the Chinese style.

He had set the table in her small formal dining room and even found the bungalow's one remaining candle that he artfully placed in the middle of the table. He was in the process of lighting the candle when he heard her turn the knob of the front door.

Dr. Pai Lin Song entered the bungalow and recognized the smell of the cooked fish.

"William," she almost screamed, "Are you back? Why didn't you call or let me know, I must look like hell after being at the hospital all day."

Elliott walked through the door and took her in his arms. They kissed deeply for several seconds until she slowly broke the embrace.

She pounded him good-humoredly on the arm and exclaimed, "I can't really believe you are home. Not one word in almost three weeks and suddenly here you are . . ."

"Shuuu," he countered softly. "You knew it would be almost impossible for me to contact you. I would have loved to be able to write or even call you, but I really didn't have the chance."

"A likely story," Pai Lin replied, stroking the back of his head. "If you *really* wanted to you would have found a way," she added in a playfully. "At least I have you back for now, and that's the important thing."

"Yes, you most certainly do. And just what are you going to do with me now that you finally have me back?"

Pai Lin thought and answered teasingly.

"Well, for starters we are going to dive into these wonderful fish I smelled when I first came into the bungalow. We will eat them until we are both very full. Then we will adjoin to my nearby bedroom where I will make love to you for the next day or so. How does that sound?"

"Very fitting indeed, since it now seems that I don't have a great deal to say about it."

"No, you most surely don't, " she added. "Follow me, Lieutenant."

She took his hand and led him into the dining room. When she saw the lit candle in the center of the table, her heart started pounding again.

———————

It was almost noon on the following morning before Pai Lin and Elliott finally began to stir. Their lovemaking had lasted for hours, and both had silently agreed it was probably the best they had ever experienced during their entire relationship. Elliott was now completely exhausted, as much from his extended trip and lack of sleep as from the couple's unmitigated lovemaking session.

When he finally opened his eyes, he found Pai Lin's lovely brown eyes staring back at him.

"You are quite beautiful when you are sleeping, my love" she said softly. "You sleep so peacefully, as if you haven't a care in the world."

"Exhaustion does that to you," he answered a bit slyly, "and, too much lovemaking." He reached for her, drew her to him and kissed her deeply.

"There can never be *too much* lovemaking," she countered. "At least that's what I believe."

"Whatever you say, my love. Anyway, I just happen to agree with you about *too much* lovemaking."

"You better had, it would do you no good to disagree anyway."

"Oh yes, and what if I did?"

"I'd just make love to you more and more until you surrendered and agreed."

"That might take some time," Elliott added mischievously. He kissed her again.

"I really don't think so," she fought back. "I am very persuasive when I want to be."

"I have already found that out," Elliott smiled.

"Good, then that's settled. We'll live happily ever after."

"Right," he paused, reflecting on something that had clicked in his memory.

Sensing his thoughts, Pai Lin asked rather plaintively.

"What is it darling, is something bothering you?"

He waited another moment and finally answered.

"I guess it has to do with where I've just been and what I've managed to see, that's all. Once you see something for yourself, it becomes all the more realistic. I guess I was just thinking back to Indochina."

The mention of the word Indochina sent a chill down the naked spine of Pai Lin, who attempted not to show her uneasiness.

"Tell me what you saw," she said reassuringly. "Once you get it out it might be easier for you."

Elliott thought for a moment and replied.

"I'm not sure I want to involve you in all this. After all, it's mostly my own sense of what I saw that's bothering me. I don't know if you really need to be aware of all this."

"Whatever it is, we are in this *together*, Lt. William Master Elliott of the British Royal Navy. Do you understand?"

Elliott thought again and finally capitulated. When she looked at him like that he knew it was foolish to resist.

He settled back and reshuffled the bed's pillows to lend support his aching back. Something connected about telling Pail Lin about his sore back but he chose to wait on that for the moment. He tied to choose his words carefully, not wishing to unnecessarily alarm his wonderful partner.

"I'm not sure exactly where to begin, it's sort of like a gigantic puzzle with lots of interactive parts. In the end, they all seem as if they should fit together."

"Start wherever you want, my darling. After all, we have *all* day to figure it out."

Elliott began at the outset. He hoped he wasn't making a big mistake.

June 23, 1941, Singapore Recreation Club outside bar, Raffles Road, The Padang, Singapore, 1400 hours

The Outside Bar at Singapore's Recreation Club was definitely more inviting to Lt. William Elliott's taste than some of the other more prestigious watering spots on the island. Located at one end of the beautiful Padang, it had served as the site for the island's best tennis complex for more than a hundred years.

The Recreation Club's incredible view was accentuated by the Singapore Cricket Club's extensive and meticulously groomed Australian fairways located at The Padang southern end, making the place one of the most ambient on the entire island if not the entire world.

Elliott had discovered the Recreation Club soon after arriving in Singapore and it had quickly become his favorite place for a lazy afternoon cocktail. It was also a lovely spot on which to view the comings and goings of the colonial inhabitants of the island. When he had first brought Pai Lin to the Club, she also immediately embraced it as if it were her own.

The two sipped gin slings in the breezy and humid June afternoon on the deck that contained a number of round tables with natty outside umbrellas. A couple of the other tables were occupied, but none in close proximity to the one at which Elliott and Pai Lin were seated. Sundays were particularly rewarding afternoons as the international cricket matches usually swelled attendance at the other end of The Padang.

Soaking in the sun and the atmosphere, Elliott turned to Pai Lin and said, "When we are here in the midst of all this peacefulness and serenity, all that we talked about the other night seems almost impossible, doesn't it?"

Pai Lin thought back to the preceding weekend's conversation and answered, "Well, we don't really know for sure, do we? After all, a lot of what you said was just a feeling you had wasn't it?"

Elliott shook his head affirmatively. "You are right my little Singaporean dumpling. I have no real proof other than what I saw with my own eyes.

The Japanese might very well have other motives and options that I am unaware of, and might not be thinking of making war on us."

Pail Lin looked around to see if anyone had heard Elliott's comment. Satisfied they were far enough from the nearest possible set of ears, she returned to Elliott.

"You had better be careful saying that out in public, I'm not too sure it is wise to be so open with your views."

"I can't even impress our own intelligence people with my opinions," he retorted, a bit too sharply for Pai Lin's taste. She gave him a stark glance and replied. "I know too many people who believe such talk is defeatist in nature. My own hospital abounds with persons like that. It's as if Singapore is something like a pristine garden that had been provided for our pleasure. Furthermore, this setting comes complete with the fact that we are absent of all danger. When you throw in the extensive belief that the British Crown will protect us from *any* harm, is easy to believe we are in a fairy tale land."

"Then, I will attempt to control my outbursts," he said jokingly.

"Don't be silly, William. We both know you are probably right about things. You have a great affinity for figuring out things before they happen. You even seem to know what I am thinking before I actually think it."

"Not to worry, my love. I will think of something to get us out of it, if and when the time comes."

"That's something else, William. I have been meaning to talk to you about it. I started thinking about it after you told me about your trip. What if you are correct and the Japanese attack? And, if they are successful, then what about Singapore and my patients at General Hospital? Most of them are so young and defenseless, what would happen to them? I asked some of my cohorts at the hospital about contingency plans in case of a natural disaster. I did not even mention the Japanese or an attack for fear of alarming them, but no one had any answers. As much as they knew, there are *no* such contingency plans. One doctor even laughed at the suggestion. He felt Singapore was immune to such things. Can you believe it?"

"I see the same thing all the time, each and every day. Even among the military that should know better. They all believe in this fortress thing. You know, the Impenetrable Fortress of Singapore and all that stuff."

"I've heard about it since I was young," Pai Lin confessed. "I really didn't pay any attention to the notion of such a thing until you told me about your trip."

"I now wish I had kept my mouth shut," Elliott replied. "The last thing I wanted to do was to upset you."

"I'm glad you did," she added, "it really started me thinking. Unless I can think of something, all the children under my care will be in great danger."

"Not if I have anything to say about it," Elliott spoke out, placing his hand upon hers on the table.

"I will start mulling over a possible alternative, one that might actually work."

"Thank you, darling, I knew you would think of something."

"Yes, I will try. Now, there's something else that I need to tell you."

She saw a look of concern creep into his eyes and fought to control her emotions. She looked at him apprehensively as he continued speaking.

"Brigadier Simson has decided that I need to take another trip, but this one will be confined to Malaya itself. I will probably be gone several weeks to a month, but I should be able to contact you quite freely. I will be visiting some of our upland army and air bases to see how they are coming along. It all seems a bit routine to me."

For some reason, the word *routine* struck a severe chord with Dr. Pail Lin Song.

She unsuccessfully tried to quell a rising sense of unease.

June 23, 1941, along the beach below Khota Baru, Northern Malaya, 1145 hours

His present trip to Thailand on an intelligence-gathering mission had been uneventful so far and newly promoted Major Shigeharu Asaeda of the Imperial Japanese Army was pleased with the information that he had been able to gather thus far.

His journey had started in Singapore, a place where Asaeda found himself a bit uneasy. After taking the Straits inland-island railway from the station on Keppel Road on Singapore City's southwestern side, he changed to another northbound train at Jahore Bahru that was part of the FMS (Federated Malay States) Railways System. The system conveniently branch-ended at Singora in Thailand, the northernmost point that Col. Masanobu Tsuji has instructed Asaeda to reconnoiter.

Both Singora and its neighbor city to the south, Patani, were similar in nature, with fishing being their most evident commerce. Asaeda spent a day at each town and noted each town's similarly aging run-down airfield that showed no evidence of upgrading or modernizing.

His most important discovery came almost by surprise.

Asaeda spent one late afternoon with a number of fishermen at a run-down barroom near the Singora waterfront. After buying a few rounds, he was surprised to find out that the fishermen were actually afraid of the conditions during the northeast monsoon period that often produced waves as high as nine feet.

During the years a number of fishing boats had been lost to the elements and the local fishermen no longer tempted the gods during that period. With his perception that the planned Japanese invasion could easily occur during the period of the northeast monsoon, Asaeda realized that any disembarking troops or equipment could face serious problems if the conditions the fishermen described were indeed correct. He was pleased to have secured such information. He was also happy that the group thought enough of him to suggest he visit a local establishment around the corner from their location. It was there that Chinese girls were available who were rumored to possess certain skills and abilities that worldly men could easily appreciate.

Since it has been a long time since he had shared the pleasures of a woman, Asaeda took the men up on their offer. He proceeded to the building and was surprised to find a clean and well-appointed brothel that did offer a number of Chinese and some Thai ladies that were delighted to help him part with some of the money Colonel Tsuji had given him for his expenses.

He enjoyed himself to the point that he contracted with a second and, finally, a third young woman during the course of the evening. Those ladies were in turn delighted to see a man of Asaeda's physical statue, uncommonly tall for the average Southeast Asian. The fact that his athletic body was perfectly muscled and taut was an added pleasure for the ladies. That fact was not entirely lost on Asaeda, who couldn't remember a better evening. In the end, it was a struggle for him to get up the following morning and walk to the train station for his relatively short ride to Patani.

In Patani, it was much the same as Singora with an old dilapidated airfield and little or no defenses apparent anywhere along the beach. It amazed him that neither the Royal Thai Army nor Air Force had little or no presence in either city. He made a few cursory notes on a notepad Tsuji had provided and had dinner by himself at a small hotel he found near the train station.

He went to bed early, still a bit exhausted from his efforts the preceding evening.

The final leg of his journey had brought him to his present location at Kota Bahru, where he immediately found that Malaya was a different story.

Located as it was some five miles up the Kelantan River on the northeastern coast of Malaya, Kota Bahru was a bustling environment of shops and restaurants. A number of British soldiers were enjoying a day of liberty and buying rounds of ale for each other.

Asaeda found a small table near the wall of one of the restaurants and basically spent the early afternoon watching and listening to the soldiers enjoy themselves. From the conversations he concluded there were serious mine-laying activities underway all along the beachfront that could prove quite difficult for any Japanese invasion. He heard reference to a Royal Air Force Station that was located nearby and made note to go and see it when he left the restaurant.

After several hours, he ventured out in the general direction he expected the air force facility to be. After rounding a bend in the road, a guarded compound came into view that was obviously what he was looking for.

Asaeda assessed the situation and realized it would be difficult getting on the grounds since the entire place was surrounded by fencing and guards were apparent at several points along the fences.

He found a small grove of coconut trees and assured himself that these trees were not visible from either the facility or to the casual walker on the road he had just traveled from Kota Bahru. He removed his belt and used it to help shimmy up the largest of the trees that was located the farthest from the road. It took several minutes, but Asaeda reached a spot approximately thirty feet in the air. While the view wasn't a perfect one, it did provide Major Asaeda with a relatively clean view of the Kota Bahru Royal Air Force Station.

Asaeda could tell that this was an important military installation, but saw no aircraft. What caught his attention was a series of antennas and radar domes that signaled a communications location. He made a mental note to write down his findings and quickly went back down the palm so as not to create as little attention as possible.

The complex seemed important enough to Asaeda that he decided to attempt to visit it the following day.

Early that morning he visited the Japanese Consulate. He was given a set of forged credentials that afforded him a Malayan nationality. He also carried a letter that introduced him to the cleaning outlet at the airfield that was run by a Japanese man whose sympathies were with the Empire. The letter and forged papers were thought to be enough to get him past the main gate sentries.

He approached the main entrance and was stopped by a British Royal Marine. He produced the forged papers and letter and waited for a response from the marine.

"Goin' to see the cleaner, are 'ya?" the marine asked in a chilly manner.

Asaeda nodded, realizing his English left a great deal to be desired.

The marine peered again at the papers and then at Asaeda, who fleetingly thought he might be in trouble.

"Well, be off with 'ya," the marine added. "It's down that road," he concluded, pointing at a road off to the right.

Asaeda nodded again and took the papers back. He started walking in the direction of the cleaners.

Along the way, there were numerous signs of activity at the Kota Bahru Airfield that were evident to the casual observer.

New fortifications including pillboxes were strewn amongst the buildings and what seemed to be the active runway was no more than five hundred yards ahead.

If only I could get close enough to see the planes and fortifications, Asaeda rationalized. That would be too much to hope for.

He passed next to a building with a small sign in front reading

FACILITY CLEANERS

and stopped. He intended to see the proprietor and find out what his chances were of actually getting to the flight line.

He entered the small building where they were several customers collecting various uniforms and clothes and waited until the person behind the counter was alone.

Bowing, he introduced himself to Hanshi Soto, the cleaning store's owner.

Soto bowed back and motioned his visitor into a small room behind the counter.

"It is better back here, no one will see you," Soto explained.

"I am here on a most delicate mission, Mr. Soto. I was told I could expect your full cooperation."

"I was expecting you, Sir, the Japanese consulate told me of your journey."

Asaeda was inwardly pleased at the Empire of Japan's thoroughness. He wouldn't have to waste a lot of time explaining everything to this new face.

"I wonder if it is possible to get onto the flight line?" asked Asaeda. "I want to see the installations for myself."

"No, that would not be possible. Every one going there is thoroughly checked. However, I might have another option."

Asaeda listened carefully as the man outlined his plan.

"These is a feeder road that nearly circles the entire area," Soto continued. "We could drive around it in my little truck and perhaps you could see what you need."

"If that is all that is available, well, so be it. When can we go?"

"I'm afraid we must wait until my store's expected closing time, around 7:00 p.m. That is when I usually leave and our trip will arouse no suspicions. Will that be okay?"

Asaeda nodded in agreement. He could not believe that the gods had favored his mission with so much luck.

He would make an offering to them the next chance he had.

July 5, 1941, Sungei Patani Air Base, Kedah Province, Malaya, 1215 hours

The sun beat down mercilessly on the tarmac of the Royal Air Force Base at Sungei Patani in northern Kedah Province, Malaya. The base was located slightly east north east of the Island of Pedang off Malaya's western coastline. While the sun was relentless, the tropical winds that often brought relief to the Royal Air Force airmen and support crews operating out of Sungei Patani were almost non-existent at the noon hour of this early July day.

For Royal Navy Lt. William M. Elliott, it was definitely time to move to the next stop on his travel agenda; he had definitely seen enough of Sungei Patani to last a lifetime. Elliott initially thought himself lucky to have grabbed a hop with a flight of Bristol Blenheim Mark I bombers heading for Sungei Patani, but his arrival and subsequent time at the base proved to add little to his report.

Sungei Patani was a typical Royal Air Force base, which had been designed to protect the northern part of Malaya in the event of an attack. Facilities and conditions at the base were primitive at best and morale was what you could expect from such a remote location. The squadrons assigned to duty there could be considered as reasonably ready for most eventualities, but Lieutenant Elliott found the base defences practically nil. A series of small bunkers placed in strategic spots on the base and a number of sandbagged gun stations containing three-inch hundredweight anti-aircraft guns served as protection for the base. The emplacements and positions were staffed by various elements of the 11th British Indian Army.

Elliott quickly surmised that very little real thought had gone into the development of a defence plan should the base be attacked. It was also Elliott's subsequent findings—during conversations he conducted with various personnel at the base—that few airmen actually thought such an attack on the base was even feasible.

It was the same story for much of Elliott's wandering trip throughout central and northern Malaya. His fact-finding mission on behalf of Brigadier Ivan Simson, Chief Engineer Malaya Command, was very eye opening to the young Royal Navy officer.

Only once during his entire trip, on a visit to an Indian Army Unit, the 2nd Argyll and Sutherland Highlanders, was he actually impressed with a unit's preparedness and flexibility. The 2nd Highlanders was an old-line Scottish element that had been made part of the 12th Indian Infantry Brigade upon arriving in Singapore in September of 1939.

The Highlanders presented a mixture of pageantry and military perfection. With their bobbed caps and colorful skirts, the unit seemed better prepared for a parade than a skirmish with an invading enemy.

But, as Elliott witnessed, once these fierce fighters donned their pith helmets and tropical pants, they were immediately transformed into an intense, predatory fighting unit. Elliott was party to a typical jungle exercise that proved the 2nd Argyll and Sutherland Highlanders could stand up to anyone given a reasonably fair playing table on which to compete.

During his brief time with the unit Elliott was assigned to A Company,

Eighth Platoon, for the field exercises. The small group was comprised of men from all over England and Scotland, and even contained a private who went by the name of Bill Elliott, who good-naturedly accepted the naval lieutenant with the same name into the Eighth Platoon's ranks.

Elliott soon became friends with the platoon's leaders, Second Lieutenants Gordon Schiach and Derek Montgomery-Campbell. Elliott found these two to be able leaders who were both thoroughly versed in the rigors of modern jungle warfare.

"If it ever comes to it, we'll show 'em a thing or two," Schiach offered matter of factly during a training break. "We have learned a lot about how to fight in the jungle. We have turned the bloody wilderness into our friend and have learned to use what is given us, and no more. My men can shoot from the hip and can cross any stream within reason. I would trust my life to these men, and feel I would be quite safe in doing so."

Elliott considered the bravado and then watched as Schiach and his men backed up his fierce talk. At the conclusion of the exercise, Elliott made a note to see if he could persuade some of the higher ups in Malayan Command to have a number of the 2nd Argyll and Sutherland Highlanders sent to other units to teach their effective warfare methods to other British forces in Malaya. Elliott knew that if all British troops could fight as well as these men, then the Royal Army forces might just have a chance if real conflict ever materialized.

After leaving the Highlanders, Elliott proceeded directly to his next scheduled stop, the headquarters of the 1/13 Battalion Force Rifles at their headquarters near Kota Bharu on Malaya's northeastern shore.

From the onset it was apparent to Elliott that this unit was typical of many of the British Indian Army Units throughout Malaya. The 1/13th was not essentially prepared for any future military endeavors save ordinary peacekeeping missions in its own designated area.

After spending the better part of the day waiting around the headquarters building, Elliott took it upon himself to spend some time with members of the unit who were engaged in various activities throughout the base. He interviewed a number of the men who were mostly professional soldiers that were in the army for the long haul. As such, they had a number of specific viewpoints as to how things should be done in their unit, but nothing out of the ordinary that caught Elliott's attention. They went about their daily duties with little real regard for the future.

When he felt he had seen enough, Elliott made immediate plans to continue his mission for Brigadier Simson. He was now firmly convinced that the near apathetic attitude of British commanders in Malaya had indeed filtered down through the ranks of a number of elements of the British army. Elliott was also amazed at the number of exceedingly youthful soldiers he saw at practically every stop, soldiers untested in battle and therefore an unknown factor should trouble ever pop its ugly head through the clouds of war.

He made some final notes on the Kota Bharu infantry unit and settled back into his first-class accommodations on the Straits Railways train that was taking him to his next stop.

He thought to himself about what he had just seen.

We had better do something about this situation, and it had better be done quite quickly. Maybe the direction the 2nd Argyll and Sutherland Highlanders has taken will serve as a spark for the other units, but that will be up to the high command to act upon. I hope Simson has enough power to see something like that put into action, because I really don't have much else to suggest to him.

Lt. William Elliott finally let himself go and dozed deeply as the train relentlessly swayed and clicked its way through the dense summer's night air of Eastern Malaya. Tomorrow would provide another stop.

July 15, 1941, Flight Operations Center, Alor Star Airfield, Kedah Province, Malaya, 1020 hours

Capt. Patrick Heenan was becoming convinced that his military career was finally turning creditable even after some recent career setbacks had made it seem he would never get anywhere as an officer in the British Army.

It was true that it still rankled whenever he recalled the appalling episode with his former Punjab Regiment and his unceremonious departure from its officer ranks. He promised himself he would deal decisively with the 3/16th's asinine commander, Lt. Col. Franklin Moore, if and when their paths next crossed. Heenan realized that such a confrontation with the senior officer would hinder his immediate career plans, but decided to cross that bridge whenever it occurred.

Capt. Patrick Heenan's duties at the newly-finished Alor Star Airfield in Malaya's Northern Kedah Province were actually quite exhilarating when compared to his former mundane role in the infantry. He had finally managed to complete the Air Intelligence Liaison Officers course in Singapore even though he was forced to take the closing examination three times. Heenan was now officially termed an AILO and was entitled to a staff officer GSO3 grade.

Northern Malaya also provided a most enjoyable respite from his former rudimentary infantry surroundings that were generally located in remote areas. His new, much more scenic surroundings also enhanced his lifestyle in several ways. Ever since his youthful school days in England, Patrick Heenan considered himself a natural athlete. Here in northwestern Malaya, he was once again able to show his skills in a number of sporting endeavors, including his favorite game of tennis.

Heenan's stationing at Alor Star also provided the dashing young captain numerous opportunities for meeting and seducing a number of young ladies from the expatriate British colony. These forays usually took place in and around the Cameron Highlands, a hill station east of Ipoh. This charming resort area had become extremely popular with the British officers corps seeking rest, relaxation and the company of the opposite sex.

The landscape around Cameron Highlands was among the most beautiful in Malaya.

After passing through the small town of Tapah and traveling toward the six thousand-foot peak known as Guong Batu Brichang, the road twisted and turned through some of the most breathtaking scenery in South Asia. Cameron Highlands was located about two-thirds up this road.

The resort itself was a four-tier affair, with shopping bazaars at each level. The top level, Tanah Rata, contained several hotels and a number of vacations homes for wealthy Malays and colonial plantation owners. Visitors to Cameron Highlands could enjoy golf, tennis, horseback riding and other natural amenities, always in the company of their peers. Magnificent views abounded around each curve in the road, covering thousands of acres of untamed jungle doted with picturesque tea and rubber plantations as far as the eye could see.

This entire scene and its incredible natural ambience impressed Capt. Patrick Heenan to no end, and he continually reminded himself he was naturally destined to spend time in a spectacular setting such as this. He attempted to apply himself to his work schedule so as to appease his new superiors and also to secure his position at this near-perfect duty station for as long as possible.

He found his new responsibilities unchallenging and repetitive, consisting of following the training and deployment activities of the British squadrons at Alor Star's main airfield and several auxiliary airfields including Sungei Patani and Butterworth.

After several months on the job and with Air Intelligence officers in short supply in Malaya, Capt. Patrick Heenan was given a few minor additional responsibilities. Foremost of his new tasks was local liaison for the newly-developed British plan for the defense of Malaya from potential attack.

This latest piece of good luck pleased Heenan immeasurably. In his wildest dreams he could not have imagined himself so lucky as to be given the new air defense liaison responsibilities for Alor Star and northwest Malaya. More importantly, Heenan was delighted with the fact that he had not actively sought the job; it had simply been placed in his lap.

Patrick Heenan could not wait to report his newest good luck to his contact in Japanese Army Intelligence who was located north of the town of Jitra, not far from the British base at Alor Star.

He would finally be able to provide some useful information to the Empire of Japan.

III

PLANS FOR WAR

30 July, 1941, British Naval Headquarters, Singapore Naval Base, Singapore, 0800 hours

The silent whir of ceiling fans did little to move the hot, humid air inside the main conference room at British Far Eastern Fleet Naval Headquarters on the Island of Singapore. The time of the hastily-called meeting, eight o'clock, was designed to utilize the coolest part of the day for the collection of high-ranking British officers and their staffs, who were all settled quietly around the large table in the center of the conference room.

Lt. Gen. Arthur E. Percival, General Officer Commanding Malaya (GOC), was instigator of the meeting and raised his right hand to start the proceedings. At the first perception of the general's hand movement, the room came to complete quiet.

Percival surveyed the room and was pleased that everyone had been able to make the meeting on such short notice. To his left sat his chief adversary, Lt. Gen. Sir Lewis Heath, commander of the British Army's III Corps and a military hero in the action at Keren in North East Africa several months before. Also in attendance was Air Vice-Marshal C.W.H. Pulford, newly arrived AOC (Air Officer Commanding) for the Far East, who had flown into Singapore on a civilian flight the day before. Pulford was forced to attend the meeting in a borrowed uniform due to the fact that his trunks containing his uniforms and personal belongings had not arrived on the flight with him.

Across from Pulford sat Air-Chief-Marshal Sir Robert Brooke-Popham, at sixty-two, several years older than the other major officers at the meeting. Well regarded by his peers, Brooke-Popham had been hastily called out of retirement by London to lend his expertise to the developing Far East situation. The former governor of Kenya was considered an air operations expert and a key appointee for extended British military planning.

Admiral Sir Tom Phillips represented the British Navy, Commander in Charge of Great Britain's Eastern Fleet; he sat next to Australian Maj. Gen. H. Gordon Bennett whose duty it was to serve in command of the 8th Australian Division, part of the Australian Imperial Force (AIF).

The meeting's final participant was quasi-military Brigadier Ivan Simson, chief engineer of the Malaya command, whose specialty was considered a most important aspect of the defense of Singapore.

"Gentlemen," General Percival barked as he opened the proceedings, "thank you for arriving here so early for our meeting. I though it best to try and get through as much of this while it isn't so bloody hot."

From around the room came several muted acknowledgments, as the general lowered his head to follow the notes he had arranged in front of him on the table.

"I have been in recent communication with London, and I am afraid that there are several new developments in world affairs. A couple of these might be considered as to affect us directly here in South East Asia."

Again, the group uttered a smattering of low noises, along with a cough from the table that cut through the silence.

"It seems that intelligence has surmised that the Japanese have continued to increase both their troops and supplies into Indo-China. Last year you may recall it was Northern Indo-China they were interested in. More recently, our little brown friends have also occupied the southern part of Indo-China. Our French sources now report a rather large number of troops arrived by ship two days ago in Saigon, and that's not jolly good news for any of us in this particular part of the hemisphere.

You are all aware that our political and economic sanctions against the Empire of Japan have not really worked as well as we had hoped. We were able to stop export of aviation fuel a good while ago and, by last November, we were able to add both iron and steel to the list. While those actions might have slowed the Nips down a little bit, economic sanctions certainly haven't stopped their general military build up."

"That's mostly old news, General," Gordon Bennett, the Australian general spoke up. "With the exception of the news about the occupation of southern Indo-China, we are all aware of the rest of the facts."

"I am about to make a point," Percival retorted, somewhat annoyed at the Aussie's blatant interruption.

"The real news I bring to the table concerns the war in Europe, gentlemen, and its ongoing effects on our efforts here. The war in Europe and elsewhere has not proceeded according to our country's earlier projections and our forces have continued to experience heavier opposition than initially expected. This scenario has forced the War Department to change some of their projections and I am afraid this action will affect us here in the Far East."

"In what way, General?" The speaker was Air-Chief-Marshall, Sir Robert Brooke-Popham, who had now served in Singapore for some nine months. "When I left London last November, I was assured that all commitments regarding aircraft, equipment and personnel would be met on a timely basis."

"Sir Robert, I would imagine that at that time, everyone involved most certainly felt that they could live up to their commitments, but, clearly, things have changed," Percival answered somewhat defensively. "From the latest dispatches we have received it seems that Jerry has been pounding the RAF quite brutally, and a larger number of aircraft have been allocated for the defence of our homeland. Also, the fact that the Germans invaded Russia last month has forced Great Britain to send a number of aircraft to Russia to help them stop the German invasion. Our country's needs for either situation could not have been accurately forecast."

"So where does that leave us?" Brooke-Popham inquired again, his tone somber and concerned.

"I guess you might say that we will have to make do with what we have. I have been given some figures but I've already fired back a reply that the allocations are quite unacceptable."

"You mean to say that I am to defend our entire region with the odd assortment of Swordfish and Wildebeests we are currently flying, and the American Brewster Buffaloes we received in February? Lord knows these are sturdy enough planes but they are no match for the Japanese Zeros in actual combat conditions. Where are the Hurricanes and Spitfires I was promised? Damn it, man, how am I to carry on any sort of sensible defence with my hands tied?

"Sir Robert, it seems that London is of the mind that the political situation in the Far East is not as critical as the one involving Europe and Russia. Our experts have thoroughly studied the Japanese and do not believe they have neither sufficient forces nor necessary aptitude to become a formidable adversary. Several of my dispatches have warned me about overestimating the capabilities of Japan and the Imperial Japanese Army and Navy. After all, they were our allies until a few years ago and it seems to make sense that our intelligence fellows have a good line on their capabilities."

"That might make for a convincing argument in Parliament," Brooke-Popham shot back, " but out here I prefer to deal in reality. Are you able to tell me just how many aircraft I can expect in the next few months?"

Percival considered the question and took several moments to formulate his answer.

"As of right now, military planning is sticking to its initial target of 336 aircraft, and it is their opinion that that number cannot be increased before the end of 1941, and will remain subject to the general state of military affairs in Europe and elsewhere. I have made an immediate priority request that the first of these aircraft be shipped to us as early as is humanly possible. If this request is granted and the ships reach here safely, we could see some results as early as October."

Percival paused and let the rudiments of his statement sink in.

Sir Tom Phillips, the diminutive commander-in-charge of the Eastern Fleet, saw his opportunity, pushed his chair back slightly and stood. He asked flatly, "So what about the navy and the support we are supposed to receive. You seem to be the only one who has any real up-to-the-minute information to share. Exactly where does the Eastern Fleet stand in all this, General?"

Percival shuffled the papers spread in front of him and selected one. He studied its contents and addressed the white-uniformed, naval officer.

"Admiral, I am afraid I am not any better informed than you are in this matter. It seems London cannot make up its mind on one course of action or the other. First I get a dispatch indicating a certain plan will be followed and then I receive another amending the first dispatch.

I think the chiefs-of-staff and Mr. Churchill are somewhat perplexed by the situation on the high seas. Our navy has met with unexpected difficulty in attempting to control the German Navy and that has put a premium on our ships and resources. It has always been assumed that the navy's reaction time for relief of the Fortress of Singapore was around one hundred eighty days, and that figure has been in effect for over two years. The general thinking has always been that even in the event of a major military action by any aggressor, the British Navy would have sufficient time to react to such circumstances. After all, even under the direst of circumstances, Great Britain and our allies have sufficient men and resources to hold Singapore for a minimum of three to six months."

Phillips retorted back. "Again General, what you say is perfectly correct and is what I also believe to be accurate. But the fact remains that our intelligence chaps in different parts of Southeast Asia are picking up bits and pieces of information that say the Japanese are intent on putting together a viable force that could easily threaten the safety of much of our territories in the Far East."

"I agree completely with your assessment, Admiral Phillips, and have cabled London thusly. What I have received in return is the admonishment that the chiefs-of-staff are completely aware of the emerging situation and will take appropriate steps to defend us if the situation deteriorates and Japan's future actions warrant it."

"If everyone waits for something to happen, it will probably be too late to react conclusively. I have taken the liberty to request an immediate carrier group to be dispatched to our waters as soon as possible. Even if the action is instantly approved, it might take several months for the ships to arrive here on station." Phillips sat back down with a gloomy stare that was clear to all present.

"Gentlemen," General Percival exclaimed, his patience seemingly eroded. "It is vitally important that we all work together in our cause, and that major decisions affecting us all are reached by a majority of opinions. I realize there are a number of commands assembled here, but the defence of Singapore and Malaya will only be successful if we all pull together."

"Here, here." Several voices came together at the same time voicing support for the speaker.

Air-Chief-Marshall Sir Robert Brooke-Popham waited for quiet around the table and confidently asserted himself in the general direction of Percival.

"I am delighted that everyone seems in agreement with your sentiments, General. For everyone's good and the good of the Crown, we had better remain unified in our decisions.

In all my years of service, both military and civilian, I am at a loss to recall any more difficult situation facing me. I think it prudent that each of us take the hard line with regard to our future communications with London. Somehow we must convince the powers that be that the Fortress here, and indeed, all of Malaya should be considered as particularly vulnerable without correct air and sea support. I do not feel it is the proper time for any of us to push the panic button, but the signs the Japanese Empire have begun to spread are simply too ominous to disregard. General Percival here needs all our help and support and it is up to each of us to do his part.

Also keep in mind that all of us at this table are all military and view the conditions facing us from a military viewpoint. When the Colonial Office joins in on our discussion, I need say that there will be contrasting viewpoints."

Another muted vocal noise greeted the chief air marshall's remarks.

"Thank you, Sir Robert," General Percival added, allying himself to the respected soldier and diplomat. "Your advice is well taken.

Gentlemen, I have decided to schedule a meeting like this every so often from now on to help us remain advised of current events both here and abroad. I also intend to meet with each of you individually and I earnestly solicit your support and counsel.

As you can see, there is a typed report I have classified Extremely Top Secret that I want each of you to take with you. It contains much of the information we have already discussed here today plus some other information that you might find interesting. I want each of you to bring your individual staffs up to snuff on the report's contents, and get back to me in rapid order with any comments or feelings you might have.

Is that understood?" Percival surveyed the faces and assumed he had made his point.

"In that case, we can now consider this meeting at an end."

"Attention," came the bark from the ranking staff colonel.

The officers stood at attention as General Percival and his adjutant exited the table and the room. Upon his departure, the room burst into a subdued jumble of voices.

August 6, 1941, Headquarters, Australian Imperial Force, Kluang, Malaya, 1200 hours

The series of visitors he had received in recent weeks had nearly unnerved Gen. H. Gordon Bennett. As commander of the 8th Division AIF, he expected the high-level government people in Melbourne to show the confidence in him that they displayed when he was appointed to his position in late January.

For some reason, the individuals in Melbourne seemed to be put out by some of his decisions and a number of high-ranking officers had been sent to Malaya to see Bennett. Part of the trouble had to do with the upstart commander of his 22nd Brigade, Brigadier Harold B. Taylor.

None other than Maj. Gen. Sir Vernon Sturdee, the Chief of the General Staff, opted to send the much decorated Brigadier C.A. "Boots" Callaghan to meet with Bennett about his relationship with Taylor.

Brigadier Callaghan met with Taylor first to hear his side of the story, and then listened to Bennett's view of what had occurred and what was expected in the future. Just to be sure, Callaghan also privately interviewed Bennett's chief of staff, Col. Harry Rourke, who was only too happy to pass on his less than flattering impressions of Bennett's heavy hand in managing his command. Upon his return to Australia, Callaghan convinced General Sturdee that he should seek another command for Bennett, implying Bennett's age acted against him in making important decisions.

The next visitor was Lt. Gen. Sir Sydney Rowell, who had also filed a negative report on Bennett to his superiors. Rowell's report brought a visit from General Sturdee himself–who immediately filed a classified report with Canberra asking for a replacement for Bennett , and citing Bennett's health as the reason for replacing him. As he left Malaya, Sturdee realized it would all take time because Bennett was simply too politically entrenched to be quickly removed. Sturdee also approached General Percival, GOC Malaya, for his assistance in helping to oust Bennett, but Percival refused to become involved in the internal politics of the AIF.

None of these events fazed Bennett, who continued to press Percival for the reassignment of his force. The fiery general was still determined to see the British give his Australians their just do by making them a frontline defense force.

"It will happen sooner or later," Bennett was heard to say on more than one occasion. "Then they will realize the correct course to take. I have to be patient and wait it out."

Less than four weeks later, Bennett's patience was rewarded when sealed orders arrived in Kluang that released the 8th Division from Command Reserve status and sent them directly to a location that, in most military expert's opinions, was directly responsible for the defence of Malacca and Johore.

The embattled 22nd Brigade, and its capable Commander Brigadier Taylor, was sent to the Mersing-Endau area in northeastern Malaya, while the 27th Brigade was moved from Singapore to northwest Johore where it could easily support the 22nd's frontline actions.

Bennett greeted the news with genuine optimism and a great deal of patriotic flag waving. Seizing the opportunity, he also immediately moved his headquarters to Johore Bahru in order to be closer to his troops.

Upon his arrival, he called a meeting of his brigade commanders and outlined his new plan of action. Bennett was now of the opinion that his

8th Division was in the perfect position to thwart any enemy invasion or attack, provided the Japanese or anyone else even dared to attack this particular part of the British Empire.

None of the other Australian officers present uttered a single word during the briefing. They were only too aware of the potential consequences of his action.

August 20, 1941, Command Pill Box, Fort Canning, Singapore, 1520 hours

Ever since he had returned from his mission to Northern Malaya, Royal Navy Lt. William M. Elliott felt he had hit the proverbial roadblock. He was now feeling frustrated about the matter and had no idea what to do about it.

His initial meeting with his boss, Brigadier Ivan Simson, chief engineer of the Malayan Command, was well received, but after that the young naval officer had seemingly hit a brick wall about what he would do next.

Simson had eagerly plowed through Elliott's copious set of notes from his trip, since Elliott's information confirmed the attitude Simson thought prevalent throughout the British military forces that dotted the entire country.

Simson was also quite keen on Elliott's suggestion concerning cross training by the 2nd Argyll and Sutherland Highlanders, and had even proposed its implementation to a number of his superiors. When he found little real interest, Simson ordered Elliott to report to his office. It was almost two weeks to the day after Elliott's return from his mission.

"I'm afraid I have some disappointing news for you, William," he began. "I have just gotten some feedback from the last of the general officers I approached about cross training the Argyll jungle fighters you found."

Elliott did not reply and waited for his commander to continue.

"I guess you could say that I was unable to get anyone interested in such a project," Simson, paused, "I took your idea to anyone whose units I thought could benefit from the idea. You wouldn't believe some of the comments I got back."

"Not exactly breaking down your door, huh, Brigadier?"

"I simply cannot believe it. Such things as, depleting the 2nd Argyll and Sutherland Highlanders would reduce its own fighting efficiency— to what does a *naval* officer know about *army* jungle fighting? I must admit I cannot follow the reasoning or logic from a number of my fellow officers."

"That sort of philosophy follows the London line of thinking, Brigadier," inserted Elliott. "From what I have been able to gather by listening in at the right places, as long as London feels there is no chance of a conflict breaking out, it stands to reason that no one around here will either. That sort of view seems rather short sighted to me, but then I'm only a lieutenant and no one has even asked my opinion."

"Well, I certainly have asked and I respect what you have uncovered, William. And it is somewhat my responsibility to see that we are prepared for *any* eventuality, no matter what the brass around here believe to be correct."

"So what can we do about it, Brigadier? It seems as if we are sort of dead in the water if I can borrow a naval term for it."

"We might be dead for now William, but I intend to pursue it even further. I have sent a cable back to London to a friend of mind in the High Command, to see what he thinks I should do. He carries a lot of weight in the right circles, and I hope he will see it our way.

Until I hear back from him, I have one more piece of business for you."

"Certainly, Brigadier, I'm up for practically anything," Elliott answered hopefully.

"My staff has just discovered the fact that a number of machine-gun pillboxes were partially completed in the jungle near Kota Tinggi, not very far from the causeway that connects Singapore to the mainland. From our records, we learned that General Dobbie started these emplacements in 1939 at intervals of a mile or two, but, for some reason, stopped on them.

I want you to go and see if you can locate them and report back to me what condition they are in and what might be needed to do to bring them up to snuff, you know what I mean. I could send someone else on my staff, but I have enjoyed working with you and I like the way you detail your reports."

"Thank you, Brigadier, that means a great deal to me."

"And, William, I will assign a staff car to you and a driver if you want. You might want to take that lovely creature I met at the club with you not so long ago, I believe she was a doctor of some sort."

"A doctor of pediatrics who specializes in children's traumas, to be correct. Her name is Pai Lin, Brigadier."

"Pai Lin it is, William. In any case, she is certainly most beautiful."

"Thank you, Brigadier, I will be happy to take you up on the offer. That is, if Pai Lin can get away."

"No hurry, any time in the next few days will do."

"I think she has some time off later this week."

"Just get back to me if you find anything. I will give you these folders that contain the general descriptions of the locations. I hope they help."

"Yes, Brigadier," Elliott added, taking the manila folders in his hand.

"Well, on to it, William. And jolly good luck in finding them."

The Brigadier returned his attention to the paperwork on his desk as Elliott rose and departed his office.

As luck would have it, Dr. Pai Lin Song was scheduled for two days off from her duties at Singapore General Hospital beginning on Friday, August 22nd. The prospect of spending additional time with her favorite British naval lieutenant was most appealing since it meant she would actually see him involved in some of his military duties. Elliott hinted at a bit of suspense and intrigue when he told her about the short trip. The possibility of a romantic evening outside Singapore made Pai Lin even more eager to go with Elliott.

Elliott had negated the driver and chose to drive himself. He skillfully guided the staff car up to a space in front of Pai Lin's bungalow just after

104 / Jack DuArte

nine o'clock in the morning. It was a stately Austin Ascot that was painted a deep purple as opposed to most of the staid motorcars that Elliott was used to seeing around military installations. It was formally known as the Austin Heavy 12 and was the most spacious touring car that Elliott had ever set foot in.

He squeezed Pai Lin's hand as the car accelerated northward until finally reaching the causeway to the mainland almost an hour and a half later. Once across, Elliott noted the roads became much more narrow and of poorer quality as the surroundings became more curvy and mountainous. He considered the difficulty of defending such hilly territory as he consulted the map that Brigadier Simson had provided him. Pillboxes in this locale could provide a valuable asset to the defenders should he find them in decent condition. He spoke to Pai Lin as the car neared a crossroad about six miles southwest of Kota Tinggi; the small town that Simson had suggested was the starting point for his search.

"I think this is one of the roads we need," he remarked, not really convinced he was correct. "If the directions are accurate, we need to go almost two miles up here and begin our search." Pai Lin said nothing, attempting to take in the breathtaking beauty of the natural Malayan landscape.

The Austin wound its way around the curved and overgrown road that narrowed appreciably as it turned northward. For a moment, Elliott was of a mind that a smaller car might have been a better option for the search.

When the odometer showed they had traveled two miles, Elliott stopped the car. "Now we can really begin looking," he announced with a degree of authority.

"And just what are we looking for, Lieutenant?" Pai Lin asked, somewhat amused with his show of power. She alighted from the Austin as Elliott opened the door. The thick humidity and ever-present heat blasted them from above the treetops.

"You will know when you see it," he replied. "It will definitely stand out in the jungle."

"Whatever you say, this seems almost too mysterious for me."

"Just fan out a bit and keep your eyes open. We might do better if we aren't in the same spot."

"Okay, darling, er, Lieutenant. I'll just look over in this direction."

The two parted and continued to make their way up the road, bolstered by the fact that the sun had fallen behind some ominous black clouds that had formed overhead and given some relief to the incessantly high temperature.

About five minutes later, Pai Lin suddenly saw something on her side of the road and exclaimed loudly, "William, could this be what we are looking for?" She pointed in the direction of a small rectangular edifice protruding from the floor of the jungle. It was overgrown with plants but commanded a formidable position on the jungle road.

"I believe you are on to something," Elliott answered. "Good eye, my love, I knew you could do it."

Pai Lin blushed, happy to have been of help.

Elliott approached the concrete structure that was about three feet above the floor of the jungle. As he got nearer, he could see the rear portion was dug out even further and offered a back entrance. He cleared away foliage from the front and a narrow slit of about ten inches came into view.

They had found the first of the machine-gun pillbox emplacements that Brigadier Simson had mentioned!

Elliott took out his notepad and began making some notations. He stepped to the rear and entered the pillbox. Various small creatures scurried about, suddenly roused from their daily routine. He examined the remainder of the emplacement and made additional notes. During his time in the pillbox, Pai Lin had chosen to remain outside.

"This is really great, Pai Lin, the pillbox was right where it was supposed to be. I hope we are as lucky with the rest of them."

"How many are there?" she asked, afraid of the answer.

"According to his notes, about fifty, I think. But it won't be necessary to visit all of them. If they are all in the same condition, I think it would be okay to let the engineers locate the rest of them. We can make do with three or four."

Pai Lin was relieved to hear that from Elliott. Maybe her idea of a romantic getaway could still be salvaged.

They got back into the Austin and drove another mile up the road. Elliott stopped and the entire process of finding another pillbox was repeated. Since they now knew exactly what they were looking for, this time the search proved to be much easier.

Pai Lin was delighted when she again spotted the pillbox.

"Maybe I have found my calling," she said playfully.

"Maybe," he answered. "There certainly seems to be a growing need for pillbox spotters around here."

She playfully punched him on the arm for his sarcasm.

"You're just mad because I saw them first . . . and, because I'm a girl and girls aren't supposed to be good at these sort of things."

Elliott finished making his notes on the second pillbox and gestured her back into the car.

After locating two more structures off an adjacent road, Elliott was convinced he could report back to Simson that everything was in order regarding the emplacements.

It was already past four in the afternoon and it was time to pay some attention to Pai Lin and their upcoming evening.

He managed to turn the car around on the narrow road and headed back toward Kota Tinggi. When he finally saw signs they were entering the town, he slowed to a crawl. Heads turned as the big touring car entered the main thoroughfare, something of a rarity for the remote town.

A two-story building with a large sign, Grand Hotel, caught his attention. He pulled up to a stop and cut the motor.

"This will do," he pronounced. "I just hope the inside is a good as the outside."

Stepping out of the car, Pai Lin nodded and placed her arm on his elbow. They entered the door and looked around. A huge ceiling fan dominated the main lobby and a spiral staircase led to a series of upstairs chambers.

Elliott spotted the desk and moved in that direction. An aging Malay greeted him in perfect English.

"Can I help you, sir?"

"Most surely, my good man. We are in need of a fine room and maybe a suggestion for dinner."

The clerk produced a register that Elliott signed. The man motioned up the stairs.

"Up there, last door on the right. It's our best room and has a marvelous breeze throughout the night. You will have a wonderful rest."

"Thank you, I'm sure we will. And what about dinner? Any suggestions?"

"That is a little harder, Mr. Elliott. I'm afraid there is little here to offer. But since you came in such a fine motorcar, I can suggest a wonderful little place about fifteen miles from here. The road is fairly well traveled and you should not have a problem. The place is called Teluk Sengat and the village is devoted to seafood. There is a wonderful small restaurant there, and I know you will be satisfied."

Elliott handed the old man a bill that the Malay accepted graciously. The pair climbed the stairs and opened the door to a room with a larger than average bed and adequate side furnishings. A cooling breeze traversed the room that contained an unexpected view of the town's central garden area, which was in full bloom.

Pai Lin walked to the window and looked out.

"It's absolutely beautiful," she exclaimed. "It should be in a picture."

"With you in it, my love, then it would be entirely perfect."

Pai Lin turned to him and kissed him deeply.

"You say the most remarkable things, William. It makes me love you all the more."

"And I you, my darling." He kissed her again, his passion taking hold.

"What about dinner?" Pai Lin played along.

"Dinner will just have to wait. Right now, we have other things to attend to."

He took her in his arms and carried her to the bed. In a moment they were entwined as if one. Their mouths fought for each other's affection and were rewarded at once.

It would be awhile before they left for dinner.

───────────────

THE FOLLOWING MORNING, PAI LIN AND ELLIOTT SLEPT TO WELL PAST noon. The preceding evening had been part of a dream, a wholly fulfilling dream, particularly to Pai Lin. She was a person who always believed such euphoric experiences could be had by simply applying one's imagination and unyielding determination.

She knew she loved Elliott wildly and last night's wonderful experience simply added to her deep-rooted feelings.

The meal at Teluk Sengat was a joy, in much the same manner as their idyllic sexual experience at the Grand Hotel was, but in an obviously less sensual manner. The two ate fresh seafood until they were stuffed, drank native beer and toasted each other as well as anyone and everyone else they could ever remember.

Several of the local fishermen were seated at the next table and after a while the two tables became fast friends. After several exchanges of beer, the two tables were joined to the exclusion of the remainder of the restaurant. One of the fishermen was a former teacher in Singapore who had given up teaching to pursue his passion for fishing and the call of the great outdoors. He lived for the call of the forever-rolling ocean. About forty or forty-five, he immediately told them his name was Chan. Elliott and Pai Lin took to him straight away and the three became fast friends. After several hours, the trio closed the restaurant. Chan said goodbye and Elliott and Pai Lin began the drive back toward their hotel.

The drive home was a blur with Pai Lin nesting near Elliott's left elbow as he tried to navigate the mostly unlit and unmarked road back to Kota Tinggi. When they finally arrived back at the Grand Hotel, they went noiselessly to bed since they were the only inhabitants of the town up at that hour.

After they had risen and bathed, Elliott had one last surprise for Pai Lin, a trip to the nearby waterfalls at Lombong, and a scant eleven miles from Kota Tinggi.

After a light brunch, they boarded the Austin for the short trip. They arrived to find the place deserted, except for a Malay warden who wandered by. The falls itself was lovely, falling some one hundred twenty feet from the nearby Gunung Muntahak Mountain into a series of shallow pools that seemed ideal for swimming to both Elliott and Pai Lin.

They chose the most secluded of these pools and quickly rid themselves of their clothes and stepped in. The water was clear and cool and brought a brief respite from the heat and humidity of the late August tropical afternoon.

"This is the way it is in paradise," Pai Lin cooed, as she treaded water next to Elliott. He could see the sparkle of her bronzed figure through the water and suddenly became aroused.

She looked at him and understood. They swam to the far side of the pool and walked behind some dense palm leaves and shrubs. He cut several of the large leaves and made a natural bed for them to lie down. He knelt beside her and took her in his arms.

She started to cry softly and he looked into her eyes that were filled with deep pools of tears.

"Tears of happiness, my love. Tears that I have always wanted to shed."

He nodded back to her, appreciating her pure emotion. After a moment, he laid her down and entered her again. Pai Lin stirred and soon the rhythmic sounds of her shortened breath filled the air. In a few moments, they were again together as the same person.

The waterfall was indeed a part of paradise.

August 21, 1941, Seremban Sungei Ujong Club, Seremban, Malaya 1900 hours

She was twenty-nine years old, the possessor of a remarkable pair of gray eyes, along with an overtly attractive figure, set off by a more than an ample bosom. Baptized as Gyda Jean Robertson, she was known by anyone who knew her even remotely as Pinka. The name evolved from a childhood nickname that had begun as Pinky, but had assumed during her teenage years, the more adult application of Pinka. Secretly, Pinka cherished her name, feeling it set her off from many of her more ordinary-named friends and acquaintances.

It was additionally observed by practically everyone, that Pinka Robertson also possessed a most fiery nature, and on numerous occasions was totally argumentative with most of her peers, particularly males. Moreover, owing to her advancing age and attitude, Pinka Robertson had gained a reputation among the British bachelors of northwestern Malaya as "entirely unseduceable."

That all changed for Pinka Robertson the first time she met AILO Capt. Patrick Heenan who had just returned from Singapore. That was almost two months ago and even though Heenan's reputation as a ladies' man had preceded him, Pinka Robertson did not care one bit. She took one look at the handsome young officer's rugged, athletic build and craggy good looks and immediately concluded that *all* men, and Heenan in particular, just couldn't be bad.

When she noticed the attraction was more than mutual, she immediately consented to begin the affair, the first such dalliance in her adult life.

When she found out that Patrick Heenan was more than a year older than her, Pinka was perfectly satisfied. After all, a younger man just wouldn't have set right with certain members of her inner circle of friends.

For his part, Heenan was right at home with the half-Norwegian woman whom he learned ran a riding school in the Cameron Highlands, the only such school in the region.

Their relationship had begun with an argument. When Pinka Robertson saw that Patrick Heenan would not back down from her stubbornness, she took an immediate interest in the young officer. Within two weeks, Patrick started snatching any time off he could manage in order to make the trip up the mountains to Cameron Highlands. There he found Pinka's company cheerful and warming. For her part, Pinka Robertson considered Capt. Patrick Heenan the first man she had met that she would actually *consider* marrying.

The two sat together on lounge chairs around a squared table on the wrap-around porch of the Sungei Ujong Club in nearby Seremban, as the late afternoon sun started its slow egress into evening. The club was the premier gathering place for the younger set in the area and had also been the scene for their eventful first meeting. She recalled those first moments and looked over at her new lover who seemed inappropriately distant for such a romantic setting.

Pinka looked closely into Heenan's soft, medium blue eyes and saw from his troubled face that he was miles away from their table.

"Patrick, my dear, where are you at this moment? You are certainly not anywhere around here," she chided, sipping the last refreshing drops of her second gin sling.

Heenan regarded her question, turned toward her and answered, "You are most perceptive Pinka. I was deep in thought."

"About what, if I may ask? From the look on your face, whatever you were thinking about was quite unpleasant."

"I was thinking about my work," Heenan lied. "And it wasn't all that unpleasant. I am having a little problem with some of the people I work with, that's all."

"Well, I hope you can straighten everything out, Patrick. When we are together, I am quite selfish and want you all to myself."

"And you shall have me all to yourself my darling. Remember, I gave up the favors of a number of other young ladies to begin this bout with you," he quipped.

"*Bout?* Is that all you think this is, a bloody bout?"

"Well, we did start off our relationship with an argument, didn't we? Heenan teased back.

"And, as I recall, it was really a beaut."

"When two stubborn people decide to argue about something, it is entire possible the argument will experience a good deal of duration. At least you didn't back down during the argument. It was the very first thing that impressed me about you."

"The first very thing?" Heenan posed, drawing her onto his lap.

Pinka Robertson looked around to see if anyone had noticed their bantering, because her good taste and formal training dictated that public displays of affection should always be undertaken for sufficient good reason and in the proper setting. Satisfied that they were unnoticed, she drew herself near to him and stroked his wavy, blonde hair.

"Well, maybe not the *very* first," she conceded. She looked into his eyes and knew that she must have him again in the very near future. Maybe then, the deep need that had developed when she first met Capt. Patrick Heenan could be satisfied. She took his head into her full chest and pulled him closer to her.

The two remained that way for more than a few moments until Heenan straightened his back and pulled away slightly.

Pinka considered his action and thought to herself.

Worried about his work? I don't think so . . . there has to be more to it than that, I wonder . . .

Pinka's concentration was interrupted by the club's head-boy, who dutifully announced their table for dinner inside was now available.

Pinka and Heenan got up and followed the head boy inside.

Pinka Robertson would get to the bottom of all this at a later time.

September 2, 1941, British Naval Headquarters, Singapore Naval Base, 1100 hours

Lt. Gen. A.E. Percival, GOC Malaya, looked up from the stack of papers on his desk as his orderly beckoned the visitor inside the spacious room that served as his office. It was unusual for Air-Chief-Marshall Sir Robert Brooke-Popham, commander in chief Far East, to have requested a meeting on short notice and Percival knew that such a distinctive action usually meant trouble.

"Good morning, Sir Robert," Percival intoned, hoping to lighten the air with his older counterpart.

"Good of you to see me on such short notice, General, but I thought it important I see you right away."

"Certainly, Sir Robert, I am always at your disposal."

"Thank you for that, Old Chap, I appreciate the thought."

"Before we start, can I get you a spot of tea? I have some excellent Formosa Oolong brewing that is simply marvelous. It won't take a minute."

"Yes, quite. That would be nice," agreed Brooke-Popham.

Percival walked to the closed door, stepped outside and uttered a few words to someone outside. He shut the door and returned to his chair.

"Now, that's done. It won't take a minute until it is brewed. What is it you wanted, Sir Robert, has something happened?"

Brooke-Popham settled his weight into the large sofa facing Percival's chair and began his explanation. He spoke evenly, a hint of urgency definitely apparent in his voice.

"General, I'm here about this *Matador* thing, referring to the existing British plan to defend Thailand and Malaya from attack. I'm afraid I am beginning to believe the entire affair is spooked."

Percival tried to hide his reaction to the name *Matador*, but failed.

"I'm not sure what you mean Sir Robert, as far as I know, everything involving *Operation Matador* is in place."

"Quite," Brooke-Popham answered respectfully, "on paper it all seems to make sense. The problem I have is its timing and implementation."

In theory Percival and the planners at British Military Headquarters believed that *Operation Matador* was simplicity itself. The plan called for the British Army and Navy to take the initiative and occupy key military positions *after* Thailand's sovereignty was breeched by an invading force such as the Japanese.

Matador was based mainly on the contention that the British Fleet would have great superiority in surrounding waters and on the fact that a reasonable number of British aircraft would be available to cover the operation. Percival had been briefed on the plan in London prior to his appointment in Singapore, and before long he realized that *Matador's* apparent fatal flaw was the fact that the plan was developed *prior* to Great Britain's involvement in Europe with Axis Germany.

Percival waited a moment and replied," Can you be more specific, Sir Robert?"

"Of course, General." Sir Robert's tone became more aggressive as he spoke.

"You are aware that the main reason I was sent here is to find out if we are ready for a *real* shooting match. I have studied everything and talked to a number of key people since my arrival. The main premise of *Matador* is that it may not be put into effect without consulting London. It also works under the impression that we will have ample warning and that we will be beyond reasonable doubt that anyone, and in this case the Japanese, are approaching the shores of Thailand.

What if the Japanese catch us by surprise and we have little or no advance warning? By the time we wade through the red tape of seeking London's permission, it will probably be too late. Our opportunity to act decisively would be lost."

"That thought has crossed my mind too, Sir Robert. I've even included my misgivings in dispatches back to London. The answers I get are that it is a political point that cannot be resolved. Our beloved Great Britain cannot be regarded as an *aggressor* under any set of circumstances."

"I am of the opinion that we should immediately consider moving some of our forces into Southern Thailand," Brooke-Popham said forcefully. "We must seize the ports and landing areas that could accommodate Japanese Army supplies and equipment. If we take away the places where they can land, we basically deny them the ability to invade us in the first place. Don't forget the fact that it would also be nice to have soldiers in place in case they decided to attempt to come ashore."

"I cannot fault your logic, Sir Robert. In fact, I agree with some of your points. But, as I explained, my hands are tied in what I can do. And I get little help from the Colonial Office who seems to have its own set of unique problems. I also want to point out the fact that it takes more time than imaginable to get anything approved there."

"I am quite used to dealing with political matters, General. My concern here is that Thailand is the key to the Malayan Peninsula. It's the Achilles Heel of the Fortress of Singapore and, depending on the actual scenario, it is possible that *Matador* leaves us entirely exposed."

"My dear, Sir Robert. Let me put your mind at ease on that regard. I have had numerous discussions with the General Staff in London and with the powers that be, including of course, Mr. Churchill himself. To a man, and I must certainly include myself in that number, we are mostly of the opinion that if and when Singapore is attacked, such an attack will most definitely *not* come by land.

By God, man, do you realize what an advancing army would encounter in trying to cross the god-forsaken jungles of Malaya? It would be a logistical nightmare for anyone to even attempt to try. You must also consider the fact that we have just completed two new airfields in that very region to strengthen our positions. No one in his right mind would ever attempt such a undertaking." Percival paused to let his words sink in to his visitor.

For several moments, Sir Robert Brooke-Popham remained silent. When he was ready, the highly decorated naval officer spoke again to General Percival, but in a tone much more subdued than before.

"You might be right, General, along with everyone in London . . . it is just very difficult for anyone, and in particular me, as a military planner, to put all my eggs in one heavily defended basket. Singapore sits much like an ancient storied citadel just daring anyone to attack it. God knows what will happen if we are all wrong. It could be disastrous . . . it might even change the direction of an entire war."

"Well, we must all pray that God is on Great Britain's side," Percival added wistfully. "After all, it wouldn't be the first time."

"Quite," Brooke-Popham agreed. "Quite. I pray that we are all correct in our thinking."

September 13, 1941, Just outside Divisional Headquarters AIF, Johore Bahru, Malaya, 1330 hours

It was the first time since being assigned to Brigadier Ivan Simson that Royal Navy Lt. William M. Elliott had actually not taken pleasure in the orders he had been given by Simson in Singapore just a day ago.

When summoned to Simson's busy office at Fort Canning, Elliott was his usual eager self as the brigadier laid out his ideas on Elliott's upcoming mission. As he listened to the older officer, Elliott felt something of a mental change take place in his mind, a feeling that he was not completely able to control.

Simson was now in the middle of his explanation as Elliott's attention returned.

"And you can easily see from what I have told you, William, this is no easy situation to control. What I need to know is just how far our Australian brethren have slipped regarding their attitude toward our defensive plans against an attack, exactly where their morale is at this point and what is necessary to put them back into working order as a viable defense force."

Elliott shook his head, as much in skepticism of the content of Simson's words as his uncertainty as to the meaning of what he had just heard. If his assumption was correct, Lt. William Elliott wasn't at all comfortable about his upcoming mission of spying on the officers and men of the Australian Imperial Force.

"Brigadier, let me make sure I understand you," Elliott said evenly, choosing his words with due care. "You want me to go and visit the headquarters of the AIF and try to get close enough to General Bennett with the express purpose of deciding in my own mind whether Bennett and his forces actually represent a fit fighting force or not, and if so, is their discipline sufficient to wage an aggressive and considerable battle against the enemy?"

"Well, I wouldn't have put it *exactly* that way, but I guess you have the gist . . . "

"Brigadier, I'm not sure why you think I am the right person for this sort of mission. After all, I am part of the Royal Navy and . . . "

"Precisely my point, William. They would never suspect you were on this type of mission."

"But I would be reduced to being a spy, Brigadier. *And*, I would be spying on our country's closest *allies* to boot."

Simson looked somewhat frustrated and rose from his chair. He faced Elliott directly.

"Sometimes we must do that which is not really pleasurable, William. And sometimes it involves people who are our friends and allies. Let me explain it to you like this; if push becomes shove and we are ever attacked, the AIF will be expected to shoulder a great deal of the responsibility for defending Malaya. Right now they are penciled in to fill some major gaps and I just want to know if they are up to it. Lord knows it's hard enough to tell how battle-prepared they are in the first place and how objective their progress reports are. I also need to know how they have progressed with our defensive positions. I have all their reports here, but I'm not really comfortable with anyone self-reporting on their own progress.

Furthermore, General Bennett seems to actively dislike *any* British officer or practically *any* outside military unit he's involved with. And, the common Australian soldier wants to take a poke at every British Tommie he meets, in or outside of a bar. Since the AIF polices itself, we cannot be sure their fitness reports are totally impartial and there are so many reports of disciplinary breakdowns at all levels that I have lost count.

General Percival was impressed with your earlier reports I shared with him from Saigon and also from Northern Malaya, and we both thought you might be able to give us some real insight into the matter of the Aussies' morale. No one ever would suspect a minister would be a spy, and you have already had a good deal of practice being a minister."

Elliott looked at the brigadier, who was smiling, and saw that further protest was useless. Besides, he had internally started to agree with his superior that he might be able to find out the information Simson needed without any compromise of his own values.

Elliott shook his head affirmatively and asked, "Brigadier, I think I might do something a bit differently . . . that's if you agree."

"I'm listening. Just what do you have in mind?"

"Since this is a *really* delicate matter, I think I would like to change my nationality and become a New Zealander. I have a bunch of friends from there and know the layout of the country quite well. I can imitate the accent quite easily and I think the Aussies will be much more relaxed with a blinkin' Kiwi than with an Englishman, even if he is of the cloth."

Simson thought a minute and agreed. "Sounds good to me, can you leave right away?"

"Tomorrow for sure, or I can take the late train tonight if you prefer."

"Tomorrow will be fine. Stop by the intelligence office and get yourself some realistic credentials in case you happen to need them. We wouldn't want something to happen to you, would we?"

"No, Sir," Elliott replied. "I will see to it this very minute."

"And, William, one more thing."

"Yes, Sir?"

"Take as long as you need on this one. It might very be the most important mission I've ever sent you on."

"I understand. Will do."

"Good, then I'll see you when you get back. Keep safe."

"Always, Brigadier. Always."

Elliott started out of the room and was already thinking of Pai Lin before he reached the door. He had to decide just how much of this new mission he would confide in her. He already knew it would be just about everything.

THE SHORT TRAIN RIDE NORTHWARD TO JOHORE BAHRU HAD BEEN uneventful for Elliott with the exception that the starched white collar he was wearing was unusually stiff and uncomfortable. He finally unbuttoned the collar and allowed it to hang limp around his neck. So much for church discipline regarding personal attire while traveling, Elliott surmised, as if anyone around him seemed to care.

The somewhat rumpled lieutenant-turned-minister arrived at Johore Bahru's smallish train station around noon on a lazy Saturday afternoon. He soon inquired as to the nearest military watering hole, a question hardly expected from a man in minister's clothes. Given the directions to a not-too-distant pub, Elliott made his way to a rather large, single-story building some six or seven blocks away from the railroad station of Johore Bahru. The spot was just off the town's main road that eventually led to the causeway back to Singapore.

What he found when he arrived gave instant meaning to the fears expressed by Brigadier Simson before his departure.

Outside the building, a motley assortment of Australian soldiers in various sorts of undress stood and swayed in the moderately dry September afternoon sun. Each held a beer in one hand and a cigarette in the other. They eyed the neatly attired man in grey as he approached the front door. A simple sign 'DRINKS' appeared above the door.

Elliott entered and a collection of more Australian soldiers became immediately evident. The large main room was about half full with men along with a compliment of native Malay girls in colorful, native sarongs who mixed in with the clusters of soldiers.

Elliott stepped up to the bar and ordered a beer. The bartender seemed surprised, but complied and poured him a draft. Elliott paused and then gave the sudsy brew a decided chug. When he was finished, he put the glass back on the bar with a deft movement.

A red-headed, grandly mustachioed man with a staff sergeant's chevrons moved into the space next to him.

"G-day, mate," the man said in Elliott's direction.

Elliott returned the greeting, "G-day to you."

The man leaned over, attempting to catch Elliott's accent.

Elliott spoke first, as reassuring as possible. "New Zealand, but I hardly have any accent."

"Ah, Ah can hear it now," the staff confided, bolstered by several beers. "All you Kiwis sound alike, it's easy to spot."

"Whatever you say, mate, and that's the truth."

"Ah say it's a great fuckin' day, that's what!"

"To today," Elliott offered, trying to be friendly. "Barman, how's about another for me and my mate."

At that, the red-haired man slapped Elliott on the back and announced to the rest of the room, "You 'eard it right 'ere. My mate is buying me a round." He offered Elliott his hand.

"My name's Boyland. Cleve Boyland."

"Nice to meet you Cleve. I'm the Reverend William Elliott."

"Reverend?" Boyland seemed clearly confused.

"You heard right, I'm a reverend in the Anglican Church of New Zealand, Christchurch actually."

It was way too much information for the staff sergeant to handle. He simply dropped his head and propped himself up against the bar.

"Whatever you say, mate. Makes no difference to me."

Elliott decided to have a bit of fun with the sergeant.

"We in the church are allowed a pint or two each week, preferably on Saturdays," Elliott smiled. "The rest of the week we must abstain."

The sergeant considered Elliott's words and decided that was also okay with him.

"Whatever, mate. It's all okay by me."

Elliott smiled and took a sip of the next beer. He was already well on his way of gaining the trust that would be necessary for him to complete his mission. Getting to see General Bennett in person would be another matter, but he was already in the process of developing a plan for that eventuality. For the present, he was willing to sit back and enjoy himself.

September 13, 1941, Above Robinson Waterfall, Cameron Highlands, Malaya, 1800 hrs

Of all the places Capt. Patrick Heenan brought her during their developing relationship, none were as special to Pinka Robertson as the spectacular waterfall that locals called Robinson's Waterfall. Heenan had originally taken Pinka to the place under the guise of finding the "natural handiwork of God that bore her name." Pinka went along with the game and even though the actual name wasn't perfectly synonymous, the duly impressed young woman came to enjoy the idyllic spot as if it were her own.

The water that passed this pristine spot was slowly making its way from the higher elevations of the Malayan mountain system. It passed near Brinchang and through most of the Cameron Highlands before arriving at its final destination of Ringlet Lake and the sprawling Sultan Abu Bakar Dam, named for the former Sultan of Johore.

Heenan had earlier discovered an isolated cliff that overlooked the entire area and offered an unobstructed view to the north and northeast that was breathtaking in both scope and grandeur. When he first shared the spot with Pinka Robertson, she immediately knew the falls was destined to have a very special significance for their relationship.

In his civilian slacks and a light brown silk shirt, Patrick Heenan was the most handsome sight Pinka Robertson had ever seen.

"This is the most beautiful place I have ever seen in all of Malaya, my darling," she whispered softly into his ear as Heenan held her tightly on a high rock cliff that constituted the couple's favorite view. "I wish I could just stop time right here and now and this could be the background for the rest of our lives."

"No reason to think that's not possible Pinka," Heenan returned. "Like everything in life, it's what you want to make of the bloody thing."

Pinka broke the embrace and pushed him back.

"You are totally unromantic, Patrick. Some times I think you are the most insensitive man I've ever met."

"That's not what you say when we are under the sheets," Heenan teased back. "Right then you say I'm the most wonderful bloke in the whole world."

"Don't you confuse love and sex," Pinka replied lightly, attempting to gain the upper hand in the conversation. To her consternation, Pinka knew that she truly enjoyed verbal sparring and Heenan's reluctance to cave in to her verbal jabs was one of the first things about him that had fascinated her about the attractive British captain.

"I won't if you won't," Heenan returned, ready as always for the verbal fisticuffs.

"It isn't exactly easy for a woman, " Pinka explained. "Men can trifle around and play with women's affections and the whole world is ready to condone their actions. When a woman starts experiencing feelings for a man, it is a much more personal sensation. I think it takes a woman longer to know she actually is in love, but, once it happens, she becomes powerless to do anything about it. It envelops her entire being and even dictates how she should handle whatever comes along in her life."

Sensing the seriousness of the subject, Heenan decided to forego any further sparring and answered.

"You know, Pinka, I do agree with *some* things you say."

Pinka gazed into his deep blue eyes and reached out for him. She pulled him close and reached for his lips, parting her mouth as they touched. She kissed him deeply and held the kiss for several moments. She reached down and felt the beginnings of his sexual arousal. She looked around for a level spot and pulled him down on the heavy grass.

"I want you this very instant, as much as I've ever wanted anything."

"I can never refuse you anything, my Pinka," he replied, attempting to unbutton her blouse with his teeth. When the process proved undoable, he reverted to his skillful fingers for the job.

As he removed the final button and helped her out of her pink silk blouse, Capt. Patrick Heenan managed to check his wristwatch without Pinka Robertson being aware. It was already well after six o'clock and the time was drawing near when he would have to transmit his latest message.

Since that meant taking out his Bible and also making an excuse to leave Pinka for a few minutes, Heenan knew that their lovemaking would have to be an act of relatively short duration. He could justify such shortness with the passion of the moment, but the excuse he would use to extract himself from her company for even a few minutes would be another matter.

With those thoughts, Heenan returned to the prone, pulsing body of Pinka Robertson.

Whatever the causes or circumstances, Patrick Heenan simply could not afford to be late on his weekly shortwave transmission to Japanese Intelligence.

September 14, 1941, Australian Imperial Force Officer's Club, Johore Bahru, Malaya, 1845 hours

At least the past day and a half could not be considered completely wasted for Lt. William Elliott in his disguise as a minister for the New Zealand Anglican Church. Despite some early setbacks, his decision to frequent the favorite bar of the AIF's soldiers in Johore Bahru, or simply Jo Bah as the Aussie soldiers called it, finally proved to be correct.

Towards midnight of his first night, a group of low-level officers had appeared and befriended the half-plastered Elliott, who had forgotten just how much Australian soldiers could actually drink. Several captains and an AIF staff major named John Wyett invited him to their table. By the time the place closed, the group all considered themselves fast friends. Wyett was an interesting man who was attached to General Bennett's staff and was remarkably personable to boot. He informed Elliott that he was also a New Zealander and took to Elliott immediately. He eventually offered him accommodations at the AIF's visiting officer's quarters, a chance happening that Elliott immediately accepted. Also included was an invite extended to Elliott for dinner the following evening at the AIF officer's club, an invitation that Elliott gratefully agreed to.

He arrived at the AIF club around six o'clock, and was immediately shown to the bar. Major Wyett and a few of his friends from the night before were there, joined by a large number of other officers who all seemed in a truly spirited mood. Elliott had managed to keep up his charade, and silently hoped that he would not come into contact with anyone else who was really familiar with either New Zealand or Christchurch for that matter.

His gray minister's suit stood out against a veritable sea of khaki in the long room that served as the bar. Off to the left, another similarly large room seemed to be set for dinner, or so it seemed at first glance to Elliott.

He promised himself to go sparingly on the booze, as much to enjoy the remainder of the evening as well as to enable him to remember the details of what would be said during the rest of the evening.

About half past seven, Maj. John Wyett approached him and spoke.

"Okay, Reverend, I think it's about time for us to start on some dinner, you up for that?"

"Sure am, John, I guess I might have had a bit too much to drink last night. I really haven't had much to eat today."

"Sounds like a wee Kiwi shortcoming to me," Wyett chuckled, to the expense of his own New Zealand heritage. 'Yur drinkin' was what we admired the most about you."

"Well, as you could easily see, I really don't drink all that much. Not to mention the blasted tropics and the toll the temperature and humidity takes on you. Man, you really feel like hell the next morning."

"Takes a bit of gettin' used to, I guess, "Wyett replied with a thick accent. " I never really had any trouble with it myself."

"Bully for you, Major, wish I could say the same."

Wyett gestured toward the open room that was now about half filled with tables. Only a few females were present, most native Malays from their varied dress.

Elliott followed the officer to a large table that seated eight. The places were already filled with the exception of two seats. The officer gestured again and Elliott took a seat next to him.

Introductions were exchanged and Elliott was given a simple printed menu. The choices were varied and indicated a well-stocked kitchen.

"Looks good to me. What are the specialties?" he asked in general.

"Everything!" came a voice from his right, a burly artillery captain. A series of 'rightos' resounded from the remainder of the table.

Elliott though a bit and selected a steak with a rice accompaniment.

Better feed the stomach something solid or suffer the consequences. These guys can really drink; it seems like they can go all day long and most of the night.

Elliott engaged in small talk, mostly with Wyett who mentioned that in all his thirty-three years, he had never enjoyed himself as much as he did in his present duty. Even though he was a graduate of the University of Tasmania and was a pharmacist in civilian life, Wyett had had to pull strings to even get into the AIF despite extensive reserve training, both in the navy and the militia. He was delighted to have been posted to Malaya, and particularly to Bennett's staff where he was "in the middle of what was going on." Wyett offered an almost friendly, if candid, view of Bennett.

Outwardly, he enjoyed the general, but also found him incredibly egotistical, particularly regarding his views on handling the European war and the inferiority of British officers and their staid thinking on tactics and training. Elliott was careful to let Wyett speak his peace, particularly since Wyett served on Bennett's staff. Elliott paid close attention to the seemingly innocent talk between Wyett and the other officers, particularly when it involved the British or the defence system.

Elliott was engrossed in a side conversation with two young artillery captains when Wyett casually spoke to the men at the table.

"Better drink up now boys, the old man is coming in a few minutes and yew wouldn't 'wanna miss any of what 'e has to say."

Elliott perked up at the news. The 'old man' was Maj. Gen. Gordon

Bennett to whom the group had referred to several times at the bar. Elliott was elated at the prospect of seeing Bennett since he had few practical prospects as to exactly how he was going to get in to see Bennett in his guise as a minister. A physical meeting of some sort with Bennett was one of the prerequisites of Simson's instructions.

Elliott settled down to his steak, a manly cut that was sizzled to perfection and covered by a deft lemon butter sauce. He applied the sharp knife and cut into the meat. He tasted the first bite and was duly impressed. The meat was fresh and expertly prepared. The AIF certainly knew how to live and eat, at least with regard to the basic necessities of life.

The table settled down to some serious eating and small talk, with no one paying particular attention to Elliott. That was fine with him, since less attention meant less chance of being discovered.

A half hour later, Maj. Gen. Gordon Bennett arrived with a small posse of staff officers and occupied a table directly across from Elliott. The group ordered quickly and the food was brought out in a few minutes.

Another fifteen minutes passed and the noise surrounding the tables was at a low roar. It wasn't until Elliott started hearing a clinking of glasses, the universal signal for silence in an officer's mess, that the room suddenly became quiet.

Bennett waited until the last sound had died and rose to his feet. He wiped his mouth one last time and pushed his chair away.

"G'day," he said, his voice raised as if in challenge to the assembled officers.

"G'day," came a chorus of answers from the eager gathering, a pitch of excitement fueling the roar.

"It is great to be with 'ya all again, under such pleasant circumstances, men. I much prefer this type of exchange to the more formal type of meetings."

A cry of 'hear, hear,' emanated from somewhere in the group.

Bennett paused a long second, then continued.

"What I want to tell you is that you are all continuing to do a great job in this sticky situation, even though I would prefer it if we were somewhere else on this planet actually doin' some real fightin'. "

Again, a brief spattering of applause followed his words.

"But as you can plainly see, we are here in this god forsaken tropical jungle and probably will be for some time. I have been asking the Brits to change our status and give us some territory to defend that would actually mean something, but so far I have been unsuccessful."

Not a single sound echoed throughout the room.

"But, I have not and *will not* give up on that, and in that regard you have my promise. Right now we are surrounded by all our Indian buddies, and I'm not too happy about that. Morale in the Indian Army seems low to me, and many of those soldiers don't look old enough to shave. From their general demeanor, I take most of them to be a bit homesick."

The room shook with laughter at the obvious joke.

"I'm sure each and every one of you has given some thought as to your individual jobs here, so I won't try and prop you up, as it were. We must all follow orders here, no matter how distasteful they might be."

Elliott looked around, and everyone seemed in agreement with Bennett's words.

Bennett continued. "I've just returned from down under, and the truth is there are some in our government who don't want the status changed, no matter how unfair it is to us. But, I will simply have to work thorough that sort of defeatist thinking. Too much of that going on around here if you ask me."

Again, several 'hear, hears' resounded throughout the room.

"I want us all to be on the same page, gentlemen, the very life of the AIF depends on it. Even if our British mentors are all wet in their thinkin' and plannin', we must overcome these adversities. Agree to whatever they say and then find a way to do it or make it better. Lord knows we're the best fighters in the entire British army, I just don't know how many times we will have to prove it before they realize it."

This time, several officers rose and a loud round of applause followed his lexis.

Bennett put his head down as if in deep thought. When he raised it, he spoke again in a more controlled tone.

"Lads, I know this sort of postin' is disgustin' to many of you. I know our morale isn't what it should be and I have looked the other way on several occasions that could have called for stricter discipline. That's the way it is when your mission is strictly support and not first-line defence. But I hope that's all comin' to an end. I intend to keep pesterin' General Percival to give us a front-line defence position, and I won't give up until he agrees."

The group rose and applauded. Bennett waved his arm to the room and sat back down.

Royal Navy Lt. William M. Elliott thought profoundly about what he had just gleaned from the Australian commander.

He couldn't wait to get back to Singapore and report it all to Brigadier Simson.

September 15, 1941, side room off the main bar, Eastern and Oriental Hotel, George Town, Penang, 1700 hours

The meeting brought together an engaging group of professional men who gathered at the request of the resident counsellor of Penang, Leslie Forbes, the de facto head of civil authority on the Island of Penang. Also present during the first real vestiges of the equatorial fall season were Penang Fortress Commander C.A. Lyon, George Town attorney Charles Samuel and a smattering of men from various important sections of the Penang community.

When the room was filled, Forbes assessed the attendees and motioned to the person closest to the door to shut it.

He gestured for everyone to sit down and began speaking.

"Gentlemen, I want to thank you for taking time off to attend this little meeting. I wanted to do this both unofficially and informally, since the subject matter I want to cover is a bit sticky. I will ask from each of you your assurance that what we talk about in here will be considered as strictly confidential and will remain within the confines of this room."

His statement produced a bit of low-level muttering, but each of the men attending nodded their agreement to the conditions outlined by the resident counsellor.

Forbes began talking and the men in the room returned to silence.

"As you can see, I have gathered the leaders of our island community together for this meeting, and I might easily have left a few out. To those who fall into that category, I must apologize in advance. I really wanted this meeting to be low key and not raise any undue fears for anyone."

At that statement, several of the men turned and looked at each other, questioning the statement.

Forbes continued. "The Brigadier and I," he motioned toward Lyon, "have started to perceive a few things in meetings with our superiors and counterparts that we feel should be put on the table. It is nothing really concrete, rather a feeling that we both have reached from entirely different directions." Another low murmur filled the room.

"It seems to us that a number of important people, both from the Colonial Office and also the British military, have begun to believe that it is entirely possible that Great Britain and the Empire of Japan might take courses of action that would bring the countries together in an other than favorable position."

"Do you mean war?" The question came from a man seated in the middle of the room.

"Quite possibly," Brigadier Lyon offered. "Right now it's still a long shot, but there are more and more people talking about it every time the subject is brought up."

"But that's impossible," another long-time veteran of the Straits Settlements spoke. "The Japanese are our friends and our allies. And, we have treaties, not to mention the great trade that currently exists between our countries."

"Point well taken," replied Forbes. "And I must tell you that the official stance, taken recently by London and, indeed, Mr. Churchill himself, is that such an action is most unlikely. Mr. Churchill has been quoted as saying that the Japanese have their hands full with the Chinese in Manchuria and many in British Parliament agree with him completely.

"However, there is also a faction within the government that takes an opposite stance and feels that Japan is actually looking down the road, a road that requires expansion, and a road that can only be accomplished through war and conquest. If these people are right, our nearly idyllic spot here on Penang could be in great danger."

Charles Samuel, the respected lawyer and former civil servant, now stood and began to address the group.

"Gentlemen, I think most of us are in agreement that this premise of a potential war is a bit stretched, stretched so far as to not have a great deal of credibility in. I have heard a bit of such talk, but for the life of me I cannot place much stock in its chances. We have lived in a most comfortable climate with our Japanese neighbors and have traded successfully with them for generations. I have several Japanese friends and even a Japanese client that I have represented in litigation. None of these people have given me the slightest inkling that anything is up with regard to the Japanese Empire."

"With the distinct sense of nationalism that the Japanese people possess, do you think they would actually give you a warning?" Brigadier Lyon answered, getting straight to the point.

"No, Brigadier, but I feel that I would be able to detect some feeling about the matter, that's if it actually existed," replied Samuel. "Exactly what evidence can you produce to support your feeling, er, you did say it was just a *feeling*, did you not?"

"Yes, quite," Leslie regained the floor. "It's not something we can put a distinct finger on. It's more an impression, if you like, something we both have begun to feel. When we discussed the premise between ourselves, both of us were convinced we were on to something."

"Gentlemen," Samuel spoke to recapture the momentum of his argument, "I think that a number of us seated here in this room would be able to detect changes in the Japanese approach to business or at least their unwillingness to continue our relationships on the same level."

"And I say that if their plan was to attack us, we would certainly be the last ones to know," shot back Brigadier Lyon, now visibly perturbed. "What I am simply saying is that we should consider some degree of increased planning that would include any eventualities. God knows I've asked for additional troops to be sent here, but that simply has not happened. I'm always told that men and resources are needed more desperately in other places. I'm also told that Penang and this entire western coastline does not figure to be attacked in case of trouble."

"I have heard the same thing," another voice from the back said.

"Well, I certainly hope they are all correct," Brigadier Lyon continued. "Because, with the meager troops I have to defend this place I would not want to be responsible for everyone's ultimate safety."

"Does that mean we are all in great danger?" It was Charles Samuel once again asking the question.

"It simply means that I am of the opinion that there are insufficient troops to produce a complete defence of this island," Lyon answered, attempting to moderate his tone.

"This might be a case of much ado about nothing," another voice countered from the side.

"Gentlemen, we seem to be getting nowhere," Resident Counsellor Forbes countered. "This meeting was simply to bring our apprehensions to your attention."

"And you have most certainly done that Mr. Forbes and Brigadier Lyon. I think I can speak for everyone in saying that we will continue to monitor the world situation," Charles Samuel finalized. "If there is nothing else, I suggest we adjourn to the outside bar and buy each other a series of early evening cocktails."

The group rose and began exiting the room.

Brigadier Lyon looked at Leslie Forbes and shook his head.

"I thought it might be like this. These people have been too comfortable and too isolated in this colonial civilization to take note of the realities of the outside world. I don't know exactly what to do. If we held a united front of concerned citizens, it might make a difference to the Colonial Office. But the way it is, we don't stand a chance in hell of convincing anyone that we are unprepared for what might lie ahead."

"We will continue to do our best, Brigadier, and hope that it is enough. That's the British tradition that's been our standard for centuries. We'll simply pull our belts in a notch, British spirit and all that rot."

"Right, Counsellor, and all that rot."

The two left together in the direction of the main bar. Maybe a few cocktails would make the pain of the disastrous meeting a bit easier.

September 20, Pinka Robertson's Riding School, Tanglin Girls School, Cameron Highlands, Malaya, 1215 hours

Pinka Robertson had just finished her third set of student riders and was wiping off the last of the bridles and saddles when Capt. Patrick Heenan stuck his head through the main entrance of the stables that served as her riding academy.

Even though she had expected him for their noontime luncheon, the sight of the handsome uniformed man brought a pleasant sensation to the formerly resolute woman.

She smiled as he walked in and planted a kiss squarely on her lips.

"Hi gorgeous," she said effusively. "What took you so long?"

"I got behind a lorry on the trip up and it took me longer than usual," Heenan replied, matter of factly. "I'm not really late, am I?"

"When you are on my time and you are even a few minutes late, I start to worry. I guess I've really fallen for you, you big lummox. Don't you know what it's like to be in love?"

"I've never been in love…until now," he added a bit later, attempting to correct himself.

"It is well you added the 'until now,' it would have really hurt my feelings if you didn't."

"I wouldn't have wanted to do that, no reason to."

"Well now, what about our lunch date? Want to pack a lunch basket?"

"I don't really care, I'm not really hungry to be honest."

Pinka noted Heenan's indifferent response and sensed something was bothering him.

"Are you all right?" she asked. "It's not like you to not want to eat."

"I'm okay," Heenan responded unconvincingly. "Don't worry about it."

"I'll worry about it if I wish," Pinka Robertson answered back. "And I will worry if I choose to worry."

"There's nothing you can do about it, and I don't really want to get you involved. It would be better for you to just piss off, if you know what I mean."

Pinka looked at Heenan in utter disbelief. It was the first time since she met him that he had used that tone with her, not to mention the sophomoric phrase that capped his sentence.

"What did you just say to me? I'm not used to anyone speaking to me like that. What made you use the term 'piss off' to me?"

Heenan chose to look downward and drop his head.

"I'm sorry for what I said. I told you that I didn't think you should get involved."

"Well, it looks right now as if I am involved, wouldn't you say?'

Heenan paused, attempting to find the right words.

"I guess I could tell you, you might even understand."

"Thanks for giving me some credit, even if it is a bit back handed."

"It has to do with my commanding officer…and the British military. In fact, it has to do with the entire British people if you want to know the truth."

Heenan stopped in mid sentence, wondering if he had gone too far.

Should I tell her all about it or should I make some excuse and change the entire direction of this conversation. She is the first woman I have ever considered as an equal so maybe she would understand. And, she is only half-British so she might not be so closely endeared to the British Crown. Besides, I really like her, or at least I think I do.

Something about Heenan's tone and the part about the *'entire British people'* didn't ring quite true with Pinka Robertson, so she probed him again.

"What an interesting combination. Your commanding officer, the British military and the *entire* British people. Whatever on earth are you talking about, Patrick?"

Heenan decided the conversation was taking a decided turn for the worst. Perhaps this was not the best time to go into any of his reasons for being unhappy.

Pinka saw his hesitation, but pushed her point forward.

"What about it, Patrick? You brought it up and it's up to you to finish it."

Patrick began to see and feel the aura of British superiority begin to manifest itself in her questions. He shuffled his feet together and looked around for a distraction. He found none.

"I'm waiting, Patrick. Why won't you answer me? It all seems quite simple."

"It depends on your point of view I guess," he answered, still hoping to find a way out of the question.

"Look here, Patrick. You are an adult as well as an officer and a gentleman. We should be able to discuss anything bothering you anytime we wish. If we cannot, it certainly doesn't speak very well of our relationship."

Heenan looked at her, becoming more incensed with her words by the minute. He tried to control himself, but blurted out instead.

"I told you when we started all this that I really didn't want you involved. Why can't you accept that?"

"Involved? Is that how you look at it?" This was a side of Patrick Heenan that Pinka Robertson had never before seen.

"Yes, involved. It's just like you British to always stick your noses in things that don't involve you."

It was now Pinka Robertson whose turn it was to become annoyed.

"I'm not sure what you mean by 'you British,'" she shot back. "After all, unless I'm mistaken, you yourself are quite British."

"You know I am originally from New Zealand, I already told you that."

"So why are you so insistent on faulting the entire British people? Just what have they done to you?"

Heenan again tried to gain control his temper, but found himself becoming angrier at each word.

"There's a great deal that you don't know, Pinka. Things that have been going on my whole life."

She stopped a moment and contemplated his last words.

"So if it is so awfully bad, are you then unwilling to tell me about it?"

"What good will it do?" he asked plaintively. "No one has ever listened to me before."

"Sounds like you feel sorry for yourself, Patrick. If you can't talk to someone about it, it might never be resolved. I can't see why talking about it will do either of us any harm."

"I think you just want to butt in," he blurted out. "It really is *none* of your business."

Pinka stood back, reflecting on the situation.

Finally, she turned her back and began to walk away.

"Pinka, I didn't really mean that."

"I think that perhaps you did, Patrick, and for that I am truly sad."

"But, I . . . "

"Don't," she interrupted in an unassailable tone. "I just want to end the conversation here. I seem to have just lost my appetite and think it is best we allow ourselves the luxury of some time and distance before we see each other again. Maybe that will help us sort out the problems that suddenly seem to be present. At least, that seems to me to be the smart thing to do."

Heenan remained silent, as her profound words sunk in.

"If, at a later date, I think continuing our relationship makes some sense to me, then I will contact you. Until then, do me the honor of respecting my request not to call me."

She looked regretfully at Heenan and turned her back. In a moment she was through the stables entrance and out the building.

For one of the first times in his entire life, Capt. Patrick Heenan was totally speechless.

September 26, 1941, 25th Japanese Imperial Army Headquarters, Saigon, Indochina, 1800 hours

The tedious, lengthy air trip to reach his new unit's present headquarters was a welcome respite for recently appointed Staff Officer in Charge of Military Operations for Japan's 25th Army, Col. Masanobu Tsuji.

After an unceremonious, early morning departure from his wife and children, who were still sleeping in Tokyo, Tsuji caught a scheduled, passenger airliner from Haneda Airport bound for Hanoi in northern Indochina. The long flight provided him with a chance to catch up on the heavy pile of paperwork that he had found waiting upon his return home.

The Greater Japan Airways flight also allowed Colonel Tsuji to reflect on his upcoming birthday, a date when he would pass the forty-year level of his life. He thought about various aspects of his career and, in the end, admitted to himself that both his life and career to this point could both be considered as highly successful.

The Douglas DC-3's engines droned on in constant, fixed rhythm and, for the third time since he received his orders by special military courier, Tsuji reread the papers assigning him as staff officer to the 25th Army. Tsuji was keenly aware of the upcoming mission of the 25th Army, since he had enjoyed being part of the planning team at *Doro Nawa* Unit, which had developed the plans for Japan's proposed invasion of Thailand and Malaya.

But, getting himself assigned to the key job in the upcoming invasion wasn't as easy as Colonel Tsuji had expected. It had been necessary to call on several old friends in high places to actually secure the orders. In the end, his long-standing relationship with important government figure Hideki Tojo won out over the protests of other high-ranking officers and government figures — ones that felt that as planner for the most important mission, Colonel Tsuji's expertise could be better used in a non-combat environment.

But Tsuji was growing tired of the endless paperwork required in his old job, and fought hard to land the prized job of staff officer. In addition to filling a need to be where the action was, he desperately wanted to be in a position where he could be assess the quality and planning that went into the *Doro Nawa* Unit's work. He realized the tactical importance of the Malayan campaign and the strategic jewel of Singapore that would be acquired if the campaign were successful. Singapore held the key to military advantage of the Pacific for the Empire of Japan and Masanobu Tsuji was willing to do anything to insure its capture. For the past ten months, he had worked harder than he ever had in his entire career, had lost nearly ten pounds from his smallish frame, and had offered his very existence for his plan's ultimate success. His new position as staff officer assured him that he would see his work reach fruition.

When the aircraft finally touched down in Hanoi for the overnight stop, Tsuji passed on dinner and went straight to bed at the small hotel the airline provided for its passengers.

He awoke early the next morning completely refreshed and rejuvenated.

Because the only flight to Saigon was scheduled for midafternoon, Tsuji took a break and walked from the hotel along the tree-lined streets of Hanoi, eventually making his way down to the busy harbor. A number of ships were being unloaded; including several that carried the Japanese flag. Tsuji wondered if any of the goods were ultimately destined for military use, but there was no way of knowing. With the planned invasion of Malaya's starting date scheduled for a little more than two months in the future, Tsuji was sure that at least a portion of the stores and equipment that the Imperial Army required were already on their way to Indochina. Pleased by that thought, he continued his walk and eventually made his way back to the hotel where a bus would take them to Hanoi's airport for the short flight to Saigon in the south.

Several uneventful hours later, Tsuji's plane touched down on Saigon's recently upgraded runway and pulled to a stop in front of the main passenger terminal. From the small window beside his seat in the cabin, Tsuji had been able to observe what appeared to be busy activity at an adjacent part of the airport. There a number of military aircraft, all bearing the *Hi-no-Maru* flag of Imperial Japan. Workers were engaged in various activities, and a large cadre of Japanese military personnel scurried around in their duties.

It is all beginning to come together. We Japanese are about to fulfill our historic destiny and I have been fortunate to have been selected to play an active part.

As he stepped upon the airport's tarmac, Tsuji was aware of a distinct difference between Saigon and its northern neighbor Hanoi. The early evening coolness of Saigon tended to mask an earthy, practically foul-smelling aroma that permeated the air. During his stay in Hanoi, Tsuji was acutely aware of a similar offensive sensation no matter what time of the day or night.

A young Japanese lieutenant beckoned to Tsuji as he turned a corner inside the terminal. It was obvious he was waiting for Tsuji to arrive. The lieutenant bowed and bid his superior to follow him. A staff car was already waiting at the curb with its motor running. Tsuji motioned for the lieutenant to assist him with the small, wooden trunk that contained his personal effects that he had brought with him from Tokyo. The two lifted the case to the top of the staff car, a Toyota AA sedan, and in another minute's time the vehicle was on its way to the headquarters of Japan's 25th Army.

Tsuji was impressed with the young lieutenant and the 25th Army staff's attention to detail that allowed him to be met in such a timely manner.

"How far is the drive?" Tsuji asked after the car departed the grounds that constituted Saigon's airport.

"A little over twenty minutes, Honorable Colonel. The streets of Saigon aren't in very good condition and there is a lot of foot and cart traffic."

Tsuji settled back and took in the scenery. At length, the car pulled into a palm-laced driveway that led to a large, sprawling country villa. A questioning glance from Tsuji to the lieutenant produced the following explanation.

"These are actually the officer's quarters, Honorable Colonel. I was told to take you here so that you could relax. I will pick you up again tomorrow morning and take you to the general's office."

Tsuji accepted the explanation and waited until the vehicle stopped. He opened the door himself and stepped outside. Around the grounds, a number of men could be seen in various stages of relaxation. Most were dressed in bathrobes and many were holding beer bottles in their hands.

Tsuji checked his watch and confirmed the time, which he noted was approximately six thirty.

He made a mental reminder to take up the matter of the officer's seeming relaxed environment with the commanding general of the 25th army as soon as possible.

Tsuji realized that — given the short amount of time left before the invasion actually began — scenes of excess such as the one that he had just witnessed upon arriving at his new quarters could not be tolerated.

October 2, 1941, Operations Center, Alor Star Air Base, Malaya, 0950 hours

Normal, daily air operations at Alor Star Air Base in extreme northwest Malaya had almost doubled during the past year, thereby placing a premium on space and adding strain on the understaffed base operations personnel. Talk of potential war abounded within the operations section as well as at the Base Officer's Club, where practically every other conversation contained a theory as to exactly when and where British military forces would come to grips with the armies of the Empire of Japan. For some reason, this common feeling was neither shared by many of the general officers stationed in the area, nor by the higher echelons of the British military or government.

Since Alor Star was the largest British air concentration on Malay's western coastline, it was, by necessity, the strategic staging area for aircraft from several, other smaller British and Malayan bases located throughout the region. It also served as a regional maintenance facility for most of the British squadrons dotted throughout Malaya.

For Royal Air Force Maj. Geoffrey Cone, second-in-command of the base's operations center, the entire Alor Star scenario was becoming a little too grueling to handle. The daily influx of pilots and machines was taxing his personnel's abilities to perform their jobs at sufficiently high levels as to meet his own exacting standards. His request for more manpower was met with the same basic answer as other requests from similar field commanders. As long as the existing war in Europe continued to expand, the probability of additional personnel for Southeast Asian bases was bleak at best.

A strong proponent of the courses he had taken some time ago while attending Army Staff College, Major Cone attempted to delegate some responsibility to some of his junior officers. On most occasions, his junior officers had risen to the occasion.

That was not the case in the person of Capt. Patrick Heenan, one of the Air Intelligence liaison officers currently assigned to his unit. Ever since the cocky New Zealander had reported several months ago, Cone had found Heenan's performance listless at best. Heenan also displayed a tendency toward indifference particularly regarding his dealings with enlisted men. One particular incident had caused him to assign Heenan to Air Liaison School in Singapore soon after his arrival.

Cone was disappointed upon Heenan's return to Alor Star, observing that the officer continued his intolerance toward most of the enlisted men under his command. Off duty, Heenan's attitude tended to be somewhat better, and on a rare occasion, Cone and Heenan had even shared a pint in the Aloe Star Base Officer's Club. On those occasions, Cone found that Heenan was also incredibly over opinionated about many things, but somehow managed to be extremely popular with members of the opposite sex who happened into the club on social occasions.

Something about the way Heenan conducted himself prompted a chord in Major Cone's dispassionate mind, and the thirty-seven year old career army officer soon resolved to get to the bottom of his nagging concern.

But what bothered Major Cone the most about Captain Heenan was Heenan's undue concern about British Air Squadron deployment and training exercises, especially in the more remote areas of Malaya in deference to the sorties around Alor Star itself.

On one particular occasion the prior week, Heenan had verbally abused a desk sergeant who had failed to provide him with a timely report on two Blenheim squadrons that were rotating to Kota Bharu from Singapore. Heenan redressed the startled sergeant in front of a number of onlookers that included Major Cone.

After the tirade, Cone ordered Captain Heenan into his office where he questioned the new AILO about the incident.

"Just what was all that about out there, Captain Heenan?" Cone asked, as Heenan stood at ease before him.

"The sergeant didn't have all the information I had requested ready for me when I wanted it, Major," came the quick reply. "I can't be expected to do my job properly if I do not receive proper information from my subordinates. Don't you agree?"

Cone considered Heenan's answer and waited a long moment before replying.

"And just what information are you talking about, Captain Heenan?"

"I wanted the details of the two Blenheim Squadrons that were rotating to Kota Bharu from Singapore," Heenan replied guardedly. After a moment he added, "I need the data as part of my job with our existing air defense plans."

"And just how does two squadrons deploying on the east coast of Malaya affect us here at Alor Star, Captain Heenan?"

"I just like to be thorough, Major. If I know where all the aircraft are, I get a better idea of what is happening."

Major Cone considered the explanation and looked up at the taller, blonde-haired man in front of him.

"Captain Heenan, I do not I completely agree with your way of thinking, and I definitely cannot condone your way of handling the situation in front of the rest of the men. Your outlandish actions appalled me as an officer and I intend to so something about it.

From this point on you are to concentrate on the air squadrons and deployments that affect Alor Star and northwest Malaya *exclusively*. There's certainly enough to do around here without barging into the other area's business. Do you understand?"

"Yes, Sir, if you wish," Heenan answered weakly.

"Consider it an order, Captain Heenan. And, oh yes, one more thing." Sir?"

"If I *ever* witness you dressing down another non-commissioned officer in public as you did a little while ago, I shall make it my business to do the same with you . . . and, I promise you, the result will not be pleasant. Do I make myself clear?"

"Perfectly. May I go now?"

"By all means, Heenan. Things are difficult enough around here without adding unnecessary stress and intimidation."

Heenan saluted and turned to depart. He walked to the door and opened it. Major Cone watched the man's movements until he had passed through the door.

When he was sure the junior officer was out of hearing distance, Major Cone picked up his desk phone. When his staff sergeant answered rigidly on the other end, Major Cone spoke slowly.

"Sergeant Potter, please get the senior air liaison officer in Singapore on the phone for me. There is a matter I need to discuss with him."

Major Cone replaced the phone on his desk and thought about the episode with Captain Heenan. Something about the entire confrontation rankled him. It was time that something was done about it.

The phone rang back in less than a minute and Cone picked it up.

"Cone here."

"Major Cone, this is Colonel Ashcroft, the SALO on duty. What may I do for you?"

"Colonel, I have something of a problem up here and I am hoping you can help me. It might be nothing, but one of my officers has been a little off of late and I am not buying the answers he gives me when I question him. It is just a feeling I have, but something is not quite right with him."

"Go on, Major, just what do you have in mind."

"Well, Sir, I was wondering if I could send him to temporary duty down with you and possibly feed him some bogus information. I'd only want him down there a month or so, then I will bring him back up here. If he was away from his normal surroundings, he might just drop his guard and spill something about what he is doing."

"Well, we are all quite busy here, Major, but if you think it is all worth it, I'll make the arrangements. What did you say his name was?"

"Captain Heenan, Colonel. Capt. Patrick Heenan."

October 19, 1941, 18th Independent Chutai (Squadron), Saigon Aerodrome, Saigon, Indochina, 1545 hours

Col. Masanobu Tsuji, staff officer for military planning for the Japanese Imperial 2th Army, realized he was in a deep pickle and wasn't sure what he was going to do about it. By way of his past experience in military planning, Tsuji had always held that one of the most important aspects in developing the specific details of the upcoming invasion of Malaya was to be as accurate as possible with regard to the strength of the enemy. Tsuji had been able to gather detailed information from several of his intelligence sources, but was keenly aware that several important details were still missing—details he needed before he could accurately report back to the Imperial Japanese general staff. He was also bolstered by the recent news reaching Saigon that his long time friend and political mentor, former Lt. Gen. Hideki Tojo, had been named Prime Minister of Japan just days before.

However, the astute, career military officer also was keenly aware that time was beginning to run out on the basic window of opportunity for the southward advance that he truly embraced. He also realized it was only a short time until the advent of the northeast monsoon season and its providential cover for Japan's basic invasion plan. In fact, recent weather reports had begun to track the beginnings of Southeast Asia's historically rainy season.

Tsuji had decided that his only option at the time was to see Malaya and Thailand for himself and that would require a reconnaissance flight from Saigon to points in both countries. He made that decision earlier this Sunday morning and as soon as his luncheon meeting was concluded, had his driver transport him immediately to Saigon's newly-renovated aerodrome.

When he arrived there, Tsuji's present dilemma began. When he sought out Flight Lieutenant Omuro, regarded as the unit's best pilot, Tsuji was dismayed to find the man in no condition to fly. Lieutenant Omuro was actually part of the Imperial Army air force, and along with the other members of the 18th Independent *Chutai,* was presently assigned to the Imperial Army for reconnaissance work.

Tsuji approached Omuro, who was slumped unceremoniously in a large chair in the pilot's lounge.

"Lieutenant Omuro, I must ask that you fly me on a secret reconnaissance mission tomorrow. The matter is of the highest priority."

Omuro attempted to rise and groggily attempted to focus on the diminutive Colonel standing before him. His effort failed and he slumped back into the chair.

Another nearby pilot spoke to Tsuji.

"You can forget about Lieutenant Omuro for the next few days, he is completely exhausted. He has been flying for the last thirty days straight and can't even stand up. We tried to get him to go to the officer's quarters for a rest, but he didn't have the energy. We are all in the same state here; we haven't had any rest for weeks."

Tsuji studied the young aviator who had spoken up and saw immediately that the man was telling the truth. He silently cursed the fact that members of the Imperial army and air force were currently being asked to perform their duties and accomplish their goals in incredibly unrealistic short timespans . . . details that could normally be spread out over many months and even years.

The colonel paused to consider his predicament and regarded the rest of the pilots who were all slumped around the room. From the general condition of their uniforms and overall demeanor, he knew he was going to have a problem finding a pilot.

Colonel Tsuji walked over to a window overlooking the flight line and studied the busy tarmac. It was evident that Japan was preparing herself for war—and that thought gave him a renewed sense of direction.

He was about to leave the window when a figure approached his side and bowed.

The young officer was dressed in a flying corps uniform that bore the rank of *Tai-i*, or captain.

"Honorable Staff Officer, I am Captain Ikeda from the Kanto Army, just arrived to take command of the One Hundred Type Reconnaissance Plane Squadron." It was evident to Colonel Tsuji that the young aviator was extremely proud of his new assignment and was in extraordinarily high spirits.

Unsure of how to answer, Tsuji replied, "Thank you for seeking me out."

Captain Ikeda acknowledged the greeting without answering.

Tsuji continued. "Tomorrow I wish to go flying over the southern part of Thailand and northern Malaya, will you be able to do it?"

Captain Ikeda pondered the idea for a few seconds and replied.

"Yes, I can do it. If you, Mr. Staff Officer, can go, I shall manage it." His words brimmed with confidence and enthusiasm that impressed Tsuji and lifted his own spirits.

"Well then, Captain Ikeda, I ask you to make preparations immediately to set out at five o'clock tomorrow morning. By way of precaution, have the *Hi-no-Maru* (Japanese flag) painted off the plane. We will both wear military uniforms in case something happens during the flight, but I want us to attract as little attention as possible while we are in the air."

Captain Ikeda bowed and Tsuji took his leave.

Tsuji was relieved that he would now be able to perform the most important reconnaissance flight himself, and that would answer his lingering questions. He realized that his flight tomorrow would provide the last bit of strategic information the Japanese army would need for its invasion plans.

The gods were indeed smiling on his worthy cause.

October 20, 1941, 18th Independent Chutai (Squadron), Saigon Aerodrome, Saigon, Indochina, 0430 hours

It was still very dark and particularly humid when Colonel Tsuji arrived at the briefing room of the 18th Independent Chutai, who were also known around Saigon as the Reconnaissance 100 Type Squadron. There was practically no activity at that hour of the morning and Tsuji was apprehensive that something had gone wrong—that Captain Ikeda would not be on time for the pre-dawn flight.

He looked around the building, becoming more restless as the minutes wore on. Presently the outside door to the flight line opened and Ikeda peered in, his face rounded with cheer—much as it was the day before when Tsuji first met him.

"Ah, Honorable Colonel, all is ready for our departure. I was just checking the plane before we take off. I trust you had a restful night."

"Yes I did, Captain Ikeda," Tsuji lied. Tsuji's labored sleep had been marginal at best, and he had risen a little after three o'clock when he realized that he could sleep no more. He spent the better part of an hour going over some figures he had recently received, until he felt it was time to begin to make his way to the Saigon aerodrome.

Captain Ikeda held open the door as Colonel Tsuji exited the briefing room.

"I have a flying suit for you out at the aircraft," Ikeda remarked, noting the colonel was attired in an air force uniform as opposed to the regular army uniform of the prior day. "You can throw it on over your uniform. I made sure it was a little large for just that purpose."

"As long as I have my uniform on I am satisfied," returned Tsuji. "If anything happens and we are forced down, I would not appreciate being treated as a spy."

"Nothing will happen, Colonel. I am an excellent flier and this is the finest reconnaissance aircraft that Japan possesses."

Tsuji nodded as they reached the plane. He took the flight suit and easily climbed into its spacious confines. It was way too large for his small, narrow frame, but he was otherwise comfortable as he climbed into the back seat immediately behind the pilot.

Captain Ikeda took the pilot's seat in the cockpit and within minutes the Mitsubishi Ki-46, which was also known as the 100 Type, was rolling toward the end of the runway. Since it was the only aircraft moving at that time, permission was quickly given to depart.

Once the twin-engine plane cleared land, it immediately turned right and headed toward the Malayan Peninsula. As the plane gracefully executed its turn, Tsuji was amazed as the first rays of light heralded the new day.

Captain Ikeda also noticed the reddening sun and clicked his intercom.

"Beautiful isn't it, Honorable Colonel? We always get the best views up here. Such sights are truly gifts of the gods and should be revered."

Impressed with the young pilot's ability to appreciate and express such beauty, Tsuji answered in agreement.

"If I would have known it was this beautiful, I would have chosen to be a pilot instead of an intelligence officer. The colors are truly inspiring." Tsuji relaxed and concentrated on the trip's first landmark, Cape Cambodia, a natural landmark that jutted out into the water some distance to their starboard in the blue-gray distance ahead.

An hour later, Ikeda again click the intercom.

"Colonel, I wanted to let you know about our flight plan."

"Certainly, Ikeda, please go ahead."

"I figure we have about five hours of flying time between Saigon, the northern part of Malaya called Kedah Province, and the return to Saigon. We should have sufficient time to see what you want provided the weather remains favorable, and we do not encounter strong headwinds or enemy fighters along the way. We will need the blessings of the gods, or something similar, to be successful."

"I will ask for their help," Tsuji answered jokingly. He had already decided that he liked the pilot's cheerful disposition and uplifting attitude.

After another hour of uneventful flight, Tsuji became aware of the bitter cold he was experiencing. Ikeda had informed him that they would be cruising at eight thousand feet and that the altitude would require the use of oxygen tubes that were placed in the mouth.

Tsuji also became aware of increasing cloudiness ahead of their plane that warned of the approach to the Malayan coastline. Ikeda identified the thick, heavy clouds as unstable cumulonimbus clouds that differed greatly from regular nimbus clouds, and which covered the skyline ahead. Tsuji looked and saw no perceptible break. Ikeda also pointed out the fact that cumulonimbus clouds usually contained severe up-drafts, and when many of the huge towers came together, generally produced a squall line. The largest cumulonimbus clouds always produced thunderstorms.

It was obvious to Tsuji that the weather was now a severe impediment to his mission, even thought its existence meant that few British patrol planes would likely be in the area.

"Let us fly lower," he ordered Ikeda through the intercom. They had been flying racetrack patterns for the past hour with no success.

Ikeda dropped the nose of the Ki-46 and leveled at two thousand feet. Seeing no break in the clouds, he pushed the steering wheel forward and passed through one thousand and finally down to five hundred feet. The intense cold of the higher altitude changed immediately to an uncomfortable warmness that caused the two aviators to start to sweat. Encouraged by Tsuji, Ikeda descended to three hundred feet before the aircraft finally dropped out of the clouds. Spread out below was the Malayan shoreline, with gentle waves braking on the beaches, and an assortment of shorebirds scattered along the beach and in the air.

To Tsuji's dismay, the land inside the beach was completely covered by a dense fog.

Ikeda was instructed to circle around and made several passes, attempting to find a break in the curtain of fog, but with no success.

After prudently consulting his guages, Ikeda spoke to Tsuji.

"It appears that we are close to our maximum endurance, Colonel. If we don't start on our return to Saigon, we will most surely run out of petrol. I know that it is but a step to Kota Bharu, but there is no alternative. It is very disappointing."

"Very well, "Tsuji answered. "We will try again."

The remainder of the return flight was uneventful and the Ki-46 touched down a little after eleven hundred hours, dangerously low on petrol.

"You rest tomorrow and also the day after. When the weather predictions are favorable, you and I will fly again."

Tsuji was pleased to see the bitter face of disappointment on the young aviator. He knew it would take such dedication from Ikeda and many others if his plan were going to succeed. There was so much to be done . . .

October 20, 1941, Civil Engineering Headquarters, Fort Canning, Singapore, 1115 hrs

Several weeks had elapsed since his visit to General Bennett and the Australian AIF headquarters, and Royal Navy Lt. William Elliott was again restless, with little to actually occupy his time. He had filed his all-but negative report about Bennett and discussed the matter thoroughly with Brigadier Simson. In the end, Simson said in confidence that he held out hope for a leadership change for the AIF, but he also confided to Elliott that he wasn't exactly holding his breath. Simson, too, made his report on the matter to higher channels but expected little would come of it.

Elliott had also come to the realization that his continuing services on behalf of Brigadier Simson had made him practically useless to his actual assigned unit, the Far East Combined Bureau in Singapore. Except for his ability in languages, Elliott wasn't even sure why he was assigned to the FECB in the first place.

This was all okay with Elliott, since he considered himself a naval officer first and an undercover intelligence operative second. He had enjoyed his temporary duties for Brigadier Simson; since Simson seemed to be the only person he had come into contact with since arriving in

Singapore who actually seemed to understand what was going on. Upon further thought, Elliott expanded the area to cover the rest of southeast Asia, if not the remainder of the entire British Empire

Elliott thought back about Simson's initial reaction when he had returned after visiting the AIF.

"Blimey," Simson scoffed, "I really don't like the message the general seems to be sending to his men. If I read between the lines, he wants to be the hero of practically everything that's done in this region, and won't be satisfied until he's given the spotlight."

"Precisely, Brigadier," Elliott agreed, "that's exactly the way he struck me."

"Damn shame, doesn't make for a great ally should push come to shove. Much too self centered, and not much of a team player."

"Brigadier, you would not have believed it. The attitude some of those Aussie chaps have toward the Indian army and towards our own British troops is utterly amazing. They think they're the only bloody fighters in the entire army. They're always talking about this battle or that battle that they won by themselves, until it becomes quite boring to listen to it all."

Simson did not reply and thought about his next statement.

"This entire defensive network is held together by a string, William, and that's for your ears only. I have not shared this view with my own men because of the morale factor. It's hard enough to motivate them when they feel that no one cares about what they are doing, and they see the funds for our work repeatedly withdrawn or expropriated or something.

Lord knows I have enough important projects at hand to keep a unit twice our size busy for several years. It's just that I am beginning to believe I won't have the time to put many of them into effect."

Elliott looked at Simson, and felt a genuine affinity for the hard-working career officer. His own experience had taught him that people in command seldom had anyone to confide in and that fact made Elliott's bond with Simson even closer. He longed for a way of helping the brigadier even more, but realized he was powerless to do anything about the present status of what he and Simson had discussed.

Even though he knew it was fruitless, Elliott made the gesture to help.

"Brigadier, I just want you to know that I would be happy to help in any manner whatsoever. The chaps at Far Eastern Bureau have practically stopped thinking of me as one of their spooks and I find myself spending more time over here at civil engineering than I do at Far Eastern. I don't know what you have in mind for the future, but I am willing to do whatever it takes."

Simson smiled, genuinely touched by the offer from his subordinate.

"That's quite good of you to offer, William, you know that I think that your work is really first rate. It's just that what I really need is for someone to wave a magic wand and tap some of the bigger heads around here and make them see that our little Shangri La is actually in a world of trouble. It's hard for me to believe that others in command can't really see the handwriting on the wall.

I realize that a lot of the problem is circumstantial and originated with London's present predicaments on the other war fronts, but the risk to us here in southeast Asia is almost incomprehensible. If the Japanese decide to get involved in the European war, we could really be in for it. According to my calculations, we could not really stand up to a formidable strike force for more than a month or two, certainly not the six months that everyone in command feels secure in speaking to each other."

Elliott let the Brigadier's words sink in and finally spoke.

"So, what do you suggest, Brigadier? We can't just sit here and let all this happen. Isn't there something we can do?"

Simson squared his head and looked directly into Elliott's plaintive face.

"If I knew the answer to that I would already be doing it, wouldn't I? The fact is that I have already sent out the red flag message on numerous occasions. I have even sent some cables to London to see if some of my inside people in high command can ruffle some feathers. What I get back is simply the fact that there are greater priorities to be considered in the grand scope of things, and my urgencies are based on suppositions of what *might* happen as opposed to what is *actually* happening."

"It seems terribly sad, Brigadier, that nothing can be done."

"It's true, William, and until something happens to make the status quo change, I guess we are just going to have to suck it up."

Elliott shook his head in agreement.

"And, William, one more thing."

"Yes, Brigadier?"

"If what we think might happen actually does, this place could get quite dicey in a very short time. It might be smart to start thinking of contingencies and about the people we love and want to protect. Since this is an island that is connected to a peninsula, escape routes and methods of escape might become quite tricky, if you get what I mean."

Elliott thought for a moment and replied.

"I see what you are saying, Brigadier. It might be pertinent to involve one's self with a plan of some sort, just to keep handy in the event of problems."

"Precisely, William, something out of the ordinary that you could count on. But, keep it to yourself; I wouldn't want any defeatist talk around here."

"Certainly, Brigadier, you can count on my discretion."

"Good, it is nice that we see eye to eye."

Elliott returned his thoughts to the present. He had considered what Simson had said, but had taken no real action—since nothing had really materialized in his mind.

He suddenly thought of Pai Lin and how she would fare if problems arose. As his mind focused on his true love and her problems, another thought suddenly entered his mind.

He recalled the wonderful experience he and Pai Lin had enjoyed on their expedition to find the pillboxes for Brigadier Simson. He thought again about the wonderful evening and the marvelous dinner with the fishermen at Teluk Sengat, and in particular with the fisherman named Chan.

It might just be a good time I paid my friend Chan another visit, maybe next weekend if all goes well. He might very well be the answer to my problem if anything starts up around here.

For the first time in the past several weeks, Lt. William Elliott could actually feel his spirits rise. It was a good feeling to have.

October 22, 1941, 18th Independent Chutai (Sqd), Saigon Aerodrome, Saigon, Indochina, 0545 hrs

The weather forecast for Colonel Tsuji and Captain Ikeda's second attempt over the northern Malaya Peninsula was about as optimistic as one could expect. Captain Ikeda spent nearly an hour with his *Chutai's* top forecaster the preceding evening and was assured that conditions for the early morning flight on the 22nd would be near perfect.

At precisely 0545 hours Captain Ikeda was finishing his pre-flight check at the tail of the Ki-46 when Colonel Tsuji approached the aircraft. Captain Ikeda bowed and raised his head.

"Wonderful news, Honorable Colonel," Ikeda gushed. "The weather for our flight promises to be much of an improvement over the conditions that we experienced on our first attempt. In fact, this flight should be a breeze." He smiled at his light attempt at early morning humor.

Tsuji smiled, considering the pilot's attempt at levity a benign sign on an important morning.

"I will hold you to your word, Captain Ikeda. If the weather is beneficial, we might even be able to do more than I expected."

Ikeda replied cautiously, "Perhaps so, Colonel. Just keep in mind that we were practically on fumes when we landed last time."

I should have told him that the petrol was nearly exhausted on our last flight. By not wishing to scare him, I might have done us both a disservice.

Dismissing the thought for the time being, Ikeda walked around the tail and stood next to Tsuji. He was impressed that Tsuji had made several small alterations to the flight suit he had worn on their previous meeting. The suit now fit Tsuji as if it had been made for him. Tsuji colonel's insignia was also apparent on the suit. Ikeda also noted that Tsuji held a pair of blankets in his arms, along with a camera.

"For the coldness at eight thousand feet," Tsuji said, noting Ikeda's interest.

Ikeda smiled and motioned the colonel to mount the aircraft.

An hour into the flight and a cloudless horizon sprawled expansively before the Ki-46. The craft's two Ha-102 twin radial engines purred effortlessly as the silent expanses of the Gulf of Thailand passed placidly underneath.

Little had transpired between Tsuji and Ikeda so far, except for a brief conversation when Ikeda explained that he was a graduate of Ichigaya Military Academy's 49th class, and also the fact that he had most recently served with Japan's Kanto Army in Manchuria. From his attitude and general demeanor, it was evident to Tsuji that Captain Ikeda possessed a true warrior's spirit and that he would go far in the military service of the Empire of Japan. It was a shame that Ikeda was in the air force because Colonel Tsuji was sure he could find an important role place for an officer like him in the 25th Army.

Tsuji's main job was to scan the horizon for British patrol planes and hope the Ki-46's tactical speed advantage would keep the plane out of danger. While opportune skies meant better viewing conditions, it also meant the possibility of increased British surveillance patrols, and Tsuji wanted desperately to keep his mission secret.

The plane droned along and Ikeda was able to increase altitude to conserve fuel. Finally, the first sight of the Malayan coast appeared as a thin line on the horizon. Ikeda's expert eyes spotted it first and he relayed the fact back to Colonel Tsuji.

"There, Colonel, the Malayan coastline," he exclaimed as he pointed forward.

It took Tsuji's weaker eyes another two minutes before he could clearly see the thin line in the distance.

"We must be careful from this point on," Tsuji reminded the pilot. "There will probably be a great deal of activity in the vicinity of Kota Bharu."

Ikeda acknowledged the remark with a nod of his head and peered intently ahead.

As the coastline took form, Colonel Tsuji carefully checked his camera to insure that everything was prepared for the mission. He decided that whenever he took pictures he would remove his warm gloves that were much too bulky and severely limited operation of the small camera.

Tsuji glanced to starboard as the Thai cities of Singora and Patani became clearly visible on the perfectly cloudless day. Off the port nose of the plane, the environs of Kota Bharu were also coming into view. Ikeda had managed to hit the IP point Tsuji wanted dead on, another good sign for the mission. Directly in front of the nose were the three separate channels comprising the mouth of the Kelantan River, each reflecting vividly in the early morning sun.

The entirety of the picture in front of him triggered Tsuji's sharp tactician's mind. It was evident that the British could easily control the fate of both Singora and Patani from the newly-completed aerodrome at Kota Bharu. If his intelligence reports were accurate, the large number of torpedo bombers the British had on hand at the base could also control any sea force attempting to land at either Thai city.

Tsuji instantly realized that it would be necessary for the Imperial army to capture Kota Bharu at the same time the landings took place in Thailand. He now firmly believed that any other strategy could doom the entire operation to failure.

The flight turned northward and in a few minutes passed over Singora. Tsuji began taking pictures including the seemingly primitive airstrip at Singora. As the terrain passed below, all that was visible among the sea of trees was a single asphalt road and a railroad right of way that both ran north to south. Tsuji also noticed that a series of rubber plantations lined both sides of the road, extending sideways about a mile or two into the dense forests.

Upon seeing this, Tsuji breathed a sight of relief. Even with superior numbers, such a small amount of usable space would be disadvantageous to the British army that would be limited by such narrow frontage. From his early days at war college, Tsuji specifically recalled that whenever battles are fought with narrow frontage, the limits of such frontage directly affect the number of troops who can effectively engage each other.

Since Japan would always be in the position of the smaller army in terms of usable manpower, Tsuji felt the terrain of southern Thailand and northern Malaya gave his side a distinct advantage. He clicked more shots and opened the door to take some pictures with the Ki-46's aerial cameras. The cold wind formed icicles on Tsuji's eyebrows and narrow beard and made the picture taking almost impossible, but he continued on his task.

Ikeda banked the plane and in another ten minutes the high mountain range that composed the Malayan frontier passed beneath. Tsuji glanced to the starboard and saw that the entire west coast of Malaya was covered by thick storm clouds and what seemed to be heavy rain.

He clicked his mike and pointed to the west. Ikeda understood and came back on the intercom.

"What you see is an incredible anomaly, Colonel. Whenever it is good weather on the east coast of Malaya, the west coast usually has the kind of weather you see in the distance," Ikeda related almost verbatim from the crash course given him the previous evening by the squadron's weatherman.

As they approached the ominous weather system, Ikeda dropped the Ki-46 to two thousand feet. Breaking through clouds, the British aerodrome at Alor Star was immediately visible. Both Tsuji and Ikeda saw the field at the same instant and Ikeda instinctively pulled the steering wheel back and quickly gained altitude. He hoped that the rain and inclement conditions would keep most British aircraft on the ground while they were in the area.

The flight south carried the Ki-46 over two more aerodromes, Sungei Patani and Taiping. Tsuji knew little of these two places but was aware of their importance to the British in being able to repel an invasion.

The silvery belt that compromised the important Perak River came into view. Its three bridges held the key to unobstructed movement south and Tsuji knew it was important he photograph the bridges as they stood.

When this goal was completed, he inquired as to the petrol reserves remaining in the aircraft.

Ikeda reported back that they were now at maximum range and even though he wished to continue the flight south, Tsuji reluctantly ordered the pilot, "End the reconnaissance. Turn back."

Ikeda changed his course and leveled at three thousand feet. As the plane emerged out of the clouds and into clear weather, the British stronghold of Kota Bharu came into view. Ikeda immediately ascended to six thousand feet from which the pair was easily able to view both of Kota Bharu's large and impressive aerodromes.

Tsuji snapped additional pictures, but was unsure as to their quality at such height. After passing over Kota Bharu, the plane continued eastward toward Saigon. He thought about the fact that they had not seen a single British plane on the entire flight. He also silently thanked the gods for such wonderful luck.

The flight progressed uneventfully until it passed the Cape Cambodia checkpoint and started its descent into Saigon.

"How is our petrol status? "Tsuji asked Ikeda when the lights of Saigon could be seen in the distance.

"I do not believe it is prudent to ask, Colonel, I wouldn't want to tempt the gods," Ikeda answered. "It will be close."

Tsuji chose not to worry and placed himself squarely in the hands of divine providence.

Fifteen minutes later, the Mitsubishi reconnaissance plane glided to a short landing and taxied to a stop in front of 18th *Chutai*.

As the ground personnel climbed aboard to assist Ikeda and Tsuji from the aircraft, Captain Ikeda forced a long sigh of relief.

Tsuji observed the gesture and spoke first.

"You see, Ikeda, we made it easily."

Ikeda looked at him, but his usual smile was gone for the first time.

"You are quite right, Colonel, we did arrive safely."

It was also Ikeda's decision to keep to himself the fact that the Ki-46 had *exceeded* its maximum endurance figure by a full *ten* minutes.

Some things are better kept to oneself.

The pair dismounted from the plane and made their way back to squadron headquarters.

Tsuji's mind was filled with recollections of his flight as he conciously assured himself tht he had included all pertinent facts in his notebook. In truth, he had never expected the bonanaza of intelligence information he was able to gather.

It was, after all, a most incredible day for the Empire of Japan.

October 24, 1941, Southern Army Headquarters, Japanese Imperial Army, Saigon, Indochina, 2100 hours

Since his return from the reconnaissance flight over Thailand and Malaya only two days before, Col. Masanobu Tsuji had managed a grand total of four hours of sleep. Most of this could be attributed to the fact that southern Army commander General Hisaichi Terauchi had ordered his entire staff to drop everything and concentrate their time and efforts in redesigning the entire invasion plan for the Malaysian Peninsula.

For the last thirty hours, Tsuji had been in the very middle of the planning. He was chagrined that his aerial photographs were all useless, and not one had survived the rigors of the flight and his inexperience as a photographer. He turned instead to the intelligence section that managed to produce a number of illustrations of various aircraft believed to be in the British inventory at the present time. Tsuji enhanced the information that was gleaned from this effort with his near perfect memory for details. In the end, the facts apparent from the flight collaborated some of the theoretical premises Tsuji had discussed with General Terauchi.

For instance, it was definitely established that the types of aircraft present at both Alor Star and also Kota Bharu were mostly older, obsolete models like the bi-plane Fairey Swordfish and the Vickers Wildebeests. A number of Bristol Blenheim bombers were also visible on the airfields' aprons but the intelligence staff considered the Blenheims to be highly vulnerable to the superior speed and tactics of the newer Japanese Zeros.

"I think you will be amazed at just how well our new Zeros perform, Colonel Tsuji," General Terauchi had remarked. "I believe our enemies are completely underestimating their capabilities. We will achieve air superiority in a relatively short time."

While Tsuji considered his superior's contentions as correct, his experience in the intelligence field taught him to always consider the opposing viewpoint. What could go wrong usually did, and nothing was written in granite as far as air superiority in *any* scenario was concerned.

But, in reality, the main points that troubled Tsuji and the senior staff were mostly logistical in nature and would require the addition of several additional ships if the general staff were to finally approve the daring plan. During the discussions Tsuji made an excellent point to everyone involved.

He believed that the key to the invasion's success lay in the rapid movement of troops once the landings had been achieved. He proposed an increase in numbers to the *Doro Nawa* Unit's initial suggestion of bicycles for the infantry, a suggestion that was first met with total silence. When Colonel Tsuji pointed out that this would reduce the requirement for both personnel carriers and the petrol to fuel them, the entire army planning staff eventually embraced the idea.

The process had taken a little less than thirty hours, but a new operations plan covering the proposed invasion of Malaya and Thailand now existed. It was now up to Col. Masanobu Tsuji to gain the concurrence and approval of the Imperial army's general staff back in Tokyo.

Six copies of the proposal were placed in Tsuji's briefcase and a staff car whisked him immediately to the Saigon aerodrome where a Japanese Naval Aichi Type 94 bomber waited with its engines running.

A slightly groggy Colonel Tsuji climbed aboard the aircraft and the craft departed without further delay. It was soon airborne and heading toward Tokyo. Its solitary passenger was fast asleep minutes after the craft's wheels left the ground.

Tsuji knew he would need a decent rest before meeting with the Imperial general staff the following day or his entire presentation would suffer. Before he dozed off, Tsuji rethought the events of the past few days as well as he could recall. In the end he was thoroughly satisfied with the efforts of everyone involved. It was the first time in weeks that he knew he would enjoy a truly peaceful sleep.

October 27, 1941, Imperial Army Transport Department Offices, Uzina, Japan, 14:15 hours

Along with the approval of the Japanese Imperial Army general staff, Col. Masanobu Tsuji's new operations plan called for an immediate logistical meeting in Uzina at the Army's transport department offices.

Tsuji readily agreed to go since he knew he was the only officer available that would be able to pull all aspects of the huge undertaking together. Besides, the new plan was Tsuji's own invention and he wasn't about to let another less experienced officer explain its meaning and circumstances— leading to the final strategic details.

The general staff dictated that elements of several operating entities attend the Uzina conference. Since Tsuji would be there on behalf of the 25th Army, he would do so singularly. Lt. Gen. Masaharu Homma, commander of the 14th army that was to attack the Philippine Islands and his entire group of staff officers were to attend, along with the commanders of every army corps to be engaged in southward operations. As Tsuji entered the room, he realized that there were nearly forty officers gathered inside.

Once everyone had been seated around a large rounded table, with the less senior officers seated behind their superiors, the meeting began. Even though he wasn't the ranking officer, Tsuji knew it was up to him to open the discussion.

"Honorable Officers, thank you all for coming here to Uzina for this most important conference," Tsuji began. "Our glorious upcoming campaign will bring great honor to the Japanese Empire and to the officers and men who are given the various roles to help secure its honorable outcome.

I have been personally involved in this great campaign's planning since its inception, and, due to some personal observations I was able to recently make during a secret reconnaissance flight over Malaysia. I have suggested some changes to the initial plan that we developed. Some of these changes you might already be aware of, others will be new to you. The 25th Army and general staff have given their support to the modifications I have suggested and I must now call on many of you to also help in this effort.

Because of the strategic nature of the Malayan peninsula and the location of our main goal, the Fortress of Singapore, the following changes were proposed and accepted. In light of some newly-developed intelligence, it has been decided to boldly attack both southern Thailand and northern Malaya simultaneously."

Tsuji paused as a number of murmurs filled the room. He waited a moment as the noise subsided, and continued.

"I feel there is great tactical advantage to our empire in attacking multiple targets. I feel that by swiftly dismantling the British military's ability to respond, it is entirely possible that we can capture the entire six hundred miles of the Malayan Peninsula with only moderate losses to the Japanese military, both in men and equipment.

Such a bold move would be completely unexpected by our enemies—I feel they would quickly become demoralized, and lose a good deal of their will to fight back. If we are correct, this could be the first great Imperial army victory of this war, and a great aid to its eventual conclusion."

Tsuji glanced around the huge table, noting that all eyes were keenly fixed on him, intent on what he was saying. He realized for a brief moment that this was one of the true high points in his military career and, indeed, his entire life.

He started again. "In order to accomplish this end, it will be necessary for the 14th Army and some other specialized units to give up a portion of their allotment of ships and equipment. Speed is essential to this plan and our army and navy's ability to react to each and every potential scenario— as it tends to develop—will determine our new plan's overall success.

I am here to ask the commanders of each unit to most carefully consider the implication of such actions that we will discuss here today. I know each of you will do whatever you feel is best for the empire as a whole. Now, are there any questions?"

At least ten hands spiraled upward around the table, but Tsuji detected little or no hostility.

He had entreated the gods the night before for their help in this matter. It seemed as if his prayers were being answered, at least so far.

October 28, 1941, 5th Division Army Headquarters, Shanghai, China,
0100 hours

With the concurrence of the general staff of the change in plans, and
with the unifying mutual confidence provided by the prior day's important
Uzina logistical meeting, Col. Masanobu Tsuji found himself stepping off
yet another military aircraft that had just landed in Shanghai, China.

As he acknowledged the bows of the young *Sho-i* (second lieutenant)
who met the flight, Tsuji attempted to set his priorities for his upcoming
meeting with Lt. Gen. Takuro Matsui, the commanding officer of the
Imperial Army's 5th Division that was expected to play a vital role in the
upcoming invasion of Malaya.

He knew that he was dealing with one of the Imperial Army's top
fighting units that had repeatedly distinguished itself in a heroic fashion in
both North China and Shansi during the past few years. The 5th Division
was comprised of specially-selected troops and numbered about sixteen
thousand officers and men. Presently concentrated in Shanghi's bustling
suburbs, the division was already operating and training under secret
orders.

Tsuji was also aware that for more than two decades, the 5th Division
had been considered a specialist force, purposely trained in disembarkation
operations. He knew that the disembarkation aspect of the upcoming
Japanese invasion was absolutely critical to its success.

Upon arrival at 5th Division headquarters, Colonel Tsuji was
immediately shown into a large room where Lieutenant General Matsui
had assembled his entire staff. As Tsuji entered, the entire room bowed.
Tsuji bowed back in respect.

Lieutenant General Matsui spoke first.

"Please come in, Honorable Colonel, I understand you bring us good
tidings and the destiny that the gods will provide our unit."

"Yes, General." Tsuji answered politely. "I believe I have good news to share with you. After this operation is successful, your glorious division will have even more banners to add to your division's heralded flag."

Matsui gave the command to be seated to the room and offered Tsuji the seat next to him on his immediate right.

"Honorable officers, let me begin by saying it is a distinct honor for me to be among you," Tsuji started. Several officers around the table openly beamed with delight at Tsuji's words. From the response to his opening remark, Tsuji knew the 5th Division was literally brimming over with self-confidence and determination, the finest qualities any fighting force could have. He continued with his opening statement.

"The 5th Division has been specially selected by the Imperial general staff to lead our army's invasion of southern Thailand and the Malayan Peninsula. Specifically, officers and men of the 5th Division will go ashore at two points in Thailand, those being Singora and Patani. These are the keys to success and the basis for our planning. You and your men will spearhead our *entire* invasion . . ."

Tsuji looked around the table as he spoke. Several of the officers were on the edge of their chairs.

November 2, 1941, Imperial Staff Headquarters, Tokyo, Japan, 1100 hours

The three field-grade officers had arrived early for the meeting, and were now seated around a large, oblong teakwood table in a windowless room adjacent to the offices of the chief of the Imperial Army general staff, Gen. Hajime Sugiyama. Each officer had brought his staff adjutant to the meeting, each of whom was positioned slightly behind the field-grade officers, and, as military decorum dictated, to the officer's right.

The three were all proven veterans of the Imperial Japanese Army, and well known to each other. They included senior officers Lt. Gen. Masaharu Homma, Lt. Gen. Hitoshi Imamura and Lt. Gen.Tomoyuki

Yamashita. At first the trio had engaged in minor pleasantries, but now chose to concern themselves with more specific affairs in moderated tones with their adjutants.

All rose as General Sugiyama entered the room, followed by several staff officers. He bowed politely as did the officers standing around the table.

"Good morning, Honorable Gentlemen," Sugiyama began, "I hope each of your journeys here was comfortable and you find your quarters to your liking."

The three officers nodded affirmatively as General Sugiyama took his chair at the head of the table. Small Japanese flags decorated the table in front of each officer, along with water glasses that had been recently filled.

"I believe in getting right to business," Sugiyama continued moderately. "I am sure none of you knows the purpose of this meeting. From now on, the contents of this meeting must be guarded with utmost secrecy. The fate of our empire will rest on what you are about to hear. Am I understood?"

The generals nodded in unison, unaware of what was to follow.

"A number of important decisions have recently been made here at the *Daihonei* (Imperial General Headquarters) that will affect each of you.

You are all aware of the political courses of action that have affected our empire for the past several years." General Sugiyama paused a moment, seeking the correct sequence of words for his audience.

"The Imperial staff feels that a war between our empire and our enemies is imminent, and by our calculations, no more than a few weeks away. From our point of view, it is unavoidable despite our most sincere attempts to avoid such a course of action.

It is also incumbent upon us to insure that we are victorious in this action, as any other outcome would totally dishonor both the *Tenno* (emperor) and the *Dai Nippon* (Mighty Japan).

You are all aware that the *Kodoshugisha* gives Japan a divine mission to bring all our enemies under one rule. Well, my fellow Imperial officers, the emperor had given us his blessing to initiate an honorable end to such a mission."

Lieutenant General Homma was the first to his feet.

"*Hai!*" he exclaimed excitedly.

"*Hai, Hai!*" came from the others, as they also rose.

"Thank you, gentlemen, I am delighted you agree. Please take your chairs, we have more to discuss.

Everyone complied, and General Sugiyama continued.

"Each of you has been designated to play an important role in the upcoming chain of events. Each of you has been given command of an important campaign that is designed to completely demoralize our enemies. It is necessary that each aspect of these campaigns be thoroughly planned and executed; our *entire* success depends on each of *you* succeeding.

General Homma, you will command the 14th Army in our victory in the Philippines while General Imamura will have charge of the 26th Army for the Dutch East Indies Campaign.

General Yamashita, you have been chosen to lead our 25th Army against Malaya and the Fortress of Singapore.

Gentlemen, as you can imagine, a great deal of planning has already been made by the general staff and all will be made available to you immediately following this meeting."

General Sugiyama paused—expecting the generals to express their thanks for the great honor bestowed on them by the *Daihonei*.

He was a little surprised when General Homma stood up and asked, "Honorable General, just who has prepared the intelligence estimates about enemy forces and who has picked the target dates for the operation? Also, who was in charge for the allocation of the troops involved?"

Since Sugiyama and Homma had crossed swords on numerous occasions in the past, Sugiyama was not completely unprepared for his old foe's remarks. He studied the officer for a moment and prepared to reply to the questions.

Before he could, Sugiyama was interrupted by General Imamura, who spoke firmly and politely to his colleague standing next to him.

"Homma," he began. "You must accept your fate in this matter. Target dates are necessary in any military action, and I have not heard anything as yet of guarantees from the commanders. You should accept your mission like a good soldier always does. No soldier could do any more."

Homma reflected on his colleague's words and chose to remain silent. He finally muttered a respectful "*Hai*," and sat down again.

Sugiyama spoke again. "Then, Gentlemen, I will release you to your respective meetings. It is a honor to serve with you all."

The officers all stood, and then turned to walk out of the room.

General Sugiyama looked directly at General Yamashita and said, "General, if I could have one more word."

"Surely, General," Yamashita bowed.

When the room was cleared, General Sugiyama began in an even tone. "Yamashita, we are both from *samurai* families and realize what our duties mean to ourselves and others."

Yamashita nodded his agreement.

"Your task in the upcoming months is the boldest of all our actions and therefore could be expected to reap the greatest rewards. That's why you were chosen for the honor of leading. The fall of Malaya and Singapore will have a devastating affect on the morale of all our enemies.

When I was an military attaché to Singapore some years ago, I saw the strategic importance the place held, and that hasn't changed a bit in today's world. A victory there would be glorious for us all.

If we are correct in our thinking, the whole war should not take more than a few months, six to eight at most. Our lightning-like thrusts will catch everyone by surprise. It will be a most honorable way of deciding the war. I have already informed the emperor of that."

"*Hai*," was Yamashita's definitive reply. He knew he was more than capable of performing the incredible honor just handed him.

November 8, 1941, Tokyo Military Academy, Tokyo, 0800 hours

The top leaders of Japan's extensive military apparatus were ordered to convene by the emperor at a neutral site to thrash out final plans for the commencement of Imperial military actions against the enemies of Japan.

The Japanese Military Academy was chosen to begin the second week in November due to the fact that both, Japan's Imperial navy and army, considered the place a training ground for all military operations and not geared to any specific branch of the Imperial military. The meeting was held in a windowless inner room around a large teak table that provided more than enough room for the assembled officers and their staffs. Water glasses and small silk napkins were placed directly in front of each chair on small bamboo mats. Guards from the Imperial Marines stood outside the single door to the room insuring complete privacy.

Every officer who figured to play an important role in Japan's upcoming war plan was present at the meeting.

The commander in chief, Combined Fleet Adm. Isoroku Yamamoto, his chief of staff, Rear Adm. Matome Ugaki and also, the commander in chief of the Second Fleet, Adm. Nobutake Kondo, represented the Imperial navy while commander in chief Southern Army Count Hisaichi Terauchi and his chief of staff, Gen. Osamu Tsukada, represented the Imperial Army.

The reason for the meeting was well known to both staffs, and all were attempting to overcome internal squabbling that could threaten Japan's plans for waging war.

Count Terauchi, whose father had served as Japan's prime minister a number of years before and was considered the leading officer in attendance, opened the meeting politely.

"Honorable Fellow Officers, it is a great pleasure to sit down at this meeting between our two great officer staffs, a meeting that our Emperor hopes will bring accord to our two parts of our military."

The others officers bowed in respect to the emperor, and Count Terauchi continued.

"The problem exists in the fact that both the army and the navy believe it is imperative that each strike first in our upcoming operation, thus ensuring our ultimate success. Speaking for the army, it is necessary for us to begin the 25th Army invasion at Kota Baru after dark on the night of December 7 to insure its complete achievement. This date is just a month away and takes into account the effects of the anticipated northeast monsoon, and also the most advantageous tides for the area. I don't need to remind our worthy naval officers seated here of the importance that Malaya and, ultimately, the conquering of the Fortress of Singapore, are to the plans of the Imperial Army."

"Honorable Count Terauchi," Admiral Yamamoto interrupted, choosing the most moderate manner he was able to muster, "I think it is time to share with our worthy army officers our entire plan regarding our attack on Pearl Harbor. Once you have heard what we want to do and when you consider its affects on the entire plans for war, you might then feel our convictions have some merit."

Count Terauchi shifted his weight slightly in his chair as if to consider the comment, and gestured for Yamamoto to continue.

"To our planners, the element of surprise is paramount to achieving our honorable goals. Some of the details of our plan have already been put into effect since they take longer to actually reach fruition. Submarines and mini-submarines have already been dispatched that will attempt to disrupt the activities of the U.S. navy at Pearl Harbor."

At the mention of Pearl Harbor, Count Terauchi glanced over at General Tsukada. While there was rampant army speculation as to the actual main target of the Imperial navy, the navy's exact objective was a closely-guarded secret. Pearl Harbor was but one of many targets of opportunity the army planners had discussed in relation to their navel counterparts. Terauchi saw the expression of wonderment on his subordinate's face and returned his gaze to Admiral Yamamoto.

Yamamoto continued. "We have a great deal of intelligence that indicates it might be possible to catch the entire U.S. Pacific Fleet at its base in Pearl Harbor. The fleet includes numerous battleships and aircraft carriers as well as a number of other top-line ships. Our spies have made a number of actual visits and no more than a handful of these ships depart the safety of Pearl Harbor at one time. If we choose the day and time correctly, it might be possible to destroy the entire fleet with one strike."

Yamamoto paused, allowing the intensity of his words to take effect. After a few moments, he began to speak again.

"Our naval staff has put a great deal of effort into the planning of such an attack and have taken many factors into consideration. It will take a large force that must include several aircraft carriers to achieve this mission for the empire. That means a great deal of preparation on our part. Also, it is incredibly important that we not alert either the Americans or the British as to what we are doing, so almost all our preparations must be done in secret.

We will attempt to make use of certain weather patterns that will allow our task force to sail unobserved to a position close enough to Pearl Harbor to be able to launch our torpedo bombers against the U.S. fleet. The earliest possible time for such an attack is during the early morning of December 7. Our meteorologists tell us that by the morning of December 8, the northeast monsoons will start to wreak havoc on the seas and will greatly affect your army landings. That's why December 7 is the last possible day for us to begin our invasion.

We also chose that day because it falls on Sunday, which is something of a religious day for the Americans. Our spies tell us that most regular work is suspended by the American navy on Sundays and that a great many of the officers and sailors are given weekend passes and are not even aboard their ships. I must say that this is a wonderful opportunity to strike an honorable blow to the Americans, a blow that would seriously affect that country's ability to wage a decent war against us.

We estimate that our bombers will arrive in Hawaii some time around 0900 in the morning. But, you must realize on a mission as extensive as this, it will be practically impossible to tell exactly what time the first planes will arrive. Nothing could be that precise."

Count Terauchi carefully considered Admiral Yamamoto words and after a while leaned over to speak to General Tsukada. In a very low tone that could not be heard by Admiral Yamamoto or the other naval officers, he whispered to his chief of staff.

"General, for the life of me I cannot find fault with what has just been told to us. It seems as if the navy will have the great honor of initiating this honorable war on behalf of our empire. The possibility of sinking the entire U.S. Pacific Fleet is simply too important to ignore. I wonder what affect it would have on our 25th Army to have to wait until *after* the navy's attack. Would too much be lost if we push back our invasion plans? How much time would we actually lose?"

Tsukada opened some documents he was carrying and looked at his watch. He put some figures on a paper and made some calculations. When he was finished, he whispered back to Count Terauchi.

"I looks like about six or seven hours difference, that is, if my calculations are correct. That would put our invasion time at sometime around two or three in the morning. I would have to check my figures more accurately, but I believe I am close to the right time."

"That would mean that a great deal of our landings would have to be done during daylight," Count Terauchi pondered. "That exposes our troops to much more accurate fire from the English defenders. I don't like that aspect one bit, and I don't think our staffs will either."

"It is never easy when it comes to a situation involving the navy, the rivalry to be the first and greatest is sometimes too intense."

"Yes, but it is also ultimately good for the empire, it makes both sides try that much harder. In the end, everyone wins, and particularly, the Japanese Empire."

"You have a point, Count Terauchi, but we will have to sell it to the other army staff members."

"You forget, General Tsukada," Terauchi whispered softly. "Our presence here is to *resolve* any problems. If we say yes to something, everyone at army command headquarters will have to agree."

General Tsukada nodded his agreement and Count Terauchi again turned his attention to the Imperial navy delegation, speaking in an even, measured tone.

"Honorable Gentlemen, in considering your request, we realize that it comes down to deciding exactly which operation is most important to the war effort. The individual needs of either the army or navy must be subservient to the needs of the empire and it is upon that consideration that I must weigh my choices."

The naval officers sat rigidly, awaiting Terauchi's next remark.

"And, Admiral Yamamoto, what about the political aspects of such an action? What thought has been given to an honorable statement of our intentions?"

"That problem has been addressed and referred to our foreign office. I am under the impression that our ambassador in Washington will make a formal declaration of our intentions in advance of the actual attacks. It is important that the honor of both the emperor and the Japanese Empire be observed."

"Of that we are in complete agreement," Count Terauchi added. "It is most important for *everyone* involved."

"Now, what about the details of the attack?" questioned Admiral Yamamoto. "Is the army willing to bend to the needs of the navy? After all, if you attacked first, the element of surprise would undoubtedly be lost, and the results could be fatal to our cause."

"I hear you well, Admiral, and I agree in principal that surprise will be your greatest ally when you attack. I wish it could be done simultaneously, but the logistics of such an action would be practically impossible. I believe it is better for us all that your attack be allowed to proceed first, even though I am an army officer in my heart. I know I will have a great deal to explain when I return to Imperial army command, but so be it. It will take a long time to persuade some of the staff, but in the end, I am convinced that everyone will agree."

An apparent sigh of relief crossed Yamamoto's face, but he was quick to hide it from the others.

"Good," the lean-faced naval officer said flatly. "Then it is up to our staffs to work out the details. I feel this has been a most advantageous meeting, and I want to thank the army for its help in this delicate matter. I know you won't be sorry."

Count Terauchi rose as a signal for everyone to rise. The group bowed politely to each other as Count Terauchi pushed his chair aside and strode toward the door.

"Gentlemen," General Tsukada called to the remaining officers, "the remainder of our staffs is waiting outside to begin the process of working out the exact details. It is important that you impress on them the need for *absolute* secrecy in this matter, or else our well-laid plans could meet with untimely ends."

"*Hai, Hai!*" resounded from the navy group.

"Good. Then I leave it up to them to settle the details. May the gods favor us with a swift and decisive victory.

Again the sound of "*Hai, Hai!*" filled the room.

It was a fitting ending to the meeting that would bring war to the enemies of Japan.

November 10, 1941, Royal Air Headquarters Operations Office, Singapore, 1140 hours

Capt. Patrick Heenan couldn't begin to believe his increasing good luck. Even though his first week in Singapore had gone smoothly, Capt. Patrick Heenan found himself bored with the unexciting jobs he had been assigned since arriving on the island.

He was initially pleased with the orders assigning him to thirty days temporary duty at the Royal Air headquarters operations office in Singapore, since Singapore meant plenty of entertainment and also the chance to visit several Japanese businessmen he had met while attending Air Liaison School there earlier in the year. Major Cone had handed the orders to Heenan himself, along with the stinging admonition that "You can now cause someone else trouble instead of me."

Heenan had jumped at the chance—being in Singapore meant he would be close to the major British operational air center and thus, the possibility existed of being able to glean more information about the movements of all British and Australian aircraft throughout Malaya. Such feelings fueled optimism for Patrick Heenan, who now believed his status could not fail to rise in the service of the empire of Japan.

He was in the Singapore air operations room when Col. Herbert C. A. Ashcroft approached the desk Heenan had been assigned.

"Good morning, Captain Heenan, " Ashcraft spoke, " how is everything going? Have you had your lunch yet?"

"No, Sir. As a matter of fact I was just finishing up on these forms and was about to grab a bite," Heenan answered. It was only the second time Ashcroft had spoken to him since his arrival.

"Could you postpone your lunch a while, Captain, I have a new project for you."

"I would be delighted, Colonel, I wasn't very hungry anyway."

"Good, it should not take too long, as long as we get right down to it."

"What is it?" Heenan asked eagerly, looking at the pile of papers Ashcroft was holding.

Ashcroft pulled up a nearby chair and sat down. He looked around the room as if the matter was secret and spoke in a low tone.

"This stuff is all classified, Captain. No need to tell you what that means."

Heenan smiled, "No need, Sir. My lips are sealed."

"Good, then let us begin. What I have here are all the future defense allocations for both machines and manpower for the next six months. We just received it in coded fashion from London. Since we are so terribly understaffed here at the AOR, I thought you might like to take a shot at it. We need to match the numbers and see if everything comes out even. Then we must compare them to the old numbers that are in these reports. It's a big job, but I have been pleased with your work here and, frankly, I have no one else to give this to at this time."

Heenan felt a surge of adrenalin as he took the papers from his superior. He attempted to control his emotions as he answered in the most casual tone he could muster.

"Certainly, Sir, I'll be happy to give it a look."

"Be sure to take your time and get everything correct," Ashcroft again advised. "We wouldn't want any mistakes."

"Yes, Sir. I'll be very careful. I wouldn't want to mess anything up."

"I have full confidence in you, Heenan, please let me know when you have finished."

"Will do, Sir. Anything else?"

"That will do it. The project is big enough to take a good bit of your time."

Ashcroft rose and started down the hall toward the door. Heenan followed his progress and returned his gaze to the precious documents on his desk.

Across the top of the pages, the unfailing stamp of military and government secrecy read:

Confidential Items—Handle With Utmost Care

Patrick Heenan couldn't believe how much his luck had just changed. He also failed to notice the backward glance Major Ashcraft had given in his direction.

Maybe he will take the bait our intelligence types want to feed to him. If he is what they believe he is, all the false information I have just given him will be put to our good use.

November 15, 1941, 25th Imperial Army Headquarters, Saigon, Indochina, 1000 hours

The much-anticipated gathering of top Japanese military officials was finally scheduled for the morning of Saturday, November 15th, after several other proposed dates proved unsuitable to one of more of the participants. Its necessity was a result of the Japanese Imperial Staff's inability to smooth out a number of complications, which had arisen about various aspects of the Malaya Operation.

From a personal standpoint, Col. Masanobu Tsuji found the Japanese military's inability to resolve such lingering problems all the more frustrating since the window of opportunity for the invasion of Malaya was fast approaching. Fortunately, according to Tsuji's logical way of thinking, a number of important primary concerns, including the all-important logistical calendar, had already been addressed and were presently in motion.

This morning's conference was to bring together all commanders from Japan's army, navy and air forces to settle final matters and insure proper cooperation would be maintained between the three services. The proposed Malaya invasion and its related military operations elsewhere in Southeast Asia and the Pacific were the largest the empire of Japan had ever attempted. The necessary strain and tension involving such operations were beginning to take their toll on Colonel Tsuji, along with a number of other high-ranking staff officers.

As he took his seat at the large table, Tsuji surveyed the others. Across the table sat General Staff Officer Lt. Col. Prince Takeda, who was representing Field Marshal Count Terauchi, the commander in chief of all of the empire of Japan's southern armies. Several places away, Lt. Gen. Tomoyuki Yamashita, fresh from service as commander of the Kwantung Army in China, and currently commanding general of the 25th Army, busily conferred with several of his staff officers, his back to the table. Vice Adm. Jisaburo Ozawao, commander in chief of the Southern Squadron, represented the Imperial navy, while Lt. Gen. Michio Sugawara, commander of the 3rd Air Group, headed the air corps contingent.

All in all it was a most impressive gathering Tsuji decided—and a most necessary one if Japan's military forces were to ever act as a cohesive unit.

This time, it was General Yamashita who opened the meeting. A week before, Tomoyuki Yamashita celebrated his fifty-third birthday with little fanfare. The son of a village doctor, Yamashita was a 1906 graduate of the Hiroshima Military Academy who had formerly served as a military attaché in Germany more than twenty years before. He had just returned from another brief period in Berlin with high-ranking members of the German army.

A somewhat portly figure with graying temples, Yamashita was a favorite of the new Prime Minister Hideki Tojo and an officer whose reputation preceded him. He was currently in disfavor with the emperor of Japan, but Yamashita hoped to present the emperor with the gift of

Singapore to celebrate the beginning of his Imperial dynasty. It was also widely known that General Yamashita was a man used to getting results, and was the first Imperial army officer to totally embrace Colonel Tsuji's daring plan for the invasion of Malaya.

"Honorable officers, I am happy to welcome you all to this most imperative conference. You will all play important parts in the execution of the invasion of Thailand and Malaya, the target date of which is now less than three weeks away.

There is a great deal for each of us to do if our operations are to be successful and I need not remind any one of you that the future of our empire is at stake. We are here today in Saigon to discuss various aspects of this invasion, and it will be necessary for us to all agree beforehand on the details of cooperation between the different services.

The invasion of Malaya will be the largest military operation of the twentieth century attempted by Japan, or by anyone else for that matter.

Thanks mainly to the efforts of my staff officer, Colonel Tsuji, a bold new plan has been developed that will conceivably lessen the time it will take us to capture Malaya and also the Fortress of Singapore. Tsuji's new plan will also drastically cut the number of casualties we can expect from such an operation, and for that fact alone, I know we are all extremely grateful.

To accomplish our goal, unrivalled cooperation from both the navy and air corps is needed and will be appreciated by my men and me. Our invasion will be three-pronged and will cover two spots in Thailand, along with the important British military bases at Kota Bharu. All three places will be assaulted simultaneously with great determination from our troops. When we capture these key areas, the resulting turmoil should send the British troops into a general retreat.

From that point, it will be up to us to keep the pressure on our enemies until we are able to cross the causeway and occupy Singapore itself.

Vice Admiral Ozawao rose. He was relatively thick lipped and clean shaven, a slight man with excellent military bearing. At age forty-five, Ozawao was eight years younger than Yamashita. He had been a vice admiral since 1940 and was previously given the prestigious position of president of the Japanese Naval Academy.

Ozawao addressed the officers in a formal tone, his voice strong and filled with resolve.

"Honorable officers, I want it understood that I will do everything that is desired by the military forces. I will assume responsibility for the protection of the convoy of ships and of the disembarkation at Kota Bharu."

Silence followed the admiral's simple statement of intent. Through these few unpretentious words, everyone in the room now realized that the fate of the Japanese Empire would be irrevocably placed in the hands of the gods.

Tsuji had not uttered a single word since the conference had formally opened. He had expected a series of verbal arguments as the different military services attempted to secure their relative positions for the upcoming invasion.

Vice Admiral Ozawao's poignant declaration filled Tsuji and the others gathered around the table with a profound sense of purpose that was bordered with a hint of tragic sense edged with a vague sense of impending tragedy.

The fate of the Japanese Empire was now cast and Tsuji knew his plan was at the very heart of the undertaking. He considered that fact as the conference settled into discussions about specific details and comprehensive assignments for the participating units.

Once again, Tsuji was sure that the gods had spoken on the side of Imperial Japan. He was more than willing to stake his life on it.

November 30, 1941, outside veranda, George Town Cricket Club, Penang, 1610 hours

The news that dotted the day-old copy of the *Straits Times* that finally reached Charles Samuel, contained basic information and stories when it pertinent to the daily lives of the inhabitants of Singapore and of Malaya itself.

Samuel usually devoured the paper, and formed many of his own opinions based on information he gleaned from its pages. The way the *Times*, as it was simply called, reported the news was mostly straightforward, and did not always follow the line of the colonial office concerning events affecting the region.

During recent months, Charles Samuel had become aware of a trend in the periodical that caused him concern. That concern involved certain international events and their relationship to Malaya. The stories were generally reported factually, and to the ordinary reader were no cause for concern. But for Charles Samuel, who poured over each and every story with a magnifying glass, the problem lay in the way certain events he considered important to everyone were not really examined in the paper's editorial section. The main point in question was the relationship between Japan and the United States of America.

Samuel was well aware of the long-lived relationship between his mother country and its former colony, and also of the fact that trouble seemed to be brewing with regard to Japan's relationship with the industrial-rich United States. True, there were brief stories about economic talks and the like between the two countries, but little was written about the actual meaning and ramifications of such talks.

It's almost as if we would offend our Japanese trade partners by mentioning the fact that they were having problems with the Americans. Good lord, it's the Americans who are our real allies and no one seems to want to point out that salient fact!

Samuel returned to his copy of the *Times* just as the afternoon cricket matches ended.

A few of the participants waved to Samuel as they passed the extended deck of the Tudoresque mansion, which served as the main clubhouse for the George Town Cricket Club. He cheerily waved in return. Cricket was mostly a year-round sport here, near the equator, except during the northwest monsoon period when the playing fields were generally soggy or under water. That time was fast approaching, and Samuel knew that playing time from this point on would be at a premium.

A few moments later, Charles Samuel was pulled from his newspaper by the approach of his wife Vi, and several of her friends.

"Darling," she greeted her husband, "we are about to sit down to a spot of dinner. Are you up for it or should I wait for you?"

Samuel considered his options and replied, "You go ahead and enjoy yourself. I'm not really hungry at this moment and I'll grab something later if I feel the urge."

"Certainly, darling, have you enjoyed your reading?"

"Yes, thank you, I always enjoy getting caught up on the real world."

"You most certainly do," Vi replied, smiling. She signaled to her friends and they turned and moved toward the interior of the club.

Samuel followed their movements until they disappeared and returned to his paper. After a few moments the attorney paused, recalling the short meeting a few months ago with Resident Counsellor Forbes and Brigadier Lyon. At the time he considered their positions on Penang's defense as implausible at best, but lately he had begun to wonder.

What if Forbes and Lyon were indeed correct and Penang is attacked one day? It would be extremely unlikely that much of a defense could be mounted unless the attack came after a great deal of early warning. If the attack was a surprise, there really weren't a lot of troops around to defend the island. And the airfield at nearby Butterworth was mostly equipped with those old British warplanes; at least that's what the people who know about such things always said.

He returned to his paper, but his concentration was capricious at best. The meeting with Forbes and Lyon kept recurring in the back of his mind.

Charles Samuel was a person who always considered himself as someone who acted on important matters in a most timely manner. As he pondered his thoughts over the past few minutes, an inner sense—developed throughout his adult life—told to him that some of these matters were important enough to act upon.

Now that I have come to this conclusion, just what am I to do about it?

He thought a moment more and an idea came to him. He would call Brigadier Lyon the following morning when he got to his office.

December 1, 1941, Commander's Office, Penang Fortress, Penang, 1100 hours

"It was good of you to see me on such short notice, Brigadier," Charles Samuel began as he entered the stark military office at the military complex known as Fort Penang, outside George Town on the Island of Penang.

"You said it was important, so I made the time," Brigadier C.A. Lyon replied. "So, what's on your mind to bring you all the way out here?"

"I have been doing a lot of thinking of late, Brigadier, and the meeting we had a few months ago about the island's defences came to mind."

"So . . ." answered Lyon, preferring to allow his visitor to complete his statement.

"Well, it now seems to me that some of the points you and the resident counsellor made at the meeting might have some real meaning to me, according to conditions around the world. I am here to see what I can do to help you in these matters."

Lyon reached for a meerschaum pipe laying on his desk, picked up a match from a small jar nearby and lit the bowl. A puff of smoke emitted from the thin, caramel-colored device.

"So you now think there is some 'real meaning' attached to our present situation, Mr. Samuel. If I recall correctly, you didn't think such things were possible a short time ago."

"Things are changing in our world if my perceptions are right, and I'm a big enough person to admit I might have been wrong."

Lyon hesitated, and continued in a more hospitable manner.

"I must say that I agree with you, Mr. Samuel, only there's a little problem involved with your thinking."

"Problem?"

"Yes, Mr. Samuel. I probably shouldn't tell you about this because I don't want to start a panic, and I'll have to ask you to take what I tell you as under strictest confidence. I must have your word on that."

Samuel looked perplexed and nodded, "You have my word."

"Good, then let's get on with it. You might just be too late with your concern, and I'm not sure what that means in the short term. We have been received updated intelligence reports, only partially substantiated I might add, of increased Japanese army and navy buildups in Indochina. No real proof that the little brownies are up to anything, only there's no real reason for all the buildups, if you catch my reasoning. Bad thing about it all is that Indochina makes for a tidy little jumping-off place if you intend to invade Thailand or Malaya, at least that's what our intelligence people think of the matter. I personally think they are up to no good, and that it is simply a matter of time."

"Matter of time? There had been no mention of any of this in the newspapers."

"Leak what little intelligence we have to the newspapers, are you insane?"

"Well, I just thought . . ."

"Hate to say this," Lyon interrupted, " but it's a little late for thinking. Now we have to get around to the fact that our way of life might easily be challenged, and, in the not-too-distant future."

Samuel stared vacantly at the brigadier. The man—who excelled in his business life through the clever use of words—was completely wordless.

Brigadier Lyon again broke the silence.

"There's one bright spot, if you can actually call the situation bright."

"What do you mean?"

"The fact that the buildup in is Indochina actually favors an invasion on the eastern shore of either Thailand or Malaya or both. Unless the attackers specifically target Penang at the beginning, we might just have a chance at getting everyone off this island."

"Off this island? Will it be that bad?"

"Mr. Samuel, look at the facts. I only have one group of real soldiers here, the 5/14 Punjab Regiment. They have a bunch of youthful soldiers and are just really beginning to become trained. My Singapore Straits Volunteer Force Battalion is all volunteers with practically no weapons or real military training. I do have a heavy Battery of the Royal Artillery and some Royal Engineers, but Penang is a big island to defend and I daresay my troops will not last all that long in the face of hardened enemy troops. If we are bombed from the air, heaven help us—we are practically defenseless."

Samuel sat silently, digesting the Brigadier's statement.

"That's another thing, Mr. Samuel. I recently received a contingency plan for the evacuation of Europeans from the island should anything happen."

"Europeans? What of the others? What will happen to them?"

"My directives only cover Europeans, and that's not to my personal liking."

"But I have several people—loyal and wonderful people of mixed backgrounds that work for my business and my family. What about them?"

"We all are in that position, Mr. Samuel. I don't have a realistic answer for that question."

The room went silent until Brigadier Lyon spoke again.

"Look, Mr. Samuel. I have to face the fact that we are really in a mess here should hostilities break out. If I were a prudent man in your position, I would begin making some immediate contingencies."

For some reason, the conversation with Martin Ogle flashed back through the brain of Charles Samuel. What a fool he had been to not heed his friend's sense of impending problems. He nodded to Lyon and nodded his head.

Brigadier Lyon sighed and spoke in a much softer tone.

"We are all waiting for an order to begin preparations to defend Malaya from attack. The plan is called *Matador* and probably should have been placed in effect by now, but for some reason it has not. If we start right now, we might still have a fighting chance. If we don't…"

"If we don't, Brigadier?"

"If *Matador* is not implemented in short order, Mr. Samuel, I am of the opinion that we do not stand a chance in hell of repelling an invasion of either Thailand or Malaya, and we will undoubtedly suffer the consequences thereof."

Samuel waited a moment and asked.

"Well then, just what can we do?"

"Pray, Mr. Samuel, pray. And hope everyone else is praying with you . . ."

December 1, 1941, Far East Intelligence Bureau Offices, Singapore Naval Base, 1400 hours

"Gentlemen, if I could please have your attention."

The assembled British army and navy officers were seated in a theatre-style room in the concrete structure that was the home of the Far East Combined Intelligence Bureau. They immediately settled into their seats and gave their attention to the speaker.

Lt. Gen. Arthur E. Percival, the angular GOC Singapore, waited a moment for the last murmurs to cease and spoke again.

"I called this short meeting at what I consider a neutral site," Percival began casually, "one free from any distractions and also proximate to the latest in military intelligence." He paused and glanced around the room to insure that all the principals he needed for the meeting were indeed present.

Percival sought out two in particular, Air Chief Marshal Sir Robert Brooke-Popham, commander in chief Far East and Lt. Gen. Sir Lewis Heath, commander of the Third Indian Corps. Both officers, surrounded by their respective staff, were seated close to each other in the first row. Satisfied that the main adversaries under his command were accounted for, Percival continued.

"I am beginning to believe that things are becoming critical regarding our future," he said. "Intelligence reports show some Japanese activity that warrants our immediate attention. Brigadier Simson sent one of his men on a fact-finding trip to several countries and received reports of large Japanese troop buildups around Saigon that could easily be used against us. There is also the fact that London continues to be worried about the status of the Japanese talks with the U.S. in Washington. The way things are dragging on, London feels that the longer this process takes, the less inclination there is to have an agreement.

The reason I wanted to get everyone here together is to reiterate my feelings on the implementation of *Operation Matador* should the need or occasion arise.

"General Percival," Brooke-Popham spoke, "unless you have new intelligence reports I have not yet seen, I *still* do not believe there is sufficient evidence to invoke *Operation Matador*. Even though I realize that my tenure here is comparatively short lived, I am reluctant to make any real changes. I have studied the reports thoroughly and, along with my staff, feel there are simply not enough hard facts to begin an action that would basically declare war on the Japanese Empire. You know how London has changed the responsibility for *Matador* to my position and to my position alone. To be blunt about it, I simply need a great deal more proof."

"If you wait for them to take the first shot and *then* react, it will be way too late for all of us," intoned Brigadier Ivan Simson bleakly. "In fact, it might be too late now the way we have put off shoring up most of our defences."

"None of that defeatist talk, man. That sort of gibberish just aids our enemies and does us no good," Brooke-Popham retorted. "I've always said if I can see some real evidence, then I am prepared to make my decision."

"Gentlemen," Percival broke in, attempting to keep the conversation civil. "It does no good to fight among ourselves. It's up to us to see beyond what's happening now and make preparations for the future."

Brooke–Popham sighed distastefully, "Quite."

Percival spoke again, "I have ordered our aero squadrons at Kota Bahru and Kuantan to commence reconnaissance sorties to Cape Cambodia, then southwest to Anamba Islands and thence west to Kuantan in the hopes of spotting something, but so far we've had no real luck. With the bad weather that currently exists, it is a hit-and-miss situation at best."

"I simply have no other choice," Brooke-Popham again offered unenthusiastically. "My staff and I are in complete agreement on the terms of the arrangement with London. They put these limitations on me to insure there was no senseless action that could precipitate a political mess of truly great magnitude."

"Political mess, so that's what it's all about," chimed Brigadier Simson.

"No one really cares about the people involved at all. It's sheer lunacy, that's what it is...I wonder if all those Nips showed up in full military dress at the Raffles Hotel one afternoon for tea, would London consider that a prudent sign of their intentions?"

Some in the room chuckled a bit, easing the tension. But Simson had no intention of backing down from his position and spoke again.

"I have tried to make everyone see that we are in a very weak defensive posture for some time now. If we add the factor of surprise to the equation, then I would not want to be responsible for the outcome."

This time, Chief Air Marshall Brooke-Popham took exception.

"You must remember that our Prime Minister continues to be of the opinion that the Japanese will never attack Singapore," he droned. "And you know that Mr. Churchill is seldom wrong about such things. It's the reason our strategic planning has shorted the Fortress on so many basic necessities. I am afraid it is just a basic fact of life."

"I can see that this is getting us nowhere, Sir Robert," Percival added. "I just ask that you pay very close attention to our intelligence dispatches and then act accordingly. I have the greatest hope that your judgment will prove to be correct.'

Brooke-Popham nodded and turned to whisper instructions to one of his staffers.

Percival stood up and again addressed the officers.

"Since everyone here deals directly with the Far East Bureau, I suggest you stop at your individual liaisons and insure that we are all on the same page. That makes for good teamwork and fewer mistakes. Any questions?"

Seeing none, he dismissed the group and quickly left the room.

December 2, 1941, Keppel Harbor, Singapore, aboard H.M.S. Repulse, 1215 hours

Accompanied by a deepening sense of foreboding, Sir Thomas Phillips, acting admiral and commander in chief of Great Britain's Far Eastern fleet and his staff strode quickly into the formal quarters of the battlecruiser H.M.S. *Repulse's* commanding officer, Capt. William Tennant. "I am happy to see you made it here safely, Captain," Phillips offered as he extended his hand to Tennant. "I realize that the past few weeks were a bit of a stretch, but everything seems quite in order."

"Most certainly so, Sir Thomas," replied Tennant. "None of us are the worse for wear."

"Quite. Well then, let's get on with it. I'm afraid I have a bit of bad news."

Tennant, who was joined by his ship's senior staff around a large, rectangular glass table, looked apprehensive as the diminutive speaker continued.

"We have received confirmation that the *Ark Royal* was sunk off Gibraltar on November 14 by a U-boat. The staff at Naval Command has since determined that our Force Z must therefore operate our ongoing mission without naval air cover since we have just enough carriers left to fight Jerry in the Atlantic."

"What about the *Indomitable?*" asked Tennant, referring to the carrier that had run aground in Jamaica and was part of the original naval Force Z.

"I'm afraid she is still undergoing repairs, but I am of the opinion she will be redirected to the Atlantic when she is again fit."

"It won't be the first time we have operated with sea-based fighter cover," one of Tennant's senior officers remarked. "And it probably won't be the last," another chimed in good naturedly." There were chuckles around the room and Phillips smiled.

"That's the spirit, lads, we've just got to make up for it with superior seamanship."

"Exactly what will we do for the immediate future, Sir Thomas?" Tennant again asked.

"Do you have any idea what's in store for us?"

"No one can really know for sure, it's all rather secretive. London still thinks the Nips have too much on their plate with so many of their troops deployed in China to do much else around here, and, for once, I'm rather inclined to agree with them. We have no real intelligence to the contrary, so I imagine we will simply have to play it by ear.

One thing for sure, I want your re-supplying and the rest of Force Z's stores to be put aboard as soon as humanly possible. That way we will be able to take immediate action no matter what happens.

We also must remember that we have increased our air presence in Malaya with several new airfields that should be able to help us in a pinch. Coordination with these squadrons will take some time to reach fruition so I suggest we hop right on it. I can't begin to tell you what I could do with a few months more time to adequately plan things, but I'm not sure that is entirely possible.

Until then—this small group of ships, our own Force Z—happens to represent an almost miraculous sense of rapture to the inhabitants of Malaya, and in particular to the residents of Singapore.

Remember, here in Singapore, they can see you with their own eyes. Rumors have persisted for nearly a year that a huge flotilla of ships would soon appear in Keppel Harbor that would act as a deterrent to anyone who wished to do Singapore and its residents harm. We have taken the position in the news media that Force Z represents the first such aspect of that flotilla and we want everyone, and in particular the Japanese, to believe that such is the truth."

Audible murmurs from the officers around the table filled the room.

"So it is up to us to perpetuate the myth of the giant flotilla," Sir Thomas Phillips continued. "Whenever a group exits a ship for leave, they should be reminded that their sister ships and men are not that far behind. It will also be quite good for their own morale, which we all know needs a bit of shoring up every now and then."

The officers nodded in agreement.

"But be sure to keep in mind that this is a most serious time for us and our nation, and that we must be ready to act if anything goes down. Am I understood?"

Captain Tennant stood. "I believe everyone here is in complete agreement, Sir Thomas. They will insure that the correct word leaks down to even the most basic seaman. By god, after listening to them, our enemies will think a whole squadron is on its way."

"I'll hold you to that, Captain, now let us get down to serious business. Everyone can leave except for our immediate staffs. We have some important paperwork to go over."

Many of the group rose and filed out of the large room.

"Now, gentlemen, for the first order of the day. If and when necessary, I intend to make the *Prince of Wales* my flagship. Since it is a larger ship, I feel it can accommodate me and my staff and our various needs. It also has a long-range communications center and that will be of great importance to me.

As I said before, I have very little intelligence on what the Nips are planning or what they intend to do about us, and that's a bit disarming. There are only a few things that I really know, and one of them is that our two capital ships are relatively safe unless the Imperial Japanese Navy decides to commit some of its capital fleet to meet us head on."

"What about the build up of Japanese bombers in Indochina?" Captain Tennant asked. "Some of our movements to the north or east could bring us within their range."

"Those reports are not completely confirmed, Captain. I've seen various ranges on their exact numbers. And another thing, I am still unconvinced that long-range aircraft can handle the armament and pure steel of the likes of *Prince of Wales* and *Repulse*. I know they can do damage, but the rest is pure speculation.

Now, let's get on with the details."

December 6, 1941, Office of Commander in Chief Far East, Singapore Naval Base, Singapore, 0745hours

Air Marshal Sir Robert Brooke-Popham had felt the pressure building for the past few days as he sat at his desk pondering his daily reports. There was something different in the air, yet he couldn't put his finger on it.

Throughout his long and varied career, he had never felt the degree of stress he was currently experiencing. Even during his tenure as governor of Kenya, when several political issues were brought to a head, nothing reached the magnitude of what was going on in early December in this particular part of the British Empire.

For the third time that morning, he again fingered the file marked *Operation Matador* and flipped through its pages. He knew sections of the file by heart, the ones that directed him to actively begin the defence of Thailand and indeed, the entire Malayan Peninsula.

The concept of *Matador* had caused him numerous sleepless nights, including the preceding evening when he simply could not force himself to sleep. Even his own time- honored recipe of several sips of fine Amotillado sherry did not help, he was simply too wired to fall into a prolonged sleep.

Sometime in the early morning, he had given up trying to sleep and had risen from his bed and taken a quick bath. He brewed himself a pot of tea and sat down with some paperwork, but found he was not really able to concentrate. He returned to his bed with the stack of papers.

He was relieved when the clock at his bedside said 6:48 and he could justifiably head to his office.

A communications officer brought in a telegram from London marked *Exceedingly Urgent* the minute he stepped into his well-appointed office.

"This just arrived, Sir Robert. I was going to bring it over to you when I was told you were on your way in," the Lieutenant explained.

Brooke-Popham took the telegram from the officer and opened it.

The dispatch from the British High Command read:

H.M. Government has now received an assurance of American armed support in the following contingencies:

```
(a)  If we undertake MATADOR either to forestall
     attempted Japanese landing in the KRA ISTHMUS
     or as a reply to a Japanese violation of
     any part of Thailand.
(b)  If the Japanese attack the DUTCH EAST INDIES
     and we go at once to their support.
(c)  If the Japanese attack us.
Accordingly you should order MATADOR without
reference to home in either of the two following
     contingencies:
(a)  You have good information that a Japanese
     expedition is advancing with the apparent
     intent of landing on the KRA ITHSMUS.
(b)  The Japanese violate any other part of
     THAILAND (SIAM).
```

In the event of a Japanese attack on the NETHERLAND EAST INDIES you have the authority without reference to home immediately to out into operation the plans which you have agreed with them.

Brooke-Popham read and reread the telegram, making sure he understood its contents clearly. While the telegram eased his mind about certain aspects of his responsibilities, he still had lingering doubts about when to *actually* implement *Matador*.

The responsibility of plunging his country into a major military conflict weighed heavily on the sixty-two-year-old man. He knew there were certain steps that were necessary for him to have a clear picture of what was happening.

It would be essential to step up actual reconnaissance flights into the South China Sea, the only real path the Japanese could follow if they were indeed intent on invading anywhere. Also, the various intelligence agencies involved should be put on highest alert for any information that might make his decision easier.

He picked up the phone and asked for the Air Operations office. While he waited for the call to go through, he realized there were more sleepless nights ahead.

December 6, 1941, aboard Royal Australian Air Force Hudson reconnaissance aircraft, Gulf of Siam, 1340 hours

It was already several hours into his aircraft's mission and Royal Australian Air Force Flight Lt. Tenny Ramshaw was beginning to experience the first signs and fatiguing effects that a pilot experiences during a long flight. His American-built Lockheed Hudson Super Electra had departed its home base at the Royal Air Force's airfield at Kota Baru on Malaya's eastern coast a little over four hours ago. A check of the Hudson's fuel guage made the Australian flier aware that in about fifteen to twenty minutes time, his plane would have reached its maximum range. At that point, Ramshaw knew would he have to turn around and return to his base at Kota Bharu.

The Hudson's mission in early December of 1941 was strictly reconnaissance that required the smallish, converted bomber to fly a series of zigzag patterns across the Gulf of Siam. Prior to Flight Lieutenant Ramshaw's departure, and, for the past several days, the British intelligence officer assigned to brief all flight crews flying patrol duty over the Gulf, had advised of increased likelyhood of Japanese naval activity. The briefing officer was adamant that added diligence on the part of the aircrews should be given to each surveillance mission.

Since he was a professional flier with over a dozen year's service in the RAAF, Ramshaw heeded the advice and was in the process of admonishing his crew over the intercom to do the same.

"Heads up now, you blokes, we wouldn't want to miss any Nip activity down there. Goodness knows it would be easy to do, there's plenty of water down there for them to hide."

Ramshaw checked his altimeter that held steady at the Hudson's optimum cruising altitude of ten thousand feet, his aircraft's designated altitude for most of the mission. Ramshaw looked over to the officer seated next to him, who correctly guessed what was on the pilot's mind.

"We change course in about two minutes, Captain, to a heading of 045 degrees," the second officer cheerily offered. "Looks to me as if the clouds are beginning to move in," he added, "certainly more than when we first started this patrol."

Ramshaw had been aware of the increasing cloudiness for the past few minutes and nodded his agreement. Heavy cloud cover would cut down his aircraft's effectiveness and force him to a lower altitude. The lower altitude would also cut into his mission's flying time and conceivable range, neither of which would make his squadron commander happy. Tense as things were back at Kota Bharu, worsening weather would make things even more stressful.

The Hudson's pilot immediately decided to reduce his craft's altitude to five thousand feet—where he hoped to be below the base of most cloud formations, still scattered but clearly visible ahead. He pointed the steering wheel forward and felt the change in propeller pitch as the Hudson started down. Two minutes later, the altimeter gage reached five hundred and Ramshaw leveled the Hudson off. He was pleased that most of the thick clouds ahead appeared to be somewhat above him.

The airmen returned to peering across the horizon, a distance Ramshaw now judged to be about thirty to forty miles below. He adjusted the engine mixture slightly to compensate for the lower altitude and returned his gaze to the port side of the Hudson.

A series of black specs appeared suddenly on the lightly-rippled bluish expanse, causing him to yell out.

"Good lord, what have we here?" Ramshaw exclaimed excitedly.

The second officer swung his gaze to the left and suddenly caught sight of the same objects. He reached for his field glasses and quickly focused on the specks.

"Yes, yes, I see them too! Must be twenty or thirty boogers down there."

"Right," Ramshaw returned, checking the sky above. I hope there is no air cover with them. If they even catch notion of us, we would play hell trying to outrun them."

"Quite" came the weak reply from his right seater.

"Okay then, let's get back upstairs and first report what we have seen. No need wasting ourselves."

Ramshaw clicked on his intercom: "Sparks, radio back to base the following . . . large formation of Japanese ships sighted . . . and give its heading as . . ."

As it climbed, the Hudson executed a soft right-hand turn away from the specks on the surface as Ramshaw gave the twin Wright Cyclone 1100 hp engines more power and started the long return-flight back to home base.

Ramshaw smiled broadly at the second officer, confident he and his crew had surely accomplished their mission.

IV

INVASION

December 7, 1941, aboard SS Ryujo Maru, Gulf of Siam, 1210 hours

The first three days of the 25th Imperial Japanese Army's voyage aboard the crowded *Ryujo Maru* was much less problematic than Col. Masanobu Tsuji had anticipated. Even though the flagship of the convoy was Vice-Admiral Ozawa's Takao-class Cruiser *Chokai*, the Imperial Staff considered the *Ryujo Maru* the principal focus of the twenty-ship convoy since she carried the commander and general staff of the 25th Army.

As the convoy passed through the moonlit, silver-streaked waters of the South China Sea, Colonel Tsuji repeatedly recalled to his mind the setting three days earlier. The first streaks of the deep red morning sun had just appeared when the siren sounded signaling the order for the first ships to weigh anchor at Samah Harbor, Hainan Island. For Tsuji, the occasion prompted a warm inner feeling to be finally leaving occupied China, and the accompanying mind-boggling logistical pressures of getting the Invasion of Malaya under way.

The *Ryujo Maru* was a ten thousand-ton transport that had been specially built for the Imperial Army and externally resembled an aircraft carrier. She was a ship where great attention had been paid to space usage, which also included the thirty-odd boats that would serve as the invasion force's landing craft. The *Ryujo Maru* contained quarters for a large number of infantry but, in actuality, the accommodations for the soldiers were cramped and exceedingly unpleasant. The fact that the 25th

Army's General Staff was also aboard the *Ryujo Maru* was the result of a last minute switch from the accompanying *Kashii Maru,* a converted luxury liner that had formerly served international routes for Japan.

In retrospect Tsuji readily admitted to himself that the poor accommodations were his own fault. He knew now it was a mistake to have ordered the switch of the 25th Army Staff to the *Ryujo Maru.* He vowed in his mind to investigate the matter more fully should the possibility of a future invasion arise on another occasion.

As he again focused his thoughts on the present, Tsuji became aware that a petty officer was approaching the ship's bridge on the run. The petty officer moved toward the *Ryujo Maru's* captain who stood about four paces away from Tsuji's own position near a large plate glass window that looked out the ship's port side. Even at that early hour of the afternoon, the bridge was crowded with staff officers, including Lt. Gen. Tomoyuki Yamashita, commanding general of the 25th Army. The group stopped their individual conversations, and regarded the note that was handed the ship's captain. They sensed something important and waited expectantly as the naval officer examined the message.

The captain finished and turned toward General Yamashita and bowed, offering the paper in his hand to the officer. Yamashita offered a slight bow in return and reached to take the paper.

A few silent moments passed as Yamashita carefully considered the contents of the message. At length he turned and addressed his staff. His tone was relaxed and self-assured.

"Gentlemen, it seems that some of our air cover have succeeded in downing a long range British patrol aircraft a number of miles to the east of our present position, which is now east north east of Cape Cambodia. While this is a significant event, we do not know if the British plane was able to radio its position back to its base or whether there was more than one patrol plane in the area.

I feel it will be necessary to take extra precautions. As you can see, the weather around us seems to be worsening, a fact that could be a blessing from the gods. We are scheduled for a significant course change in the near future and it is imperative that we are not discovered after that time!"

Tsuji and the other staff officers grasped their leader's words with mixed feelings. After a few minutes of conversation it was generally agreed that the downing of the British aircraft was indeed a benevolent sign and should be taken in that spirit. The news tended to provide an added air of tension to the already taut situation existing among the officers and men aboard the *Ryujo Maru*.

Several possible scenarios involving British reconnaissance aircraft rolled around in Tsuji's mind, after which he decided to place the invasion in the hands of Divine Fate. As he did so, he became more aware that the pitch and roll of the *Ryujo Maru* had increased noticeably during the past few minutes. This he interpreted as a good sign. He glanced at the pitching horizon where the clouded blue sky had been replaced with an ominous gray and black background.

Naval Commander Taro Nagai approached him, a tallish lively man who served as the Navy Liaison staff officer and with whom Tsuji had developed an immediate friendship.

"This bodes well for our journey, Colonel," Nagai offered cheerfully. "It now appears that most of the Gulf of Siam will be covered with dense fog and low clouds. If this weather holds, it will cover our course change at around 0200. It will be impossible for any patrol aircraft to detect us through the overhang."

"Yes, Honorable Friend, it seems so. So far we have been extremely lucky. It is as if the gods have taken us under their wings. I have already offered a prayer that our luck will continue."

"When we first met you told me that you felt our path was controlled by destiny. I am beginning to believe you are correct."

"We need all that destiny can offer us if we are to be ultimately successful," Tsuji replied. "Remember, we are trying to capture a large area of land that is defended by hundreds of thousands of enemy troops with a relatively small force. That in itself is an almost unfathomable feat. If we are successful, we will all earn our places in our country's history books."

"Perhaps even in the world's history books," Nagai added.

"If it is meant to be . . ." Tsuji finalized, returning his gaze to the horizon that was now more purplish-black than gray.

December 8, 1941, aboard SS Ryujo Maru, off Singora Harbor, Gulf of Siam, 0200 hours

The moon appeared dimly on the surface of the Gulf of Siam, almost completely obscured by an unbroken sea of endless light to medium clouds. The Japanese invasion force that had just dropped anchor consisted of some fourteen ships that carried the men and equipment of the 5th Division of the Imperial Japanese Army. Several Imperial Japanese Naval destroyers that had escorted the invasion convoy since it left Samah Harbor nearly four days before remained silent, close to the outer ship of the convoy, carefully protecting its rear from any unseen visitors from either the sea or sky.

Aboard the ship, everyone's attention was directed to a blinking light that resurfaced every few seconds. When it was definitely identified as the Singora Lighthouse, everyone of board breathed a deep sigh of relief.

The ship was pitching and rolling in heavy seas and was buffeted by a strong northeast wind that had arisen just after the anchor had been lowered. To Col. Masanobu Tsuji, the advent of such strong winds cast a doubt on the ship's ability to unload both men and equipment safely.

A number of officers and men from the division engineer detachments stood at the rail with their heads shaking. The waves were at least eight to ten feet high—disembarking men loaded with heavy equipment under such conditions was almost out of the question. Even under the worst peacetime conditions, such a landing operation would have had to wait.

"What will we do?" one non-commissioned officer asked his fellow engineers whose responsibility it was to insure the landings. "Such waves will surely swamp our small landing boats and all the men inside them."

"Yes" was the consensus from everyone else. "We must wait for the winds to die down or we will all drown trying."

Their conversation was for naught as the light signal located on the masthead of the *Ryujo Maru* was illuminated to signal the beginning of the disembarkation process.

Throwing caution and their impending fears to the proverbial wind, the engineers quickly raced to their assigned positions and began the unloading process. In a matter of minutes, more than one hundred small boats bobbed and weaved alongside the transport. The engineers took it as a sign from the gods that their mission on this dreary night would be favorable.

Soon thereafter, a second signal started the actual boarding of the boats by the soldiers of the Imperial Japanese Army. This was an arduous task and involved army engineers utilizing long poles to keep the small boats apart while they waited to the *Ryujo Maru's* leeward side to pick up their nervous cargos. It took nearly an hour to complete the entire transfer and a number of soldiers became ill with the twisting and turning of the small boats.

An attempt was made to form a line to proceed shoreward and finally a three red light signal appeared on the gunwale of the *Ryujo Maru* to signal the entire group to proceed shoreward.

As the small flotilla approached shore, the lapping of the waves against the shoreline drowned out their engine noise. The lights of the port of Singora appeared silently while the continued thrashing of the waves against the boats made life difficult for those aboard. Yards from shore a few of the boats crashed roughly into each other sending the inhabitants into the water. Those who could made their way onto the beach, while a few others drifted and bobbed in an eternal rest.

Col. Masanobu Tsuji glanced at his watch as he finally stepped ashore. The hands were fixed perfectly at four o'clock. The entire disembarkation operation had taken about two hours, practically according to schedule as far as the high-ranking staff officer was concerned. The invasion of Thailand and the eventual trek southward toward the Island of Singapore was now a reality.

Tsuji realized there was still a great deal of work to be done if his plan was to be successful.

December 8, 1941, aboard SS Awagisan Maru, off Kota Bahru, South China Sea, 0500 hours

It didn't take Japanese Imperial Army Maj. Shigeharu Asaeda long to realize why he had chosen a career in the army over one in the Imperial Navy. His trip aboard the *SS Awagisan Maru* after leaving Samah Harbor on Hainan Island had been bad enough due to frequent periods of inclement weather, which caused the ship to continuously roll at severe angles.

Now he was intently watching the smaller boats that compromised the actual assault fleet attempt to maintain course and noted their incessant bobbing in the waves. He knew his stomach would again violently react the way it had twice before on the long trip from Indochina.

He silently thanked the gods that had placed him with temporary duty and attached him to the Ando Regiment (42nd Infantry) of the 5th Infantry Division of the Japanese Imperial Army. The force with its various support units that totaled about 16,000 men and equipment.

Asaeda had agreed with Col. Masanobu Tsuji that it was important that a member of the *Doro Nawa* Unit be present when the important landings at both Patani and Kota Bharu take place. Kota Bharu was the northern gate of Great Britain's military fortifications in Malaya. As the capital of the province of Kelantan, Kota Bharu was also the site of the Royal Air Force's largest air base. As a result, the city was considered the earliest possible prize for the Japanese Imperial Empire if its plan for the invasion of Malaya was to be successful. It was also one of the places Asaeda had scouted on his northern intelligence-gathering foray some months before.

But, Patani was equally important, since it was the gateway to one of but two major roads extending southward—Patani was the key to the rapid movement of troops toward Singapore. In the end, it was decided that Asaeda join the Ando Detachment after its landing at Patani, but that he go ashore with the Takumi Detachment at Kota Bahru. More defenses were expected there, and he could judge its effectiveness in fighting. How he would ultimately get to the Ando Detachment was left up to Asaeda's judgment.

Asaeda was still on board the *Awagisan Maru* off Kota Bahru when it took its first direct hit from the British shore batteries. He had unsuccessfully tried to get into one of the first wave of launches but was unable to do so since every space was already pre-assigned and taken. Even though he was a staff officer, the debarkation officer told him to wait for the launches to return. Asaeda reluctantly followed that order and waited.

When the Japanese Imperial naval bombardment signaled a start to the invasion, Major Shigeharu Asaeda was able to take in the ensuing spectacle. At first he could only hear the navy guns, but soon he was able to see splashes that indicated the return fire was coming from shore. This went on for about fifteen minutes until the first shell hit the bow of the *Awagisan Maru*, the southernmost stationed member of the invasion convoy. The solid explosion shook the entire ship. At once, the ominous *ah-oo-gah* of a Claxton horn began sounding with its resounding frequency. Asaeda watched nervously as the ship's crew instinctively reacted to bring a deck fire under control.

He realized the seriousness of his position and inched toward the station on the port side where men were beginning to move into the now-returning launches.

An Imperial navy lieutenant was discharging the men into the boats and Asaeda grabbed him by the arm.

"I need to go on this boat," he said somewhat forcefully. "I need to go *now*."

The navy lieutenant looked at Asaeda's uniform that was somewhat different from the other soldiers waiting to step into the launches, and then at the man's huge physique. He correctly surmised that this staff officer meant business. He held his hand out to stop a corporal from beginning his descent into the launch.

He nodded to Asaeda, "Okay, go now. You can be the last one on this boat."

Asaeda stepped forward and then judged the distance to the bobbing craft to be about four feet. He waited for the small boat to rise and then jumped perfectly into a small space near the stern.

Once aboard, the engineer operating the small craft turned the bow and revved the motor, causing the bow to slowly turn shoreward. Once he was satisfied with his progress, the engineer yelled into the wind as loud as he could.

"Keep your heads down as much as possible, they are shooting at us and have hit several who stood up to see what was happening. Look at the blood they left behind. Be smart, and the gods will surely keep you alive."

Asaeda needed no such encouragement and hunched down as much as possible. He looked up to see the engine flares of a British fighter plane that had flown overhead strafing the landing boats. It seemed to him that the British were putting up a pretty good fight of it.

The launch neared the beach and Asaeda felt the jolt as the boat's bottom hit something solid. He looked up and was astounded to see that he was still some distance from the beach. He turned around to the engineer who saw the look of exasperation in Asaeda's eyes.

"I am sorry, Major, but the winds pushed us down further than I wanted. I think we hit some sand dunes or something, but my craft is much heavier than it should be. I won't be able to refloat it until it is much lighter. I am truly sorry for my error."

Asaeda turned around to see some of the soldiers in the front scrambling over the sides. The water was about waist high on the heavily-armed men and made their shoreward progress slow. It also made them excellent targets for British gunners on the beach.

Asaeda silently cursed the gods for this particular predicament and decided it was time to get over the side himself. He cradled his backpack and pushed his way off. The water was unexpectedly cold and he sought to find his footing. Another aircraft appeared in the sky directly in front of him and began firing at the soldiers in the water. A private about three yards in front of him fell backward and several rounds from the fighter splashed around him. Asaeda continued pumping his legs and forced himself forward. The water was now only knee deep and his traction suddenly improved. Another ten yards and he began to feel the firmer sand and small pebbles of the shoreline under his boots.

He continued forward and flung himself at a small rise of sand that appeared to his left. He stopped for a moment and attempted to catch his breath. He realized his heart was pounding in a manner that he hadn't felt since his last great hand-to-hand battle in frozen Manchuria. He silently thanked the gods that he was still alive on this glorious morning and looked back to sea as a loud explosion ripped the heavy, early morning air.

He could see the blazing outline of a large ship that was completely engulfed in fire. A second explosion sounded and another huge fireball erupted in the sky. Even though it was still somewhat dark, Major Shigeharu Asaeda was fairly sure the ship was the *Awagisan Maru.*

He watched silently as it began to slip below the surface of the South China Sea.

The invasion might not be quite as easy as everyone at the *Doro Nawa* Unit had expected.

December 8, 1941, Office of the Commander in Chief Far East, Singapore Naval Base, Singapore, 0620 hours

A million possible alternatives had visited Sir Robert Brooke-Popham's mind since the report of the Japanese convoy's sighting was received by his Far East Headquarters almost three days ago. Immediately after the Australian Hudson's fortunate sighting, Sir Robert had called his chief of staff, Major General I.S.O. Playfair into his office for a conference. The pair moved to a brocade coach in the CIC's office where Brooke-Popham spoke bluntly.

"General, I need your take on what is taking place out there," said Sir Robert, referring to the Japanese convoy. "I must be totally sure of the Japanese intent or my actions could easily place our country in another blasted war."

Playfair hesitated a moment, as if to choose his words. Even during his extensive European duties in military actions against the Italians, he had not been asked to comment on anything so expansive as the Japanese threat that was looming before them.

"I've seen the initial reports, Sir Robert, and I am still trying to fix in my mind possible explanations. On one hand, the fact that the Japanese made no attempt to shoot down the Hudson says one thing, for that would have been an outright act of war. We can also conclude that if the Hudson saw the convoy, the convoy surely saw the Hudson. That very fact could cause them to alter their plans."

Brooke-Popham nodded, considering Playfair's argument.

General Playfair started again.

"The position of the sighting we have verified as approximately 110 miles southeast of Point Camau (Cape Cambodia) and steaming in the direction of Thailand, which is not a good sign. It does appear that this force intends to head in a direction that could prove negative to our interests."

"And what if this is an attempt to provoke *us* into taking the first shot?" Brooke-Popham asked. "Then *we* would have initiated the warlike posture."

"That's certainly something to consider, Sir Robert."

"Dammit, General, I need more conclusive proof of their intentions before I commit our country to war. I need to be absolutely sure."

"I agree, Sir Robert. You have an awesome responsibility."

Brook-Popham thought aloud, "I initially thought it was good when London gave me the final responsibility for implementing *Matador*. Right now, I'm not too sure. There are too many damn political implications to any move we might make. Bad stuff, what."

Brooke-Popham paused for a moment and again addressed his subordinate.

"I want increased reconnaissance activity started immediately. I want a new flight every two hours if need be. I want to know where those ships are every moment."

"Very well, Sir Robert. I'll take care of that. I just want to remind you of the nasty weather situation that exists out there. Shadowing the convoy might not be all that easy."

"I am aware of the weather, General," Brooke-Popham answered testily. "I need to know *exactly* what those ships are doing, understood?"

"Yes, Sir Robert. I'll see to it."

THE FOLLOWING DAY, DECEMBER 6, ADDITIONAL REPORTS WERE received at Brooke-Popham's command regarding the Japanese convoy that was initially spotted the day before.

This time, a second, smaller convoy was reported, but the direction of both convoys proved a question to the British commander.

He summoned Vice Adm. Sir Geoffrey Layton, commander of China Station, and Rear Admiral Arthur Palliser for a noon meeting. The trio discussed a number of possible options for several hours. When it was over, the conclusion was reached that, in all probability, owing to the deteriorating weather conditions, the convoys were most probably attempting to make anchor at Koh Rong on the west coast of Indochina.

On the basis of this conference, Sir Robert Brooke-Popham decided against ordering the implementation of *Operation Matador*.

Brooke-Popham had returned to other pressing matters when received a call from General Percival on the secure line in his office just after seven o'clock.

"Sir Robert, I have just returned to my headquarters from Kuala Lumpur and I have just been told by my staff that *Matador* had not yet been ordered. May I please inquire why not?" Percival nearly shouted, highly irritated.

"I felt there was not *adequate* reason to do so, General. Please try and calm yourself."

"I am calm, Sir Robert. I just cannot believe you have failed to initiate *Matador*. I received a message around three o'clock that had the convoy's position located at eighty miles east southeast of Point Camau and steaming westward. That clearly shows their intent to attack Thailand. Don't you see that?"

"I received the same information, and have had a conference with the Navy who sees it a bit differently. They feel the weather is going all to hell and that the convoy will put up in Indochina and ride it all out.

I have, however, ordered more reconnaissance flights to monitor the convoy's progress."

"Sir Robert, I am compelled to tell you that I think that is a huge mistake. I have already ordered both the 3rd Corps and the 11th Indian Division to a state of higher readiness based on the information I have."

"You are perfectly free to do that, General Percival. But before I commit our forces to war, I really must be sure of our enemy's intent."

"If you wait any longer, it will be *too late*, Sir Robert. If we can't catch the Nips before they come ashore, it might be impossible to contain them."

"Nonsense, General Percival. You are talking about British forces that are among the best trained and equipped in the entire world. The Japanese, on the other hand, have to be in a state of near exhaustion after their long war with China. They would be crazy to attack us now. That's why I am so hesitant to invoke *Matador*. I really don't want the blame for a war to be placed squarely on British shoulders."

"I sincerely hope you are correct, Sir Robert. I would hate to be responsible for what might happen if you are wrong."

"So far, I am right, General, so no more of that sort of defeatist wag."

"By all means, Sir Robert. But please keep me informed as quickly as possible."

"You will be the first to know, I promise you. You will be the first."

———————————

IT HAD BEEN AN UNCOMFORTABLE TWO DAYS SINCE BROOKE-POPHAM'S disturbing phone call from General Percival, and the career naval officer was becoming aware of the fact that the strain was finally getting to him. He had spent several sleepless nights, and had tried to nap each following day to make up for the lack of sleep. That hadn't worked very well either, for the rests were light and filled with unpleasant thoughts of all types.

Additional dispatches had been received from coastal units and one had even sighted strange ships standing offshore, although positive identification could not be made.

The sinking feeling that he had been wrong in his estimation of the Japanese intent was making Brooke-Popham queasier than he expected.

What if everyone in London and most of my staff here are wrong and those are Japanese warships standing off our coast? The original plan for Matador called for seventy-two hour implementation from time of actual order. If I give the word now, it would still take three days to implement. Even though I don't agree with the seventy-two hours, I think twenty-four would be sufficient, I would order Matador now if only I was sure that it is necessary.

He found himself seated at his desk early on this foggy and rainy morning. He looked at his desk calendar for the exact date, December 8. He fixed on the date and pondered what his next step could be.

A soft knock on his door was followed by the figure of Rear Admiral Palliser, who hurried through the door.

"Sir Robert," Admiral Palliser said weakly, "I'm afraid it's started to happen . . ."

Brooke-Popham stared back at the officer, not really wanting to hear what was coming next.

"We've just received word from our forces up the coast. It seems the Japanese have started an invasion in the face of some really nasty weather and are storming our positions at several locations. We are trying to verify everything, and we are also attempting to make contact with our liaison operators in Thailand. All I know for sure, is that it is a coordinated attack on a fairly large scale."

Brooke-Popham looked at Palliser blankly until Palliser asked, "Any further orders, Sir Robert?"

He gathered himself, put his head down and summoned all the strength he could muster.

"Send a message to the commanders, Admiral. Tell them it's now time to push those little brownies back into the water. With God willing, it won't take all that long. And tell them I am counting on them, along with each and every British man, woman and child in this part of the world. Tell them that, will you."

"I'll see to it, Sir Robert." Palliser turned and left.

Brooke-Popham walked over to the window and looked out into the drab, wet landscape laced with dark, menacing clouds.

Help us, O Lord, for we are in great need. You have helped us before and I hope you will again. Your faithful servants need you and your presence here would be most welcome.

It was the first time he had called on his God in a number of years.

December 8, 1941, Office of GOC Malaya, British Army Headquarters, Singapore, 1330 hours

The minute Lt. Gen. Arthur E. Percival, GOC Malaya, realized an actual invasion had occurred he sprang into action. At first he detailed a number of orders to subordinates and then left for the regularly scheduled meeting of the Straits Settlement Legislative Council where he reported to its members on what had occurred during the preceding night and early morning.

He hurried back to his office at Malaya Command and immediately attempted to telephone Lt. Gen. Sir Lewis Heath, commander of the III Indian Corps, to take up defensive positions on the Singora and Kroh-Patani roads. The most important call to Heath was not completed due to the fact that there was but a single civil line that was shared by both the military and civilian users. This afternoon, it was completely jammed.

Percival had already resigned himself to the fact that the struggle ahead would be a defensive one rather than the opposite, since the well-conceived *Matador* offensive posture was now a thing of the past. He knew he must protect the British aerodromes at all cost and fight a defensive battle in Malaya, with the defence of Singapore the ultimate goal. He reasoned that if he was able to delay the invasion forces long enough, sizeable British reinforcements could arrive and save the day for the British Empire.

Part of Percival's initial defensive strategy was to send a force northward toward Kroh in Thailand to prevent the Japanese from reaching the coast and blocking the trunk road east of Butterworth Airfield. If this action were not successful, it would adversely affect the forces that were also being sent to a position that was immediately termed by Percival's staff as the Jitra line.

It seemed to the battle-hardened general that the Kroh column, or *Krohcol* for short, had a relatively easy job. All it had to do was get to a spot on the road called The Ledge ahead of the now advancing Japanese. The

Ledge was a highly defensible six-mile stretch of road cut into the hillside above the Patani River. Whoever reached the spot first held a commanding position and could be easily reinforced.

Things began badly for the British troops expected to reach The Ledge. Two key units that made up part of the *Krohcol* force were late in arriving due to internal problems. The final *Krohcol* element, the 3/16 Punjabs under Lt. Col. Henry Moorhead, started into Thailand by themselves. Lorries driven by Australian 2/3rd Reserve Motor Company drivers carried the troops northward to the Thai border where three hundred Thai policemen brandishing guns met them at the border. The Thais delayed progress until the following afternoon when the troops were finally allowed to advance.

That night, sporadic sniper fire from the Thais made the night's rest an agonized one for the young Indian soldiers of the 3/16 Punjabs, most of whom had never even heard a gunshot in action.

The column started early in the morning and soon arrived within six miles of The Ledge.

From there, the weary Punjabis proceeded on foot. Less than a mile later, the advance guard came into contact with the Japanese 42nd Regiment, which had beaten them to The Ledge. The 42nd Regiment was made up of battle-hardened veterans of the China War and immediately took the fight to the young Indians.

The 42nd also brought into action the remarkable Type 97 Shinhoto *Chi-Ha* medium tanks, the backbone of the Imperial Army's infantry. With its low silhouette, aerial spread around the vehicle, top and asymmetrical turret, the Type 97 's unique appearance terrified the Punjabis who had never even seen—much less faced—advancing tanks and infantry.

The Japanese inflicted heavy casualties on the 3/16 Punjabs. Fearing the worst, the following morning Lieutenant Colonel Morehead requested permission to withdraw his remaining forces to Kroh where he could reorganize his battered troops. But, he waited too long to withdraw and, when the hour of withdrawal arrived, found himself surrounded. The Japanese attacked and killed practically all of his command. Morehead himself was lucky to escape in one of the four vehicles still remaining under his command.

It was an inauspicious start to the ground war in Thailand and offered the Japanese Imperial Army a marvelous opportunity to traverse a valuable main road with very little opposition.

Meanwhile, General Percival's other main defensive position, the Jitra Line, was not faring much better.

The 11th Division was given the order to defend the Jitra line, but had spent so much time waiting for an affirmative decision on *Matador* that the Jitra Line resembled a building site on the early morning of December 8. It had rained all night and was still raining through mid-morning when the soldiers of the 6th and 15th Indian Infantry Brigades began the tedious job of first bailing out, then digging and finally wiring the flooded trenches.

The Jitra Line actually consisted of a conglomeration of small wooded hills surrounded by marshlands and cultivated rice fields—very difficult terrain to defend under any circumstances. There were only two main roads to protect, but the expanse involved made defending them quite difficult.

On the morning of December 10, Japanese Col. Shizuo Saeki's armoured reconnaissance detachment ran into British defenders along the Singora Road. The extended action lasted the better part of the next two days and was fought in mostly monsoon-like conditions.

While the British defenders were able to inflict some serious casualties on the invading Japanese, Maj. Gen. David Murray-Lyon finally requested permission to withdraw his troops early on the morning of December 12. The permission was not given and the fighting continued. Nearly twelve hours later, Murray-Lyon again requested permission to withdraw, this time fearing his division would be ripped up by the advancing Type 97 *Chi-Ha* Japanese tank columns.

General Percival, who had by now moved to new headquarters on Sime Road, was more receptive to such an action.

"Go ahead and move your forces, General, but keep one thing in mind," Percival warned. "Your task is to fight for the security of North Kedah. We consider that you are only opposed by one Japanese division at most. We think the best solution may be to obtain considerable depth on both roads and obtain scope for your superior artillery."

Murray-Lyon took the conversation to heart, but the implementation of the plan was far more difficult. The logistics of moving an entire division and its guns and ammunition was no easy chore under the best of conditions, but doing so at night in a driving rain was practically impossible. The only road leading south to Gurun was clogged with every type of moving vehicle and progress was exhaustingly slow. A number of foot soldiers started out across country on their own, hoping to join their division units further south. Some units did not receive the pull-out orders and were still in their trenches the following morning.

The entire scenario was a setting for disaster for the reeling British troops. When the Japanese advanced, scores of British guns and ammunition were found in perfect working condition. Casualties were incredibly high for some units. The 15th Brigade was reduced from twenty-four hundred men to just over six hundred, a level that rendered it unfit for duty.

More than one thousand troops were taken prisoner. Many of the bridges that were to be blown up to cover the retreat were still in tact, owning to the rainy conditions that dampened the explosive charges.

The rout of the Jitra Line was a phenomenal blow to British troop morale and the notion of British troop superiority over a supposed-inferior Japanese Imperial Army.

It foretold of difficult times ahead for British forces in the defense of the Malayan Peninsula and the Fortress of Singapore.

December 8, 1941, aboard HMS Prince of Wales, South China Sea, 1800 hours

The shoreline of the Malaysian coast was barely visible in the failing light of the darkening December evening as the small fleet force made it was through the final currents that comprised the Straits of Johore. The task force, again officially marked as Force Z by the British Navy, included the battleship *Prince of Wales* that served as flagship to Adm.Sir Thomas Phillips, the battlecruiser *Repulse,* and four destroyers, the *Express, Tenedos, Vampire* and *Electra.*

The four destroyers were basically anti-submarine factors, while the two capital ships were intended to create havoc among the Japanese troopships and supply ships that, according to first reports, were carrying on landings further up the coastline of Malaya.

The *Prince of Wales* was a modern, first-class capital ship that had already distinguished itself in actions against the German Battleship *Bismarck,* sinking the German battleship early in the war. She was full plated and seemingly impervious to anything the enemy could throw at her.

On the other hand, the *Repulse* was a WWI cruiser with conventional thin armor plating that had been refitted at the end of the Great War and, again in 1936, when it received improved deck armor and a catapult airplane configuration for reconnaissance. It was commanded by Capt. Bill Tennant, an excellent sea tactician with a remarkable record and keen perception for acting with grace and distinction under battle.

The entire force had managed to get under way within six hours of notification of the initial Japanese landings at Kota Bahru, Patani and Singora earlier that morning.

Sir Thomas Phillips was adamant that his small force put to sea "as quickly as humanly possible," in an attempt to stem the tide of the vicious Japanese attacks to his north. As he passed the boom at the entrance to the Straits of Johore, he received a visual signal from his chief of staff, Rear

Admiral Arthur Palliser, at Changi Signal Station who reported, "Regret further fighter protection impossible."

Phillips had made the decision to leave Palliser behind so that he might attempt to produce cohesive coordination between the varied British airfields in Malaya that could afford his force a degree of protection from Japanese aircraft. British naval intelligence was expected to identify approaching aircraft as potential trouble to him and his ships.

Palliser's negative message was exceedingly ominous to Phillips who had hoped for ground-based air cover. Informed of the Japanese multi-landings to his north, Phillips realized that the British Army—now fighting for its very existence—would probably utilize all fighter-aircraft resources.

Phillips checked the force's formation and was pleased to see the four destroyers deployed off both the port and starboard sides of his battleship, already engaged in defensive-crossing zig-zag maneuvers designed to locate enemy submarines in the area.

Satisfied that his ships had fulfilled their initial requirements, he retired to his quarters to mull over the numerous charts and intelligence folders he was able to grab from the Singapore naval staff files before heading out to board his ship.

He also reconsidered the other parts of Rear Admiral Palliser's coded message. Palliser warned that he had received new information on a large concentration of Japanese bombers in Indochina and the possibility of other bombers as close as Thailand.

He also flashed that the key Kota Bahru aerodrome had been evacuated and that he felt the British were losing their grip on other northern Malaya aerodromes due to the lightning-fast actions of the Japanese.

Sir Thomas considered the alternatives and ultimately decided that two factors should determine the direction his force would follow in the upcoming days. Most importantly, he *must* uphold the honor of the British navy while the forces of Great Britain's army were slugging it out with the Japanese army on shore. Secondly, he must take the initiative to the enemy despite the fact that there was no availability of friendly air cover for his force.

Phillips and Force Z were extremely lucky for almost the entire the first day, December 9th. Frequent rainstorms and low visibility managed to conceal his ships from any peering enemy eyes until around five in the afternoon when a trio of Japanese reconnaissance seaplanes spotted the ships.

"Send an immediate message to Singapore," Phillips instructed a junior officer on the *Prince of Wales*. "Tell them that we will continue sailing on our present course until dark and then we will reverse course and head back to Singapore."

Early the next morning, December 10, Admiral Phillips received an unconfirmed report from Palliser about a Japanese landing at Kuantan, not far off Force Z's present course. Phillips decided to investigate. Force Z reached Kuantan at eight in the morning to find a peaceful harbor and no sign of a Japanese landing fleet.

Instead of departing the area with great haste, Phillips decided to first investigate some barges and a small ship they had passed on their route into Kuantan. At a little past ten, a radar operator on *Repulse* spotted radar dots on his scope and immediately signaled the *Prince of Wales*. A few moments later, a lookout spotted another Japanese reconnaissance plane that was close enough to see the entire force.

The Japanese aircraft was actually a long-range element of the 22nd Naval Air Flotilla under the command of Rear Admiral Sadaichi Matsunaga based in Saigon. Within minutes of the sighting, the majority of Matsunaga's bomber force was heading toward the reported location of Force Z.

When Phillips learned that enemy aircraft had, in all probability, sighted his ships, he realized he had put his ships and men in a precarious position.

Adding to his trouble was the fact that one of his escorts, *HMS Tenedos*, had just signaled the flagship that during it's return to Singapore with engine trouble, Japanese aircraft had attacked it.

Phillips made a decision to continue his course and maintain radio silence rather than attempt to contact one of the northern airfields for fighter cover. His decision would later prove to be another incredible blunder.

Shortly after eleven o'clock, a large formation of Japanese bombers was sighted coming from the southwest, the order for battle stations was broadcast throughout the force.

It has been *less* than forty-five minutes since Force Z had been spotted from the air. Capt. Bill Tennant took it upon himself to break radio silence and contact Singapore requesting any available air assistance. The 453 Squadron of Royal Air Force Buffaloes was immediately dispatched, but precious time had already been lost for the two great ships

The sailors and officers aboard Force Z quickly assumed their emergency firing positions and waited for the enemy bombers to come into range. At nearly eleven fifteen, the first orders were given and the 5.25 high angle guns of the *Prince of Wales* opened up on the bomber formation with a dazzling array of gunfire. Starbursts and black cordite bursts appeared within the raiders' formation and the first of the enemy bombers was hit and fell out of the bombing configuration.

The other Japanese bombers pressed forward as the giant battleships and their escorts attempted to change course and avoid the oncoming swarm of attacking bees.

The first wave of aggressors was high-level bombers that attacked with precision and accuracy. One bomb actually hit the *Repulse* and landed on her deck but failed to pierce her newly-installed deck armor.

By this time, full battle maneuvers were in force for the entire group. These initial maneuvers had proved fairly successful in thwarting the Japanese bombers' attempts to destroy *Prince of Wales* and *Repulse.*

Just before midday, another wave of planes appeared—a squadron of torpedo bombers.

Repulse was successful in evading the first torpedoes, but two gigantic explosions rocked the *Prince of Wales* as she veered to port. The explosions stopped her propeller shafts and the now-doomed lady of the sea went immediately out of control. In a few minutes she began listing to port and her speed declined to around fifteen knots.

Meanwhile, *Repulse* had fared much better, thanks mainly to the maneuvering skill of Captain Tennant. Time and again she had dodged torpedoes and for a brief moment seemed to be clearing the action.

Captain Tennant was about to go to the aid of *Prince of Wales* when the two-ball pennant was raised signaling *Prince of Wales* was out of control. He signaled 'Can we help?' to Admiral Phillips, but received no reply.

In a matter of minutes, *Prince of Wales* took three more direct hits from torpedoes and began burning fiercely, and was still making headway even though her deck was already awash. The situation had quickly become hopeless.

Finally, another torpedo from the relentless Japanese bombers found *Repulse*, and the giant ship shuddered at the initial impact. Additional torpedo bombers appeared and continued the unrelenting assault on the suddenly stricken ships.

Repulse's rudder jammed and she took additional hits. *Repulse* was now listing almost thirty degrees to port and Captain Tennant sensed his position was hopeless. He ordered his men topside and gave them a well-deserved tribute.

"Men, you have fought bravely against overwhelming odds and have made your king and country quite proud. It is now time for us to abandon ship and save ourselves so that we can fight another battle on another day. Our destroyers will attempt to pick you up, of that you can be sure. I wish each and every one of you good luck. Now get going, I'm very proud of each of you."

Repulse continued her list to port, which was now some sixty or seventy degrees. She hung there for several minutes until she rolled and slipped beneath the water. The time was twelve thirty three.

The *Prince of Wales* had continued limping further north, but by one o'clock it became apparent that her wounds were simply too grievous for her to survive. A half hour earlier, *HMS Express* had managed to get alongside and take off a large number of the ship's company until she herself was forced away when the larger ship began the rolling process that was the precursor to her sinking. The order to abandon ship was given and preparations began immediately to save as many of the remaining crew as possible.

At approximately twenty after one, the majestic *Prince of Wales* also slid beneath the waters of the South China Sea, leaving most of her crew of 618 to be rescued.

Neither Admiral Sir Thomas Phillips nor her gallant Capt. Jack Leach survived. It took the destroyers almost five hours to fish out the living survivors and a great deal longer to bring the dead aboard.

The sinking of these ships was the greatest tragedy to ever hit the modern Royal British Navy during the period known as the British Raj.

There was now no real British naval presence in an ocean that it had commanded for the past two hundred years.

December 10, 1941, residence at 116 Jalan Kampung Perak, Kedah Province, Malaya, 0600 hours

The sun had finally risen on a relatively dry day for the town of Alor Star, considering this small dot on Malaysia's western side was already the recipient of several doses of this year's version of the dreaded northeast monsoon season. Only scattered puddles remained of the torrential downpour that had drenched the area during the past week—a tribute to the sound local Malay engineering, which provided tremendous run off during peak storm season.

The small cadre of five British Royal Marines alighted silently from the half-ton lorry that provided them transportation to the one-story wooden cottage that bore the number 116 Jalan Kampung Perak. The street was slightly north of the middle of Alor Star's main commercial district, while the city of Alor Star was itself not far from the southern border of Thailand.

Four of the marines were enlisted men, and were all armed with new .303 Inch No 4 Mk1 rifles that had arrived in Penang via freighter just a week before. The unit's leader, Major Ashley Cundiff, wore his treasured Browning HP 35 pistol high on his hip, as was his unit's custom. Cundiff carefully unlatched the holder's leather flap and fingered his weapon.

"All right now, men," he barked softly, "let's not make a mess of this. I want a clean job in here, and I want it done snappily."

The Royal Marines stiffened attentively, each checking his weapon to insure it was ready to fire with the safety off. Cundiff mentioned to the rear of the house and two of the marines moved away to cover that area. Cundiff stepped to the doorstep and firmly knocked several times on the door. He waited a few moments and knocked again.

Finally, a light appeared under the door and a voice from within asked.

"Yes, who is it?"

"Major Cundiff of the Royal Marines, Captain Heenan. Can I have a word with you?"

"For what, man, I'm still in bed," Heenan countered.

"It will only take a minute Captain. If it wasn't important, I wouldn't be bothering you."

"All right, let me get my robe."

A few moments later, the lock began turning and the somewhat irate figure of Capt. Patrick Heenan peered out into the dawning light. He saw the drawn weapons and immediately stepped back.

"What is all this?" he demanded. "What do you want?"

Cundiff was ready for this move and immediately stepped inside the cottage, placing his weapon directly in front of Heenan's eyes.

"Please do me the pleasure of not moving, Captain, I'm afraid my pistol has something of a hair trigger. I certainly wouldn't want it to fire, would you?"

Heenan nodded in disgust, now deflated by the presence of the armed men.

Major Cundiff spoke again.

"I have an order here to search your cottage and confiscate anything I find that I consider of interest, and I intend to do just that. For our safety and yours, I am placing you in handcuffs until our search is over." He motioned and a Royal Marine corporal came forward to place the cuffs on Heenan.

"You won't find anything here," Heenan said defiantly, "I have no idea what it is you are looking for."

"For some reason I think you do, Heenan, so just remain quiet. Corporal Twithers, go and fetch the other chaps from out back so we can get started."

Twithers nodded and left the room. He returned a few seconds later and the search began.

It took the better part of ten minutes until Twithers returned with a leather-bound Bible securely nestled inside a small box. He handed it to his superior.

"What have we here?" Cundiff mocked the subdued officer in front of him. Heenan's face froze as he saw the box. Cundiff opened the box to reveal a small radio transmitter. He held it up to Heenan who suddenly turned belligerent.

"So, what's that prove? I just use it for my own pleasure. You can't prove nothing. Just like you British, always out to get someone."

"But, Captain Heenan, you too, are British, aren't you?"

Heenan remained sullen and dropped his head. He searched for something to say but couldn't find the words.

A minute passed, and another of the Royal Marines came into the room carrying a machine that resembled a typewriter. He handed it to his major.

"And what's this?" Cundiff asked the group in general. "Just what might this gadget be?"

"I dunnot know," the Marine replied with a severe cockney accent. "At first I thought it was some sort of typewriter. The more I looked at it, the more it didn't look like a typewriter at all. It seems to be some sort of radio, but it's unlike any one that I've ever seen."

"Anything to say about this?" Cundiff turned and asked Heenan. "You might as well come clean with all this evidence we've found."

Heenan stared back at the Royal Marine officer with a menacing stare, but declined to speak.

"All right, then, we'll continue our search here if it takes all day. When we are finished, we will all go over to divisional headquarters. I know the lads there will be happy to see all this stuff of yours."

Heenan stared back disgustedly at the officer. All he could hope for now was that the Japanese would continue their advance to the south and rescue him from his captors.

He hoped they would really hurry.

December 10, 1941, Office of GOC, Sime Road Headquarters, Singapore, 1400 hours

It was an ashen-faced British naval lieutenant commander named Hartston, attached to his staff as naval liaison, who brought the news to Gen. Arthur E. Percival. At first, the officer could not bring himself to speak. He gathered himself and spoke weakly.

"I'm sorry, General, I'm afraid I have some rather bad news to report."

Percival looked up from his desk and spoke clearly, "Good heavens, man, out with it. With what's going on around here, just how bad can it be?"

"The worst, sir . . ."

"Okay then, let me have it."

"We have just received an air confirmation from No. 453 squadron that was dispatched to try and cover the activities of Navy Force Z. The commanding officer reports that, upon reaching his target, he found no evidence of either *HMS Prince of Wales* or *HMS Repulse*. He was only able to detect three destroyers that were all involved in picking up survivors from the two ships."

"What? *Both* of them . . . but that's impossible, it simply couldn't happen."

"I agree with you, General," the naval officer added. "I find it quite unlikely that such a thing could take place. There were no Japanese capital ships reported in the area that could inflict such damage. If you want, I'll recheck the report. Perhaps there has been an error."

"Yes, do that if you will. What about Sir Thomas? Any word from him?"

"We did not receive any reports from *Prince of Wales* during the past twenty-four hours. We did get a message from *Repulse* and that is why the 453 Squadron was sent to intercept Force Z."

No word from either Admiral Phillips or Prince of Wales is definitely not a good sign. Sir Thomas was sure that his force could withstand an enemy aerial attack and told me so on several occasions. That could be the only answer. And, if it is true that both the Prince of Wales and Repulse are lost, that means we have given up control of the seas around us for the foreseeable future. When Brooke-Popham hedged on ordering Matador, I knew it was a big mistake. The Japanese came ashore at precisely the spots I would have picked if I were planning an invasion. Any fool with sufficient military experience under his belt could see that, it was plain enough.

Now these bloody sinkings have turned our plan of sea protection into a bloody mess—what an absolutely horrible sequence of events for everyone involved.

Percival sighed and returned his attention to the navy officer standing in front of him

"Commander Hartston, it is best you set about getting me some firm facts on what has transpired as quickly as possible, and that better jolly well be quick. I need realistic figures on exactly what was lost and what was saved. Do you understand?'

"Quite, Sir. I'll be back to you as soon as we have been able to figure things out."

"Good, I'm not going anywhere."

The commander shrugged at Percival's attempted sarcasm and turned to leave.

"And one more thing, Hartston. If all this proves to be true, please let Admiral Palliser and everyone on the naval staff how sorry I am personally to see this happen. Sir Thomas was a very likeable person and a good comrade to everyone."

"I certainly will do, General, and thank you for your consideration."

Percival waited until the officer left his office, but was unable to immediately return to his paperwork. He glanced at the official picture of the king hanging on the wall in front of his desk and thought deeply.

What we need to do now is simply hang on until help arrives, and that might be a long time coming. This entire situation had turned into an incredible predicament and there doesn't seem to be an acceptable answer anywhere. I must be very wise with my decisions from here on; we British and our allies can't afford any more mistakes.

December 10, 1941, Imperial Japanese Army 5th Division Staff Headquarters, Northwestern Malaya, 1440 hours

The invasion had gone according to plan, even if the British resistance had been more than expected in certain sectors along the Malayan coastline, as far as Col. Masanobu Tsuji had been able to tell from his intelligence reports. The really bad weather could be held accountable for some of the problems, but Tsuji was confident that the overall plan—developed by his *Doro Nawa* Unit almost a year ago in Taiwan—would be successful over the next few months.

One of the most important elements of the plan, in Tsuji's opinion, still needed to be addressed. For that reason, he had summoned Major Shigeharu Asaeda to his temporary headquarters tent on this particularly humid and close December afternoon. He was reading the latest dispatches when the tall figure of Asaeda appeared at the folds of the tent, his head lowered in a perfunctory bow.

"Come in, Asaeda," Tsuji said warmly, "and tell me all about your landings with the Takumi Detachment at Kota Bharu and also about the people at Ando Detachment. I have been so busy since we landed that I haven't been able to see you until now."

Asaeda finished his bow and raised his head.

"It was all very exciting, Honorable Colonel, but the landing was particularly difficult. The area we finally came ashore was not where we had planned, and the enemy fortifications inflicted heavy losses on our brave soldiers. I was pinned down for a while but was finally able to make it to the beach and then into a grove of trees that offered some protection.

It took us almost half a day to secure the area and then our remaining troops were able to make it to shore. The weather was so bad that I actually became seasick, as did many of our men. I don't know how important the weather was, but I know I really wasn't prepared for the worst. The best thing is that it's now behind me and I can concentrate on killing our enemies."

Tsuji looked at the tall, gaunt warrior in front of him and realized this man's acute need for combat.

How many other Japanese officers feel this same call to battle and attack their duties with such admirable bravado. Asaeda is truly a remarkable man, and the emperor and the Imperial Japanese Army are fortunate to have him in their service.

"And what of Ando Detachment? Did they fare well on the invasion?"

"I think their landing was somewhat easier, Honorable Colonel. When I reached their position, they were already preparing to move out from the beach area. I spoke with a few of their officers and they were in fine spirits. I think they lost a few soldiers, but nothing like the losses suffered by the Takumi Detachment. Their troops' morale was very high and they were all eager to engage the enemy further. I think Ando Detachment will be hard to stop for anyone who comes into their path."

"That is good to hear, Asaeda. I prefer a report from someone who has been to the unit rather than the daily reports we receive that vary so much according to who has produced them."

Asaeda shook his head in agreement with his superior.

"Now I have another important assignment for you, perhaps the single most important of the entire campaign."

Asaeda's head perked up as he waited for Tsuji's next words.

"You know that the bicycle aspect of the *Doro Nawa* model is incredibly important to our army's overall success. It was developed with speed in mind. We anticipate moving very swiftly through the jungles of Malaya and cannot do this unless the ordinary soldier is able to keep up. Since we were not able to bring along sufficient cars and trucks to haul them, the bicycle seem like the most practical way to travel."

Asaeda knew about the bicycles and of their importance to the mission, but out of respect for Tsuji, he remained quiet as the colonel continued.

"Our plan calls for each person not assigned to a truck or vehicle to have his own bike, and these are being brought ashore as we speak. There are also two members of each company whose duty is to keep the bikes and tires in good condition. Supplies of extra tires and parts are also on the transport ships. We know that many bridges will be destroyed and will need to be repaired. We hope that our troops will be able to ford the smaller creeks and rivers and cross the repaired bridges with these bicycles on their shoulders.

I want you to personally see that we start utilizing these bicycles correctly from the very beginning. If you encounter any problems with officers or the like, you will let me know at once. Some of these officers are used to having horses and wagons as we did so competently in China, but this is the jungle and the terrain is completely different.

Each division has some six thousand bicycles assigned for its use, and that figure represents a lot of bicycles and parts. This project won't take you too long to oversee; I just want to insure it is correctly perceived from the start. A staff officer asking about bicycles will get everyone's attention and that will insure its success. I promise you that I will find some real action for you after you finish, you have my word."

Asaeda smiled and bowed again. Tsuji returned the gesture.

"I have given you some important credentials to allow you to pass through practically any area under our control, but I hope you will not really need them. If I am correct, we will slash through the British defenses and be ready to attack Singapore in less than two months."

"*Hai*," Asaeda agreed. "The gods will look with favor on our honorable actions."

"*Hai,*" Tsuji concurred. That would be the greatest accomplishment, Tsuji thought.

December 11, 1941, Bishop Street, George Town, Penang 1040 hours

It was pretty much business as usual in George Town, the capital city of the Island of Penang, at mid-morning on Thursday, December 11. The myriad of shops and teeming bazaars of Chowrasta market were filled with people buying the essentials of life and preparing for the noontime lunch period.

Along Bishop Street, people walked leisurely to and from appointments in the relative heat that was part of the early December Malaysian climate. At the main fire station on Beach Street, several members of the volunteer fire brigade polished their equipment as part of their unit's daily drill, when suddenly, all eyes turned skyward.

Approaching from the east was an extremely large formation of airplanes that formed a perfect V-formation, much larger than anyone in the town had ever seen. The planes droned along, their engines in perfect pitch high above the streets of George Town.

When the first bombs fell along Bishop Street, people began running and screaming, attempting to find shelter from the ceaseless punishment of screaming metal. Bombs seemed to explode everywhere, with no deference to buildings or persons. The leading aircraft completed its run and turned to starboard away from the Island of Penang, the red Rising Sun symbol clearly visible on its wings.

After the first Japanese bombing run, the entire city of George Town seemed to be on fire, from one end to the other. A number of bodies littered the streets along with parts of exploded buildings, overturned cars, rickshaws and just about anything else imaginable.

There had been no air raid warnings. Such warnings would have done little good since there were no shelters for the inhabitants to run into.

People were just returning to the streets some twenty minutes later to aid the injured and dying when a second wave of Japanese bombers reappeared and began another low altitude run. This time the intent was to strafe anything that moved and numerous additional casualties were soon inflicted on the mostly civilian population of the Island of Penang.

Since no British fighters were apparent during either of the raids, it was evident to all involved that the Japanese had complete control of the airspace around the island.

When he realized what was happening, attorney Charles Samuel immediately left his offices on Union Street and told his staff to close the office and return to their homes.

He dodged some burning vehicles and a lot of smoldering debris and slowly made his way up "The Hill" where Vi and his children were waiting.

It suddenly came to him that his worst fears had just been realized. The Japanese had decided to make the Island of Penang a major target of their invasion.

It would now be necessary to figure out a way to get his family to safety as quickly as possible. At that particular point in time, little else mattered to Charles Samuel.

December 13, 1941, legal offices of Charles Samuel, Union Street, George Town, Penang, 1600 hours

The four days after the first Japanese bomber attack on Penang had been something of a shocking hollowness for Charles Samuel. The Japanese planes had returned for successive days, but were being somewhat more repelled each day by British Buffaloe fighters from the nearby airfield at Butterworth.

The city still smoldered from the large number of fires that were out of control due to the complete destruction of the main fire station on Beach Street along with many of its volunteer firefighters. Only the frequent torrential rains each day kept the entire city from burning down.

On some of the bombing runs, the Japanese had dropped leaflets aimed at the non-European inhabitants of Penang. In these propaganda leaflets, the Japanese disseminated the fact that the empire of Japan was "waging war solely against the 'White Devils', and urged the Asian inhabitants to 'burn up the whites in a blaze of victory." While these papers caused increased concern among the Europeans, they also drew a weary eye from the many Chinese civilians on the island whose native country was also involved in a military encounter with the Japanese. The Malays for the most part paid little attention, choosing to ally themselves with their British employers and friends who had treated them quite civilly for many past decades.

Samuel was in a quandary as to exactly what course to take. His daughter worked for the naval office on the island that was abruptly closed the same afternoon as the first bombings. That signaled to Samuel that the Island of Penang was in immediate danger and would, in all probability, be left undefended to any great extent by British forces.

Since he was fifty-eight and considered a pillar of the island's professional business community, Samuel attempted to keep up a good front and had traveled down from The Hill each day to his office. He was generally alone with the exception of a few of his partners and staff who came to collect personal files and treasures they had left after their sudden departure four days before.

Rumors were rampant and no one really had any idea what was happening or what course to take. A handful of stores still operated, but provisions were getting low, as re-supply was practically impossible.

Samuel was seated at his desk when the phone rang. He picked up the receiver.

A voice on the other end identified herself as a staff person for the resident counsellor, for the Island of Penang, Mr. Leslie Forbes. She read from a prepared statement.

"All persons under the direct responsibility of the resident counsellor should prepare to evacuate Penang as soon as humanly possible. This order applies to all European Service families, women and children, and all patients of area military hospitals."

Samuel shot back at once.

"Can people be *compelled* to go?" he asked shortly.

"No," the voice replied, "but they must be *urged* to, in their *own* interest."

Samuel hung up the phone, knowing he would have to comply with the instructions. He reached for the phone and gave the operator the number for his home on The Hill. Even though he had already discussed the matter of evacuation with his wife Vi, he realized the reality of actually being forced to do so was, in fact, incredibly difficult to comprehend.

She answered after two rings.

He began in as calm a tone as he could muster, trying not to seem too excited.

"Vi, darling, I'm afraid the time has come. I've just gotten the call we had talked about."

"Oh, God," Vi exclaimed. "So soon?"

"Yes, it seems so. Everyone at our level is being asked to leave, as quickly as we can manage."

"Right," she returned, "If that is the way it has to be."

"I'm afraid it must. I'm sure I'll be expected to set an example, having been a commissioner and all."

"Charles, I'm afraid of what's going to happen. Where are we to go?"

"I'm sure that will all be explained to us, my darling. They wouldn't be asking us to go if there weren't contingency plans for our safety. I'm sure they will send us to Singapore and there we will be safe. After all, Singapore is Singapore, not Penang."

"Oh, Charles, can you hurry home so we can pack? I'm not sure what we will be able to fit into the trunks."

"You had best forget the trunks, Vi, I think we will probably be limited to what we can carry."

"But Charles, that means leaving all our family valuables that have taken so many years to collect. What about them?"

"We can always come back and claim them after the Japanese have left," Samuel reassured his wife. "There will be ample time then."

"Oh, I just hate the Japanese for starting all of this," Vi screamed, her voice trailing off.

"I wish I had been smarter and listened to the right people," Samuel confessed. "I might have made a different plan and we might have wound up in another position."

"Position, smishion," she replied angrily. "It's too late for all that now. Come on up and help me gather together our stuff. Did they tell you when we had to be ready?"

"No, I'm afraid I hung up too quickly to find out. I was in a state of shock."

"Well, I know the telephone operators will know the details, they know everything that goes on around this island. I'll give them a buzz when we ring off and see if I can find out. You just get yourself up here as soon as you can."

"I'm on my way, love, see you soon."

Samuel replaced the phone and looked around his office for the last time. There were numerous mementoes he treasured that he fleetingly considered taking along with him until his better sense clicked in.

He left his office and turned the fans and lights off and stepped out of the front door. He put the key in the lock and turned it to the left. Satisfied, he turned to see the city of George Town.

There was really not much left to see in the smoke and debris.

December 14, 1941, Sime Road Headquarters, Malaya Command, Singapore, 0950 hours

It was almost a week since GOC Malaya Arthur E. Percival learned of the incredible decision of Sir Robert Brooke-Popham not to invoke *Operation Matador*. He had always envisioned an offensive war that followed the outlines of *Matador*, where he could pick and choose his times and areas of opportunities. After more than a week of Japanese attacks and counterattacks, he was sure he was fighting an experienced and well-versed army with a gainful plan of attack. So much for the intelligence experts and military insiders who had dismissed the Japanese as a second-rate fighting power, tired of toiling in China, and ill equipped for the extreme rigors and climate of jungle warfare.

Percival was still puzzled by some of the intelligence messages he was receiving on practically an hourly basis. A single item, sent down from a post near the Thai border two days after the invasion, pointed out the fact that a small column of three Japanese trucks were identified and stopped by a column of Indian Gurkhas. When the trucks were searched, their contents were found to be bicycles, not ammunition or food supplies. Percival had circled the word 'bicycles' and had questioned his intelligence liaison, but no one had any real idea of the bicycles meaning. Percival placed the fact in the back of his mind, hoping to find out its meaning at a later time.

The general had quickly moved on to other things, mainly to the decision as to exactly where to make his next stand in northwest Malaya. He knew it was important to gain control of some section of this important part of Malaya, as much to show the Japanese that the British were willing to make a fight of it but also to give the common British soldier a spark of hope that the fight against the invaders could eventually be won. He realized that circumstances were dangerously close to providing his army a demoralized prospect, and therefore no demonstrative reason to keep fighting.

With the state of the 11th Indian Division in shambles and its leadership and men near exhaustion, Percival decided to regroup at Gurun, a road junction some thirty miles south of Jitra. Here the rice fields of the western plains were joined by the mostly rolling and heavily wooded countryside that was home to numerous rubber plantations of southern Kedah.

Percival was incensed when informed that the large civilian work force that had been hired to prepare fortifications around the Gurun area had quickly departed at the first news of the Japanese invasion. Once again, the tired and exhausted soldiers of the 11th Indian Division were obliged to perform the backbreaking labor of preparing a series of fortifications.

By the time the first advance Japanese advance elements arrived in mid morning, the 11th Division was near exhaustion. The road bridge over the River Kedah had been blown during the night, but the railway bridge had rebuffed all the engineer's attempts to blow it.

The Japanese utilized the railway bridge to ferry both lorries and tanks as well as scores of infantry. The failure to blow the second bridge cost the British dearly. A night attack destroyed a large number of 12th Brigade defenses and the rout was begun. Two days later, another retreat was ordered to a position back behind the Muda River. Another four days later, defensive positions were established further south at Taiping—a move than left the Island of Penang completely uncovered.

When Percival was informed of this series of strategic retreats, he accepted the news stoically. For some time he had been at odds with III Indian Corps Commander, Lt. Gen. Sir Lewis Heath. Heath wanted to defend Penang and its valuable supply of petrol, food provisions, and large civilian population but was ordered to evacuate the area without regard to any of its apparent advantages.

Heath was also adamant on moving his remaining forces to more carefully prepared defensive positions in the Johore area, but was overruled by Percival who wanted shorter, more concentrated battles that would delay the Japanese advance.

The rift was the beginning of a major directional disagreement between the two key English generals, who would disagree for the next two months on several crucial issues. Their discord on these matters would play a key part in the eventual battle for Singapore.

December 25, 1941, bungalow off Beach Road, Singapore 1610 hours

Overall, it had been a rather nice day for Dr. Pai Lin Song. By noon, the children's excitement over Christmas in the pediatric ward of the Singapore General Hospital had been reduced to the usual, daily noise levels with the children occupying themselves with the assorted presents Pail Lin and her staff had been able to scrape together. Since Christmas was definitely more European than Asian, the gifts were just as much for the staff as for the children, although few admitted to that fact.

The Straits Volunteer Red Cross had been its usual stellar self and between the staff and Red Cross, a wide variety of inexpensive gifts had been collected and disbursed to the children. A number of family members had also visited the children and had stayed most of the day. At three o'clock, Pai Lin called a halt to the festivities and closed the ward to visitors so that the children could begin to wind down and eventually, drop off to sleep.

After she instructed the evening staff on the overnight procedures, Dr. Song left the hospital and walked the mile to her neat little bungalow just off Beach Road. The evening was damp from an earlier rainstorm, but the approaching evening air was actually refreshing and tinged with a hint of coolness that energized her walk. As she neared her bungalow, she suddenly felt quite alone.

Pail Lin had not seen or heard from Lt. William Elliott for several days. She searched her tired memory and attempted to count the days, but finally gave up. She knew he was up north involved in the fighting in that area—she had been able to tell that much from the distinct lack of information he had provided when he left. Pail Lin knew Elliott wished to spare her the details whenever he was in a dangerous situation, and had given up trying to pry the particulars out of him.

She stepped up to her door and glanced at the small green wreath she had attached to it. The wreath was a gift from a satisfied family whose daughter had been her patient a couple of years before and wanted to present her with a lasting memento. Pai Lin touched the rough branches of the wreath, and realized it was the only visible aspect of Christmas that she displayed.

She opened the door and entered the bungalow. It was just late enough in the afternoon for the outside light to begin its nocturnal fade, and the emptiness and silence of the bungalow seemed a bit surreal to Pai Lin.

She made her way to her bedroom and was finishing placing her purse and jewelry on her vanity when a noise from the other room caught her attention. A moment later, Lt. William Elliott walked quickly into the room.

She leapt into his arms and started sobbing.

Elliott patted the back of her head, and asked softly, "What's all this, crying over the sight of me?"

"I'm just happy to see you, you big poop. You know that. I can't believe you made it home."

"I would have been here yesterday, but the Nips just wouldn't cooperate. Seems they have a different view of Christmas, or something. I had to keep making detours and that took extra time."

"Oh, darling, was it completely awful?"

"It wasn't all that bad. Some of our lads are putting up quite a fight, and the Nips are barely moving forward."

"Oh, William, does that mean that Singapore will be saved?"

"I don't really know for sure, my darling. We are fighting a defensive battle wherever I go. And, the Nips are quite determined. If we don't get some help soon, it just might be too late."

"I shutter to think of what would happen then," Pail Lin sighed. "It would be the end for all of us."

"I didn't come home to think about those things," Elliott squeezed her again. "I came to be with you on Christmas and have a wonderful meal and open our presents. Afterwards, we can make passionate love for many hours."

"Silly, you know there are no presents. I didn't even know you were coming. I can make you a wonderful dinner though, and then we *can* make love all night."

"If you insist, my darling. I never deny anyone a Christmas wish." He kissed her again and held her tightly.

"*You* are my Christmas present," she whispered into his ear. "The best one I have ever had." Another tear started down her cheek as she spoke. They held each other without moving for what seemed like an eternity.

THE CHRISTMAS MEAL—FEATURING A CORNISH HEN—WENT OFF without a hitch, and the lovemaking that followed was as enjoyable as she had ever experienced. Pail Lin was completely spent and stared upwardly as she lay next to Elliott in the nearly soundless dark. A drizzle provided a weak, dripping sound somewhere outside the bungalow's bedroom window and the ever-present thump of the ceiling fan in the hallway provided a relatively pleasant flow of air throughout the entire house.

Pai Lin turned and looked over at Elliott whose eyes were closed. His breathing was even and seemingly restful.

"Are you awake, darling?" she asked softly.

"Yes, my love. I'm just resting a bit."

"William, I have been thinking about something. I need to talk to you about it."

"Right now? We are both quite tired, at least I am."

"I am, too, but this is really important."

Sensing her urgency, Elliott replied, "Okay, I'm listening."

"It's about the Japanese," Pai Lin said slowly. "I'm really worried."

"I would think you have a right to be, the situation is really serious."

"I know it is. I have heard all the local bravado about stopping them and sending them back with their heads between their tails, but I don't think that's the way it is at all. I listen to Radio Singapore and I don't think they are telling us all of the story."

Elliott was happy she had been able to glean that out of the chaos surrounding them, and stroked her hair as he spoke.

"You are quite correct in your thinking," he answered her, almost matter of factly. "The truth is, we are having one helluva time containing them and have reverted to falling back to defensive positions throughout Malaya. If we don't get reinforcements soon, we will be pushed back onto Singapore itself, and the end will be near."

The two lay there practically motionless, the dire nature of his words sinking in with each passing moment.

"What will happen to my patients if the Japanese overrun us?" Pail Lin asked, her voice barely audible.

"I don't have any idea about that, but I can't believe the Japanese would be all that vindictive toward children."

"That's if any of us are left alive to care for them," Pai Lin added.

"Good point, but you must think of the positive. It's totally unproductive to dwell on the negative of a situation."

"There you go with that British thing, keep a stiff upper lip and all that. I'm really worried. A lot of my patients can't really go anywhere, and we are getting more and more every day. My ward is almost filled up, and it's never been that way before."

"Let me think about it for a bit, maybe I can come up with something."

"Could you, William? That would be simply marvelous."

"I just said I would think about it, that's all. I'll do what I can."

I had better get back to Chan and make sure everything is all set before I tell her about my plan. It wouldn't do to raise her hopes and build up her expectations. I'll try and reach him tomorrow if I can.

"That would do splendidly," Pai Lin cooed, feeling suddenly animated. "I know you will come up with something. Now, how about that all-night lovemaking that you're so well known for?" She smiled and came toward him. She opened her mouth and kissed him deeply as she moved her body on top of his. She took his arms and extended them outward.

Elliott knew it was useless to resist.

December 26, 1941, Sime Road Headquarters, Malaya Command, Singapore, 2330 hrs

Boxing Day, the traditional day many British subjects use for delivering presents to less fortunate acquaintances, fell on a Saturday this year, but its existence had little or no consequence on Maj. Gen. Arthur E. Percival, GOC Malaya. The fact that it was also his 54th birthday seemed inconsequential to the exhausted and disheartened career British army officer who dutifully accepted a few, informal good wishes from his staff throughout the day. Feeling himself in immediate need of sleep, he had decided to turn in a bit earlier than usual just before midnight, when the sound of the shrill doorbell to his quarters broke the night's prevailing silence.

He approached the door and opened it. One the doorstep stood Brigadier Ivan Simson, chief engineer of his Malaya command.

"What is it, Brigadier? It is late and I was about to try and get some sleep."

"Sorry, General, but I have just returned from a meeting with General Heath in Ipoh and was asked by the general to have a meeting with you as quickly as possible. I am reporting late due to the fact that there were two air raids along the way and during one of the bombings a Japanese bomb disabled my car. Under ordinary circumstances, I would have been here hours earlier."

Percival immediately regretted his opening remark and answered, "All right, man, if it's that god-awfully important, I guess you had better come in."

Simson entered the quarters and sat down in a covered armchair. Percival chose his favorite seat in his quarters, a Victorian couch to Simson's right. He sat and crossed his long legs.

"Now then, Brigadier, what's all this you have to share with me?"

"Sir, I had an extensive meeting with General Heath and he gave me this message for you." He handed a two-page document to Percival.

"If you prefer, I can summarize both the general's and my own feelings."

"Why don't you do that, Brigadier, it might save us some time."

"Right. Well, Sir, we both feel strongly that it is time to consider the construction of some fixed defences in Johore that can really do our lads who are fighting the battles some real good. General Heath says it is becoming nearly impossible for his troops to be expected to dig defences all day and most of the night and then attempt to repel the Japanese and their heavy armor immediately thereafter.

I know you are keenly aware of the beating the 11th Indian Division had taken so far, and the fact that Sir Lewis has so many inexperienced troops within his ranks. I personally think he has done a masterful job of retreating given the incredible fact that he has had little or no true defences to aid him in his effort.

We also both agree that it seems that time is becoming precious with regard to the actual defence of Johore, not to mention that of Singapore itself."

Percival listened passively, and fought an ongoing urge to yawn.

I cannot believe how tired I am at this moment. Maybe this is all starting to get to me, it seems as if I have had this conversation before in another time and place. Please don't let me yawn; it would be painfully embarrassing to me, not to mention Brigadier Simson.

Simson continued, attempting to follow the key components of the message he had helped General Heath draft earlier that day.

"General, I believe I was sent here to Malaya for the express purpose of creating such a defence works that was considered a necessity by the war office almost a year ago. I have more than sixty-five hundred engineers who can still make a difference. In a matter of a few weeks, we can make it quite difficult for the Nips to break through, even with their assortment of tanks and heavy artillery.

What Sir Lewis and I are asking is that I be given a chance to do what I do best, build some real defences for our troops before it is too late."

Percival pondered the last words and turned his head away from Simson. He thought some more and eventually returned his attention to his subordinate.

"Let me put it simply, Brigadier, I am of the opinion that defences are bad for morale . . . for both troops and civilians alike. When our troops see large-scale defence works being prepared, they become hesitant to go on the attack.

My position has always been that the best defence is a good offense, and I don't think I'll be changing my perception in the near future. I know Sir Lewis and his troops are tired and a bit shaken, but, in fact, they are learning to be soldiers as we speak. You cannot tell me that those troops of his have not grown up a great deal in the past three weeks. They are learning how to fight and will eventually be able to gain an upper hand."

"With all due respect, Sir, " Simons interrupted, his voice rising and becoming more agitated. "The 11th looks like a pack of whipped dogs at this point. Their morale is incredibly good considering what they have been through. Their problem is purely physical, they have been asked to work beyond their capabilities. They dig all these trenches and prepare to fight, and the Japanese appear so quickly that they are forced to abandon the defences they have spent all night preparing. It is simply ludicrous. Until we prepare a fixed set of defenses that are constructed by military experts, we are wasting their time and their lives. I cannot stand by and watch this carnage any further."

"Brigadier, you will control yourself," Percival shot back, now fully awake. "These decisions you ask are my responsibility and mine alone. Your job as chief engineer is to implement what I and my staff feel is best for everyone concerned. Do you understand?"

Simson fought the urge to shout, but controlled his increasing anger.

"Certainly I know my role, General, all that I am asking is to be put in a place to fulfill my position and utilize the men under my command.

I simply cannot believe that you can't see the reasoning behind Sir Lewis's request. You must give some credibility to your commanders in the field who are under direct fire."

Percival took immediate affront to the back-handed jab by Simson.

"I have proven myself many times under fire, Brigadier. My military career is well documented. I don't need an engineer to tell me how to act under fire or anytime else for that matter."

Simson sensed he was nearing a dangerous crossroad in the conversation. He attempted to appeal to his superior from another viewpoint.

"General, I am of the opinion that a fortress such as Singapore without a defence is a contradiction in terms. I know our position is secure from the sea, but our backside is badly exposed. I just don't want us to wind up in a position with no alternatives. I hope you can see that."

Percival considered the statement and replied.

"I appreciate your position, Brigadier, and I realize that we are all under severe strain at this time. What you don't know is that I am expecting troops to help our positions and reinforce our divisions that have been weakened thus far. We still have a great number of troops on Singapore itself and some of my staff and the colonial office still feel that the Japanese will stop short of actually invading Singapore. The feeling is that the Japs will have made their statement in occupying Malaya and will not risk losing their entire army to take the island from a vastly superior force. I must say that I partially concur with this thinking."

Simson sighed deeply as the blood rushed to his head.

"I cannot agree with you one bit, Sir, it simply doesn't make any sense. Why would they spend all the time and planning to waltz through Malaya and then stop at the doorway to Singapore? If we haven't been able to impede them on one single occasion since they began their invasion, what would happen all of a sudden for us to be able to stop them?"

Now it was Percival's time to explode.

"Such talk is defeatist, Brigadier, please be careful with the direction this is all heading."

"I'm not being a defeatist, General. I am simply speaking realistically. All I am asking is for a chance to do something that might conceivably help our forces contain an enemy who has built up a great deal of momentum in a very short time."

"Again I must call your attention to the fact that it is *my* decision, Brigadier, and I just can't make myself believe it is the best course of action for everyone involved. I will, however, give you the authority to take up the matter of north shore defence with General Simmons, the fortress commander. If he is receptive to your ideas, I will be willing to revisit the subject at a later date."

Simson shrugged and lowered his head as Percival's words sank in. He knew that further talk with the GOC was practically useless and that a great number of British soldiers and civilians were now at an even greater risk than ever before.

He didn't have the heart to attempt to call Sir Lewis Heath and tell him of the meeting at this time of the night.

The bad news could wait until the following morning.

December 30, 1941, Rajah Game Preserve off Sardhana Road, Meerut, Uttar Pradesh State, India, 1120 hours

The favorite pastime of British Army officers in India was something called pig sticking, or, boar sticking to be more polite. In it, British officers pursue a wild boar on horseback and attempt to eventually kill the animal with thrusts from their specially-sharpened sabers.

The pig sticking was thought of as great sport due to the fact that the enraged wild boar was considered a desperate fighter, and its ultimate demise required a great deal of horsemanship and tenacity on the part of the rider.

It was in this bucolic setting that Gen. Sir Archibald Percival Wavell, commander in chief of the Indian army found himself just before noon on a sunny Tuesday morning just outside the city of Meerut, in India's northern state of Uttar Pradesh.

The group of officers was just beginning to remount when a messenger from Wavell's headquarters found their location. He saluted and handed a telegram to Wavell.

Wavell tore open the envelope and began reading its contents. To his surprise, the telegram was from Wavell's old friend, Prime Minister Winston Churchill.

The group of officers waited as Wavell finished reading the message. At last, he turned and remarked, "Sorry lads, it seems as if my pig sticking is completed for the day."

The officers waited, until one finally asked, "Was it good news, General?"

Wavell thought for a moment and commented, "Hard to say what it is right now. It's from the PM and he had just appointed me head of something called the AMDA with responsibility for most of this part of the world."

"Good show, General, he knows you are the right man for the job," another of the officers offered.

"Right," Wavell countered. " I'll share this last part with all of you. It says 'Everyone knows how dark and difficult the situation is.' I think the PM might have understated everything a bit. From what I am hearing about Malaya, the situation is most critical.

I suspect I will be going there in the very near future, of that there's little doubt. Anyway, that's it for me around here right now, old chaps. It's been a fun morning."

He handed the reins of his horse to a lieutenant colonel who stood next to him and started to walk away. The remaining officers remained silent until he had departed.

January 2, 1942, Singapore Railway Station, Singapore, 0130 hours

The puffing steam engine and its following of assorted passenger cars of the Federated Malay States Railroad moved almost quietly into the ramp area of Singapore's Tanjong Pagar Railway Station at 30 Keppel Road. Its trip southward had been a problematic one, with frequent stops to attempt to accommodate its vastly overloaded compliment of passengers and military personnel.

As the Chinese engineer brought the giant monster to a stop, he wiped his brow and bowed to his chief stoker, an older Malay man, to suggest a job well done. The Malay man bowed slightly in return, acknowledging his fellow worker's genuine gesture of respect.

Three cars from the rear of the train, Charles Samuel tried to get his wife Vi to awaken from her sleep. When she first resisted his attempts, he decided to let her rest for a few more moments. After all, with the train as crowded as it was, it would take a good deal longer than usual to dismount the train. Even then, Samuel was unsure of exactly where he and Vi would go. They finally alighted and began walking through the beautiful art deco rooms of the station, also called the Keppel Road Station. The building seemed out of place to the displaced and exhausted Samuel, who glanced up at the enormous domed roof and silently wondered if it would survive the remainder of the war.

The trip from Penang to Singapore had lasted for more than two weeks and was most surely the ultimate trip from hell. As the train had crossed the Johore-Singapore Causeway more than an hour earlier, Charles Samuel had recalled the details of their trip with little effort.

All European residents had been directed to the Eastern and Oriental Hotel in George Town at half past six on the evening of the 15th of December, two days after he received the official call to evacuate at his offices.

He and Vi had taken the train down the hill from their home with little fanfare and were accompanied by many of their friends. Martial law was now in effect and few people ventured out into the streets. Vi had packed three suitcases and a small revelation case that held her personal items and some jewelry. Samuel also carried his leather brief case, which contained his papers and some important legal documents.

After several hours, an announcement was made and the group made its way to the riverfront jetty that served as Penang's ferry mooring. Once aboard, the ferry made its way to the mainland and off boarded near the railway station at Prai. Due to the problems with boarding and overcrowding, most of the Samuel's luggage was somehow misplaced or lost. The pair was left with what they were carrying, Vi's revelation case and his own briefcase. Luckily, Samuel had packed a good deal of cash with which to buy any additional supplies along the way.

By now, it was just past midnight and the crowd had grown extremely restless. Other refugees from further north brought chilling stories of impropriety by the invading Japanese and mostly unfounded stories of British defeats and blunders at the hands of their attackers.

Samuel weighed this new information and wisely decided to discount anything that could not proved to be based on fact.

The train finally arrived and the group boarded the cars that relief officials pointed out to them. The Samuels were assigned to a third-class carriage, the type usually occupied by lowest-paying passengers. The seats were all narrow and hardwood, and not at all suited to any degree of comfortable travel. The trip southward that night seemed endless to Charles Samuel. The train seemed to be barely making any progress due to a large number of indeterminable stops in the pitch black of the mild December night.

The train reached its next scheduled stop, Ipoh, just after ten o'clock the following morning. A series of air raids delayed the train's progress until the all clear sounded just after one o'clock in the afternoon. The train started its southeasterly trek again and was finally able to limp into the Kuala Lumpur Railway Station around five o'clock.

There was general mayhem as the crowd tried to step down from the train's passenger carriages. A civil official mounted a small platform and attempted to address the crowd with limited success. At last, a number in the crowd shouted "quiet" and the place fell silent.

"All of you here," the official began, "I ask that you pay close attention to what I have to say. We are only prepared to get you to this point in your journey; there simply wasn't enough time to do much else, given the circumstances of the Japanese surprise attacks.

Most of you are British citizens, and you know the British people's flair for rising to the occasion."

A low rumble greeted his last sentence.

"Anyway, there is a large British community here in Kuala Lumpur and they have been put on notice that you will be needing food and accommodations until our army and navy can put an end to this mess. Some of our military people are saying it won't take too long, and then you will all be able to return to your former homes and jobs."

A few scattered applauses and even a "hear, hear," rose from the back of the crowd.

"If you look beyond that fence, there," he pointed to a white-boarded fence almost fifty yards in the distance, "you can see a number of our friends and neighbors are already here. They are right past the Red Cross contingent on the left. They will try and assist you with what you need. Many will offer you their homes and their food. I know you would do the same for them.

I have no idea how long each of you will be here, but I hope for the best. Now, if you will please make your way to beyond the fence, you can all get started. I know many of you could use a good sleep tonight."

The interlude in Kuala Lumpur lasted a little less than two weeks.

When the city was bombed on the night of December 22, Charles Samuel knew he had better find another avenue of escape for he and his beloved wife.

By this time, an office to assist stranded refugees from Northern Malaysia had been established and Charles and Vi Samuel sought its help.

In a few days, a travel permit that allowed the couple to travel to Singapore was approved and, on either the 28th or 29th of December (Charles' memory was beginning to play tricks on him) they said farewell to the lovely couple that had befriended them with accommodations and boarded the train for Singapore. The friendly couple was truly moved by their new friends' plight and even brought them an assortment of pastries and foods for the trip south.`

Other than being unwearyingly slow and tedious, the train finally crept its way into the Keppel Road Railway Station with its exhausted crowd of passengers. The relatively short trip between Kuala Lumpur and Singapore had taken the better part of *four* days!

January 2, 1942, Headquarters No 101 Special Training Unit, Far East Combined Intelligence Bureau, Tanjong Balai, Singapore, 1120 hours

Eight days had passed since the two main factions of Chinese political forces in Singapore had agreed to bury the hatchet due to the impending invasion of Imperial Japanese forces against the Island of Singapore.

The historic meeting took place on Christmas Day 1941 and brought about the reconciliation of the Kuomintang—who were loyal to Chain Kai-shek—the Chinese Nationalists and the Chinese Communist Party that had heretofore been ostracized by all other Chinese political parties.

The intention was to raise an immediate defense force of between one thousand and three thousand soldiers to take an active part in the defense of Singapore.

Prior to the Christmas Day accord, the British colony government had been hesitant about potentially arming any of the nearly two million Chinese in Malaya, many of whom also held Chinese citizenship despite being born in Malaya.

But, with their backs to the wall and facing an impending Japanese military avalanche, an agreement was reached to raise an all-volunteer Chinese force by the fastest means possible.

To lead this group, a former police commissioner from the eastern Malay state of Trengganu named John Dalley was selected and given the rank of lieutenant colonel.

When word of the accord was reached, literally thousands of high-spirited Chinese men showed up to enlist in the new force. The existing facilities of the specially-equipped 101 Training School—part of the Far East Combined Intelligence Bureau—was immediately taken over by the officers and men of this new unit. Since the two-story bungalow in Tanjong Balai was originally intended to train potential guerillas for use in various areas of Southeast Asia, it was ideal for the needs of the new Chinese volunteers.

Even though he had little actual military background, Dalley was a sensible leader who treated his men with respect and civility. He won immediate admiration from practically everyone involved and set about to train his men as quickly as possible. It was intended that some of these irregular troops be trained as saboteurs and dropped behind Japanese lines to cause commotion and problems in the form of a guerrilla action.

It was in the small room that now served as his office that Lieutenant Colonel Dalley received his visitor, Brigadier Ivan Lyon. Lyon had recently escaped the Japanese bombing and invasion of Penang, and had been temporarily assigned to act as a military advisor to the Chinese recruits.

The two men had already started talking when the door opened after a quick knock.

A pair of special operations executive operatives, the parent organization of the Far East Combined Intelligence Bureau, walked into the room.

"Gentlemen," Dalley rose, extending his hand, "I'd like you to meet Brigadier Lyon. He's been assigned to help us and with his first-hand knowledge of the Japanese and their tactics, I think he will be very valuable to us."

The two men introduced themselves as Richard Broome and John Davis.

The men seated themselves and Brigadier Lyon spoke.

"I understand from Colonel Dalley that you two have been busy setting up some secret supply dumps between Singapore and Johore for our men to use. How is that entire coming project coming? Will they be ready for us to use in the immediate future?"

"Quite," John Davis answered. "In fact, some are already in place and the others will be ready in a day or two. I think we will be able to meet the proposed schedule. I just hope it's not too late already."

Dalley spoke up before Brigadier Lyon could respond.

"Brigadier, there is a feeling here and among a number of the British army staff, that the Japanese are simply coming too fast for anyone or anything to do much good. I'm almost inclined to agree. Our weapons arrived a day or two ago and we have practically no ammunition to speak of. Right now, there are not a total of ten thousand rounds for my entire force, and that's only eight or ten bullets per soldier. We haven't even had enough ammunition to practice firing with and there's no telling what will happen if we are ever put into the battle line."

Lyon made a note on his pad and returned his glaze to Dalley. He tried to sound reassuring. "I'm sure there is more ammunition coming, it simply hasn't reached you so far. I'll make an attempt to find out more when I return to Fort Canning."

Dalley returned a worried smile as John Davis spoke again.

"We must look at the brighter side. The morale in our troops is sky high; these men really want a piece of the Japanese for what they have done to China for the past few years. I really wasn't aware of the magnitude of their hatred for the Japanese until I saw it this week. Many of them would go out and fight the Japanese with their hands if they were given the opportunity."

Men with bare hands rarely defeat well-armed soldiers," Lyon reminded the others. "I would prefer that they have the same equipment and chances as our own men."

"They are our *own* men, Brigadier, even if their ancestry is a bit divergent," Dalley replied. "And it's up to us to make them a really viable unit in the time we have allotted."

"Understood, I'll do all within my power to see that you get more guns and a great deal more ammunition."

"One more thing, Brigadier." This time it was Richard Broome speaking.

"The men have gotten together and decided we needed a name. They respect Colonel Dalley and are now calling our unit Dalforce for short. Among themselves, they call each other Dalley's Desperadoes, but I think Dalforce is better for the outside world. We'd all appreciate it if you would spread the word around Fort Canning and elsewhere."

"Consider it done. It's got a nice ring to it and is easy to remember."

"Thank you, Brigadier," Dalley concluded. "I think we are about done anyway."

"I agree, Colonel, and I want to wish very good luck to you and your brave men."

"We'll need all of that we can muster," Dalley replied, "and maybe more."

The men stood as Brigadier Lyon stood up and walked to the door to leave the office.

When he had gone, Dalley motioned to Davis and Broome to sit and spoke again.

"Now, gentlemen, let's have your list of where your supply spots are. I have just received orders to start infiltrating at the earliest possible time and that means today or tomorrow."

Davis and Broome looked at each other and reached for the tablet on Dalley's desk.

It would only take a minute to write out the details.

January 7, 1942, 42nd Infantry Regiment, Japanese Imperial Army, about twelve miles northwest of Slim River Bridge, 0600 hours

It was considered a great honor for the 42nd Infantry Regiment to be selected to lead the Japanese charge to capture the important series of bridges that crossed the Slim River in northwestern Malaya. The 42nd Regiment was also called the Ando Regiment in honor of its intrepid commanding officer, Col. Tadao Ando. The regiment had previously distinguished itself in the China Incident by being the first Japanese regiment to break through the fabled Great Wall of China. It had also shown incredible early success in Malaya.

As the signal was given to start operations, a platoon of leading Type 95 *Ha Go* tanks under the command of Second Lt. Sadanobu Watanabe, took the lead. Watanabe was a recent graduate of the Japanese Military Academy, who was now considered a seasoned leader after battling British positions for the last month.

The British had set a number of wire entanglements that the Type 95 *Ha Gos* were easily able to trample. Next came a formidable British artillery barrage that stopped the advance for a few moments. Pressing through the shelling, Watanabe reached his first objective, a white concrete bridge on the road ahead that appeared still intact. The British infantry units provided an incessant stream of fire from pillboxes located in the nearby rubber plantations.

As Watanabe peered through the small frontal opening of his *Ha Go*, he saw that explosives had been placed on one of the supporting piers of the bridge. Watanabe quickly jerked the turret cover off his *Ha Go*, and jumped to the ground. He dodged a hail of bullets that were now directed at him and reached the explosives. He quickly pulled his saber from its sheath and cut the wire to the charge.

At the same moment, a British soldier charged toward Watanabe from the other side of the bridge, grenade in hand. He covered about three-quarters of the distance before he was cut down by a shot fired by another military academy graduate and classmate of Watanabe's, Second Lieutenant Morokuma, who had charge of a platoon of infantry.

Watanabe bowed towards his friend and quickly jumped back aboard the *Ha Go* and urged the attack forward. The ten tanks in his platoon crossed the bridge and continued southward. At length they crossed a second, third and fourth bridge. The retreating British forces had failed to demolish any of these important bridges. During one of these shorter encounters, machine gun fire had somehow found its way into Watanabe's tank and injured his sword hand.

At a fifth bridge, Watanabe found another unanticipated problem. This time the bridge had been heavily mined, with charges that were directly visible from his turret. He also was able to clearly see the electrical wires that connected the charges.

Using his tank's 7.7mm machine guns, he fired at the wires until he successfully cut them, rendering the explosive charges useless. He signaled to his other tanks and continued the charge across the sixty-yard bridge. In one fell swoop, he had led his tanks almost six miles into the midst of the British positions.

The fighting raged for another twelve hours and resulted in the first decisive battle for control of Malaya.

Almost three thousand British troops were taken prisoner in the Slim River action and the Japanese seized scores of trucks, artillery and ammunition.

The Battle of Slim River was the beginning of the end of the British defense of Malaya.

January 28, 1942, Singapore Naval Base Officer's Dining Hall, Singapore, 1410 hours

The message that had been drafted by Rear Adm. Ernest J. "Jackie" Spooner, the commander-in-chief of the Singapore Naval Base, was direct and to the point. He fingered the one-page document as he waited for silence among his assembled military and civilian staff in the base's large officer's mess.

When the room became silent, he began speaking.

"Men, it gives me no pleasure to have to say these following things to you, in fact, it actually breaks my heart. You are all no doubt acquainted with the rumors and insinuations that have been rampant concerning the Japanese army's success against our forces in Malaya. I am sorry to tell you that most of these reports are true."

Loud grumbles swept across the crowded room.

Spooner waited for a moment and continued.

"The Japanese have executed a swift and deadly invasion that has virtually assured them of victory and our own forces have been powerless to stop them. I have felt all along that their eventual goal was the occupation of our Singapore Naval Base and our vast store of rubber and tin, along with our equipment and facilities.

I must tell you that most of our remaining aircraft have also been directed to fields where they can live to fight the Nips on another day. This means we are practically defenseless here at the naval base.

For that reason, I am ordering all of you, both military and civilian, to vacate the naval base at once, and report to Singapore City. Right now, we are scheduled to be sent to Ceylon where we can do some good for ourselves and for our country.

Remember, men, this war had just begun and the heart of the British Lion is stout indeed!"

A number of men in the audience applauded.

"Men, we have but two days to get off the island, the forecast is that serious. I want you all to go home and get what little you can carry and then get down to Singapore City. Your families, if they are still here, can come with you.

The place for our rendezvous had not been fixed as yet so I will tell you to go first to Government House. Someone there will redirect you to the proper meeting spot.

I wish you all good luck and God's speed. God bless the King."

From around the room, a chorus of "God Bless the King" resounded.

January 30, 1942, just above Johore Causeway connecting Johore Bahru to Singapore Island, 2320 hours

For some unexplained reason, Royal Australian Maj. John William Caldwell Wyett of the 2nd Australian Imperial Force had felt uneasy about the planned demolition of the Johore Causeway, as ordered by Maj. Gen. Gordon Bennett. Wyett wondered if it was because he was tired of seeing bridges blown up prematurely in the British retreat through Malaya, but decided there were also other plausible explanations. Those demolition actions had resulted in cutting off a number of retreating British Indian army units as well as some of his own AIF troops, many of whom had been forced to surrender to the Japanese.

On each succeeding occasion, Wyett had promised himself to make sure it would not happen again, but the reality of the situation was that there was really little he could do as a staff officer. The information usually came to him as the demolitions were taking place or after they had occurred, much too late to do anything in the way of prevention.

This time, the demolition of the Johore-Singapore Causeway was different. Opened first in 1923, the span was the only link to Singapore from the Malayan Peninsula. Since the causeway was the *only* exodus road for all British military units, a certain degree of pre-planning had taken place that Major John Wyett was fortunately privy to. His sixth sense told him that it would be wise to investigate the situation further, if nothing more than to ease his mind that no more British military units would inadvertently be cut off.

He had sat in on the briefing, which resulted in the decision as to how to blow the causeway to prevent its use by the Japanese, but the exact time of the demolition was left to the dictates of specific events as they unfolded. Later that same day, Wyett was apprised of the withdrawal schedule of a number of units from various sectors of the Johore fighting area—they would need to cross the causeway to reach the relative safety of Singapore Island. He made a mental note to check on the status of these units as the day wore on, since there were significant numbers of men and equipment involved, not to mention a large supply of ammunition that was also scheduled to be moved south for use in Singapore.

Due to numerous interruptions, it was approaching midnight before Wyett was able to make his way onto the southern entrance of the causeway. A number of sentries placed strategically along the causeway observed his movement as he approached the main demolition site just north of the center of the long bridge.

Wyett looked at the significant amount of charges that had been set and wondered what their effect would be on the structure. Judging from the sheer number and distribution pattern of the charges, Wyett was confident the entire structure would be rendered useless for a long time to come. His curiosity got the best of him and he wandered north toward the bascule bridge that allowed boats to pass under when it was raised.

He could see a few men from a Fortress Command sapper detachment that was just finishing placing the charges on that part of the bridge.

He sought out the person in command of the demolition operation and was referred to a sergeant. The man turned his attention to Wyett and saluted.

"Evenin,' Major, what can I do for you?"

"What time have 'ya set to blow everything up here, Sergeant?" Wyett inquired casually.

"My orders say midnight, and midnight it will be, Sir."

Wyett looked at his watch in the near dark and was astounded to see it was already nearing the appointed hour.

"That will not be possible, Sergeant," Wyett replied forcefully. "I know for a fact that some of our lads, actually a good number of them, can't possibly be here by midnight. Even if they encounter no resistance, they would still need at least two more hours to make it here to the causeway. By the time they all get across, it could take another two or three hours. You must delay the demolition until they have all reached safety."

The hardened sergeant looked toward the ground and slowly raised his eyes.

"Meanin' no disrespect, Sir, but my orders say to blow the bridge at midnight and that's what I intend to do."

"Now see here, Sergeant," Wyett raised his voice, attempting to control the situation, "we both know it's perfectly acceptable to change the bleedin' time of the demolition if the course of action dictates it would be best for all involved. I'm telling 'ya that thousands of our troops will be cut off if you blow it at midnight. If that happens they will probably all fall into the hands of the Japanese. 'Ya don't want that to happen, do ya?"

The sergeant thought for a moment and raised his chin again.

"Orders are orders, Sir. I intend to carry them out."

"All right, I'll give you an order if that's what you want. You will *not* attempt to carry out this demolition until I say so.'

"I'm not about to take any orders from any blinkin' Australian," the sergeant shot back. "You can take your order and shove it right up your arse."

Wyett saw that a stronger course of action was needed, sooner than later.

He calmly drew his Enfield #2 Mk 1 .38-calibre service revolver and pointed the gun directly at the sergeant's head about two feet away.

The sergeant's eyes widened as he looked directly into the barrel of the handgun and then back into Wyett's unyielding gaze.

Wyett spoke again, this time more evenly.

"If you make any attempt to blow that fuckin' bridge before I say so, I am going to blow your bloody head off. Is that perfectly clear?"

The sergeant backed down and shook his head. He shrugged and walked back to where his men were still working. Major Wyett returned the pistol to its holster and continued walking across the causeway to the Johore Bahru side where a British military unit had just arrived. Wyett quickly identified them as the remnants of the Argyll and Sutherland Highlanders that had finally made its way to the causeway's entrance.

The Argyll's leader, recently promoted Brigadier Ian Stewart, approached Wyett and was informed of the earlier confrontation on the bridge. Stewart took the news in good spirits and decided to place a guard at the demolition site to insure the bridge's safety. He sent a detachment to the bascule bridge section of the causeway with strict orders to keep an eye on the demolitions team.

Stewart also informed Wyett of his intention to be the last unit across the causeway.

Wyett again glanced at his watch. It was exactly midnight as the two hands stretched together. January 31st was already creeping out as he sat down alongside one of the Argyll's parked armoured cars.

He would try and grab a quick nap before the arrival of the AIF troops.

THE SOUNDS OF HEAVY MOTORS AND SHOUTING BROKE HIS BRIEF respite almost two hours later. Major John Wyett rubbed his eyes and rose to see the approaching column of trucks and troops approaching out of the semi-darkness with headlights filtered. Some of the Argylls rose to greet their comrades and welcome them to their circumstantial meeting spot. The moon flickered in and out of the cloudy night and gave the entire scene a feeling of macabre intensity.

Wyett approached the lead vehicle and waved it through after insuring it was indeed the unit he was expecting. There was not a moment to loose since the antsy demolitions team was waiting nearby with their fingers on the charges.

He tried to count the vehicles and troops as they passed in front of him, but soon found he was much too tired to keep an accurate count. He made a mental note to contact the forward mustering point and get some accurate numbers that he could pass along to the AIF staff. With the incredible pace of the British retreat, Wyett was sure that most of the troop strength numbers were completely erroneous and of little value to the staff. He hoped the AIF forces could stop long enough to count themselves.

Two hours later, the last of the vehicles were passing when one of the lorries pulled to a stop. A figure in khaki jumped out of the back and approached Wyett.

Wyett glanced at the man, who appeared familiar to him. The man approached and extended his hand.

"John Wyett, it's nice to see you again."

Suddenly Wyett recalled the somewhat familiar face and circumstance of their former meeting.

"Why it's our bleedin' Kiwi preacher," he exclaimed in his slanted New Zealand accent, still unsure of the man's presence in front of the causeway.

"Well, it is me, but I'm not really a Kiwi at all," responded Elliott. "That's what I wanted to explain to you. When the lorry rounded that last bend and I saw you standing here, I knew I had to stop and explain."

Wyett was completely taken back, but remained silent. From the direction of the Argylls, another officer approached.

He looked closely at Elliott and exclaimed, "It is you, isn't it. I thought I recognized you but the light was so bad."

"Yes, Lieutenant, It's me all right," Elliott answered in surprise, "nice to see you again."

"What are you doin here?" Lt. Gordon Schiach asked. "This is one dangerous place to be."

"I was just going to explain that to the major here," Elliott responded. "Now I can tell you both.

I'm actually a lieutenant in the Royal Navy. My name is William Elliott and I was assigned to gather some information on different allied units' morale and attitudes," Elliott explained. "The Brigadier I work for needed to know that he could count on different units for certain things. In the case of your forces, Major, it was his idea to dress me up as a minister, since he didn't think you would all be comfortable with me in my Royal Navy uniform."

Wyett digested what he had just heard and confronted Elliott.

"It takes a lot of balls to do something like you did, mate, and even more guts to stop now and tell me about it. We have all really taken a bloody, great beating since we last met and have probably learned a lot about life and its little eccentricities, know what I mean?"

Lieutenant Schiach added his agreement with a nod of his head, as did Elliott

Wyatt continued. "I guess your brigadier did what he thought best and I hope your input helped 'im with whatever he needed. Too late now to cry over spilled milk, now we are all fightin' for our lives."

All three officers turned as the high pitch sounds of bagpipes emanated from the grassy knoll that held the Argyll and Sutherland Highlanders. In another minute, the soulful sounds of '*Hielan Laddie*' pierced the humid and breezy night.

"The Scots do it in style every time," Wyett offered, impressed with the battered battalion's bearing and pride as they began their spirited march across the causeway to Singapore. "They march like they just got off the boat."

Lieutenant Schiach seized the chance to speak. "We are part of a grand old tradition, Major, and we are among the best fighters in the entire British army. I'm not sure just how many Japanese soldiers have joined their ancestors fighting the Argyles for the past six weeks, but I know it's significant."

"I must agree with you, Lieutenant," Wyett approved. "I've always enjoyed watching you people march into action."

"We won't see much more real action with what's left of us—there can't be more than a couple of hundred total that are actually alive and able to fight."

"You might be out of action for a while, but I met your commander and he will be back in the thick of it as soon as he can," Wyett added. "Now, Mister Elliott, would you be interested in a ride back to Singapore with a lowly AIF staff major? I just happen to have a jeep and room for one more."

"It would be an unexpected pleasure, Major Wyett. I would love to get to know you better under different circumstances. You Aussies are actually great fighters in your own right."

"That's what General Bennett has been saying for the past eight months," Wyett smiled.

"I'm delighted the British have finally taken note."

"I'll pass it along even further, and, in the right sort of places."

"I certainly hope so," Wyett joked, throwing his leg into the jeep. "Wouldn't do a bit to have it in the *wrong* places."

Elliott shook hands with Gordon Schiach as the last remnants of the Argylls passed toward the causeway entrance.

"Best of luck, old chap," Elliott offered.

"Good seeing you, too, best of luck yourself," Schiach answered and departed to rejoin his unit.

Elliott climbed aboard the jeep as the vehicle's engine slowly coughed its way into life. The crucial ride back to Singapore wouldn't take all that long to complete.

February 8, 1942, Imperial Palace Tower of the Sultan of Johore, Johore Bahru, Malaya 1200 hours

It had been a difficult decision, but Lt. Gen. Tomoyuki Yamashita, commander of the 25th Imperial Japanese Army was hopeful his instincts would prove correct. Over the objections of several staff members, he had chosen to occupy the luxurious *Istana Hijau* or Green Palace that was built by the Sultan of Johore without regard to cost some years before.

The palace, or more precisely, the palace's imposing tower, offered an uninterrupted view of the northern extremities of Singapore and therefore, an exceptional opportunity to watch the upcoming invasion. It was also true that the tower was in easy range of British artillery, but Yamashita was convinced the political aspects of the British firing artillery shells on the Sultan of Johore's Imperial Palace far outweighed any chances of his being hit should the shelling ever begin.

It was exactly the noon hour when he finally peered out of the tinted windows at the vastness of the Island of Singapore. Stray rounds had hit the large glass panels and damaged a number of the windows.

"The view here is even better than I could have imagined," Yamashita intoned to Lt. Gen. Osamu Tsukada, the visiting chief of staff of the Imperial Japanese Southern Army who had joined him at the large windows. "It makes one humble to see such grandeur."

"Yes, it does, Yamashita, it makes one wonder what it will be like after the conquest," Tsukada replied.

"It will not change much, the scars of war are easy to heal in an equatorial setting. Nature takes care of itself. Whatever we destroy, nature will replace in a few months."

"Yes," Tsukada agreed. "For that we can thank the gods."

Yamashita did not reply, and was deep in thought.

Tsukada noted the commander's edgy silence and eventually asked a question.

"How long do you think the actual invasion and conquest will take? I know you had hoped to have the fortress under our control for *Kigensetsu* (the anniversary date for the founding of the empire of Japan) as a present to our emperor, but that occurs in only three days. I hope the extensive notes I brought with me have been a help to you in making your decisions for the invasions."

Yamashita considered the statement for a moment and answered.

"I do not think three days will be enough, it will probably take a week or even longer. The British have too many men and our own supplies are limited. I hope to be able to capture additional British stores and thereby resupply our men and equipment. We have done that throughout our invasion because the British have been unable to cope with the speed of our troops.

As far as your staff notes are concerned, I looked them over and discarded them as irrelevant. Do not feel bad, for it is difficult to know the needs of an actual battle commander from as far away as Saigon.

Tsukada gasped, not believing what he had just heard. He chose not to respond.

"The news you bring does not help either, and I don't mind telling you that in an official manner." Yamashita's tone had taken on glacial insinuations.

"The troops and aircraft are needed elsewhere," Tsukada replied defensively, referring to the soon-to-be departure of the Imperial Guards Division and the 18th Division, along with a major part of the 3rd Air Group. "Besides, your invasion is proceeding very well and according to plan. You can't really tell me you are worried about the loss of a few troops."

"A few troops?" Yamashita shot back. "You take some of my best fighters and most of my air support just as the deciding battle of the campaign is about to begin. We are starting to run short on food and ammunition ourselves and it is taking our artillery too long to get into correct position. From your perspective, just *who* will be responsible should Singapore not capitulate on schedule."

"You will find a way to make it happen, Yamashita. That's why you were chosen to lead the 25th Army in the first place."

Yamashita wanted to reply but found the strength to hold his tongue. Besides, Tsukada was probably just following orders in spite of his arrogant attitude. There was no point in throwing more fuel on the burning fire, so Yamashita decided to hold his tongue.

"I must be leaving right after lunch, Yamashita. I am needed back in Saigon. There are other operations besides yours that require attention."

"*Hai,*" Yamashita replied, glancing over Tsukada's shoulder.

Yamashita's orderly had just entered the room to signal the beginning of lunch. The invasion of Singapore could wait for at least another hour.

February 9, 1942, Pediatric Wing, General Hospital, Singapore, 1150 hours

The rising swell of patients had forced the doctors and staff of Singapore's General Hospital into near desperate disarray. The neat rows of beds and supplies had given way to portable beds and floor mats that now occupied every square inch of the pediatric wing, as well as every other section of usable space in the large hospital.

Dr. Pai Lin Song had fought a losing batter with the hospital's administrator to keep the rooms entirely filled with children, but at this point she admitted that she no longer cared that much about who would occupy empty beds. There were no unfilled beds and no more room to put any wounded, adults or children.

Pai Lin stood over the bed of a pair of children, a brother and sister about eight years old who had both been wounded in recent Japanese bombings. Shrapnel had torn through their tiny bodies and seemingly endless amounts of bandages had been applied in an effort to stop the bleeding. Since they were related and space was at an absolute premium, it was felt that it was okay to allow the pair to share a bed for the time being.

Pai Lin checked the charts and felt the bandages. Both youngsters were dry indicating the bleeding had stopped, at least for the moment. She sighed, and replaced the chart on the foot of the bed. She turned around to see Lt. William Elliott standing behind her.

"What?" she started as he put his hand to her lips. "I didn't know you were coming."

"Thought I would surprise you, my dear. Isn't that allowed anymore?"

"I can't say for sure what is or is not allowed, I don't even know what day it is," Pai Lin replied. "I haven't been out of here for days."

"For your information, today is Tuesday, February 9th, not that it makes much difference. I just got back myself from trying to help clear up some of the messes with the refugees that are trying to leave Singapore. No one can believe how utterly insane everything has become."

"The hospital sent a number of nurses from here to the docks a couple of days ago, but I don't have any idea where they were going," she recalled. They were mostly European nurses and most really wanted to leave."

"I believe I saw some of them at the docks; I recognized their uniforms. But there's no telling what happened to them. Someone put Brigadier Simson in charge of the boarding documents for all the people, and it's been a nightmare since then. He asked me to help and I said I would. There was really nothing much for me to do other than grab a spare gun, so I thought I might be able to help out."

"I'm sure you did, my darling, you always make a difference no matter what you are doing."

"When was the last time you had any real sleep, Pai Lin?" Elliott asked, looking at the deep circles under her eyes. "Tell me the truth, when was it?"

"Oh, I don't know," she answered truthfully. "A day or two ago, what's the difference?"

"I'm not sure how long you can act on no sleep, that's all. It has to affect your performance."

"Act, smack," she replied testily. "With all these injuries, it is quite impossible to be completely professional about everything. Besides, it's just a matter of time according to the hospital's grapevine. From the shelling and stories around, it seems as if the Japanese are no more than a day or two away."

"Maybe a bit more than that," Elliott countered. "I think we can hold out a little longer."

"To what end?" she questioned, looking him squarely in the eyes. "And then, what happens to all my children? Do you honestly think they will be given any care?" She put her head down as if searching for an answer.

"That's why I came, Pai Lin, I just might have an idea. It all goes back to our talk around Christmas, don't you remember?"

Pai Lin looked up, searching his face for a clue as to what he was talking about. The strain and lack of sleep affected her powers of recollection.

"What can you do? The situation seems so hopeless. I have just about given up."

"We can never give up; it's not the British way of handling things."

"I'm not exactly British and I'll handle it any way I choose," she answered sharply. Realizing her shortness, she spoke again, much more softly. "I'm sorry, darling; I guess all this is getting to me. I... I have no idea . . ."

Elliott drew her closer and almost whispered. "It's all very simple, but it will require a great deal of luck if we are to be successful in this."

Pai Lin looked deeply into his eyes, feeling her own eyes beginning to well. "Go on, my love, you have my complete attention."

He smiled at her. "Right. You remember last summer when we went for the overnight to that little town above Johore."

"Yes," she replied, drawing from her memory. "It was all quite wonderful, almost like a dream. In fact, right now it seems as if it *was* a dream."

"Well, it wasn't a dream at all. And do you remember the restaurant near the coast were we had such wonderful seafood and met the local fishermen?"

"Yes, vaguely."

"And do you remember the one called Chan, who used to be a teacher here in Singapore?

"Chan, yes, that was his name. I do remember him."

"Well, it all came to me a couple of months ago, after I had a talk with Brigadier Simson.

He warned me of what could happen to Singapore and I thought about you and the children that you love so much. That's when I first thought of Chan. He might be someone who would be in a position to help. Since the place where he lives, Teluk Sengat, is sort of off the beaten tract, and probably wouldn't be involved in any Japanese invasion plans. I went to see him and feel him out about the chance of his being able to assist us.

Chan remembered us fondly and said that he would be honored to help in any way he could. He contacted a couple of other fishermen from the town to see if they could also help. The fact is that the locals there hate the Japanese as much as we do and they all agreed to help.

I managed to get word to him through one of our Straits Volunteer Units that was nearby him to let him know to put the plan that he and I worked out at that time into effect.

If it all works out, we might be able to get something going in a few days. I told him to aim for the night of the 13th, and he said that would work for him. Our plan will involve all of your children who can travel and enough nurses to see them to safety. It won't be easy, but it is entirely possible we can get them to safety."

Pai Lin looked at Elliott as a delighted smile filled her overwrought face.

It was the first time she had been able to do so in the past three weeks.

February 10, 1942, Headquarters 8th Australian Division AIF, north of Bukit Timah Village, Singapore, 2010 hours

In the opinion of Maj. Gen. H. Gordon Bennett, commander of the 8th Australian Division, little had gone right for him and his men for as long as he could recall during the past two months.

He now controlled a sizeable force that included his own to Australian Brigades, the 44th Indian Brigade, another battalion-sized group and the two companies of Chinese volunteers that were known by his men as Dalforce.

Thinking for a moment about the Chinese irregulars, he suddenly wished to himself that he had more of them. With no uniforms to speak of and inexcusably ill-equipped with a variety of weapons, the Chinese had shown themselves as marvelous fighters who were willing to die for their beliefs and their hatred of the invading Japanese. In the hand-to-hand fighting for Bukit Timor, first reports had reached him that the Chinese of Dalforce had been almost completely decimated.

Give me a couple of more thousand of these lil' Brownies and a month or two to train 'em and equip 'em, and I could easily stop the Nips. After all, with 'lil or no ammunition and in mostly hand-to-hand fighting, they 'ave already sent a large number of the emperor's sons to meet their maker. Too bad so many of 'em were killed in doin' so.

Bennett's thoughts returned to the present and the almost unsurmountable problems that faced him.

He admitted that the present situation he faced was becoming out of control, and there was very little he could do about it. It was the first time in his military career that he couldn't realistically come up with a solution to his problem.

The Japanese army's onslaught was so tenacious that there was little his outgunned Aussies could do, although, he also admitted to himself, they had offered a pretty stout defense and taken one hellluva lot of Nips with 'em. Even though Percival had told him to hold his defenses at all costs, Bennett was more concerned with his immediate problem of holding onto the reservoirs and varied food depots of Bukit Timah. Once these fell, the British position would be completely compromised, and surrender would be the next step.

And there was also the ongoing matter of escaping the blasted fortress, even though he had already formulated a plan in that regard. He had sent his aide, Lt. C.W. Walker, to secure the Sultan of Johore's fast motor launch that he knew was docked in Singapore Harbor. The Sultan was his good friend and Bennett was sure he wouldn't mind if he borrowed the craft for his escape. As of Sunday morning, February 8, Lt. Walker had reported the launch was still moored in the inner confines of the harbor known as Telok Basin.

The sleek boat was to be Bennett's ticket out of Singapore.

February 11, 1942, Private Home off Grange Road, Singapore, 1000 hours

Charles Samuel was absolutely bewildered at the toll the past two months had taken on him and the other evacuees he had the occasion to mingle with in Singapore. He and his wife Vi were now living in another assigned house, after moving from the home of the first family they had been assigned when they initially arrived on the island.

Charles' fifty-ninth birthday had come and gone two day earlier, the occasion celebrated with a simple cup of his favorite Formosa Oolong tea and a toast to each other that they were still alive.

Vi had busied herself with the Singapore Red Cross sewing branch and was also working at the local YMCA Services canteen. Samuel had volunteered for a number of minor jobs, but he mostly busied himself listening to radio broadcasts on Radio Singapore. He attempted to decipher the content of short-wave radio broadcasts courtesy of the small short-wave receiver his new residence happened to possess.

Like everyone else in Singapore, Samuel was devastated by the news of the sinking of the *Repulse* and the *Prince of Wales* slightly more than two months to the day earlier. Like most British expatriates, Samuel considered the British navy as something closely akin to invincible, and the sinking of these two capital ships at the very beginning of the military action with Japan had been particularly hard for the now-exhausted lawyer to swallow.

He continued to listen to his fellow refugees try and convince each other that the British and their new American allies would soon push these invaders back to Japan. But, inside his own heart, he knew better. He realized the invasion of Malaya had been a well conceived and meticulously carried-out plan that had been met with little or no resistance.

He chided himself for his culpability and naïve assessment of the ultimate goals of the Japanese and their willingness to bring the fight to their enemies. When he heard other Brits laud about the might of the

British and allied military machines he endured it all silently, knowing that whatever might happen later, Singapore was in for a terrible time in the foreseeable future.

Samuel kept most of these feelings to himself, not wishing to burden Vi with his forecast of continued misfortune. He was bent over the short wave this particular morning when the first artillery shells whizzed over the house and landed a short distance away. A minute later, more shells exploded in close proximity to the house and literally shook its foundations.

Ten minutes later, there was a distinctive knock on the front door.

Opening the door, Samuel saw the chevrons of a staff sergeant in the Royal Australian Army.

"Sorry, Sir, I'm afraid everyone is going to have to move out of this house."

"For what reason, Sergeant, we've only been here a couple of weeks?" Samuel replied a bit testily.

"The brass decided to place a gun battery on the hill above here and another directly below," the sergeant explained with a thick Southwestern Australia accent "That makes this area a good target for the Nips' artillery. I think they have already started trying to locate its exact position. You should have heard the shots a few minutes ago."

Samuel considered the absurdity of the statement and fought to control his temper.

"So, where do you want us to go now?" he questioned. "I would think you are beginning to run out of places for the likes of us to stay."

"Righto, sir. My captain has told me to direct you and the others in this area to the Fullerton Building in the center of the city for the present. It is a very strong building with adequate walls and provisions. You should be quite safe there."

"That's what they said about this place," Samuel shot back, looking around the house.

"Look, mate, I don't make the rules, and I don't care if you are not happy with what I'm telling you, but I really don't want you killed for no reason, you understand that?"

"Sorry for jumping on you like that, Sergeant, I know you are just following orders."

"Righto. So I can count on you leaving?" The sergeant seemed pacified that he was finally accomplishing his mission.

"As soon as my wife gets back from her work at the Red Cross, we'll pack what little belongings we still have left and be out of here, I promise you that."

"Thank you, sir, and best of luck to you both."

"We'll need it, by God. Every poor soul on this island will."

"Yes, sir." The sergeant half-saluted, turned and departed.

Samuel followed the man's progress until he was out of sight. He turned his head in the direction of another shrill noise as an artillery round exploded about three hundred yards away.

Vi had better bloody well hurry home today or there might be nothing left of me to evacuate. This is one hell of a mess we've managed to get ourselves in. What more could happen to us? How much longer will we be able to survive?

His senses returned as another incoming round went off a short distance away from the last.

February 13, 1942, Battle Box Bunker, Fort Canning, Singapore, 1400 hours

Even though it was one of the few air-conditioned buildings in Singapore, the air within the Battle Box Bunker Complex at Fort Canning seemed unseasonably thick as the senior British commanders sat around the large desk in the command center.

Lt. Gen. Arthur E. Percival, GOC Malaya, stared stoically forward as Lt. Gen. Sir Lewis Heath, Commander of the III Corps of the Indian Army, continued his remarks. It was at Heath's insistence that this meeting was held on this Friday afternoon on relatively short notice.

". . . that the Japanese troops have now driven down the peninsula more than five hundred miles since their first invasion troops hit a little more than a month ago. It is apparent to me and to anyone who looks at the matter that we have done little in the way of stopping this assault. It is not my intention at this time to lay blame, but simply to point out how fruitless it is to continue in the manner that we are currently doing." Heath paused and sipped the glass of water in front of him. He then continued.

"I also realize that many of us have given a great deal to this struggle and are exhausted to the point of being practically useless. I include myself in that group. I have had almost no sleep over the past three days and now find it difficult to concentrate on really important matters. I have seen a number of horrible situations involving both our military and civilians that have caused me to rethink my initial position on defending the island. There is almost no Bofors ammunition left and without it the Japanese aircraft can come and go as they please.

There are casualties everywhere and my medical staff fears some dire consequences cannot be far behind. My Indian army troops are without water supplies for the most part. I will ask Brigadier Stringer to address that topic after I finish. I also have some personal grounds that are swaying my judgment right now, I hope not adversely. As some of you know, my dear wife is pregnant and she has remained here rather than be evacuated. I have seen little of her and have been unable to assure her that she will be safe if she remains. Under any case, the situation is dire and the consequences even more so." He paused again.

"My intelligence reports that the Japanese are now within three miles of the center of Singapore City. The Japanese artillery is relentless and their air force has complete control of the skies. They are bombing us at will and do not seem to care about which targets they bomb, military or civilian. There are even some reports that we have been unable to bury some of the dead because there aren't enough people to search the bombed-out buildings to locate them. General Percival, Singapore has become a living hell and I call on you to do something about it.

Our troops are very downhearted and completely exhausted from their duties over the past month. I think many of our units have fought bravely, but we have little to show for it. My own divisions are at a fraction of their initial strength and some are scattered through the island, fighting with whomever they can attach themselves.

Please, General, give some immediate consideration to a truce or cease fire of some sort. We still have the upper hand as far as men and resources go, so that could be put to some use. I urge you to seek some solution, before it is too late."

"For once I agree with Sir Lewis," injected Maj. Gen. H. Gordon Bennett, Commander of the 2nd Australian Imperial Force. "And most of you know, I have seldom agreed with him of late."

A few chuckles around the table broke the abject rigidity of the meeting.

Bennett continued, his accent seemingly more severe in the cutting atmosphere.

"I cannot see much hope either, General. My lads are plum wore out. They're givin' the Nips all they can handle, but the tanks are beginnin' to take their toll. I cannot see much hope ahead since there is so little actual land left to defend. I urge you to consider Sir Lewis's plea, while we still have somethin' left to bargain with the bloody Nips."

From around the table, several muffled voices agreed with the Australian's last words.

The room became silent as Percival searched for the right words. Finally he lifted his head and addressed the assembled group.

"Gentlemen, I have already given great thought to what has been said, of that you may all rest assured. I have thought about the consequences since the first reports of the invasion reached my offices. I am keenly aware of the predicament we are currently facing and obviously, what lies ahead for all of us.

My staff keeps me updated hourly on the status of everything and everyone involved, since it is all my ultimate responsibility. I want you all to know that I take that responsibility seriously and I want to pursue the best course for all involved.

But, gentlemen, I am not at all convinced that an immediate surrender is the best possible resolution to our present situation."

The heads of those officers who were turned down as Percival spoke suddenly focused on their commander, waiting for his next sentence.

"As a matter of fact, I have already started on something that I hope will benefit all of us. My staff is currently working out the details on the organization of a counterattack that will recapture the food depots at Bukit Timah and also relieve the pressure on our defenses. Once we break the Japanese ranks, we will be in a position to encircle the Japanese and then regain most of the territory we have lost."

From around the table, an assortment of grumblings arose.

From the center of the table, Brigadier C.H. Stringer, commander of the Fortress Medical Services, stood.

"General Percival, if I may have a moment."

"Certainly, Brigadier, please go ahead." Percival was somewhat relieved it was neither Heath nor Bennett that had risen to speak.

"Gentlemen," Stringer began, "I want to set the record straight on a couple of items. Let me first say that I agree with both General Heath and General Bennett, for what they have said is absolutely correct."

Percival glanced up at Stringer with a quizzical look, but remained passive as the officer continued.

"I approached General Percival two days ago about the medical situation we are facing. I told him then that only an immediate surrender could prevent a number of horrendous consequences. These include an almost certain outbreak of malaria and also a number of other hygiene-related diseases. My staff is doing everything they can to combat these problems, but the number of casualties is so high and our ability to deal with them correctly is greatly compromised."

The number of voices around the table that grumbled their agreement with Stringer's statement grew louder.

"What about the civilians, General?" one of the corps commanders asked. "We have tried to help them whenever possible, but of late we have been so busy dodging enemy artillery, I'm afraid they have been forgotten for the most part."

"I have the civilians and their safety in mind," Percival answered. "Do not forget that we have evacuated a great number of British civilians during the past few weeks."

"What about the native lots?" Sir Lewis Heath countered. "Some of them are also British citizens, so why have they not been treated accordingly?"

"We have had limited means of evacuating people, and a limited number of ships. We evacuated those whom we thought needed evacuating. Remember, we had the colonial office to deal with in those matters. It wasn't always my own decision."

More dissent could be heard as the officers discussed the topics among themselves.

Once more, Percival raised his voice and returned to speaking.

"I have specific orders from General Wavell that Singapore is to be defended to the very last man if necessary. These orders are very explicit and I intend to follow them to the letter."

Sir Lewis Heath rose and the side chatter died out. He addressed Percival directly.

"General, I have been sitting here, thinking about what you have said and what the others have added to our conversation. Since it was my idea to have this conference, I believe it is up to me to state the obvious.

You have already tried one counterattack, and it proved to be a complete failure. There are no fresh troops available for another counterattack and from what I have recently learned, there are no reinforcements due in the foreseeable future. Given the circumstances, I do not think a counterattack has the least chance of success."

Percival sat passively as Heath's words sunk in. This time there was complete silence around the table.

"Sir Lewis, there are other things to consider," Percival replied finally. "There is my honour to consider and then there is the question of what posterity will think of us if we surrender this large army and this valuable fortress."

Heath could not believe what he had just heard and shot back, "You need not bother about your honor. You lost that a long time ago up in the north."

Percival felt the air go out of his lungs as Heath's words hung relentlessly in the humid air.

"Gentlemen, I must tell you all that I do not know what to do at this point. I am a soldier who follows orders and have done so my entire military career. To do anything different here is simply out of the question. I would ask the same of any British officer, regardless of rank. It is what separates us from our enemies and has done so for centuries. General Wavell, our commander in chief, has ordered that we should continue our struggle at all costs and without consideration to what may happen to the civil population. It is our duty to continue fighting as long as we can."

Again, Sir Lewis Heath broke in.

"How can General Wavell command this battle from Java?"

Percival stared intently at Heath but offered no reply.

"Will you at least approach General Wavell one more time?" Heath asked plaintively. "Under the present circumstances, I can't believe he won't change his mind."

Percival thought for a moment and replied. "All right, gentlemen, if that's the consensus, I'll approach the Chief and see if I can change his mind."

There's about as much chance of that happening as it snowing tomorrow morning. Lord knows I have already tried. But, if that what my commanders want, I will make another effort. After all, all he can say is no.

Percival rose and dismissed the gathering. It was now almost three o'clock.

February 13, 1942, Old Chinese Fishing Pier off Singapore City, Singapore, 2140 hours

Dr. Pai Lin Song was pleased to have had four days to get things organized at the pediatric section of the Singapore General Hospital. After initially hearing Elliott's plan to save the children under her care, she had been so tired that she couldn't find a place in which to begin.

She decided a nap was in order and awoke nearly twelve hours later.

"No one wanted to wake you up, Dr. Song," the old Chinese head nurse, Sun Loo admitted. "It had been so long since you slept and you looked as if you really needed the rest."

Pai Lin had to admit the head nurse was right, and knew she felt much better for it. For the first time in a long spell she felt refreshed and ready for the challenges ahead. She gathered the senior nurses on her staff and explained what was happening.

At first, Elliott's plan was greeted with suspicion and doubt.

Fishing boats that reeked of the smell of their trade? Sick children who barely survived the confines of the Singapore General Hospital, being thrown into an ocean-going trip with no idea of their final destination?

There were more questions than answers. It was the head nurse that put everything into perspective for the rest of Pai Lin's pediatric staff.

Sun Loo reminded everyone of the Japanese attitude toward Chinese civilians in the Manchurian War and of the stories of genocide that practically every person on the staff had already heard.

"Do you really expect it to be different here?" she chided the other nurses, about half of whom were Chinese themselves. "If you do, you had better think again. The Japanese think of themselves as conquerors and deal with their enemies swiftly and surely. They hate all Chinese and would like to kill every one of us. They feel superior to all the other Asian races and intend to prove it to everyone from the very beginning. I for one want no part of them, and you had all better see the light along with me before it becomes too late."

Sun Loo's argument was so convincing that Pai Lin found no further opposition to her plans.

She immediately organized her forces and made a specific list of those who were going and asked for volunteers to stay with the few that were simply too ill to chance moving.

Pai Lin was pleased that a pair of younger Malayan nurses with strong ties to Singapore agreed to stay, a gesture that allowed all the Chinese nurses to leave with the children.

Next she made out a complete list of articles to bring and assigned different nurses and orderlies to handle gathering the supplies. Since there were still two days left before their departure, the group decided it was best to keep the news about the trip from the children until the very last minute. Nurses were told to discuss it with their families and no one else.

Transportation for all the children from the hospital to the dock where they would board the fishing vessels would be another problem, given the disabilities of some of the sicker children, along with the very real logistical problem of providing enough food for everyone for the extended trip. It was a predicament that must be given great consideration.

But, slowly and with a sense of growing desperation, everything finally began to come together on the afternoon of February 12, the day before the group's departure. Pai Lain carefully decided which children would go and which would stay, and in one or two cases, the decision was a very weighty one for the remarkable woman doctor. In the end, her decision was based on what she believed the individual child could handle as far as adversity was concerned.

Later that afternoon, word was received that a Chinese friend of Sun Loo would provide a small fleet of bakery trucks, thereby solving the transportation problem. It was learned that the trucks really weren't needed to deliver bread until the following morning and everyone at the bakery was eager to help the children flee from the onslaught of the feared Japanese invaders.

Food was another thing. No matter where she turned, Pai Lin was unable to prioritize her upcoming hazardous voyage. First, the General Hospital administrator pleaded the fact that his hospital now had more than four hundred extra patients and more were being brought in every day. He was beginning to worry where the hospital's own food supply would come from and was simply not able to help Pai Lin at all.

Lieutenant Elliott and Chang had agreed earlier that Chang would also provide ample water for the passengers, so water was not an issue.

When Elliott and Pai Lin met briefly around midnight on February 12, Elliott decided that as a last resort he would take a vehicle and attempt to confiscate some basic food supplies from one of several British naval storage areas. He also confided he wasn't above using a bit of force to accomplish his mission, an idea Pai Lin found to have very little merit.

"I don't want you to do that, William," she scolded. "It's not really fair to the men who will need it later."

"If the Japanese overrun the island, it will only go to them," he responded. "I think it would actually be in Britain's best interest to give us the food."

She saw his side of the argument and was too weary to contest his point any further.

"Do whatever you think is best, darling, I just can't make myself believe all this is all really coming together."

"We're not there yet," Elliott countered. "But, we are making some significant progress. There are a number of ships trying to leave from here in the next two days and some people are saying they are the last ships available. From the looks of some of the old crates I've encountered the past few days, practically everything that floats has been put in service to attempt to get people off the island."

"I don't really know what it's like out there, I'm cooped up all day and night here in the hospital."

"You are not missing much, Pai Lin, I can assure you of that."

"And Radio Singapore keeps broadcasting nationalistic stuff and follows it up with even more patriotic songs. It seems almost unreal."

"It *is* unreal, Pai Lin. Some of the things I have heard lately make me totally ill. Some things people are saying right now make me sorry I'm a Brit in the first place."

"You will *always* be a Brit. It's actually one of the first things about you that really impressed me."

Elliott moved closer to her and gently kissed the back of her neck.

"In what way did that impress you, Dr. Song?" he asked affectionately.

"Well, for one thing, you never threw the British thing in my face like some of your countrymen tended to do. You never tried to be superior or above it all. In fact, I don't remember your mentioning it except in passing."

"Bully for me," he said again kissing the back of her neck. "I guess I really know how to handle a woman like you."

"You twit," Pai Lin smiled, "Can't you ever be serious? You were doing so well and then, well, so much for the mood."

"Sorry, my love, I guess it's a sign of the times."

Pai Lin sighed deeply.

"You are so right, my love. It's hard to be in love in times like this. Makes you sort of feel like you are cheating at something when you see all the suffering and fear around you. To be in love seems like something to be experienced in another time and place."

Elliott remained quiet, letting her profound words slowly fade. At length, he squeezed her waist and spoke to her.

"My darling, we will get through all this, one way or another, and one day we will be able to enjoy each other, I *promise* you that."

Pai Lin looked into his eyes, again starting to tear up.

"I hope so, my love, I hope so." She fought back a quiet sob as the two remained in a tight embrace.

A knock from behind them shattered the privacy of the couple's solitary moment. It was the head nurse who had knocked.

"Excuse me, Dr. Song, I don't mean to disturb you."

"It's all right, Sun Loo, I need to be doing other things anyway. What do you need?"

"I have some good news, Doctor. I have just heard from my friend at the bakery and he has arranged for a large number of loaves of bread to be specially baked for the children. He also managed to secure several large bags of rice. I think it will be enough to feed the children for several days."

"Good, Sun Loo. You and your friends have done so much. I don't know what to say."

"We are all in this together, Dr. Song. Remember, the Japanese hate us Chinese more than they hate the westerners. It's been like that for many centuries. I know you have heard all the old stories."

"Yes, we all have," Pai Lin replied. "When I was younger, I never really paid much attention to the old tales. I guess I was a bit naïve or something. The legends certainly seem quite real today."

"We must never forget our history," Sun Loo replied. "It always teaches us something vital to our lives. If we learn from it, we will be better able to handle the challenges that we face today."

"Why, head nurse, I never knew you were such a philosopher."

Sun Loo was a bit embarrassed, but replied, "It is never polite to expound on a subject until it becomes necessary," she explained. "I was taught that when I was a young girl. I have never forgotten the lesson."

"It has served you well. I will try to remember its meaning."

Sun Loo bowed and turned to leave. Elliott squeezed Pai Lin's hand and made a gesture that he should be leaving too.

Pai Lin looked at him again and finally dropped his hand.

"I guess I will let you go…for now," she grinned. "But it won't be easy. I will still be thinking of you each and every minute."

"With what you still have to do to get ready, you won't have time to think about me one little bit," Elliott teased.

Pai Lin reached up and kissed him firmly on the mouth. "Remember me like this," she played. "It will make it easier."

"It will make it more difficult," Elliott rejoined. "Much more difficult,"

"When will you contact me again, my love?"

"I will try and check in before the trucks arrive, that is if the phone system is still operating."

"I will pray to God that it is. Will you meet me at the dock?"

"I will try and meet you here and we will all go to the dock, at least that's my plan."

"All right, keep safe, my darling."

"And you, my love." He kissed her once more and left.

Much to Pai Lin's relief, the bakery trucks arrived at the hospital on time the following evening and the mass exodus of children and nurses began on time. Several children who could not walk were carried on stretchers by hospital orderlies and patients who were well enough to help out.

For the children, they were told that they were starting a great adventure. The nurses also made sure the children understood that it was important that they remain extremely quite, but the children nevertheless became animated and giggled whenever anything seemed to develop a hitch. Only the sounds of the continuous shelling in other parts of Singapore brought the entire happening back to reality.

Pai Lin watched proudly as her staff saw to the children's needs. The children filed into the sweet-smelling trucks and fought for places near the two small windows. The nurses urged them to keep quiet and the children dutifully obeyed, their eyes wide open as to not miss a single event of their new adventure.

The loading process took about forty-five minutes to complete and the signal was given to start the convoy. Pai Lin looked around one last time but saw no sign of Lt. William Elliott. Even though she was worried, she fought the urge to hold the convoy on Elliott's behalf. Besides, Elliott was resourceful enough to meet them at the dock, and so she convinced herself it was best to get going.

The procession wound through New Bridge Road and crossed the river. From there it took a detour to Queen Street since there were a number of bombed-out buildings on Victoria Street. They turned right toward the water and finally arrived on Beach Road where the convoy took a left. They proceeded about a mile until the outlines of the old Chinese fishing dock came into view on the right.

Pai Lin was in the lead truck and breathed a sigh of relief that they had made it so far. The shelling was more irregular by now, but loud claps of powder bursting were still heard every minute or two. The air at the dock was heavy and smelled of the sea. She glanced upward and could see from the full clouds that rain was a distinct possibility. The sound of an airplane's heavy drone from over the city pierced the night air.

Pai Lin looked toward the water, and gasped.

There were no fishing boats to be seen!

Pai Lin alighted from the truck and walked out onto the dock. Sun Loo and the man who had driven the lead bakery truck soon joined her. The head nurse and the driver spoke animatedly in Chinese, until Dr. Song interrupted.

"That's enough you two," she said firmly. "Something must have happened and made them late. After all, we *are* in a war. We must simply wait."

The period proved to be one of the longest thirty minutes in Dr. Pai Lin Song's entire life. The children were growing restless and the nurses' attempts at keeping them quiet became more difficult with each passing minute.

Elliott had still not arrived and Pai Lin was now becoming worried.

It was Sun Loo's tired old eyes that first noticed the outline of a boat on the water, seemingly headed for the dock."

"There!" she yelled, pointing in the direction of the boat.

Pai Lin craned her head and finally focused on the outline of a fishing boat. A moment later, a second boat appeared and a minute later, a third. The first boat approached the pier and a hand leaped out and secured a rope to the dock. A minute later, the lead boat was firmly secured and Chan jumped down off the boat.

He approached Pai Lin and offered his hand.

"Sorry we are late, but the Japanese had a number of supply boats dropping troops along the coastline. We saw them in time and had to go further out to sea to avoid them."

"That's certainly all right," Pai Lin replied. "At least you made it safely."

"That's what I promised Lieutenant Elliott, Dr. Song. I always try and keep my promises."

Pai Lin smiled at the man and gave the head nurse the orders to start boarding the children. Chang called back to the boat and several more hands jumped onto the deck.

The entire process of boarding the children and nurses took a little over forty minutes.

Pai Lin was so busy that she failed to notice that Elliott had still not arrived.

Chan approached her and asked, "Is Lieutenant Elliott not coming with us? It was my understanding that he would be here and take charge of everything."

"He was supposed to meet us at the hospital, " Pai Lin replied, now genuinely worried. "I don't know what might have happened."

"Well, we have been lucky so far, but I don't want to push it too much.

We can still wait for another half hour or so, and then the tide will become unfavorable. I really don't want to take a chance beyond that point."

"We will wait," Pai Lin said firmly, "until the last possible moment."

She busied herself making sure all the children were as comfortable as possible. While the smell inside the boat wasn't pleasant, it certainly wasn't unbearable. The children were still wide eyed, but behaved remarkably well considering the circumstances.

A light drizzle began to fall, further obscuring the few remaining buildings that were visible from the deck of Chan's boat. Finally, Chan approached Pai Lin again.

"I must give the order to the other boats to cast off, the time is getting critical. I will keep my own boat here another five minutes, but then I must also cast off."

Pai Lin nodded that she understood and poked her head through the raincoat Chan had offered her to shield her from the drizzle. The other boats cast off their lines and slowly started out to sea. Pai Lin looked again at Chan, resigned to the fact that it was time to leave.

Chan raised his hand to give the order but was surprised to see the deckhand holding the mooring lines suddenly waving his arms, pointing in the direction of the city.

A jeep suddenly appeared at high speed, careening around the last barrier to the dock. It screeched to a halt and the two inhabitants quickly jumped out. Lt. William Elliott of His Majesty's Royal Navy jumped on board followed by an Australian corporal carrying a large Mark1 Bren 3.1 LMG machine gun and several pan magazines of ammunition.

Pai Lin saw that Elliot was also armed with a new Colt Tommy gun that he had shown her once before. Instinctively, she reached for him.

"Cutting it a bit close are we?" kidded Elliott, taking her in his arms.

For once Pai Lin was absolutely speechless. Instead, she chose to squeeze him even tighter.

*February 14, 1942, aboard fishing boat **Monsoon II**, 15 NM off Karimun Island, Riau Island Group, Indonesia, 1145 hours*

Throughout the night and into the hot morning hours the steady engine of the *Monsoon II* filled the air with its relentless thumping, thereby propelling the fishing boat way southward, away from the calamity and devastation that was Singapore.

The overcast, rainy night had given way to a wonderful, breezy morning, which was good for sailing but bad for the prospect of Japanese aircraft seeking boats carrying the last refugees hoping to escape from Singapore.

Elliott was sitting atop the bow of the *Monsoon II,* engaged in a fairly deep conversation with his friend Chan, the boat's owner.

Chan was explaining his plan of escape to Elliott, who listened attentively.

"We must keep our fishing nets out, even though it makes us proceed much slower," Chan was explaining. "If the Japanese see the nets, they will think us fishermen making our living. I've even taken the liberty of adding a Japanese flag to each boat's fantail. The other boats know to wave the flag if they see any planes."

"Very clever, Chan. You seem to have thought of everything."

"It is best to be cautious in such matters, but even then we might not be so safe."

"How far do you think will they pursue us? After all, they surely have other things to think about."

"I have no way of knowing. All I can tell you is that the word around the harbor was that the Japanese have implemented a sort of blockade to keep people from escaping. I know that a number of boats and ships have already been sunk."

"Too bad," Elliott remarked. "I even had a bit of a hand in getting some poor souls on a few of those ships."

"It would be well to pray for them, Lieutenant. We all need the help of God to get through this."

Elliott nodded and turned his gaze back toward Singapore. He silently wondered what was in store for the poor unfortunates who had been unable to leave.

His concentration was broken by the sound of young voices that broke the quiet air. Pai Lin appeared at mid deck with two youngsters, both of who struggled to run free on the deck.

He immediately recalled the fact that Chan had designated that each child would rotate on deck for five minutes starting on the hour, both to enjoy the freshness of the sea air and also to overcome the relatively unfriendly stench from below the deck of the *Monsoon II.*

Also, if a Japanese plane were spotted, it would only take a few seconds to get the children below deck.

Elliott had also changed to fisherman's clothes and an Oriental hat to disguise his looks, and was told to remain as inconspicuous as possible. His precious Tommy-gun was placed under a tarp where it was immediately accessible.

The *Monsoon II* and her two companion boats moved slowly south, southwest and began seeing sea birds that indicated their closeness to land. Chan pointed to the horizon and the tops of a small mountain range became visible.

"That's Karimun Island, part of the Riau Island group. We will head for Tanjung Balai where we can get food and water. I know a few people there who will help us."

"Sounds good to me," Elliott replied. "All I want is to get everyone to safety."

"That might take a few days more, depending on our final destination. We must be sure the place we finally decide on can handle the children's special needs. They are after all, just out of the hospital and . . ."

Chan's statement was cut off by the hurried shout of the forward lookout, whose arm extended straight to the northeast. A dark speck in the air suddenly grew larger.

"Get the children down the hatch," Chan ordered. "And put that Japanese flag out. It might come in handy." Chan turned to see that the other boats had also spotted the intruder and was pleased to see Rising Sun flags out on both boats.

The aircraft droned closer and started to make a low-level pass.

"He will check us out first," Chan advised. "If he sees nothing out of the ordinary, chances are he will let us go. Get ready to wave, Lieutenant, and smile. With his speed and altitude, he won't be able to tell you from a native."

The Japanese fighter approached the fishing boats and passed them with its engine whining. As he waved to the passing aircraft, Elliott was able to identify the plane as an Aichi D3A that carried a pilot and bombardier and was usually carrier based. Since he had not heard of any Japanese carriers in these waters, Elliott quickly surmised that the fighter was one of the planes brought in by the Japanese after their capture of the Singapore airfields.

The fighter executed a starboard turn and proceeded to begin another pass.

"Oh no," Elliott exclaimed. "He's coming back for another pass."

"Just keep waving, we have no idea of what he's thinking," Chan ordered. "And keep waving that flag, Hong! Make him think you really mean it."

All three waved as the fighter approached. As it passed overhead, the pilot rolled the plane's wings from right to left and started to climb.

"He bought it!" Elliott exclaimed wildly. "He bought the bloody thing with the flag."

"The flag satisfies their egos," Chan remarked. "It makes them think that all their actions are okay and that someone down here actually likes them."

"Right now even *I* fancy them," Elliott added. "As long as they let us alone."

"We can relax for now," Chan added. "We are getting to get close to Karimun. We should be there in about a half an hour."

Elliott looked again at the mountains that were beginning to take shape. He walked to the hatch where Pai Lin was waiting. He smiled as she stepped up on deck.

"Well, we survived one more thing," he sighed. "One thing among many."

"Yes, my darling, and we *will* survive it all. I just know it."

"I'm beginning to believe it too," he agreed. The couple held each other as the *Monsoon II* and its escorts slowly chugged their way toward Karimun.

February 14, 1942, Alexandra Barracks Hospital, Ayer Rajah Road, Singapore, 1300 hours

The orderlies who had been stationed on the Alexandra Barracks Military Hospital's top floor balconies sounded the first cries of alarm. The stately, white three-story colonial building was currently the home of more than 1,250 patients, far exceeding its actual capacity of 550. Every Red Cross flag that the hospital had in its inventory was prominently displayed on its balconies and doors. Members of the Royal Australian Medical Corps made up most of the staff at the military hospital.

The first Japanese troops approached the hospital led by a green-uniformed soldier carrying a large Japanese flag. Other soldiers approached in single file, their weapons at the ready with fixed bayonets. All wore camouflage of twigs and shrubbery on their steel helmets. A second group of infantry started in the direction of the Sisters' quarters that was separate from the main hospital building.

A single Aussie officer, Capt. J.F. Bartlett of the RAMC, ventured outside to insure that the hospital would be treated as an international medical sanctuary. His arms were raised and he pointed to the red crosses on his uniform's brassard. Captain Barrett started saying the word "hospital" as the first soldier, who had entered the gap of the overlapping blast wall, raised his rifle and shot Barrett at point-blank range. Barrett crumpled to the ground and died instantly. The remaining soldiers then mulled around in the courtyard until an officer gave the order to enter the hospital at around 1:40. At the order, some one hundred Japanese soldiers rushed into the hospital

In the commander's second floor office, Lt. Col. J. W. Craven of the RAMC was in a meeting with his staff discussing surrender of the facility. Included were the registrar, Major Henderson, the hospital's chaplain and a British medical officer, Major J.W.D. Bull, who had recently arrived at Alexandra.

As the cries of the soldiers advancing reached their ears, Major Bull grabbed a nearby Red Cross flag and held it at the window. A soldier outside replied with a shot that sailed over Bull's head and lodged in the wall behind him.

Pandemonium, in its worst possible form, broke loose all over the hospital. The sounds of explosions and rifle shots reverberated throughout the halls and patients screamed and cried for assistance. Everyone inside the hospital dove for the nearest cover, which was limited at best.

After about thirty minutes, the first artillery shell burst into the hospital, tearing away doors and window shutters and filling the building with an acrid dust. A number of people, both staff and patients, dove out of the windows and headed for the relative safety of nearby brush.

In an upstairs operating theatre, an operation was underway when the first soldiers burst through the doors. Five members of the attending staff were immediately bayoneted along with the anaestheticized patient on the operating table. One of the doctors, Captain Smiley of the RAMC, the surgeon performing the operation, was bayoneted in the chest. The steel struck Captain Smiley's pocket cigarette case and saved his life. His Japanese attacker then thrust his bayonet into Smiley's groin. Two more thrusts severely injured the surgeon's hand and right arm. As he fell, the wounded Aussie officer pulled another staff member, Private Sutton, down with him. The two played dead and after the Japanese left the operating room, Sutton dressed Captain Smiley's wounds.

Throughout the hospital, hundreds of soldiers and patients were equally unlucky. After the onslaught, two hundred patients and staff were herded outside and their hands bound behind them. Some could barely walk, others were missing limbs or were hindered by plaster casts.

The group was marched at bayonet point out of the hospital grounds, along the nearby railway tracks and through a tunnel to Ayer Rajah Road. Anyone who fell was bayoneted. When they reached a building about a quarter mile from the hospital, they were herded into three small, unventilated rooms. The doors were barricaded and the windows were then nailed shut. There was no ventilation, no water for the already-dehydrated prisoners, who were forced to take turns sitting on the floor for rest. During the night an additional number of prisoners died.

The following morning, the door opened and a Japanese officer spoke to the prisoners in broken English, "We are taking you behind lines . . . you will get water on the way."

The men were escorted out two by two and headed toward the rear of the structure. After a few moments, anguished cries came from the direction the prisoners had taken. "Oh, my god . . . don't, don't," and "Mother." After a while, no more cries came from behind the building.

All the prisoners removed from the building were systematically bayoneted and killed. Only a few who had played dead inside were left alive.

February 14, 1942, 25th Imperial Japanese Army Field Headquarters, Bukit Timah Road, Singapore, 1400 hours

Once again, Lt. Gen. Tomoyuki Yamashita was compelled to receive his unwanted visitor from the headquarters of the 25th Imperial Japanese Army. Lt. Gen. Osamu Tsukada, the chief of staff for the 25th Army, was shown into Yamashita's temporary field headquarters just outside the Ford factory on Bukit Timah Road in the northeast section of Singapore. It was the diminutive general's second visit in less than a month and the intrusion offended Yamashita, who had little regard for general staff officers.

Tsukada approached Yamashita and bowed slightly.

"I hope all is well and the gods are pleased with your efforts, Yamashita."

"If the gods provide me with more food and ammunition I will consider it a sign they are pleased," Yamashita answered, content he had maintained control of the conversation while still observing the basic formalities.

Tsukada chose not to answer Yamashita's cockiness, but rather spoke directly about his mission.

"The general staff and Count Terauchi, in particular, are worried that the invasion might not go as planned. We want to be sure that everything we do is well formulated and coordinated. That is my purpose in being here."

Yamashita fought the urge to shout at Tsukada, but controlled himself. Instead, he said in a controlled tone, "You want everything to be well planned and coordinated, am I to understand you correctly?"

"That is right, Yamashita. You are correct."

"Let me tell you what I understand. I understand that unless we are extremely lucky, our whole plan is capable of failing and *we* might be the ones surrendering, Tsukada," he replied. "The situation I am faced with is a dire as I can describe."

Tsukada could not believe what he had just heard.

"You had better explain yourself, Yamashita. I am of the opinion that everything is going along quite well here. Before I left Saigon, we just received fresh reports of more advances and victories for our wonderful emperor. I can't believe what you just said."

"You had better believe, because it is as I have said. The truth is that our troops are completely exhausted from their efforts of having to cover so much space in so short a time. Our food supply is almost nonexistent and will not last another two days unless we find some more food that our men can eat. The British have destroyed most of their supplies while retreating and the kind of western food we have recovered does not sit well with our tired soldiers. Our ammunition is in really short supply and there is no more coming for the foreseeable future. We have outrun our resupply capabilities and will run out of bullets in the next day or two.

We are also getting quite short of artillery shells. Thank the gods the British didn't have a chance to destroy all of their own artillery and ammunition. We have turned their own guns around and are shelling the British with their own ammunition. I have kept up the round-the-clock shelling at all costs. I don't want them to have any time to recover, and I need them to believe we have an inexhaustible supply of everything."

Yamashita paused, letting his words sink in. After a few moments, he continued.

"What I am attempting to do is bully the British into surrendering, either later tonight or sometime tomorrow. I dropped an offer to surrender out of an aircraft a few days ago, but they didn't reply. Our spies inside Singapore City say the morale is extremely low and the concern is now about the water supply that is now under our control. I have put myself in the place of the British commander and have asked myself, what would I do if the tables were changed?"

Tsukada thought for a moment and said, "You are taking a big chance, Yamashita, what if the British commander decides to stick it out?"

"I have watched his actions since the invasion began," Yamashita answered calmly, his anger mostly subsided. "He is a decent enough soldier, but not a very far-sighted one. He could have made a number of decisions after our invasion that would have provided us with much more opposition and many more problems to overcome.

I just don't think he has the desire to stand up to us under these circumstances. He can't know our supply problems, and I won't relent on our bombardment of his positions. Any let up on our part could prove fatal. If he feels we are in the least bit weakened, he might just decide to fight. If he does, well, I just don't know what will happen."

The two men stood, enveloped by the fading echoes of Yamashita's last words.

February 15, 1942, Headquarters 8th Australian Division, AIF, Tanglin Barracks, Singapore, 1150 hours

The eerie quiet on this Sunday morning was in great contrast to the nonstop shelling that Singapore Island and its inhabitants had experienced for what seemed like many months.

It was, in fact, only ten days since the first Japanese shells fell on the island.

For Maj. Gen. H. Gordon Bennett, commander of the 8th Division, the past few days had been a nightmare of epic proportions. He had just returned from his final meeting at Fort Canning where General Percival had informed the gathered commanders of the fact that he had surrendered to the Japanese. Bennett listened to the terms that Percival outlined and left the meeting as quickly as possible.

He immediately returned to his headquarters at Tanglin Barracks where he issued orders for his men to follow in laying down their arms and not resisting their new captors. His day was made even sourer when his aide, Lt. Gordon H. Walker, suddenly appeared at his office door with some disturbing news—the Sultan of Johore's fast launch had been commandeered by the Royal Navy and was no longer moored in Keppel Harbor. The news put Bennett into a near frenzy, since his nearly flawless escape plan was now torn to shreds.

He screamed some additional orders to an adjutant outside of his office and returned to a map of the area that he had spread out across his desk. He stared intently for a few minutes and motioned to the stoutly-built Walker to approach his desk.

"This is where we will head," he said, pointing to a spot on the map. "We will go north across the straits and make for Malacca. With any luck, we can find a boat that can take us to Burma."

Walker nodded and Bennett continued. "I want you and Major Moses to come with me at one o'clock for a trip to our outside lines. We'll see if there is a spot where the Nips are a bit weak and we can slip through."

"But, General, " Walker answered weakly, "What about the men we are leaving behind? What's to happen to them?"

Bennett became more agitated and snapped back. "They'll just have to fend for themselves. That's the way it is in war. They're all brave lads and will be all right.

I feel it's up to me to escape and get back to Australia and tell the world what went on here. I want you and Moses with me when we leave, they'll be plenty for each bloke to do."

Walker accepted his fate halfheartedly, knowing it was useless to argue with the almost frantic man.

At precisely one o'clock, the three officers left the headquarters building and took Bennett's staff BSA Scout motorcar to the front lines. They eventually reached the home of a naval officer off Farrer Road that was only four hundred yards from the Japanese front lines and offered an excellent vantage point to look down on the Japanese.

A young Australian captain from the 2/26 offered them tea and biscuits and served it on the house owner's fine china. The brief respite had a calming effect on Bennett who saw the return to civility as a sign that his efforts to escape had some unearthly blessing.

On the way back to his office, Bennett decided to stop at the headquarters of the Gordon Highlanders, a Scottish unit that he had always enjoyed. There, a bottle of sherry was opened by one of the company commanders and toasts were raised to all the participants in the battle. When they departed, Bennett turned to Major Moses and said, "I only have one more thing to do."

When he was informed that the armistice papers had been signed, General Bennett immediately made his way to the quarters of his old friend and subordinate, Brigadier C. A. "Boots" Callaghan, a valiant fighter and good leader who was battling a severe case of malaria and was bedridden.

Callaghan's room was poorly lit with a kerosene lamp and reeked of medicine and sweat.

He approached Callaghan's bed and said softly, "General, I am now making you the commander of the 2nd AIF. I feel it is necessary that I escape and do something about this war. I need to let everyone know what happened here and whose fault it was. I'm also making you a major general from this point on. Good luck to you, my old friend, and God bless."

Callaghan stared back, unable or unwilling to say anything to his long-time comrade in arms. He faded back onto his pillow and closed his eyes.

Bennett and his entourage then got back into their car and carefully made their way down to the waterfront. They finally abandoned their BSA Scout as they approached the Arab Street Pier. It was now almost midnight and a number of sampans bobbed and weaved at their moorings, some one hundred yards away from the shore. Still burning buildings near the waterfront cast an eerie light on the proceedings.

Bennett motioned to Lieutenant Walker, who quickly undressed and dove into the water. He swam strongly and soon reached one of the sampans. He climbed aboard and motioned to the shore.

A group of men approached Bennett and Moses. "We are all soldiers from the Straits

Volunteers and we want to escape with you," one of the men stated forcefully. "That's what you're here for, isn't it?"

Bennett noted that the men were all well armed and conceded the point without a word.

Walker returned with a mid-sized dinghy and the group stepped in for the return to the sampan.

Bennett noted additional activity on board the craft and looked over to Walker.

"The sampan's captain was sleeping on board, General. He heard me climb aboard and met me with a machete in his hands. Lucky I speak a little Mandarin, it is. If I understand him correctly, he wants one hundred Singapore dollars to take us across the Straits to the east coast of Sumatra. He has two hands on board, and I suggest we give him what he wants."

Bennett nodded his agreement and the dinghy made its way out to the sampan. The money was quickly exchanged, the sampan anchor raised and the craft slowly moved into the Keppel Harbor channel. Bennett saw that Walker was still naked and screamed at him to get his uniform back on. The others looked in amazement as the circus-like antics unfolded.

As Bennett's outburst faded, the group on board moved noiselessly to the rail of the sampan as the fiery, somewhat eerily nascent scene that was Singapore City silently slid away. There was nothing that anyone onboard could think to say.

Lt. Gordon Walker shrugged as he slipped his army blouse over his still wet shoulders. He wondered if their escape would work and if they would ever reach Australia. He also pondered about what ordinary Australians would eventually say about Bennett's decision to leave his men.

February 15, 1942, 25th Imperial Japanese Army Field Headquarters, Ford Factory, Singapore, 1830 hours

It was intensely sobering to Lt. Gen. Arthur E. Percival, GOC Malaya, to have to travel to the opposing general's headquarters to discuss the terms of surrender for his forces. Shortly after eight that morning, he had received a telegram from the commander in chief, General Wavell, that outlined a discretionary route that enabled Percival to cease his resistance. Even though his conscience was now clear, Percival would have preferred to fight it out and die as a soldier—fighting for the last precious piece of ground under his command.

But the reality of his situation had caused him to finally cave into practically all of his commanders' and staff's wishes, namely to surrender to the overwhelming and ever-pressing Japanese Army.

He had sent some of his staff, Brigadier T.K. Newbigging, Maj. Cyril Wild who acted as interpreter, and Colonial Secretary Hugh Fraser to meet the Japanese commander, Gen. Tomoyuki Yamashita. The white-flagged delegation proposed that the two meet at City Hall to discuss the surrender. The men returned several hours later in the company of a Japanese lieutenant colonel named Sugita Ichiji, who flatly demanded that the surrender take place at Yamashita's headquarters at the Ford factory on the Bukit Timah Road.

Percival had finally agreed with his commanders on a four o'clock cease-fire. He remained at his desk until it was time to go, even though the Japanese artillery was now agonizingly close. A shell hit somewhere within the fort's inner structure and the concussion resounded throughout his office. A pile of rubble and debris fell from the ceiling, but Percival calmly wiped off his desk.

At a few minutes after four, he gently said to his waiting subordinates, "We ought to go."

This time Brigadier K.S. Torrance, Percival's chief of staff, joined Percival, Brigadier Newbigging and Major Wild for the car journey to the

Ford factory. At the front lines, the motorcade stopped and the officers alighted. The walked toward the Japanese as Torrance carried a Union Jack and Wild a white flag. After a couple hundred yards, they were met by several Japanese officers who pointed them to a pair of cars. They got in and were driven to the Ford factory a short distance away.

Inside, a large table had been assembled inside the plant's canteen. Percival and his officers set on one side of the table and five senior Japanese officers joined Yamashita on the other side.

There were no introductions and General Yamashita directed his first remarks to Percival through his interpreter.

"Have you seen our terms, which were handed over through the peace envoy?"

Percival answered through Major Wild. "Yes."

"Further details are given in an annexed sheet." He placed the paper in front of Percival, within his reach. "I want everything carried out in accordance with this."

Percival glanced at the sheet and replied, "There are disturbances in Singapore City. As there are non-combatants in the city, I should like to keep one thousand men under arms."

Yamashita quickly replied. "The Japanese Army will look after that; you need not concern yourself with it."

"Looting is taking place inside the city. And there are non-combatants."

"Non-combatants will be protected by the spirit of *bushido*. So everything will be all right."

Percival replied gamely, "If there is a vacuum, there will be chaos in the city and looting. Outbreaks of looting and rioting are undesirable, whether from the Japanese or British point of view. For the purpose of maintaining order, it is desirable that 1,000 men should be permitted to retain their arms."

Yamashita thought and replied. "As the Japanese Army is continuing its assault on the city, an attack is likely to go forward tonight."

"I should like to ask you to postpone any night attack."

"The attack will go forward if we cannot come to an agreement."

"I would like you to postpone it."

Yamashita reemphasized his point. "The attack will go forward if we cannot come to an agreement."

"Because of the rioting in Singapore, I would like one thousand men left with their arms.

Yamashita then turned to one of his staff officers, Col. Hanjiro Ikeya. "What time is the night attack scheduled for?"

Ikeya answered, "Eight o'clock."

Percival spoke up again. "If there is a night attack, then you put me in a difficult situation."

Yamashita replied, "Does the British Army intend to surrender or not?"

Percival paused, and then answered, "I wish to have a cease fire."

"The time for the night attack is drawing near. Is the British Army going to surrender or not? Answer." He then spoke in English for the first time. "Yes or no."

"Yes, but I would like the retention of one thousand armed men sanctioned.

Yamashita then answered politely, "Very well."

The commanders' discussion then gravitated to exactly what time the hostilities would cease and a time of half past eight o'clock was finally agreed upon.

Percival then signed the copy of the surrender document and the two generals stood and shook hands.

The fall of the Fortress of Singapore was now officially recorded. It would soon be referred to as the greatest single defeat in the history of the British military.

February 16, 1942, Pom Pong Island, Rhio-Lingaa Island Group, Dutch East Indies, 2130 hours

It had become increasing apparent to both Charles and Vi Samuel that their actual survival could be considered as seriously in doubt. No one, not even the greatest writer with the most vivid imagination, could have predicted the pair's last five days with any degree of accuracy.

They were currently in the company of approximately five hundred to six hundred survivors of the last futile effort by the British government to get their citizens out of harm's way and off the Island of Singapore before the Japanese finalized the invasion of the island. The group had made its way, either by boat or lifeboat, to the tiny uninhabited island of Pom Pong, some eighty miles south of Singapore.

It had all happened in a hurry.

The Samuels were residing in a baggage room at the Fullerton Building in downtown Singapore when an urgent medical priority turned the room into a casualty station of the Medical Auxiliary Services on Friday, February 13th. Heeding such an ominous sign, the Samuels, homeless once again, heard about a boat leaving the island later that afternoon.

The couple managed to secure travel permits that were officially signed by F.D. Bisseker, the deputy director of Civil Defence, on behalf of Brigadier Ivan Simson, recently appointed director general of the island's civil defense forces. They were directed to go to Wharf 2 at Keppel Harbor to board the vessel. Upon arrival they found that a large crowd had gathered around the gates to the wharf that were guarded by armed soldiers. Since the order of the day was for women and children to receive first priority, Vi Samuel made it through the gates, but became worried when Charles was not permitted to join her.

Charles Samuel was beside himself when a well-built man wearing a British naval lieutenant's epaulets passed nearby. He stopped the man, who turned and addressed him.

"Yes, sir, can I be of some assistance to you?"

"Lieutenant, I seem to be in a quandary here. My wife and I are evacuees from Penang and she is already aboard the ship. It seems my permit won't allow me through and it is imperative I join her. "

Lt. William Elliott took the papers and looked at Samuel, who seemed to him in a near pitiful state. Thin and haggard, Samuel teetered a bit to his left side. "I believe I can help you, Mr. Samuel. Please come with me. I'll talk to my boss, Brigadier Simson. For the time being, he is the ultimate authority around here and no one in their right mind questions his signature."

It took the better part of an hour, but Lieutenant Elliott's strategy worked. A new permit was issued that allowed Charles Samuel on board to join his wife.

The vessel was the *Kuala*, a small steamboat that regularly plied the waters of the East Indies. It was requisitioned and immediately put to use as a rescue craft by British authorities. The *Kuala* sailed without mishap from Keppel Harbor and made its way southward to Pom Pong Island, where it made anchor early in the morning of December 14.

The island was uninhabited and the water supply limited, so a rationing system was quickly put into effect. Twice a day, at noon and midnight, a small provision of water and biscuits was given to everyone. The ship carried a number of nurses and auxiliary nurses as well as a number of men from the Public Works Department, now dressed as volunteers in the Straits Settlement Volunteer Force.

Another rescue vessel, the *Tun Kuang*, arrived at basically the same mooring sometime during the night. The men from the volunteer force attempted to cut trees to camouflage the ships, but a Japanese reconnaissance plane spotted them before the job was completed.

Before long, two waves of Japanese bombers appeared on the horizon and made directly for the two ships. On the second pass, the *Kuala* received a direct hit that threw the passengers into frenzy. Lifeboats were lowered and Vi Samuel eventually handed over her lifejacket to a young girl in one of the boats.

Neither Vi nor Charles Samuel was able to swim more than a few strokes, but somehow each managed to survive and was dragged ashore the tiny island. They turned seaward in time to see the ill-fated *Kuala* slip below the surface of the ocean. Nearby, the *Tun Kuang* rested at an odd angle. She had also been hit by a Japanese bomb and had been beached by her captain and crew. Completely exhausted and their spirit nearly broken, the Samuels knew they were close to the end of the line.

They huddled close to each other near a makeshift fire that had been provided by some of the volunteers.

Vi Samuel spoke first.

"I would say, Charlie, that we are really in a 'peach' this time, wouldn't you say?"

"You have a marvelous penchant for the understatement," Samuel answered fondly. "I have absolutely no idea of what will happen next. I have heard several of the higher ups here talk about a rescue attempt, but it seems like more conjecture to me. Fact is, there is a very good likelihood that we'll be stuck here for some time."

"But Charlie, there's little water and practically no food."

"I realize that, but unless someone in Java heard our radio distress signals, there's little that can be expected. Remember, there's a full-fledged war going on not far from here."

Vi Samuel gave her husband a scornful look that she usually reserved for special occasions. He saw her and conceded.

"Sorry, but I feel it is necessary to be blunt in this case."

"Be blunt, not obtuse," she replied. "I'm fully aware of our situation."

Charles Samuel lowered his head and mumbled, "You are right, Vi, sorry."

She took his hand and gave it a small kiss. He looked at her the very same way he had so many years before when they exchanged their wedding vows.

"For better or for worse, my love."

"This is certainly the *worse*," she said blankly.

"Yes, it most certainly is."

The pair remained in that position by the fire for several minutes, still holding hands and looking into each other's eyes. It was a point in their relationship that was as meaningful as any in their entire life together.

"Vi," Charles began again, squeezing her hand more firmly. "I want you to promise me something."

She saw a look come into his eyes and tried to interrupt.

"Charlie, I . . ."

"Let me finish, I need to say some things and there might not be enough time later."

"All right, my love. Go ahead."

"There might still be a chance that someone will come to our rescue, and I want something understood between us. Depending on the circumstances, there might or might not be room for me in the boat. If that does happen, I want you to promise me faithfully that you will go and save yourself. " He paused and continued, "It would mean a great deal to me."

Vi Samuel was silent, pondering the enormity of the situation.

Charles continued. "If we must be separated, then so be it. If the Good Lord decides that we will one day be reunited, then that will be God's will. A number of other couples here will possibly have to make the same choice, and for some reason, a number of people look up to me for this sort of thing. I guess I'm expected to set a good example."

"Poppycock on all that," she answered, her eyes welling. "I don't know if I can make it without you, especially after all we've endured for these past two months. I don't know if I have the strength left."

"Then you must find the strength, just like everyone else. We're all in the same boat here." Realizing his unintended humor, he sat back and smiled.

"I've actually stopped worrying about everything," he confessed weakly. "No matter what I do, I can't change things and I have so little energy left it takes too much out of me to worry."

Both became silent. Finally, Charles spoke again.

"Vi, I mean it. If the chance comes, you must go without me. You *must* promise."

She sighed and finally gave in. "I promise, my love. It will be hard, but I promise." She leaned toward him and kissed him for the first time in days. She moved over into his arms and in a few minutes, both were fast asleep, completely exhausted by the events of the past day.

Two days later, a loud shout from the beach caught everyone's attention. A low roar, then another followed. The noise broke the peaceful night's tranquility.

"All women and children down," came the agreed-upon call signaling a relief boat that was sighted nearing the island.

Much commotion and general mayhem resulted as families and friends shuffled around in the dark on their way to the beach. Charles held his wife's hand firmly as they approached the waiting boats.

One of the hands identified the vessel as the *Tanjong Pinang*, but was unable to say where the ship would go after leaving Pom Pong. Samuel thanked the man for the information and looked at his wife standing next to him, her arm entwined in his. He kissed her once more on her lips and helped her into the boat. She was now crying softly and so was practically everyone else within ear shot. After a few minutes the boats pulled away from the shoreline with their human cargo and the beach became quiet once again. All that was audible was the splashing of the wooden oars as they knifed their way through the pitch-black water.

Finally, there was no sound but the gentle lapping of the waves as they broke onto the shoreline.

One by one, each man who had just lost a loved one turned and walked back up the small hill that butted the beach. No one spoke.

February 16, 1942, near the intersection of Bukit Timah Road and Victoria Road, Singapore City, Singapore, 0920 hours

It was quite an honor that Col. Masanobu Tsuji had been selected by Lt. Gen. Tomoyuki Yamashita to determine whether the British soldiers would indeed honor the surrender agreement that was reached the day before in the sweltering heat of the Ford factory.

When the staff officer carrying the news of his latest task approached Tsuji, a sense of relief that the battle was finally over enveloped the career military officer. He had celebrated with the other staff officers the previous evening and had raised his ceremonial glass to the northeast, the direction of the emperor's palace in Japan. The small sips thus ended Tsuji's self-imposed fast from alcohol and tobacco.

The celebration was somewhat subdued and many toasts were raised to fallen and injured comrades. Sometime later that evening, all in attendance had departed for their first real sleep in almost eighty days.

The following morning, there was still work to be done. Tsuji picked a pair of subordinates, staff officers Okamura and Kawajima, and outlined his plan to them around a small table in his office.

"I want you to find the biggest and finest car we have been able to capture from the British, and I want it washed and cleaned. I also want a flag of our country attached to the front so that it is visible to everyone. Make it a large flag, maybe even a regimental one, so there can be no doubt in anyone's mind as to what it is."

The two officers nodded silently.

"I also want someone who speaks English to accompany us and I want each of us to take a couple of cameras. It is important that we record this historic moment and send the results of our great victory back to Japan. The staff photographers will have to wait, we still don't know if the average British soldier will accept this surrender gracefully. We will all be in danger, but to what degree I am uncertain. I also wish to leave in one hour, while it is still fairly cool in the morning. Do you understand?"

"*Hai*," was the immediate reply from both officers. They rose and bowed and left the office.

Tsuji busied himself with the latest intelligence reports and eventually took his own worn camera out of his traveling chest. It was the first opportunity to do so since he had come ashore at Kota Bharu seventy days before.

He adjusted his uniform and attached his sword, insuring it was fixed firmly at his side. He turned as one of his enlisted staff entered the room.

"The staff officers are here with the automobile, Honorable Colonel."

"I am ready. This is a historic occasion for all of us."

The staff sergeant nodded and bowed as Tsuji passed out of the door.

The car selected was a beautiful 1938 MG WA two-toned grey roadster that shined like new. A large Japanese flag, stained in several places and generally torn and pockmarked, flew from the right front bumper.

Tsuji looked at the flag and then in the direction of Staff Officer Okamura, who explained. "It was the best that we could find, Honorable Colonel. We discussed it and thought it would serve as a tribute to the fallen soldiers of the Japanese Empire," Okamura explained.

Tsuji thought and replied, "Then it will be so. Nothing could be more fitting."

The three entered the car along with a young artillery lieutenant who would serve as driver and interpreter.

The automobile headed south down Bukit Timah Road toward the center of Singapore City. The going was slow due to numerous shelled-out buildings, vehicles and craters that dotted every block of their ride. British soldiers began appearing in small groups, some still carrying their weapons. The soldiers regarded the vehicle with interest, but made no effort to stop its progress.

Now, more soldiers appeared along the sidewalks, lounging or squatting in groups in practically every available space. Some were casually smoking; others appeared to be nibbling at pieces of bread.

Tsuji leaned toward the other officers as the car slowed to a crawl. "When we stop, I want everyone to get out and start taking pictures of the buildings. If nothing happens, we will go a little further on our journey."

The car finally stopped and the officers alighted. As directed, they began taking pictures of their surroundings.

After a few minutes, the first British soldier approached.

"Beggin' your pardon, 'guvnor, but can I ask what is the purpose of takin' those pictures?" he asked in the general direction of Tsuji.

The lieuteanant translated and Tsuji replied, "Tell him we are taking the pictures to send back to Japan for the whole world to see…"

The British soldier turned around and muttered to several other soldiers who had come closer. He turned back and addressed the lieutenant.

"Can you take pictures of me and my mates, here?" he asked. "We want our families back home to know we are alive and well, even if we are goin' to be prisoners. It's really important to us, 'ya know."

Again the lieutenant translated to Tsuji.

Tsuji glanced at his two staff officers and smiled.

"We would be honored to take the pictures of such a heroic group of men," he said, and waited for the lieutenant to translate back to the soldiers. "We, too, have families back home who would be very worried."

He gave an order and Okamura and Kawajima spread out to start taking pictures of groups of the men. In a matter of minutes, there were several hundred British soldiers waiting around to be photographed.

Tsuji was glad he had brought a good deal of extra film for their cameras.

AFTERWORD

Many military experts consider the fall of the Fortress of Singapore in February 1942 as the greatest blunder in the history of the British government and military. The inability of Great Britain's military planners, and Winston Churchill himself, to correctly estimate the actual political and military goals of the Japanese Empire combined with an actual shortage of airplanes and military equipment were the fatal factors that led to the humiliating defeat. During the Malaysian campaign, approximately one hundred thirty-eight thousand British military were killed or captured. Many more British civilians were either killed or taken into confinement until the end of the war. With few exceptions, the Australian soldiers did prove to be the best fighters, even though they suffered dreadfully. While representing only fourteen percent of British and commonwealth forces, the gallant Aussies suffered seventy-three percent of the allied deaths in battle.

Though the fall of Singapore was an incredible dagger's thrust, Singapore did not signal the end of the British Empire's presence in Southeast Asia. British and Commonwealth tenacity and their alliance with the United States ultimately overcame the long odds that Singapore's fall had placed on chances for ultimate victory.

Many of the characters continued to play important roles in the later days of World War II. Here is a list of the ultimate fates of many of these people.

Lt. Gen. Arthur Percival was removed from his POW camp in

Manchuria in time to attend the formal surrender of Japanese forces in the Philippines that were under the command of his old adversary, now full **General Tomoyuki Yamashita.** When Percival entered the room for the surrender, Yamashita recognized him but never said a word. Percival was never awarded a knighthood, an unusual occurrence for a British lieutenant general.

Lt. Gen. Tomoyuki Yamashita was found guilty for 'brutal atrocities and other high crimes,' mostly committed in the Philippines, and was hanged in Manila on February 23, 1946.

Charles Samuel was captured after leaving Pom Pong Island and was interred at the prisoner's camp at Padang in West Sumatra and lived to publish his diary about the invasion of Malaysia.

Vi Samuel and the other evacuees who boarded the *Tanjong Pinang* on Pom Pong were bombed the following day with practically all passengers going down with the ship. Vi Samuel was among those lost.

Col. Masanobu Tsuji was ordered by superiors to remain incognito after the war and then helped with his fallen country's reconstruction. He was later elected to Japan's Upper House, the House of Councillors. His account of the details of the Japanese invasion is considered by many as the foremost insider's view of the Malayan Campaign.

Sir Robert Brooke-Popham retired in 1942 after being replaced as chief air marshall Far East Command. In later years, he blamed others for Malaya's conquest and the fall of Singapore. Many of the ranking officers involved, most notably Sir Lewis Heath, in Malaya and Singapore pointed the finger at Brooke-Popham's hesitation at implementing *Operation Matador* as the chief reason for their defeat at the hands of the Japanese.

Maj. Gen. H. Gordon Bennett of Australia managed to escape Singapore on the Chinese junk and was later berated by many military historians for his failure to remain with his troops. In many quarters, he was unofficially listed as a deserter. He wrote a book before the end of the war and attempted to blame his actions on others.

Maj. Shigeharu Asaeda continued to assist Colonel Tsuji throughout the entire Malayan Campaign and is reported to have been in the

Philippines prior to the Japanese surrender. Little is known of his actions thereafter.

Lt. Gen. Sir Lewis Heath was captured and interred by the Japanese. He survived and later returned to London where he was knighted and received a number of high honors.

Brigadier Ivan Simson was one of the high-ranking British officers captured when Singapore fell. He was interred at Changi Internment Camp along with Percival and others. His account of the tragedy, *Too Little, Too Late,* is well regarded by military scholars.

Capt. Patrick Heenan was tried on February 11, 1942 in Singapore for espionage and sentenced to death on for his actions on behalf of the empire of Japan. Before he could be executed, he was shot in the head and killed on February 13th by a military policeman to prevent him from falling into the hands of the Japanese who were about to take over all of Singapore. His dead body was then thrown into the sea.

Maj. John Wyett was interred and survived months of solitary confinement at the Utram Road Jail. He wrote a wonderful book about his experiences and lived to be ninety-six. He died in Tasmania in December 2004.

Check out these titles from
THE CLARK GROUP

New Cities in America Series
by Sylvia L. Lovely

The *Little Blue Book of Big Ideas* details how people can get involved in their communities and gives examples of cities and individuals already getting big results. Valuable for everyday citizens and city officials alike, it will help people gain a spirit of mission and commitment to action that can transform their communities.

In the *Little Red Book of Everyday Heroes*, you'll meet some real, ordinary folks just like you who are working to change their communities for the better by implementing the NewCities Institute's 12 Principles of Community Building.

The Lost Dispatch
by Marie Mitchell & Mason Smith

Twelve-year-old Victoria Johnson reluctantly enlists in the Union Army. She's a little late. The Civil War was fought nearly 150 years ago. But Vic's sixth-grade class has joined adult re-enactors staging the October 8th, 1862, Battle of Perryville. Vic trades her iPod, cell phone, and TV for a kepi, wooden rifle, and bug-infested tent. She's hot, itchy, and irritable, marching in a soldier's ill-fitting boots. Don't desert Vic when she needs a friend. Help her out. Enjoy your Civil War experience—without the heat. *Quantity discounts available for classroom sets.*

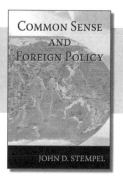

Common Sense & Foreign Policy
by John Stempel

After nearly half a century of working in the world of international politics and foreign relations, Stempel brings a unique perspective on the question of how to understand foreign policy and participate effectively to improve decisions that will determine how we live with the rest of the world. Whether as a citizen, aspiring participant in foreign affairs, or a jaded veteran of wars and peacekeeping, this book will help you understand the complexities of the subject, stimulate you to find useful information and increase your cross-cultural understanding.

For ordering information and a complete list of titles visit
www.TheClarkGroupInfo.com

The Clark Group
P.O. Box 34102 | Lexington, KY 40588-4102 | 800 944 3995 | 859 233 7623
FAX: 859 233 7421 | info@theclarkgroupinfo.com

Synopsis...

The Resistance is set in England and France during the early part of WWII. The newly appointed head of the French Resistance, Jean Moulin, is sent to England for a series of intelligence briefings. During one particular briefing, a former curator of the Polish national museum in Crackow describes the rape and plunder of his museum and other similar museums by the Nazis. His story touches Jean Moulin who devises a scheme to insure the same thing does not happen in France. Through the British Special Operations Executive-F (SOE, forerunner of today's British Intelligence), a plan is devised to have copies of the three greatest masterpieces in the Louvre secretly substituted for the real paintings, which are being secretly hidden in an old castle in the Dordogne Region of France. An American Army Captain is selected for the mission and he operates a glider to bring the fake paintings into France. With the help of the French Resistance, the switch is made. Meanwhile the Germans, in the person of an SS Colonel working under the personal direction of Reichsmarschall Hermann Goring, sets about to find the paintings for the Reichsmarschall so that they can be sent back to Germany.

The Resistance follows the actions of the American Army Air Force Captain, numerous members of the French Resistance and his beautiful French Resistance fighter-helper as they work their way through south central and finally southern France in their attempt to elude the SS, elements of the Wehrmacht and finally, the SS's Vichy equivalent Milice pursuers. The final incredibly dramatic scene is played out in the storied city of Lourdes, where a spirited gun battle finally decides the outcome of the novel.